DOLLY
IS DEAD

Also by J. S. Borthwick

The Bridled Groom
Dude on Arrival
Bodies of Water
The Student Body
The Down East Murders
The Case of the Hook-Billed Kites

DOLLY IS DEAD

J. S. Borthwick

St. Martin's Press ❦ New York

Library of Congress Cataloging-in-Publication Data

Borthwick, J. S.
    Dolly is dead /   J. S. Borthwick.
       p.   cm.
   ISBN 0-312-13052-X
   1. Deane, Sarah (Fictitious character)—Fiction.   2. McKenzie, Alex (Fictitious character)—Fiction.   3. Women detectives—Maine—Fiction.
4. English teachers—Maine—Fiction.   5. Physicians—Maine—Fiction.
I. Title.
PS3552.O756D58   1995
813'.54—dc20   95-8567
                                             CIP

First Edition: August 1995

10 9 8 7 6 5 4 3 2 1

This one is for Maddie

Many thanks to the ABCDEF BOOKS in Camden for assistance in the matter of auction prices for rare books.

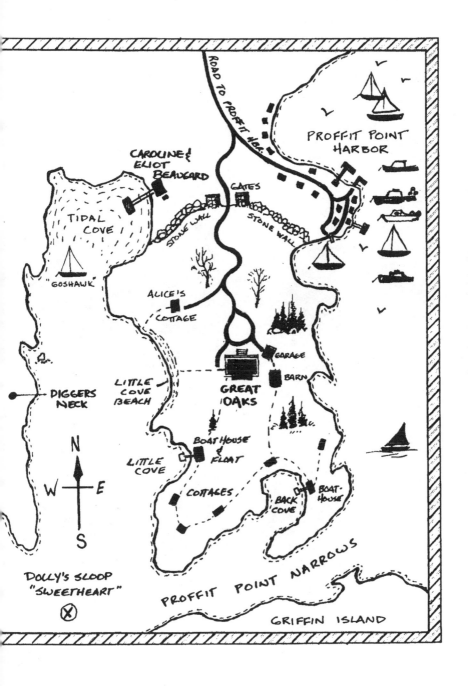

Cast of Principal Characters

Sarah Deane—Bowmouth College teaching fellow, wife of Alex
Alex McKenzie—Physician, husband of Sarah
Mrs. Anthony Douglas (Lavinia)—Grandmother of Sarah
Mrs. Arthur Beaugard (Elena)—Matriarch of Great Oaks
Dolly Beaugard—Daughter of Mrs. Beaugard, deceased
Masha Beaugard—Sister of Dolly
Alice Beaugard—Sister of Dolly
Eliot Beaugard—Brother of Dolly
Professor Lenox Cobb—Brother of Mrs. Beaugard
Jonathan Epstein—Son of Alice and Alan Epstein
Alan Epstein—Former husband of Alice, father of Jonathan
Caroline Beaugard—Wife of Eliot Beaugard
Colin Beaugard—Son of Eliot and Caroline
Webb Gattling—Friend of Alice, cousin of Parson
Parson Gattling—Cousin of Webb
George Fitts—Sergeant, CID, Maine State Police
Mike Laaka—Deputy Sheriff Investigator
Katie Waters—Deputy Sheriff

1

THE body of Marsden Gattling, pushed by a southwest wind and an incoming tide, rolled onto the seaweed-covered rocks of Little Cove one Thursday afternoon in late September. This untoward arrival on the shores of Proffit Point created among local residents neither surprise nor alarm. In fact, most of the sentiments expressed were those of relief together with an unseemly gladness. When this corpse was followed the next morning—Friday, September thirtieth—by that of his brother, Edward ("Junior") Gattling, the positive feelings animated by the first arrival were reaffirmed.

"Well, that's two of the buggers," announced Tad Bugelski, local harbormaster, as he watched with satisfaction the stuffing of Junior into the black plastic body bag.

"Two down and some to go," said a watching lobsterman.

"Nah," said Tad, who was a short, stocky man with buzz-cut

gray hair and the smashed nose of a former boxer. "This'll take the starch out of the Gattlings for a while, anyway. Those two guys should have known better. Probably poaching lobsters, cutting traps loose, or making coke deals. Chugging around in the middle of the night in an open skiff with an old, cranky motor. Found it this morning on a ledge; empty bottle of whiskey rolling around."

"So they went over the side?" suggested the lobsterman.

"Anyone's guess—but the motor was left wide open and it was out of gas. No life jackets aboard. Or on the bodies. Damn fools."

Tad turned to the dark-haired man standing next to him. "So, Alex, death by drowning? No foul-play shit or anything like that?"

Alex McKenzie was the physician and the medical examiner who happened to be on call for Knox County, Maine, which in turn included the small town of Proffit Point and the area surrounded by Little Cove. He now turned back from watching the body-removal operation, and shook his head. "Drowning or hypothermia—or who knows? Wait for the autopsy. It's an unattended and unexplained death. Just like his brother Marsden. Anyway, you'll have the state police CID boys on your neck for another few days."

"Listen," said Tad. "I can live with the state police and all of the scene-of-the-crime stuff. What I can't live with is some of those goddamn Gattlings. Bad news, half the friggin' tribe." With that, Tad spat on a rock and turned back to watch the loading of the body in the waiting ambulance.

"Bad news" about said it, thought Alex, as he trudged back to his car. The very name left a sour taste in his mouth. The Gattling clan, many of whom were settled like a malignancy across the bay on Diggers Neck, usually did spell bad news right there on the front page of the local *Courier-Gazette*. Bad news— from the eleven-year-old Gattling kid shooting a doe and two bucks out of season, to Grandpa Gattling found after-hours with his hand in the local hardware store till, to Aunt Lou Gattling now in the Knox County jail awaiting trial for vehicular manslaughter.

But this universal opinion about certain Gattlings—that they were usually up to no good—could not possibly apply to Ms. Dolly Beaugard, when three days later, the Monday morning of October third, her body washed onto the very ledge that had played host to the Gattling brothers.

Alex was called from his rounds at Bowmouth College's Mary Starbox Hospital to make his examination while the state police—still busy with the Gattling deaths—confronted the added complication of Dolly.

"Christ Almighty," said Tad, stepping around the yellow scene-of-the-crime tape—still in place from the arrival of the Gattling brothers—to meet Alex. "That's three of them. Family called late last night because Dolly didn't come home. In fact, she hadn't been seen since she took off after the Sunday noon dinner. Then in she comes with the morning high tide. But what in hell was Dolly doing? I'll bet she doesn't even know the Gattlings. Dolly's up for the good citizen award. You know, that church in Camden—St. Paul's something or other—and the hospital, the Girl Scouts. Those bird nuts, the Audubon group."

"I know, I know," said Alex. He took a deep breath, sighed, and then knelt down on the granite ledge to inspect what was left of Dolly Beaugard. One half of his brain—the recording, analytical part—took notes: condition of the sodden body, the greasy strands of seaweed caught around the collar of her blouse, the slight whitening and wrinkling of the exposed skin, the facial and skull abrasions; the other half of his brain reviewed what Tad had just said about Dolly. She was indeed a local legend, one of those indefatigable women who rise bright-eyed and bushy-tailed from their night's repose and go forth into the world to do good. There was hardly an institution in Knox County that had not felt Dolly's helping hand. Or, as some might say, Dolly's iron hand. She was the ultimate volunteer in days when such persons still in healthy middle age had long since vanished into the workaday world.

Dolly couldn't have been in cahoots with any Gattling, Alex told himself—unless she'd been trying to reform one of them. Unlikely, he decided. Dolly stuck to institutions, to group action, wasn't the hands-on type. Dolly's world of good works would never have impinged on the marauding, boozy world of the Gattlings. Then, mentally shaking himself, Alex returned to the business of determining the all-too-obvious fact that Dolly was dead—dead as a mackerel, as Tad had expressed it on the phone.

Alex rose from the ground, pulled off a shred of kelp from his trousers, and pronounced Dolly without life.

"Like Junior and Marsden, drowned?" demanded Tad.

"Wait for the autopsy," said Alex. "Besides, there's injury to the skull. A little bruising, abrasions. She was probably battered around on the rocks, or hit her head falling. Wait and see. Me, I've rounds to finish and a batch of patients lined up for the afternoon."

"Coincidence?" asked Tad. "Junior and Marsden and Dolly don't make three of a kind?"

"What do you think?"

"Never seen the lady around town with those two. Never'd expect to."

"So maybe you've just got three careless people fooling around with boats."

"Could be. Dolly used to take that little centerboard sloop of hers out in any kind of weather, and there were small craft warnings yesterday. Anyway, her boat's gone from its mooring."

"Tad," said Alex, with a certain grim satisfaction. "I'll bet you've just been congratulating yourself that you're in for peace and quiet, what with the summer people's boats being hauled out and half the population left for the winter. Well, forget it. Those Gattlings will set up a yowl from here to the Canadian border, and the Beaugards will probably outyell the Gattlings. Old Mrs. Beaugard is a tiger. Getting feeble now but probably still has a good set of claws. Watch your step, Tad."

"Hey," said a voice from behind the two men. "Tad Bugelski, you're the harbormaster who found the body, right? Hang in here. State police CID needs a statement from you."

"So have a nice day," said Alex, grinning at Tad. He turned, dodged past the police photographer, lifted a piece of yellow tape, ducked under, and made his way for the third time in a week away from a dripping, seaweed-entangled corpse.

About the reactions of the bereaved families, Alex proved only half-right. The predicted howl on the part of the Gattlings was stilled in mid-voice on the discovery of several neatly wrapped and waterproof packages of low-grade cocaine fitted under the engine mount of their large skiff. After these items came to light and after the chief medical examiner in Augusta ruled that death was indeed due to drowning, the Gattling tribe contented itself—for the nonce—with elaborate funeral preparations and the arrangement of floral tributes, real and plastic, at the Diggers Neck Baptist Church.

But Dolly Beaugard was another matter, and her lifeless arrival in Little Cove sent a series of ripples that threatened the tranquillity not only of the harbormaster but of the coast guard and the various representatives of the law.

Because it looked like the cause of Dolly's death was still uncertain. Some of the head and facial injuries had occurred before immersion in the ocean, so maybe she was hit by a swinging boom or falling mast. Alex took the phone call from Tad just after his last patient of the day had departed.

"Found Dolly's boat," said Tad.

"Capsized?"

"Yep. Sunk up to the gunwales. Hull and bottom stove in. Coast guard helped raise it this afternoon and the state police have impounded the thing and are going over it. Old lady Beaugard's on the warpath. Says I should have prevented her from going out because of small-craft warnings. But hell, I didn't even see Dolly Sunday. Wind was blowing up to twenty-five knots at least and I was helping Oscar Tabor find his mooring. It'd dragged clear across the cove. I can't nursemaid every wacko who wants to go sailing on a windy day. Besides, Dolly'd never listen to me. Dolly did what Dolly damn well pleased."

5

Alex gave a weary sigh. "I'm going home now, Tad. But call me if you hear anything else from the forensic people, okay?"

"They won't tell me. A harbormaster isn't on anyone's official list. But you've got connections in high places. You'll probably hear from your pal at the sheriff's department. What's his name?"

"Mike. Mike Laaka."

"Yeah, Mike. So you can keep me posted. And you were right about one thing. I sure am going to be spending the rest of the week dodging Beaugards."

Alex, returned home in an exhausted state, driving slowly up the long dirt road that led to the old farmhouse on Sawmill Road. Usually the road through the Camden Hills with the changing autumn colors and the flowering of the roadside asters brought some sort of anodyne after a day's grind. But the afternoon had turned to mist and cold rain and only increased the sense that all was not well with the world.

Once home, Alex flung himself into a kitchen armchair, fended off the attentions of the resident Irish wolfhound, Patsy, and stretched and then slumped back on the cushions. He was really beat. The week had been brutal. The sick had gotten sicker, the healthy had been stricken, and the three bodies that had washed in to Little Cove had certainly complicated an already disturbed week.

Then, hearing the slam of the back door and footsteps, he turned and with a weary wave of the hand acknowledged the arrival of his long-time companion and, since this past summer, his wife. Sarah Douglas Deane. Not Sarah Deane McKenzie because, as Sarah had pointed out, the only reason to yield up your own name to that of your husband in these enlightened days was if the woman's own name was something like Bugsquash or Snakeroot.

Sarah struggled out of her raincoat, put down her briefcase, sank into a neighboring chair, and ran her hands over the damp strands of brown hair that plastered the sides of her face.

"I can't believe it about Dolly," she said. "She was on her way to heaven via good works. As Grandma Douglas would say, 'She trod the path of righteousness.' "

Alex nodded. "So maybe that's it. Righteous people like that often end up in the drink. Or down a deep hole. The world can't stand too much righteousness."

"Oh, come on, Alex. Dolly was a little managing, a little bit of a sergeant major, but who else was going to be on all those committees and boards? Not me. Not you. Not anyone in our family. We're all too damn busy. God, Dolly worked at the hospital, the Scouts, was on the Midcoast Audubon board, and a docent at the Godding Museum of Art. We should be grateful. I'm spending all my time teaching and not more than an hour a month doing anything even vaguely public-spirited."

Here Sarah stood up and reached out a hand for Alex's, squeezed it, then walked over to the woodstove, flipped open the top, and began stuffing small logs into its maw.

Settled back in chairs, drinks in hand (Alex, beer; Sarah, tea), a pleasant glow and warmth emanating from the stove, they reviewed the matter of Dolly Beaugard and the Beaugard family backup team.

"You're right," said Sarah. "The family will make Tad's life miserable. He found the body. He didn't see her take out the boat. He didn't notice it was missing from its mooring until too late. I heard about it during class. In the middle of Intro Lit, this kid says out of nowhere—I'm holding forth about Chaucer, 'The Knight's Tale'—that he'd heard about Dolly from some other kid who lives on the Proffit Point Harbor. That she was covered with seaweed and had a crab fastened to one ear. I mean *yuck*. That wasn't true, was it?"

"There was seaweed here and there," said Alex, "but no crab. Kids like to embellish. But I didn't enjoy the scene, if that's what you mean. It's bad enough when the victims are thugs like Junior and Marsden. But hell, Dolly, we knew Dolly. We knew the family. Not close friends, but they were at our wedding."

Sarah put down her teacup. "Dolly and her whole family were part of the founding summer colony on Proffit Point. But most of the Beaugards live full-time now on the estate—it's called Great Oaks—or nearby. Retired or actually holding jobs."

"And doing good works."

"Dolly doing good works. The rest of the clan isn't quite as community-minded. They have a solid reputation for scrapping with each other, but they always seemed to depend on Dolly. She was the referee. She managed the estate and kept an eye on the cottages, the garden, the boats, the two docks. Took care of her mother's finances. And her mother. Saw that she got to her Shakespeare reading group, her Tuesday bridge, church every Sunday."

Alex nodded. "So with Dolly gone, there may be hell to pay. Cages rattling, toes being stomped on, push turning to shove."

Sarah grimaced and returned to her tea, and for a moment the two sat silent, both imagining the fallout of Dolly Beaugard's arrival on the rocks of Little Cove.

Sarah was a teaching fellow at Bowmouth College, an elderly institution of higher learning fitted into the lower margins of the Camden Hills in midcoast Maine. Not only was she responsible for teaching three introductory classes of English, she was also in thrall to a doctoral program with the possibility of orals on the horizon. These pressures left little time for the civilities of life and even less for any untoward goings on beyond her own threshold. So now it was with considerable effort that she dragged her thoughts away from the academic world and tried to think about the Beaugards. About Dolly Beaugard. Dolly deceased, washed into Little Cove like any random piece of flotsam. Or jetsam? Could Dolly have been pushed, tripped, encouraged to take a plunge overboard by the flat of a hand pressed into the small of her back? By a foot stuck suddenly in front of her?

"Alex," said Sarah, "it *was* accidental, wasn't it? She was out sailing in too much wind. Or is it possible . . ." She left the question hanging.

Alex looked over at her, frowning. "Not another word. We've had enough foul play this summer to last the rest of our lives. And don't you go sticking your nose into this business or I'll feed you to the sharks. Or to the Beaugards, which would be worse than sharks."

"But you're already sticking your nose into it."

"Because I'm the medical examiner. I have no choice. But when the results of the autopsy come through, that is that. You, my love, need only to go with me to the funeral. We will send appropriate flowers, write notes, visit the family, and send a donation to the indicated charity."

Sarah looked thoughtful. "Dolly wasn't everyone's all-time favorite. And she was always being held up as an example to me. When I was little, anyway. Grandmother Douglas used to wave Dolly at me like a flag. Dolly did this, Dolly won that. Social Responsibility trophy at school. Camp Spirit three years in a row at Camp Merrilark. And she taught Sunday school while I spent Sundays chasing after a good time."

Alex reached for a section of the morning paper that lay on the table beside his chair. "And I spent my Sundays concentrating on the Red Sox. Listen, let me worry about Dolly because it's my job. You go think about Chaucer."

Sarah relapsed into silence, but the order to put Dolly out of her mind only stimulated thought. Dolly had been the number two child of the family. First came Masha the beautiful. Masha the musical. Seen on posters featuring the Baroquen Recorder Consort. Masha in a white silk blouse holding her instrument and looking disdainfully into middle distance. Cool, contained, auburn-haired Masha built like a Vogue model. Then Dolly. Blonde, stubby Dolly. Vaguely porcine features, always fifteen or so pounds overweight. No student, but a mighty achiever. Or overachiever? Trying to live down the fact of a fashion-queen, musical older sister? Trying to hold her own through worthy deeds?

And then came Alice. One year older than Sarah herself—Sarah having arrived at thirty this September. In Sarah's class at Miss Morton's Academy—although suspended twice for running away. A childhood friend of Sarah's, but the kind of friend who led Sarah into escapades and briar patches from which only Sarah seemed to suffer feelings of guilt, since Alice positively thrived on the wayward life. Alice: a short-term marriage at eighteen, a college dropout by twenty-one. Another marriage, another divorce. One living child—custody to the father (which father?). Incarcerations to dry out. A brief career as a painter (oils and pastels); a try at writing (a poem published in *The Atlantic*); a period spent as a ski instructor at Sundance; a theater try in Boston; a teacher's aide in Maine. Presently holed up for a period of regrouping at the Great Oaks compound on Little Cove at the end of Proffit Point.

Last—Eliot Beaugard. The pride and joy. The son born after those three daughters. Handsome, stalwart, salty Eliot. Marine insurance, something like that. Married to Caroline, beautiful, sulky Caroline. Husband and wife living in high style outside the Beaugard compound in a "cottage" widely rumored to have at least six bedrooms, ditto bathrooms, a wraparound deck, and a outdoor, heated, saltwater pool.

And now Dolly was gone. Dolly, the good. Dolly, the force that kept the Beaugards from having each other for lunch.

"Is that someone at the door?" Alex reared his head and regarded the kitchen entrance with loathing.

Sarah, recalled from speculation, shuddered. "Can we hide?"

"No. The lights are on, our cars are outside. But we could try total deafness. Hunker down and close your ears."

This proved difficult. First the clang of the doorbell, the rapping of the brass knocker, then a solid thumping of a fist, the kicking of a foot. Then the kitchen door snapped open and the visitor strode over the threshold.

A tall woman, face pale, dark hair wet and tangled, hanging over the collar of her yellow slicker. Blue jeans and rubber boots, mud clinging to the soles.

"Bloody hell, Sarah," said the visitor. "Don't you ever answer your door? Or are you trying to get away from something? Or someone? Well, it won't work because I'm damn well going to see you. Have a nice, old-fashioned session. With you and our friend, the medical examiner. Hi there, Alex. Long time, no see."

Sarah drew a deep breath, raised her head. "Hello, Alice," she said.

2

ALEX hauled himself to his feet and extended a hand. "Alice. We're so sorry about Dolly. An awful shock. Come on in and sit down. Let me take your coat, you're dripping."

Sarah, too, was now on her feet. "What would you like, Alice? Tea? Cocoa, coffee . . . or a drink?"

Alice shrugged herself out of her slicker, tossed it into a corner of the room, and threw herself into Alex's vacated chair. "My shrink and I've worked it out so I'm allowed one blessed drink a day. The drink of my choice. One ounce. Period. Got any rum?"

Alex walked over to the kitchen cupboard. "Anything in it?"

"Put anything you want in it. Juice, butter, soda. But make it hot. So it blisters my tongue. I'm cold and wet and chilled through to my spine."

Alex busied himself with bottles and mugs, and Sarah returned to her chair and contented herself with a sympathetic look and a murmur to the effect that she, too, was extremely sorry.

"You're sorry! My God, we're all sorry. Poor old Dolly. The

family saint. Listen, I never thought I'd be saying this, but I'd give ten years of a misspent life to see sister Dolly march through the door and suggest that I shape up and make something of myself. Oh shit, why do things like this happen? Why couldn't it have been some slimeball who'd been poaching deer or running for Congress?"

"Here, Alice," said Alex, extending a steaming mug. "Hot buttered rum. The skier's drink. Or the sailor's. And I do have some idea of what Dolly meant to your family."

"Alex McKenzie, you don't have a clue. You don't know a quarter of it. We're a bloody bunch. Contentious as hell. Yap, snap, and bite. Don't deny it, Sarah," as Sarah opened her mouth to protest. A ritual protest.

"We never functioned as a family. Not really. So okay, maybe families never do function, but Dolly made us think that we did. Got us through birthdays. Thanksgiving, Christmas. The only reason we made it through holidays without cutting each other's throats was because of Dolly raving about the sanctity of the family—not that she really *liked* any of us."

Silence. Then Sarah braced her shoulders and said briskly, "Dinner with us, Alice. Just some packaged stuff out of the freezer, but we'd love to have you."

Alice put her face down into the steaming rum, sniffed, took a sip, and looked up. "Okay. If you can stand me that long. Most people can't. I'll try not to rage and thunder about the family."

"Rage all you want," said Alex. "Sarah and I have had our share of family moments. Maybe ours aren't quite as colorful as some, but there have been a few incidents . . ."

"Like my brother, Tony, trying to marry a jewel smuggler," said Sarah, "and my aunt Julia stealing horses. And Grandmother Douglas being sure if we don't start going to church, we'll all roast in hellfire."

Alice pushed a straggling lock behind an ear and gave a half smile. "Your people aren't even in the same ballpark, but I'm not here to compete. I'm here to say that with Dolly gone, we'll all fall apart at the seams, we'll combust, and maybe that's what somebody had in mind."

"What!" exclaimed Sarah and Alex in exactly the same breath. "You're not serious," added Alex. "I haven't had the autopsy results, but it looks like an accidental death."

Alice put down her mug on the table with a thump. Such a thump that the warm brown fluid splashed over the edge onto the knees of her none too clean blue jeans.

"Alex and Sarah, I'm not here to listen to sympathy and reason. But I say to hell with what it looks like. I say that Dolly was too damn useful to the family. And too damn managing. I say that someone wanted Dolly's finger out of the family pie, out of the family checkbook."

"Have you," said Sarah, carefully sorting her words, "any idea in the least that there is a someone? Have there been threats? Has Dolly any known enemies? I don't mean the sort of people who got steamed because she was a bit of a tyrant on a committee. I mean the real thing."

"No enemies," said Alice. "No threats. Nothing like that. The only people who really seriously grumbled about her were in the family, but they still hung on to her apron strings for all they were worth. It's just something I feel in my bones."

"Dinner," said Sarah. "Let me shove a few boxes in the microwave. Then we can eat and you can tell us about your bones."

The eating of dinner—Stouffer's turkey tetrazzini with salad on the side—allowed Sarah to study her guest and wonder why on earth she and Alex had been singled out for the visit. Although they'd been close when growing up, she hadn't seen much of Alice in recent years, Alice having been entirely too busy with dropping husbands, changing interests, drinking or not drinking, to be bothered with old school friends toiling in the academic world.

Alice didn't look well. A pinched look around the nostrils, fine lines around the mouth, washed-out blue eyes with red rims, a gray whiteness to the skin—at a time when most people still had a summer tan—and a limpness to the mouse brown hair that straggled in separate strands to her shoulders. Well, the red eyes might be due to recent shock, but the other details bespoke poor health. Or rotten habits. Or indifference to life. And Alice wasn't eating much, just moving her fork around her plate. Then Sarah, as she cleared the plates and began dishing out Ben & Jerry's Toffee Crunch, took a good look at Alex as an antidote to Alice. It was a relief. Alex, even though looking like some sort of nineteenth-century felon with a slash of a mouth, determined chin, dark eyes, and a shelf of black hair, and though obviously tired, still seemed like someone in his middle thirties, while Alice resembled a battered specimen closing in on fifty.

Alex, in his turn, glancing from time to time in Alice's direction, found his thoughts turning to the need of a complete workup, blood count, and a liver function test, to health spas, vitamin supplements, outdoor exercise, and the intake of protein and green vegetables. Like Sarah, he compared their guest unfavorably with his spouse and found Sarah, although thin and nervy-looking, still with color across her high cheekbones, a light in her gray eyes, and a shine on her dark short-cropped hair—hair now dried from the rain.

Dinner over, the three settled in the living room, a bare-walled space in the midst of remodeling, with books spilling out of cartons and unhung pictures leaning against the wall.

"But three decent chairs," said Sarah, removing a pile of textbooks and student papers from one and waving Alice to it.

"Now," said Alex, "let's have it. You think Dolly's boat was tipped over on purpose because someone wanted to do her in? Dolly, who, as you said, had no enemies and lived a blameless life."

"Cripes," said Alice. "I know it doesn't make sense. And I know I may be having a knee-jerk reaction because I want Dolly back. I don't want to be the new Dolly, and I can see my mother considering the possibility. Even sitting there crying over Dolly, she's said things like wasn't it time I settled home for good and began to take on responsibility for the family. For the property. The estate, Grandpa's trust fund. For the dock and the boats and the guest cottages and, of course, her. She's given up driving, you know, because of her eyesight, and she depends on one of us. Though, of course, it was mostly on Dolly. In no time she'll be going on to me about the Prodigal Son . . . or the prodigal daughter, and I don't want the job or the fatted calf. And neither does Masha or Eliot. Nor Caroline, probably, but she never says much about anything except maybe to complain. Our family zombie."

"Are you trying to say," Sarah said slowly, measuring her words, "that someone might have wanted to get rid of Dolly because none of you wants to fill her shoes and that leaves a vacancy? And some scheming evil person—like a housekeeper or a gardener or a family lawyer—is hovering, waiting to gain her confidence and seize control. Get her to change her will."

"I read gothic novels, too," said Alice, "and the answer is that I love the idea of the evil stranger, but I'm too bloody down-to-earth to believe in one. So I think if anyone's hovering, it's got to be someone in the family. And that leaves me, Masha, Eliot, and Caroline, and, of course, dear old Uncle Lenox. He's retired and moved into the family manse."

"Your uncle Lenox must be quite elderly, then," said Alex. "I can't imagine him rowing out in a dinghy in a twenty-five knot breeze just to tip Dolly over. Or banging her with an oar or a bilge pump."

"Uncle Lenox is a cantankerous bastard in quite good health. Stronger than he looks. All lean sinew and gristle. He gets by in the world by pretending to be Mr. Frail Elderly Scholar. Professor Emeritus. He thinks being a grumbling curmudgeon is fascinating. Listen, I don't trust a single soul in the whole family nest. And to repeat, I just have this feeling in my bones. Dolly's dying has left a void. A big black hole."

Sarah couldn't hold out any longer. "I just don't get it. Why, Alice, have you come to us? If there's anything amiss, well, the state police will be standing there on your doorstep, making your life miserable. It looks like Dolly went out in a big wind and pulled the wrong line or put her foot in a bucket or got hit by the boom. Something happened fast and she went over-

board. With or without the boat. No time for a life jacket."
Sarah looked up at Alex. "Dolly wasn't wearing a life jacket,
was she?"

"No," said Alex. "Not when I saw her."

"We're always glad to see you, Alice," said Sarah. "And if
you're feeling rotten about Dolly, well, use us for relief.
Friendly shoulders. Anytime. I mean it. But I don't see why—"

Alice broke in. "I'm not here to cry on friendly shoulders. I'm
here for help. I know all about you, Sarah Deane. Your grandmother told my mother that you are an expert in sticking your
nose in other people's business. That affair at High Hope Farm
this summer. People disappearing and being dug up by a horse.
I mean you two are well known, you are notorious, you and
Alex. How many married couples spend their honeymoon
working on a murder that took place at their wedding reception?"

"Spit it out," said Sarah wearily.

"I want both of you to ooze into our family circle. Sympathy
visits, condolence calls. Sarah, come for lunch. Better yet, bring
your grandmother Douglas over for lunch, and while she and
Mother are talking about the decline in morality in today's
world, you can soak up ambience. Snuggle up to Masha and ask
about her concerts. Pump Eliot and Caroline. They'll ask you
over for drinks. Or dinner. They're always looking for new people to admire that great monster of a house they've built on
Tidal Cove."

"Alice," said Sarah, her voice taking on a hard edge, "I have
just begun my semester's teaching. Three Intro Lit classes. Alex
is practicing medicine. Sick people without end. Flu season
approaching. He's one of the local medical examiners."

"What Sarah is saying," put in Alex, "is no. We will call on
your mother and tell everyone how very sorry we are. I will
explain any mysterious medical details that emerge from the
autopsy. Both of us will offer comfort and sympathy when
needed. But we won't do any oozing into your family circle."

"Hey," said Alice, rising to her feet. "No problem. I didn't
think you'd say yes right off the bat. But I'm the youngest

daughter, you know. Spoiled, devious. And very persistent. I really like to have my own way, as my two former husbands will be happy to tell you. So I'll give you a little breathing space while we wait for the results of the autopsy. Then, even if it's ruled accidental death, I think I'll zero in and pester you again. Good night and thanks for the rum. I feel more human. Ten percent human, I mean. And for me that's going some."

And Alice, followed by her hosts, marched to the kitchen, snatched up her slicker, bestowed a quick pat to the top of Patsy's head, and made for the kitchen door.

Sarah looked over at Alex, who was glowering at the departing woman. "To repeat Alice's opening remark," she said, "bloody hell."

3

TUESDAY, October fourth, the day following Alice Beaugard's visit, found Alex at noon cornered in the Mary Starbox Hospital cafeteria by Mike Laaka, deputy investigator of Knox County Sheriff's Department. Mike was a tall Nordic type, fair-haired almost to whiteness, a man more dedicated to the world of the racetrack than to that of law and order. And since Mike was a boyhood friend, there was no need for Alex to waste time on formalities.

Alex found Mike looming large over a pile of plastic trays and eyed him with suspicion. "You're not looking for me, I hope. Maybe your mother's in here for a checkup? Or you've got a splinter in your thumb? Or there's a gang of thieves in the gift shop?"

"Funny," said Mike amiably. He slid a tray from the pile, handed it to Alex, and chose one for himself. "Do you recommend the meat loaf or the Waldorf salad?"

"I don't recommend that you bother me during lunch."

"I'm going to bother you about the autopsy results," said

Mike. He chose a villainous-looking piece of lasagne, added a salad, a frosted doughnut, and a dessert dish holding what looked like whipped cotton topped by a cherry.

Alex studied Mike's luncheon selections, shuddered, and went for the vegetable soup and the Waldorf salad.

Settled in a corner, in the middle of Alex's second spoonful of soup, Mike began. "Johnny Cuzak wants to see you. You remember Johnny? Assistant chief medical examiner."

"I know Johnny," said Alex, remembering too clearly his last session with Johnny in a stable bending over a strangled corpse.

"So he wants to see you. In person. Go over first impressions. Your initial exam."

"I made three initial exams. Three bodies, three exams."

"Right now it's about those Gattling brothers. The post mortem details are kinda interesting. Interesting like peculiar."

"Nothing about Dolly Beaugard for now?"

"Wait up. Take the Gattling boys first. Looks like they both had a skinful."

"That empty bottle of whiskey?"

"Yeah, that. And what was in it."

Alex put down his fork carefully. "Not whiskey?"

"Yeah, the booze was there, all right. Or in the blood. Marsden and Junior were drunk as skunks. High alcohol level: point two one. But something was added to the bottle. Like a sedative. The lab's working full steam on it."

"Lethal dose?"

"Of which? The whiskey or the dope? Or the combo because those two items don't make the world's greatest mixers. And lethal? Well, maybe, but that isn't what finished them. Marsden and Junior didn't stay aboard their boat long enough to be killed by the stuff. They went over the side into the drink."

"And drowned?"

"Right. Lungs filled with seawater—plankton and diatoms present. Persistent foam at the nose and mouth. All the signs. So, Alex, you hit that one on the nose."

"But now you've got a complications. Doped whiskey."

"The lab people are going over their boat. Big skiff really. Sixteen-foot job. Some cloth fibers caught on the gunnels. Rips in the guys' jackets. Looks like maybe one of them fell in, the other reached for him and went ass over teakettle reaching out to grab him. Happens a lot. The rescuer dies trying to rescue. But that's all a guess. Wait for the lab."

"But you're not beating the bush for someone who might have reached over with an oar and tipped them in?"

"You mean the someone who spiked the booze with dope and then followed them out of the harbor and waited till they were liquored up and easy marks."

"Something like that," Alex admitted. "Those two guys never won any good-conduct medals, and I'll bet there are plenty of looted cottage owners around or drivers forced off the road by some Gattling or other who might have helped with the project."

"Wait and see. Now you, Alex . . ."

"We're finished. I'm finished. I'll call the medical examiner later. Now I've got to be at my office by one-thirty."

"Two things. First, go over your report on Marsden and Junior and see if you missed anything. Important since it's not such an easy death-by-drowning verdict as it seemed. Second, the state police are a bit put out by Dolly Beaugard turning up practically on the heels of the Gattlings."

"Coincidence. Dolly wouldn't have been caught dead with—"

"She just was," Mike reminded him.

"Okay, okay," said Alex irritably. He picked up his coffee cup, drained the last mouthful, and rolled his paper napkin into a ball. "What I'm saying is that it looks like Dolly was dumb enough to go sailing in a big wind and didn't wear her life jacket. But I'll bet she wasn't having a secret meeting off some island with Junior and Marsden."

"No bet. I only bet on horses, not dead bodies. But the police are going over her boat now. A life jacket's still aboard."

"The one she wasn't wearing?"

"Her brother, Eliot, said she usually didn't unless a gale-force wind was blowing. But she kept a life jacket handy. Usually hung on a cleat near the mast. Easy to reach."

"And that was in place."

"Tied around a cleat."

"So it wouldn't blow away. Besides, even with a life jacket on, hypothermia would have got her. How about time of death?"

"She must have taken the boat out late Sunday afternoon. Capsized not too long after. Lab puts the time of death between four and six—stomach contents and so forth. Trouble is, no one around Back Cove—that's where Dolly kept the boat—noticed the sloop was off its mooring. Tad Bugelski's being given heat because he wasn't around. The Beaugards themselves didn't think it was odd she didn't turn up Sunday evening. Thought she had some committee meeting. Only called us when she didn't show up later that night. We alerted the coast guard, who it turns out already were trying to track an overturned sailboat after someone called in about sighting it. Anyway, Tad and a couple fishermen went looking around the islands, but as you know, she didn't turn up until Monday A.M."

Alex stood up. "So good-bye, Mike. Call me with any reports, but no more lying in wait at the hospital."

"I have to deal in person sometimes. His high and mighty lordship Sergeant George Fitts of the State Police CID—"

"Okay, okay. We all know George. Inscrutable George with ice in the veins and frost in the mouth. He leaned on you."

"Yeah. You said it. George remembers all the hindrance and help you and Sarah have given to the world of crime, so he wants you to make a sympathy call on the family."

"We're planning to do that anyway."

"And," said Mike, rising in his turn, "see if you can sniff out the slightest odor of Marsden or Junior Gattling in the intimate circles of the Beaugards. Or any Gattling. George went to see Mrs. Beaugard and the rest last night, and they act like it's some name from inner Tibet. To which I say horse shit. The Gattlings are legend around these parts."

"Did Alice deny knowing Gattlings? It doesn't sound like her."

Mike shrugged. "Alice was out last night—over at your place, I hear. But I leave Alice out of the family picture. She's a maverick who once dated Webb Gattling—he's Marsden and Junior's cousin. Maybe that's the connection we're looking for. Alice and Webb had matching motorcycle jackets. Their names in silver studs. Cute. Anyhow, I try not to believe much of what Alice says."

Alex thumped his friend on the back. A heavy and not entirely friendly thump. "Now hear this. If Sarah and I, in the course of our condolence activities, hear anything untoward, we'll pass it along to you. If not, that's that. We're not going to— how did Alice put it?—ooze our way into the Beaugard family circle and open cupboards and cabinet drawers. Or look for bloodstains on the carpet. See you, Mike." And Alex strode off toward the cafeteria door.

"Hey, wait," shouted Mike, loping after him. "Alice? Alice has been asking you to visit? You mean she knows something? Hey!" This as Alex let the cafeteria door swing back in Mike's face so that by the time he had recovered his balance, Alex had disappeared down one of the long corridors of the hospital.

While Alex was beset by the problems of a medical practice and irritants from the world of forensics, Sarah was enduring other forms of annoyance.

That morning at seven-thirty, with an eye to making it to her eight-o'clock class in good time, her briefcase in one hand, a thermos of tea tucked under an arm, and her handbag slung over her shoulder, the telephone rang. Her grandmother.

Grandmother Douglas, a frail woman of ninety years with a spirit of stainless steel, usually avoided the telephone as an instrument of the devil. She wrote notes or sent messages just as if she lived in the mid-nineteenth century at a time when Alexander Graham Bell was yet in swaddling clothes.

But here she was. On the telephone. Sarah sighed, looked at her watch, and put down her thermos and briefcase.

"Sarah," said her grandmother, in the high-octave tones of the very old, "I have just heard about Dolly Beaugard. So tragic. I need you and your automobile."

"Now, Grandma?" said Sarah, frowning. She had student appointments, an eight-o'clock class, another at ten, one at four.

"This afternoon would be best. Say three o'clock. I must call on Elena Beaugard. And the family. I would have asked Hopkins"—Hopkins was Mrs. Douglas's housekeeper, a stalwart in her eighties—"but she's having something done about her root canal."

"But I have to teach an afternoon class . . ." Sarah began.

"Yes, I know. But see if you can make arrangements. I want you to drive me there. You know the family and went to school with Alice. It will be most suitable for you to make the visit with me."

"You mean you want me to cancel the class?"

"Yes," said her grandmother firmly. "I do. Sudden death, a tragedy like this, takes precedence over whatever poets and writers you're dealing with—most of them atheists, I believe."

Well, there was no use in tangling with her grandmother over the godlessness of certain literary lions. "It won't be easy, but I'll try, Grandma," Sarah said, looking frantically at the kitchen clock, hoping that it differed from her watch.

"Poor Dolly. What a pillar. I heard that Father Smythe is stricken. Dolly certainly whipped the Sunday school into shape in two weeks after Gloria Merton had that breakdown."

Sarah sighed. "Dolly was remarkable, but I have to go now, Grandma."

"Yes," said her grandmother. "Don't waste time chatting on the telephone. Your whole generation has given up on any other means of communication."

Five minutes late for her eight-o'clock class, Sarah found herself hard put to present Chaucer in an acceptable light to a group of heavy-eyed freshmen who no doubt wished that the computer had not dealt them an early morning class that featured an author who wrote rhymed gibberish about an antique people.

Sarah stumbled through the period and found her own interest in "The Knight's Tale" faltering, so infectious was her students' palpable discontent.

But by her ten-o'clock class, she hit her stride with *Oedipus Rex*—incest being a popular subject with youth—and after lunch made it to the English office and, pleading family problems, successfully wiggled out of teaching her four-o'clock class, which was to have centered on Defoe's *Journal of a Plague Year*.

"I can certainly do without the bubonic plague rounding out the day," she told Arlene, the English secretary.

"You're going to see that Beaugard family?" asked Arlene. "I've been reading all about it in the *Courier-Gazette*. First those two Gattlings—I went to school with Junior, and he deserved everything he got—and then this Dolly Beaugard's body coming right on the very same rock. I mean, whoa, that's suspicious."

"Arlene," said Sarah in an austere voice, "it's just a coincidence. Dolly was sailing and her boat capsized."

Arlene smiled the smile of one whose reading focused on the pages of the *National Enquirer*. "Hey, Sarah, keep me posted, okay?"

"Not okay," said Sarah, stamping out of the office.

The drive from Bowmouth College to Grandmother Douglas's house on Bay View Street in Camden wound through the lower reaches of the Camden Hills, between marshes, ponds, and wooded swales, and served Sarah as a short period of refreshment. It was a shining day, cloudless, filled with early October splendor, each maple outdoing the next in orange, vermilion, and crimson. Above the highway, the rounded hills rose, brown oak, yellow birch, red maple, all mixing with the somber clusters of evergreen, pine, spruce, fir balsam, hemlock, and cedar.

Sarah slowed to a crawl, trying to concentrate on scenery and not her upcoming visit. Then on a sudden impulse she pulled her car, a blue secondhand Subaru, into a small lakeside turnoff, cut the engine, and climbed out of the car. A killing frost had not yet turned everything brown, and the edge of the road was still thick with late purple asters.

Sarah stretched, inhaled, and then made her way slowly down the little stone beach to the water's edge. She looked at her watch. Only one-thirty. Still plenty of time. Grandma Douglas didn't tolerate lateness, but neither did she want an early arrival upsetting her after-lunch nap. On an impulse Sarah knelt down and dipped a hand in the water. It was ice-cold and so clear that she could see her pale fingers like strange polyps, the whole hand like a small sea anemone. And the moment that she had chosen to take her mind away from the upcoming visit to a bereaved household suddenly brought it home. Death by drowning, by taking great gulps of icy water into your lungs, by gasping and choking, and fighting. And losing.

Sarah forced herself to picture the living Dolly. When had she last seen her? Yes, two weeks ago at the hospital. Sarah was in the lobby waiting to meet Alex for a rare lunch together, and Dolly, dressed in the green smock of a volunteer, had stopped by Sarah's chair and smiled down at her—a professional may-I-help-you-smile—and asked how Sarah liked married life and how was Alex?

Fair-haired Dolly with her round face, her round chin, that round button nose. Pale blue eyes, invisible eyebrows, hair combed back looking as smooth as yellow satin. A full mouth with perfectly laid on lipstick. Bangle bracelets. The green smock not entirely hiding the plump contours of the body. A woman who would never do anything so messy as allow herself to fall overboard and arrive wrinkled and disordered and seaweed-entangled on a harsh coast to be found by strangers. Hauled above the tide line by strangers. Later, bagged, tabled, sluiced, probed, and eviscerated, her organs weighed and sliced by strangers. Dolly, the fastidious, the take-charge woman—if she existed somewhere as a hovering shade—must now be in a state of humiliation and trembling outrage.

Sarah withdrew her hand, now white and numb, from the water. It looked like a dead thing. She shuddered, then wiped it hastily on the side of her skirt, gave herself a mental shake, and returned to the car.

Sarah's formidable grandmother, supported by the faithful Hopkins—she of the root canal—was standing at the front door of her dark-shingled Queen Anne monster of a house. A house with half the rooms closed, blinds drawn. A house of shadows and worn velvet cushions and threadbare Oriental rugs, of large bronze vases, hat racks, and umbrella stands. Of flocked maroon wallpaper and oil paintings of dismal moors and dank pools. A house that to Sarah's mind was more mausoleum than home, but to her grandmother, an abiding refuge from the relentless stream of time.

Hopkins assisted Mrs. Douglas into the front seat of the car, and Sarah, taking her grandmother's cane, thought it was like settling a large and fragile gray moth into place. Clothes of soft gray material, gray stockings on sticklike legs, a gray shawl of weblike texture enveloping the stalk of her neck. And above the shawl, the small, almost transparent face dominated by the gold-rimmed spectacles and the thin cloud of white hair.

Sarah started the car and drove at a sedate pace down Bay View Street, all the while seeing that her grandmother was looking with disapproval at her red and blue checked skirt.

To forestall the lecture, Sarah pointed out that she was wearing her usual teaching costume. "And besides, no one gets into black anymore, Grandma. Not to make a visit. But I'm not in blue jeans and I'll bet Alice Beaugard will be."

"Alice is not my idea of an example," said her grandmother. "But I've heard she's stopped drinking, so perhaps there is hope."

"I guess Dolly earned her place as the family star," said Sarah, nudging the conversation down a different path. "She was the middle daughter, and don't they say the middle one tries harder? Dolly certainly did. And Masha's a hard act to follow. An older glamour-puss sister. Of course, she's not home much anymore, but when she is, well, who would look at Dolly? And then big hunk brother Eliot and Caroline giving those parties in that big new house. Tents on the lawn, charter boats for excursions."

"Glamour and big new houses," said Mrs. Douglas with scorn, "do not cut ice with honest people. I don't think Eliot and Caroline have been to church since their own wedding. As for Alice, what a record. Married in a hotel by a rabbi and a Unitarian somebody, and the second time in a hole in the wall by a justice of the peace. No wonder she was divorced twice. As for Masha, she only goes into church if she's playing a concert there. Only Dolly and her mother were regular attendants."

And that, thought Sarah, as she turned the car south, sums up the measure of man for Grandma. Unless you go to church—preferably an Episcopal one—you're one of the world's sinners.

"Grandma," said Sarah, picking up speed and clutching the wheel with determination. "I think you should know that Alex and I aren't exactly regular churchgoers. In fact, on Sunday we—"

Her grandmother reached for Sarah's arm and tapped it lightly. "I don't want to know. You are my dear granddaughter and I know that you have a good heart. As for Alex"—here Mrs. Douglas pursed her lips—"I will continue to pray for him."

Sarah pressed her foot more firmly on the accelerator so that by the time the car shot past the general store and made the turn for the Proffit Point Road, the speedometer was nudging fifty-five. Then, anger subsiding, she slowed.

"Tell me about the Beaugards, Grandma," she said. "Mrs. Beaugard. The whole family. Alice said they've always fought among themselves like cats and dogs. But I only visited the family when I was little and haven't seen much of any of them in a long time."

Her grandmother considered for a moment. "Well," she said slowly, "Elena Beaugard—she was a Cobb from Cambridge, although I think her mother came from Europe—Elena was always strong-minded. Difficult. The whole family seemed to go at each other hammer and tongs. Elena's husband, Arthur, usually stayed away out of sight. Spent all his time in his study working on his collections. Nineteenth-century illustrated books. Died at his desk, I am told. A pleasant man when you met him, but that wasn't often. Visiting the family could be exhausting, but I imagine that today they will be properly subdued. Elena's great cross is having a daughter like Alice who drinks and never settles to anything. Picks up husbands and drops them like used clothes."

"But Alice is the brainy one," said Sarah. "At Miss Morton's when she made an effort, she got all A's. Wonderful voice but wouldn't join the choir. Preferred being the class renegade."

"At which she was no doubt successful," said Mrs. Douglas dryly. "But what kind of a mother is she? The father has custody of the son. That's Alan Epstein, the novelist. If you call the sort of things he writes proper fiction. Jonathan is the son and quite spoiled, I hear. Sarah, you are still driving over the speed limit."

Sarah, interested in the Beaugard family life, slowed obediently. "We've said it was hard on Dolly to have Masha and Alice for sisters. But it must have been hard for those two to have a sister like Dolly."

"Nonsense," said her grandmother. "Alice and Masha received all the attention. Masha was a very beautiful child. And gifted. Gifted children usually get more than their share of attention. And Alice was a wilding from the very beginning. What was left for Dolly to do except to be good? To be dutiful."

"At which she was very successful. Saint Dolly."

"I think in the long run Dolly just wanted to be needed. She probably wished for an old-fashioned family with children and a hardworking husband." Here Mrs. Douglas folded her hands in her lap and sighed. "Dolly," she added, "was an extremely boring young woman. Ten minutes spent with Dolly lasted an age. But she did God's work."

Sarah saw ahead the stone pillars marking the entrance of the Great Oaks estate and slowed the Subaru for the road that led to the Beaugard compound and the old family house. And as she did, she thought with astonishment that her ninety-year-old grandmother, who sometimes seemed completely out of the everyday world, might have accurately summed up the Dolly phenomenon. A boring, not very bright woman who wanted attention and found a socially acceptable way of getting it. Whether God had figured in the equation was anyone's guess. But if He had, what was He thinking of to allow His dull but hardworking handmaiden to go sailing in a twenty-five-knot breeze and to capsize her boat and drown?

4

WITH Dolly Beaugard in the forefront of her thoughts, Sarah almost missed the tall, thin figure limping along by the side of the drive. Only her grandmother's cry made her put on the brakes.

"Sarah, look out. I think that's Lenox."

Sarah brought the car to a stop and peered through the windshield. A sticklike man moved haltingly along the margin of the drive, arms flapping like broken wings as if to balance himself.

"He must have hurt himself," said her grandmother. "We'll have to give him a ride. Oh dear. Lenox is such a trial."

Sarah opened the door, undid her safety belt, climbed out, and then turned back to the window to confront her grandmother.

"Alice's uncle Lenox? Lenox who?"

"Elena's older brother. Professor Lenox Cobb. I've heard he is living at Great Oaks now. As of last month."

Of course. *Professor Cobb, I know about you*, thought Sarah with a start. Former scourge of the Bowmouth English Department. Now, thank heaven, retired. She walked on toward the man, who, apparently oblivious of a car stopped behind him, continued his tottering forward progress.

"Professor Cobb," she called. "Are you all right?"

The man stopped in his tracks and gave her a look. "If you had eyes in your head," he snapped, "you could see that I am not all right. I am injured. I have had a serious fall."

"Wouldn't you like a ride, then?" said Sarah, extending an arm. Professor Cobb was swaying like a leaf in the wind. In fact, his whole body had a leaflike quality. An autumn leaf. Brown, wrinkled, and thin to the point of transparency.

"Of course I want a ride. And give me your arm. No, the one on my other side. Use your head, young woman. Can't you see that it's my left ankle that's injured?"

Sarah moved around him and extended her right arm, which was immediately and powerfully gripped above the elbow by a claw of iron. Together they walked slowly toward the waiting Subaru.

"You have a Japanese car, young woman," said Lenox Cobb in a peevish voice. "Aren't American cars good enough for you?"

Sarah fought down an impulse to drop the man in his tracks and explained the need for a four-wheel-drive that was not a truck. And that neither Ford nor Chevrolet had come up with such.

"No excuse," said her companion as they halted by the rear door. This Sarah opened and by a series of awkward maneuvers, managed to seat Lenox Cobb. In place, leaning forward, he strongly reminded Sarah of a large insect, perhaps a praying mantis. Her grandmother a gray moth, and now a mantis.

These analogies caused a sort of choked giggle so that by the time she sat back in the driver's seat, Sarah was fighting for breath.

Fortunately her grandmother and the professor were engaged in greeting each other with a minimum of civility.

"It's you, Lenox," said Mrs. Douglas. "What have you done to yourself?"

"Ah, Lavinia," said Professor Cobb, "is this your Japanese

car? I thought better of you. And I have done nothing to myself. I was knocked down. By an unseen force."

"Don't be ridiculous, Lenox. You probably tripped. You aren't wearing your glasses."

Lenox Cobb fumbled at his face. "Why, I had them on when I set out for my walk. I walk every day. Down the driveway to the mailbox and back. We'll have to turn back and search for them."

"No," said Mrs. Douglas. "Not now. I am calling on Elena and the others. Because of Dolly. And this is my granddaughter. Sarah. Sarah McKenzie."

"Sarah Deane," corrected Sarah, thinking, oh Lord, now we'll spend twenty minutes on my name. She accelerated slightly and was able to turn in to the circular drive and park before her grandmother had properly launched into the subject of taking one's husband's name and cleaving wholly unto him.

The business of unloading two breakable elderly persons took some minutes, and it was not until both were settled in the living room of the house in chintz-covered armchairs that Sarah remembered Professor Cobb's complaint.

She turned to him. "You think you were tripped?"

He inclined his head. "Or knocked from behind. Someone in the woods. I went down like a fallen tree. I began to shout and I heard someone running away. Leaves and twigs snapping."

"Could it have been a dog?" Sarah suggested.

Lenox Cobb considered this. "Yes," he said. "It could have been that dreadful animal of Alice's. A dreadful big shaggy thing. No known breed. Completely out of control. It should be tied up."

"Uncle Lenox, are you talking about Willie? He's an absolute sweetheart. You must have annoyed him." Alice was in the room, looking as if she'd been caught in a stiff wind. Scarves, shirts, vests, ties, and belts hung from various parts of her torso, and a ragged pair of blue jeans clung to her lower limbs, which were finished off by a pair of scuffed paddock boots.

Now she walked up to Sarah's grandmother and extended a none-too-clean hand. "So good of you to come, Mrs. Douglas. About Dolly, of course. It's pretty awful, isn't it? Mother will be right along. She's stuck on the telephone with the police. Bunch of ghouls. Want to know if Dolly was depressed. Had ever tried suicide. Honestly, what lamebrains."

Sarah looked up. "Was Dolly depressed?"

Alice threw herself down on the sofa next to Sarah. "Now, don't you start in. Dolly was never depressed. How could she be? She was always doing the right thing. What was depressing was watching Dolly. She depressed me. She depressed Masha and Eliot. And she probably depressed my mother. Only none of us ever dared say so."

Here Lenox broke in. "Well, there's nothing we can do about Dolly. It's all extremely sad and she was the one person who kept this house moving. I, for one, will certainly miss her marmalade muffins. Now, about your dog, Alice. Tie him up or I won't be responsible."

"Uncle Lenox," said Alice, sitting up and fixing him with a look. "If one hair on Willie is—"

But here Elena Beaugard made her presence known by the shuffling of her feet and the tapping of her heavy cane. Eyesight threatened by glaucoma, mobility limited by arthritis, bowed down by grief, she made a slow progress into the room. Lenox subsided and Alice jumped up and guided her mother to a chair, pushed a cushion behind her back, and directed her attention to the arrival of Mrs. Douglas, now settled in an adjacent chair. This produced in Mrs. Beaugard a heavy sigh and a reaching over and laying on of hands on Mrs. Douglas's arm. Who removed them, patted them briefly, and returned them to their owner.

Mrs. Beaugard was built more or less on the lines of Franklin Roosevelt's formidable mother. Dressed in gray knit with amber beads ringing her neck, she was stout, big-breasted, double-chinned, with a beak nose emerging from plump cheeks and her white hair fastened down into a net. As always, she wore silver-rimmed thick-lensed glasses that, together with her heavy eyebrows, accentuated a perpetually severe expression as if she had caught someone engaging in unmentionable activities. Although at seventy-two, she was almost eighteen years younger than Sarah's grandmother, infirmity seemed to have accelerated the aging process so that the difference between the two women did not seem great.

Following in Mrs. Beaugard's train came her oldest daughter, Masha. Masha, auburn hair in a modish chop, eye makeup and dark lipstick perfectly laid on, her slim figure wrapped in an emerald green jumpsuit, was every inch the professional performer. She paused by her mother's chair, extended a hand over to Mrs. Douglas, murmured something in a low voice, and then floated off to a window seat and turned her gaze on the outside world.

Masha was followed by her brother, Eliot, and Eliot's wife, Caroline. Eliot, fair-haired like his sister Dolly, tall, sunburned, looking seaworthy and competent, the epitome, Sarah thought, of the successful businessman. Wife Caroline, staying just behind Eliot's shoulder, reminded her of an expensive doll whose designer had failed to give her a completely human expression. Her lips were parted in a permanent half smile, her blue eyes were open and unblinking, her pale hair was tied back, and her full-skirted rust-colored dress with its white collar had an antique costume look.

Subdued greetings and expressions of sympathy were passed around, and once concluded, Sarah's grandmother and Elena Beaugard settled down for conversation, Alice and Lenox retired to a distant window seat to wrangle in a low key on the subject of untrained dogs, and Eliot and Caroline went to the door to greet an elderly couple who no doubt brought their condolences.

Seeing the Beaugard family well occupied, Sarah was free to study her surroundings and take stock of the bereaved and their visitors.

She had not been inside the old Beaugard "cottage" for years. To picnics, yes, or under a tent for Alice's wedding reception, and for weekend parties having to do with dances and tennis that had taken place on the lawn. Like her grandmother's house, it was a lumbering shingled beast with turrets and bays and protrusions and porches.

The living room was cavern-size and filled with a thicket of furniture—the summer chairs and tables having been augmented by the sale of the family house in Boston and the shipping of the contents to Proffit Point. Now weighty mahogany and dark cherry mixed haphazardly with wicker and pine and faded chintz. But the general effect, although confused, offered comfort and the sort of hominess so common in long-inhabited family houses—even if the families themselves were at swords' point.

And there over the mantel of the great fieldstone fireplace was the large oil study of the four Beaugard children. It must have been painted, Sarah thought, when Alice was about ten. Which would make Dolly, the middle daughter, fourteen, Masha nineteen, and Eliot just about eight. The artist had posed the two oldest girls on a white garden bench, Alice on a cushion at their feet, and next to her, sitting cross-legged, the boy Eliot.

Sarah, curious, got up and walked to the fireplace for a closer look. And as she approached the painting, she was aware of a small shiver running from the nape of her neck and rippling all the way down her backbone. The three girls and the young boy looked so alive. The artist had somehow managed to give a sense of animation and also catch the slightest whisper of friction between the sitters. Masha, auburn hair tied back with a white scarf, wearing a soft summer dress of the palest yellow, kept her chin lifted, her arched nose slightly elevated, her eyes upraised, her feet tucked in next to sister Alice's hand, and her shoulder turned away from Dolly; Dolly, all in white, her yellow hair swept back and held by a blue band, sat with hands folded in the lap of her full skirt. She stared straight ahead, her lips fastened in a careful smile, and somehow the artist had managed, without making her expression in the least unpleasant, to suggest a stubborn and unyielding personality.

Alice was another matter. Sarah imagined that she had been dragged into the portrait sitting by sheer force because the artist had conveyed this resistance. Alice on her cushion had one hand pressed to the ground, as if ready to spring up and away. Like her sisters, Alice wore a floating creamy summer dress, but her sash was untied and one of her party slippers had been pushed off and lay abandoned on the grass. And while Masha looked up and Dolly stared ahead, Alice gazed off to the edge of the picture as if she were searching for an escape route.

Eliot, on the other hand, sitting there with his arms folded across his chest, looked out at the world with a pleased expression. As if he owned the world. Well, he probably did, thought Sarah. The Beaugard world anyway. Eliot, the hoped-for boy born to a mother over forty. Eliot in a sailor suit, short pants, a dark tie, and a lanyard with a whistle. Did boys twenty years ago wear sailor suits even for portraits? Sarah couldn't remember any such costume from her childhood. Her brother, Tony—who was close to Eliot's age—wouldn't have been caught dead in one. But the effect, the sailor suit, the girls in their pale summer dresses, the garden bench, gave the whole a sense of an age long gone by. And it reminded Sarah of something she'd seen before. A painting? Or a photograph of just such a family? She frowned, trying to remember.

"You've seen that old thing before, haven't you?" It was Alice, a cigarette in one hand, a glass of something dark—her daily rum?—in the other.

"I must have," said Sarah. "But I haven't really been in the house for ages. You all look so alive. It's a wonderful picture."

"Well, it scares the shit out of me," said Alice. She brushed a wayward wisp of brown hair out of her eyes and poked it back into the general tangle. "It was done by an artist called Marie-Louise Dauphine. Mother found her in Quebec on some art excursion and hauled her down here to do it. Cost a fortune and we fought like cats all through the sittings. I had to be literally dragged into the scene that first day. And I didn't want to wear a dress, and Masha would sneak her foot over and try and step on my hand, and I'd pinch her ankle and put pebbles into Dolly's shoes. And Eliot would spit at me when no one was looking."

"But the painting scares you?"

"Like I said. I think that Marie-Louise Dauphine was some kind of witch. She used to drink gallons of herbal tea and cackle at us. Mother wanted a sort of period piece, the golden age of childhood. We look positively Edwardian. But Marie-Louise got right inside us, didn't she? Into our skulls. Look at Dolly. You can almost feel her jaw tighten and her hands clench, and yet she's smiling. And Masha as if she was sniffing body odor. Eliot, king of all he surveys. And me, ready to get the hell out of there. I think Marie-Louise got pieces of our souls and didn't give them back. Isn't that what the Indians are afraid of? The Hopis? Or is it the Navajos? Anyway, whenever I look at it, I feel as if someone were walking across my grave. Eliot can't believe he let Mother get him into a sailor suit—I think she had it made for the occasion. Masha says the thing gives her the creeps, and even Dolly said she tried not to look at it. Only Mother thinks it's wonderful. Which I suppose from her point of view it is. Our souls all caught and stuck up there above the mantel for ever and ever, amen."

"Alice, will you help with the tea?" It was Mrs. Beaugard calling across the room.

"Oh Christ," said Alice. "Where's Dolly when we need her? I don't do tea, I just drop cups."

"I'll help," said Sarah, thankful to have employment.

So tea was produced, wheeled in on a trolly by a handsome black-haired woman introduced as the housekeeper, Mrs. Lavender. Cups and waferlike sandwiches were duly distributed and circulated while at the same time decanters, whiskey and sherry, appeared on a side table under the supervision of Eliot.

Eliot, Sarah noticed, was playing the host to a circle of visitors. Sarah caught the repeated name of Dolly, from which she gathered that Eliot was apparently reciting amusing family tales in which Dolly was the featured player—or the featured butt. Why was it, Sarah wondered, sipping her tea, that funereal occasions often turn into slightly out-of-control cocktail parties where even simple observations take on a hysterical tinge? Where people laugh too loudly, and then look abashed and anxious.

But now Sarah was recalled to her grandmother's side. It was time to go. On their way out the door they were stopped by Masha poised to do the honors. She was sorry not to have properly thanked Mrs. Douglas for coming. So good to see Sarah. All so terribly sad. Dolly, a great loss. Mother is bereft. Dolly drove her everywhere. And what will St. Paul's Sunday school do? Or the Midcoast Audubon. Dolly was the new secretary.

"Of course," added Masha, "I never had her grit. She stuck to projects like a limpet. Got them done."

"Masha," said Eliot, coming up, with Caroline still at his shoulder, "is too damn artistic for everyday grit. Sarah, Mrs. Douglas, come sometime and see our new house. Come for drinks . . . or"—with a glance at Mrs. Douglas's disapproving face—"or tea. Just say the word." Here Eliot gave his wife a meaningful glance.

Prodded, Caroline bobbed her head. "We'd love to have you visit. Both of you." She spoke with a noticeable lack of energy.

Here Mrs. Douglas broke in and said firmly that she never went out except to church and the dentist and to make sympathy calls, but thank you.

"You, Sarah?" said Eliot. "You and Alex. Hey, we never see you anymore."

You never did see us, Eliot, Sarah told herself, but out loud she murmured about sometime and how nice and then assisted her grandmother out of the room.

To be followed by Lenox Cobb. Limping and with a cane.

"If you will take me to where you found me. I must look for my glasses. They must have fallen off when the dog jumped on me."

"It *was* the dog, then?" asked Sarah, opening the car door and lifting her grandmother almost bodily onto the passenger seat.

"Oh, Alice denies it, but Alice has never told the truth. That great hairy dog of hers counts as much as her entire family."

Sarah, whose Irish wolfhound, Patsy, was one of the loves of her life, confined herself to assisting Lenox into the backseat of the Subaru, trying at the same time not to listen to another fulmination on the subject of Japanese cars.

Sarah drove slowly until Lenox, rapping with his cane,

brought the car to a halt. Helped out and put on his feet, the professor limped into the woods that bordered the drive. "Be careful," Sarah called after him, although she was not sure quite what she was warning him about. She had seen Alice's dog asleep in the front hall as they left.

Neither Sarah nor her grandmother spoke for the twelve-mile drive from Proffit Point to the turnoff north on Route One in Thomaston. Sarah wondered whether her grandmother was thinking consoling thoughts about Dolly Beaugard passing through the welcoming gates of heaven, but then, looking sidewise at Mrs. Douglas's rather grim expression, she decided that no, it wasn't heaven on her mind, more likely some of the darker observations in Isaiah and the Psalms—all those verses about grass that is green and groweth up and then withereth and flowers that fadeth.

But when Mrs. Douglas spoke she revealed that she had not been bustling about in the Valley of the Shadow; she had been occupied with more worldly matters.

"Did you know," she began, "that Dolly had taken over most of Elena's affairs?"

"I suppose she had," said Sarah, not much interested.

"And that she had persuaded Elena to give the big house at Great Oaks to the Episcopal Church next year? To St. Paul's-by-the-Sea."

Sarah came alive. "The whole house? The whole estate?"

"No, no. Just the house and about an acre surrounding it. For a retreat. For diocesan workshops."

"Good heavens!" exclaimed Sarah, holding back stronger epithets. "What about the family? Uncle Lenox? He's living there now, isn't he? And Alice? And Alice's son if he ever turns up? And Masha? Eliot and Caroline? They have a boy."

"There are about six guest cottages, quite substantial ones, on the property. Alice is already occupying one of these, and Lenox and Dolly were each to have one. Eliot and Caroline, of course, have that new house on Tidal Cove. But now Dolly will not be here to facilitate the move. However, Elena told me that Father Smythe was quite thrilled."

Sarah made the turn onto the Old County Road, the back route to Camden, and instead of bringing the Suburu up to speed—forty-five miles per hour—she slowed, so interesting was the information.

"You really mean it, Grandma, the whole big family house?"

"As I said. Of course, the plumbing, the electric system, would have had to be redone. The house is quite dilapidated."

Sarah grimaced. "No wonder Dolly's dead. Snatching the house *and* an acre of land from her own family."

"Nonsense. The contents of the house, all those paintings—there's a Monet and a Constable and all those Whistler etchings—were to go to the heirs. And income to maintain the cottages for Alice and Lenox and Dolly. Even after various other bequests, there would have been a great deal of money for all of them. And I presume, although Elena didn't say so, that the heirs would have the rest of the property and the beach and dock to divide among themselves. Proffit Point is an extremely valuable piece of shore land. Really, Sarah, you must not go about saying things like 'no wonder Dolly's dead.' That is irresponsible. You have been involved in entirely too many criminal activities."

Sarah nodded. "I couldn't agree with you more. It's just that I'm surprised."

"I think it was a fine and generous plan. Large properties like Great Oaks need to serve more than a few family members."

"You're a socialist, Grandma," said Sarah, grinning at her.

This remark, her grandmother ignored. She simply shook her head. "But of course, any future estate plans that Dolly may have helped her mother make will be in jeopardy. That family simply lives to squabble. With Dolly gone, the contents of the house, the property, will have to be reapportioned. Elena was quite distressed and said she didn't know who would take over the estate management. Possibly Lenox, although he takes a great deal of pleasure in being contrary. Alice would be hopeless. She would probably try to turn the Great Oaks estate into a wild animal preserve. And Eliot is too interested in his own new house to be any help."

"Which leaves Masha, I suppose. But she's only available between concerts."

"I suppose so," said her grandmother in a distant voice, and Sarah could see that the effort of the visit had taken its toll. Mrs. Douglas's hands were moving about in her lap like captive birds, her eyes were drooping, her head nodding.

"Almost home," said Sarah, turning the car in to Camden's Bay View Street. Then as she drew up by her grandmother's front door, she remembered that Dolly's arrival had followed two other notable deaths. "Grandma," she asked as she held her grandmother upright and began walking her toward the door, "did Mrs. Beaugard mention the two Gattlings? You remember. Those two men who washed up in Little Cove a few days before Dolly's body came in. Did Dolly know any of the Gattling family?"

Mrs. Douglas drew herself up. "Elena mentioned the two Gattling deaths as being the silver lining to the cloud. A Gattling apparently broke into her barn last fall and stole a lawn mower. But the two families have never known each other. Why would they?"

Why indeed? thought Sarah as she turned her grandmother over to the waiting Hopkins, who, by the swollen condition of her left cheek, proved that the root canal had been attended to.

But, she reminded herself, as she headed homeward through the Camden Hills toward Sawmill Road, those Gattlings are all over the place. Two Gattling cousins had a seasonal business hauling floats for summer people—and probably casing the empty houses as they did it. Another Gattling manned a Mobil station. A Lola Gattling—Sarah had seen her name tag— worked the checkout counter at the Shop N'Save supermarket. Probably the Beaugard family, all unaware, had trafficked with Gattlings, had employed them on the estate as anonymous members of a work group, cutting lawns, fixing roofs, dealing with boats and moorings—doing the sort of work needed on any large and unruly piece of property.

With her mind busy considering the possible interfacing of Beaugards and Gattlings, Sarah almost ran full tilt into Alex's

Jeep parked smack in front of the house instead of being put away as usual in the old equipment shed that did service as a garage.

She jammed on her brakes and came to a squealing stop.

Alex leaned in the car window. "Good God, you almost wrecked both cars. I was just unloading some shingles. For the shed."

"I was thinking about the Gattlings. Whether they've been mixing it up with the Beaugards. Because I've been doing tea and sympathy over on Proffit Point. With Grandma."

"And I've been doing forensics with Mike Laaka. At lunch and later on the phone. It's just as we thought."

Sarah paused in her climb out of the car. "What is?"

"Marsden and Junior. Death by drowning. With skins full of doped whiskey."

"And Dolly?"

Alex sighed. "Also death by drowning. But complications. Contusions, facial abrasions, a depressed skull fracture, some of which occurred before she drowned. Enough injury to cause at least temporary loss of consciousness. Other injuries are postmortem from the body hitting rocks and ledges."

"You're saying she got a fractured skull while sailing?"

"Maybe Dolly was banged on the head by the boom swinging around suddenly. Because of the wind that day—squalls and gusts. Or the boat may have gone over on its side in what they call a knockdown. Say Dolly was hit and lost consciousness, then she'd fall down on the floorboards of the boat. The boat would be yawing around, boom banging, sails and sheets all over the place. Water would be coming over the side and she was facedown in it."

"But the boat didn't really sink?"

"No. It's made of wood. It would just fill up with water."

Sarah shook her head. "Could Dolly have fallen overboard before she was hit on the head?"

"Okay, that could have happened. And Dolly might have been hit on the head by the swinging boom while she was trying to hang on to the side of the boat?"

"And lose her hold and go under and drown."

"How it happened is guesswork. As I told Mike, if she hadn't drowned, she would have died from hypothermia because it doesn't take long to die of exposure in the ocean at this time of year."

"I suppose so," said Sarah soberly.

"Drowning," went on Alex, now settling into the role of instructor, "or what we call death by immersion, means that pulmonary circulation due to inhalation of water is compromised, the right heart is distended, and the great veins are filled with dark red blood. The blood is diluted by the inhaling of water, so coagulation is likely to be absent. A mass of foam— water mixed with mucous—often appears coming from the mouth and nose of the victims. All of which happened in the cases of the two Gattling brothers. And with Dolly Beaugard."

Sarah grimaced. "Okay. Okay. Enough already. I've got it. Dolly drowned. The Gattling boys drowned."

"Right. So now it's on to phase two. Or three. Anyway, into how and why. Let's go inside and put our feet up and talk about something else. Like the flu season. It's A-Beijing, this year."

"Wait a minute." Sarah waved at two wooden chairs under an old apple tree by the back porch. "Time out. No more clinical details, no A-Beijing flu. Let's sit down and admire the view. The maple trees are sensational this year."

Alex walked over, and he and Sarah arranged themselves in the chairs. Each looked dutifully at the hillsides, but not more than five minutes was given to the panorama of autumn splendor.

Sarah broke it up. "So what about Dolly's sailboat? Can't the police guess what happened by examining it?"

"Dolly's sailboat," said Alex. "Curious you should ask that. I'm being called as a so-called expert in the matter."

"Her sailboat? You?"

"Me. Old sailor McKenzie. Dolly's boat is a class of wooden sixteen-foot sloops called Weymouth Scooters. Only about thirty or so were ever made, and most of them were sailed out on Weymouth Island—my summer stamping ground. Or sailing waters. A few Scooters—maybe five or six—were built for local people like the Beaugards who lived on the mainland. The sloops are speedy devils, but they never caught on. Centerboard jobs with too much sail and too little weight below. Hard to handle in a stiff wind. My father sold ours after my younger brother, Angus, was dumped. But I learned to sail in the thing. And after one of those Scooters, handling any other boat was easy."

"But Dolly hung on to hers."

"So it seems. But Alice isn't the only one with suspicions. The police want me to go over Dolly's boat because I know what the original boat looked like and perhaps can tell if Dolly's has been tinkered with. Which seems likely because the six Scooters the police have located have been modified to make them seaworthy."

"Why not ask the builder or look at the original designs?"

"Builder is dead, and none of the boatyards can put hands on blueprints. I have a date with Mike Laaka to look at the sloop over at the coast guard station boathouse at six o'clock tomorrow."

"And I can come?"

"You're not invited, but I suppose you can lurk."

"It's what I do best."

"You're telling me. But try and keep a low profile."

"I will crawl around on my hands and knees. I will abase myself. I will kowtow. I will lick boots and polish brass."

"You see," said Alex amiably, "Alice is right. You can't resist sticking your nose into someone else's sleaze."

"Not sleaze," said Sarah. "It's the Beaugards. All of them. There's a sort of horrible fascination about them. Like some sort of bad four-hundred-page novel. And I guess I want to know how it comes out."

"Aha!" said Alex, grinning. "The truth at last. Come on, Miss Marple, it's beer and tea time."

5

THE next day, Wednesday, October the fifth, at a few minutes after six, Alex, with Sarah a step to the rear, presented themselves at the coast guard station and were led inside a long building housing a number of small boats. There, off to one side, under a bright hanging light, propped up by four metal legs, sat Dolly Beaugard's Weymouth Scooter.

A sad sight, thought Sarah, seeing sails draped over the bow, a tangle of lines hanging over the sides, the tiller cracked, stays loose, the top of the mast broken off. Part of the hull had been splintered, and here and there ragged holes showed. And over the whole, straggled dried strands of seaweed, while an amber sheet of kelp concealed part of the name painted on the stern.

Sarah moved slightly closer, squinted at the letters and made it out. *Sweetheart.* Oh dear. But somehow the befouled name, the seaweed combined with the hunks of gray muck that adhered here and there to the bottom, not only gave the little vessel a dirty and forlorn look, it gave a sober sense of what had happened that blustery day off the Maine coast.

Sarah, mindful of approaching officialdom—a uniformed

deputy and Mike Laaka—retreated to watch. It was a slow process. Alex, outfitted in a lab coat, rubber gloves, and covers for his shoes, crept about under and behind the sailboat, then up a short ladder to probe *Sweetheart*'s innards. Sarah, tired of the spectator role, decided to look for another object of interest.

Which she immediately found.

To the rear of the building at a distance from Dolly's boat, propped in the same manner, sat the *Sweetheart*'s twin sister. Only this vessel—named *Zippo*—was clean and shining. White hull, green-painted topside, green boot stripe, red bottom paint. Sarah looked around and saw a familiar face. Sheriff's Deputy Katie Waters—a person with whom she had shared a thoroughly unlawful investigation the past summer.

Katie marched over and Sarah took note of her crisp brown uniform, her trousers with perfect pleats, her Smokey the Bear hat at the correct angle. Katie was short and slightly built with a sharp little triangular face sprinkled with freckles, but she wore such an air of stern professionalism that Sarah realized they were not about to have old-home week about past misdeeds.

To forestall questions, Sarah quickly pointed to the *Zippo*. "What's this one?"

"Are you supposed to be in here?" said Katie warily. Sarah had almost cost Katie her job that past July, and she wanted nothing more to do with the woman.

"Don't worry, Katie. I won't go near Dolly's boat. I came with Alex. He's apparently an expert on Weymouth Scooters. But I thought the police couldn't find one that hadn't been altered. That's why Alex was called in. This looks exactly like Dolly's. Only it's in one piece and cleaner."

Katie melted slightly. Sarah away from the *Sweetheart* could cause no real trouble. "State police just found this half an hour ago on a mooring in Rockport. Family by the name of Baum. Joseph and Melinda Baum. Mr. Baum said he hadn't changed anything, so the police got into gear and trailed it over exactly as is."

The *Zippo* was not propped as high as the *Sweetheart*, since detailed examination of the hull and bottom would not be necessary. And this meant that Sarah could not only walk around the boat but could get a good view of its interior.

It was a tidy thing. Teak floorboards, mahogany seats, brass fittings, halyards, jib, and main sheet all coiled and clean. The sails were bent on, furled, and tied neatly with sail ties. A plastic bucket, a sponge, a boat horn, a bailing scoop, and a small hand pump rested on the floorboards.

"Did Dolly Beaugard's boat have all this stuff in it?" asked Sarah. "The pump and the bucket?"

Katie hesitated and then apparently decided that this information would probably be general knowledge. "Any loose equipment aboard the *Sweetheart* must have floated away when she filled up. Even the floorboards except one. But a life jacket was aboard, tied onto a cleat."

"They say cause of death was drowning," said Sarah.

Katie Waters clamped her mouth shut. "They, whoever *they* are, can say what they want. I don't give out that kind of information. I keep my mouth shut and keep my job."

"I'm sorry I mentioned it, Katie. But Alex told me. He's the medical examiner."

"Alex should keep official information to himself."

"Oh, Katie, lighten up. I'm not going to talk, and by tomorrow the family will know how Dolly died. So will the whole county." Sarah turned back to *Zippo*. "The boat's in perfect condition. The Baum family must not have tipped over much."

"Probably better sailors," said Mike Laaka, coming up behind Katie. "Those Weymouth Scooters are what Alex calls 'tender.' Not 'love me tender,' but mighty touchy in a wind. That's why they're obsolete. Too many people ended in the drink."

"Did Dolly make a habit of capsizing?" asked Sarah.

"We asked around. Seems she had a pretty good record. Went out in stiff winds and came back okay. Once got caught on a ledge at low tide, and this summer her tiller stuck and she drifted into an island, but that's about it."

"So why," said Sarah, still puzzled, "did she get into trouble last Sunday?"

Mike shrugged. "Because there's a first time for everything."

Sarah stood stock-still for a minute, and then, "Mike, is there a telephone around here?"

"Public phone by the town landing. And just who do you want to call? The district attorney?"

Sarah smiled at him. "Just a call to a private family."

"Sarah, butt out, okay?" said Mike.

Sarah lifted her head. "Michael Laaka, I haven't butted in. But something just occurred to me. And I'll be right back."

Sarah kept her word. In less than ten minutes she reentered the boat shed and found Alex, Mike, and Katie standing in the middle of the floor midway between *Zippo* and *Sweetheart*. An argument was in progress about *Sweetheart*'s broken mast.

"Could have snapped in the wind," Mike was saying.

"Doubt it," said Alex. "I've never heard of one snapping off just like that. It probably broke on a ledge after the capsize."

"But if the tip broke off and hit Dolly on the head," said Katie, "then that would account—"

"Unlikely," said Alex. "Because—"

Sarah felt free to interrupt. "Ballast," she announced.

The three turned and stared.

"Ballast," repeated Sarah. "*Zippo* carries ballast. "I've just had a friendly chat with Melinda Baum, who said that after their first sail in their Scooter, they decided on ballast. Otherwise she would always be on her ear in the least wind."

"Ballast," repeated Mike. "What kind of ballast? *Zippo* hasn't been modified. That's why it was trailed over."

"It wasn't modified," said Sarah. "It was added to. Lead ballast. A dozen bars of lead laid inside along the centerboard. Keeps her from being knocked down with every gust. Take a look." Here Sarah led the way to *Zippo*, and the four peered into the boat.

"Lift the floorboards," suggested Sarah.

Mike, giving her a look, climbed aboard and pulled up the long segments of teak planking and reached down into the bilge. "Lead," he announced. "Or something like it. Laid two by two."

"And *Sweetheart*?" said Sarah. "Did she carry lead bars?"

Mike stared at her resentfully. "I didn't see any. But if she had, maybe they would have been dumped out when the sloop went over. Or Dolly never carried ballast in the first place."

But Sarah shook her head. "You just said there's no record of Dolly getting in trouble before. Except for two minor incidents. Are you sure? How about coast guard records?"

Mike looked unhappy. "So far coast guard records don't show anything, but we're still at square one. Sarah, I can't believe you just went out and called the Baum family and this all came out. The state police said the Baums swore that their sloop was an original unchanged Scooter."

"So it is," said Sarah. "Only a little weight adjustment."

"One point for the home team," said Alex, who had been listening to the Mike-Sarah exchange with a certain pleasure. It wasn't often that anyone set Mike back on his heels.

"Christ," said Mike unhappily. "Now we'll have to see if *Sweetheart*—what a god-awful name for a boat—carried lead."

"There should be rub-marks, dirt lines," said Alex. "Even with the hull and bottom trashed, you should find some signs of wear from the lead. Paint scrapings, splinters."

"And," put in Sarah, "I don't think *Sweetheart* is such a bad name. It's growing on me. Dolly apparently didn't have a human one, and a pretty little sailboat seems like a fair substitute."

"A human sweetheart," said Katie, speaking after a long silence, "wouldn't have hit her on the head and dumped her into the Atlantic Ocean."

Alex turned on her with a grim expression. "You know better than that, Katie. Human sweethearts can be lethal."

"Never mind," said Sarah. "The question is whether Dolly's boat usually carried lead ballast. And if it did, then why wasn't there a single bar left even after it capsized? With one floorboard still in place, you can't tell me every one of those heavy lead lumps just wiggled loose, floated out, and sunk."

"It's possible," insisted Mike, frowning.

Alex raised his eyebrows.

"Okay, okay, okay," said Mike. "I'll call the Beaugards. I'll call

Tad Bugelski. I'll see who helped Dolly rig her boat and launched it for her every year. Who was scheduled to help haul it out. See if *Sweetheart* carried any goddamn ballast. Jesus Christ, we'll take a simple case of drowning and turn it into a suspicious death when we're already run ragged trying to find out what was going on with those drunken doped-up Gattling brothers. It'll keep the state police around everyone's necks until after Christmas."

"Around *your* necks," corrected Sarah. "Not mine, not Alex's neck. We're just vagrants passing through."

"Hell you are," said Mike. "Alex is the medical examiner, and you are very useful because you're intimately acquainted with the whole Beaugard tribe."

"Not intimately," said Sarah with irritation. "Slightly."

"If it isn't intimate now," said Mike, turning to leave, "it will be."

"Seriously," asked Alex, as the two, after a pit stop to pick up a pizza, drove back to through the Camden Hills and toward Sawmill Road. "How well do you know the Beaugards?"

"I thought I'd told you," said Sarah. "When we spent the summers in Camden with Grandma, I was taken over there to kid birthday parties. And I was in Alice's class for a few years and in the same tent for two years at Camp Merrilark. Then, when I was older—after Alice had more or less deserted the family—there were tennis tournaments, dances at the Proffit Point Boat Club. Sailboat regattas. I was invited because Mrs. Beaugard knew Grandma and I'd been a friend of Alice's. But I wasn't part of the Proffit Point scene. I always felt like someone's stray cousin being dragged in to fill out a doubles match. Be a crew in a sailing race. I was a fringe person."

"But the Beaugards came to our wedding."

"Grandma insisted."

"And you went to Alice's wedding."

"The first one. Reception at Great Oaks. Big tent, lawn, music, dancing. And Alice and her husband—Alan Epstein, you know, he writes those sci-fi psycho thrillers that have people turning into reptiles or crows. Well, in the middle of toasts, Alice began a wingding argument, Alan got a glass of champagne in the face, and Alice ended up being tossed off the dock in her wedding regalia."

"A sporting affair," observed Alex, slowing for the home turn.

"Memorable, anyway. But the second wedding was family only. A man who owned television stations. I think Alice had a vision of a media career. I don't think the marriage lasted six months. But she's got a son by Alan. Name of Jonathan. Grandma says he's spoiled, but she thinks all children are spoiled."

Alex shook his head. "I'm getting a picture of Alice, all right, and it's giving me a headache. Back to Dolly. Was she the sort to have a death wish? Ever depressed?"

"The police are asking that. The answer seems to be no. Besides, if you were thinking suicide, why would any woman in her right mind take pounds and pounds of lead ballast out of a sailboat, then sail away in a stiff wind in order to capsize and drown? It could have been done with much less effort by simply wading out into the ocean."

"The operative words are 'in her right mind.' "

"Dolly was the most sane female I've ever met. Steady, determined, levelheaded. Dull as dishwater. But sane."

"That's your view."

"It's a correct view. Ask around."

"You know, I might just do that. But it's still most likely to be ruled an accidental death. The ballast business is interesting but not earthshaking. Not yet anyway." Alex swung the car up the dirt drive leading to the farmhouse and then slowed. And swore. "Now, who in hell is that?"

Sarah looked up and ahead. There in the driveway stood an alien vehicle, a small yellow pickup truck. And under the front door light, seated on the steps of the kitchen entrance, leaning against the handrailing, a figure. Female. Long legs crossed on the stoop, the tiny red glow of a cigarette end, and music. The almost eerie sound of a clarinet.

"Mozart," said Sarah in astonishment as Alex brought the car to a halt.

"Who is playing Mozart on on our steps?" demanded Alex.

"It's not one player," said Sarah. "It's a quintet. Mozart clarinet quintet. It must be a radio or tape deck. But who in God's name?" Then she stepped out of the car and took a step closer. The profile, the cigarette, the careless sprawl of the figure, the sense of clothes in multiple and random layers.

"Oh God, it's Alice."

Then she stopped. "I didn't mean it that way. I'm sorry for her. Even in the middle of her family today she looked so alone. But tonight I wanted to correct papers and crawl into bed."

"Go ahead," said Alex with a weary sigh. "I'm not on call tonight, so I'll do the honors."

Aware that Mozart had ceased in midphrase, Alex and Sarah walked toward their guest, who rose to greet them.

"A little night music," she said. "I got sick of waiting and I didn't want to break into the house, so I settled down here with my tape player. Mozart to soothe my savage breast."

"You're feeling savage?" said Alex. "Come on in and help us with a pizza."

"I ate here last night. But okay. And some coffee maybe. I'm being picked up at your house. Hope you don't mind my parking my truck here. I'm meeting someone at your place. I've got two dates." Here Alice rose, crushed her cigarette with her bootheel. "I know you two don't have any common vices like smoking. Anyway, we've had news. Dolly died by drowning."

"Yes," said Alex. "It seems that way." He held the door open and the three trooped in and headed for the kitchen, Alice shrugging off a leather bomber jacket that looked as if it had been through at least two World Wars.

Conversation during the pizza heating and the coffee brewing ranged from the state of Mrs. Beaugard's nerves, the persistence of the police on the subject of Dolly's mental health, to Alice's loathing of Caroline and Eliot's newly built house.

"It's one of those state-of-the art things. You know, pseudo-Victorian Queen Anne shingle on the outside with high-tech goodies inside and every window facing the sea. Which reminds me. You're both invited over. Drinks Friday at six unless that's the day of the funeral. But we can't have the funeral until the police release the body. Mother wants Saint Dolly in a proper casket at the altar. She's choosing hymns and Psalms now. God, I can hear it now." And Alice lifted her head and sang out in a clear and true soprano:

"For all the saints who from their labors rest,
Who Thee by faith before the world confessed,
Thy name, O Je-sus, be for-ev-er blest.
Al-le-lu-ia! Al-le-lu-ia!"

Sarah and Alex stared. It was as if something unearthly had taken possession of the room. Then, after a moment of stunned silence, Alice herself broke the spell. "Think I should join the choir? Okay, Alex, when are the medical people going to let Dolly's body go, because let's get the funeral over. I mean, Christ, so Dolly drowned. What more do they want?"

Alex didn't answer immediately and busied himself with clearing the coffee cups. Somehow he didn't want to let Alice know that the police were also interested in Dolly's head injuries. That every inch of her sailboat was being examined. That it wasn't just a simple case of accidental drowning. Carrying the cups to the sink, he took a sidelong glance at Alice and decided that although she didn't look any better than when he'd seen her yesterday, she didn't seem worse. And somehow she'd managed to have her hair cut, and the improvement was noticeable. Straggle had been replaced by a straight clip, but Alice, like Sarah herself, had the cheekbones and chin to carry a severe look.

But now Alice was explaining why, for the second night in a row, she had invaded their kitchen. "It's not like I'm running away from the family, but the whole scene at Great Oaks gives me hives. Mother wants me to sleep in the house, not in my cottage, because she's trying to turn me into a Dolly replacement. And Uncle Lenox is driving everyone up the wall. He's acting like we're all in his classroom. He's got opinions on everything, and goes on about my dog, Willie, and his blasted glasses. Still lost in the woods. He keeps making little trips to look for them and makes me keep Willie in. He even went out searching last night with a flashlight. New trifocals, he says. What a grouch."

"He did seem a little cranky," Sarah admitted.

" 'Cranky' hardly touches it. I think he's gone a little goofy since his fall. But Mother doesn't see it. He's her older brother and she's always had a soft spot for the creep. And I'll bet he's secretly glad Dolly's out of the way because he's been itching to manage Mother's affairs himself and take over Dolly's job at the Midcoast Audubon. Run the Christmas bird count thing."

Sarah, who had been about to gather her briefcase full of student papers and retire, paused.

"Christmas bird count?"

"You know," said Alice. "Every year around Christmas the whole neighborhood climbs around in snowdrifts in below-zero weather counting chickadees and seagulls. I went along once and it's unbelievable. People arguing about whether they really saw a pink-breasted titmouse or a black-assed woodpecker. Mother loves it, spends the day counting the birds at her feeder, and Uncle Lenox leads a team, and I get the hell out of Proffit Point and do something lowlife like go to a bar or go bowling."

Alex, who had been busy wiping off the counter, looked up. "Actually, I've been asked to help. With you, Sarah. December, Saturday the seventeenth. I'd almost forgotten. Dolly herself left a message last week on my answering machine. Sorry, Alice, you're in the presence of another bird nut."

"Alex is speaking for himself," said Sarah. "I am not a bird nut. I just married one."

"The point is," said Alice, "that Uncle Lenox is in seventh heaven. He hated being organized by Dolly, and now he can run the affair by himself. At least the Proffit Point section of it." Suddenly she came to attention. "Was that a car?"

"Your date?" asked Sarah, going to the window. She peered out into the dark. "No one there. Does whoever it is know the way? Sawmill Road isn't exactly on the main drag."

"Not a real date," said Alice, reaching for her jacket. "More like a business meeting. Husband number one. Alan. He knows the way here because he's renting on this road. He's moving from New Hampshire and teaching at Bowmouth next semester. It's some sort of writer-in-residence deal. Sci-fi stuff is very big. I hope they pay him a bundle. I want Jonathan to have swimming lessons."

"Bowmouth College," said Sarah with feeling, "has never paid anyone a bundle."

"Anyway, Alan has custody. As he should because, as the judge pointed out, I'm a little on the flaky side. But I turn up from time to time to play mother. Jonathan's quite used to the whole setup. Very mature kid. Eleven going on forty. Anyway, what with Alan being in the middle of moving and Jonathan's school situation messed up because of the move, I'm taking him for the school year. Or rather Mother and I are taking him. Cocustodians. The court seems to think that his living at Great Oaks is putting him into a stable environment. Little do they know. So I'm meeting with Alan to go over the details and then have myself a real date."

"Good," said Alex, who was wondering how soon he and Sarah would have the house to themselves.

"We're going to this rock concert thing tonight," said Alice. "I couldn't meet him at home because there would be multiple cat fits and cries of anguish. Mother, Lenox, Masha, and Eliot all keening away. Caroline making little mewing noises."

"Okay," said Sarah. "Who are you going with? The Phantom of the Opera or the Vampire Lestat?"

"He's not a vampire, though Mother would probably much rather he were. It's Webb."

"Webb who?" asked Alex obediently.

"Webb Gattling. I've known him forever. Well, since sixth grade, anyway. And yes, he's one of the famous Gattlings about whom we have all heard so much. Particularly this past weekend. But there's Alan's car now. I won't bring him in. See you, and thanks for the coffee."

Sarah and Alex sat immobile, listening to the car door slam

shut, the tires crunch on the gravel, the sound of the motor accelerating, the sound diminishing down the drive. Only then did speech come.

"Gattling!" sputtered Sarah. "Well, wouldn't you know."

"Trust Alice," said Alex. "Mike told me that years ago Alice hung around with Webb Gattling, but he didn't sound as if he thought it was still going on. But here it is. The Gattling connection."

"And it's obvious the Beaugards don't have a clue that this old-time friendship is alive and kicking."

"Maybe not so much ongoing as revived," said Alex. "After all, Alice has been all over the map for the past ten years. Having husbands and a baby and visiting sanitariums."

"And who are we to judge?" said Sarah. "This Webb Gattling may be the greatest guy since Saint Peter. We shouldn't generalize on the basis of knowing that at least some of the local Gattlings belong behind bars. There may be pockets of wonderful Gattlings keeping their heads down and doing an honest day's work."

"Sure," said Alex. "There may be. I just haven't stubbed my toes on any. But I'm open-minded in all things and—"

But here the telephone rang across Alex's sentence and the idea of an honest member of the Gattling clan expired, not to be revived for some time to come.

Sarah answered the phone. Listened, nodded, made a face at Alex, and then said shortly into the receiver, "All right. Yes, he will. I will. Right away."

Alex looked up, glowering. "He will? You will? Right away?"

Sarah sighed. "That's Masha Beaugard. It's Lenox Cobb. He left for a walk around six. Or six-thirty. Into the woods, looking for his glasses. Hasn't come back. It may just be his ankle again. Or he's resting somewhere. They don't want to stir up the police over what may turn out to be nothing."

"They want to stir us up instead?"

"You've got it. We're practically family, says Masha. I love it. We haven't seen them in years except at weddings. Now we're family."

Alex reached for his windbreaker. "I'll go. You correct your papers."

Sarah hesitated, visions of schoolwork finished, hot bath taken, pillow and comforter beckoning, and then shook her head.

"'Whither thou goest, I will go; and where thou lodgest, I will lodge.' Or driveth—as the case may be."

"Hah," said Alex. "Don't put on sanctimonious robes. You are eaten up by an unholy curiosity as to the fate of the egregious Lenox Cobb. Right? You said you wanted to know how the four-hundred-page Beaugard family novel turned out. Well, this is Chapter Two."

"I'm beginning," said Sarah, opening the door, "to see the advantage of sticking to the short story."

6

ALEX, a heavy foot on the accelerator, made it to Proffit Point in record time.

"Really," said Sarah, as he slowed the Jeep at the entrance to the Great Oaks property, "if a moose ever decided to cross in front of us, we'd be raw meat."

But now a light bobbing in the end of the road forced Alex to bring the car to a halt. It was Eliot Beaugard, wearing a blaze orange vest and equipped with a long-handled flashlight.

Alex pulled the Jeep over to the side of the driveway and, together with Sarah and Patsy, made himself known.

"Yo, Alex," shouted Eliot, "you made it." He eyed Patsy. "That dog, does he track?"

"He can try," said Sarah. "He's great at finding porcupines."

"I suppose," said Eliot, "that describes Uncle Lenox. But we can use all the help we can get. That animal of Alice's—Willie—is hopeless. I've had to take charge of this circus. Mother's home shouting and banging her cane. You'd have thought Lenox was the only thing she had left in life. Me, I think he belongs in a home. He's gone wacko. Senile. Alzheimer's or blocked arteries."

"Where do you want us to start looking?" said Alex shortly. He had no liking for wild speculation on medical matters.

"And if we don't find him in the next hour, don't you think you should call the police?" said Sarah.

"Police," growled Eliot, and Sarah could almost hear Eliot's teeth grinding. "We've had police up to here. Like maggots. Forget the police. We just need a little homemade help. Like you and Alex. People who know us. Hell, this is a perfectly normal thing to happen to an elderly guy whose brains have scrambled themselves. I mean, looking for his glasses at all hours of the night and day. Tying up the entire family. Forcing us to call in strangers . . ." Here Eliot paused, realizing that two strangers had just been described as friendly homemade help.

"It's all right," said Alex. "Let's get on with it. Where have you looked already?"

Eliot subsided and produced a pad of paper, held up his flashlight, and squinted at it.

"Caroline and our son, Colin—he's nine and pretty sharp—are looking around the beach areas. And I've asked Tad Bugelski to keep a lookout by the harbor. After all, he's not the police. Mother's housekeeper, Vivian Lavender, is checking the house, the flower gardens, and the garage. I've looked in the potting shed and the pool house. Lenox isn't floating in the swimming pool; I turned on the underwater lights."

"And us?" Alex reminded him.

"Try and cover the woods by the gates here—both sides—and I'll case the middle part of the property and snoop around the guest cottages. All but Alice's. Her cottage is on your turf. Wouldn't you know that Alice is out on the town at the one time we could actually use her. I'll tell you this. Dolly could bore you to death arguing, but she wouldn't have let Lenox out of her sight. But hey, you two, we really appreciate you coming out here. And here's a whistle for you. Two blasts if you find the old buzzard."

"And if we don't?" said Sarah.

"Keep looking."

"For an hour. Two at the most. Then the police," said Sarah firmly. "And how about calling in more neighbors? Tad Bugelski could probably line up some of the lobstermen."

"No way," said Eliot, his voice rising. "It's bad enough that the whole county looks at the Beaugards like we're this bunch of weirdos because of Dolly and those Gattling brothers washing in practically on top of each other. No need to make it any worse."

"So let's move it," said Alex, now impatient to be away.

"Right," said Sarah. "I'll take the west side with Alice's cottage and the oceanfront except for the beaches, and you take the woods and the harbor side."

"I don't have two whistles," said Eliot. "You'd better work together."

"No," said Sarah. "I can whistle through my fingers. I do it loud and clear."

"You don't know Sarah," said Alex. "The Lone Eagle of detection. And we've got our own flashlights." And then as Eliot strode off down the road into the dark, "Are you sure, Sarah? Maybe we should stick together."

"Who, me? The Lone Eagle? Not on your life. Besides, Alice's cottage has a porch light on it and not many trees around. It's quite civilized. And Patsy could frighten an army."

But for all her sturdy proclamations of independence, Sarah felt a familiar crawling sensation moving from the nape of her neck down her back. Not because of unknown dangers hiding in the shadows, because indeed her search territory was crossed and recrossed with walking paths and garden benches, and Alice's cottage, just beyond a clump of birch, offered a cleared well-lighted safety zone.

Her unease had more to do with a sense of the nearby ocean. A southwest wind had sprung up; the tide was coming in, splashing softly on the lower rocks of the beach. Sarah could not help having visions of Marsden and Junior Gattling, like unearthly visitors, sodden with seawater, brains numbed with whiskey and drugs, washing in at high tide, followed by Dolly, Dolly turning in the moving waves, her blond hair streaming from her head.

Taking a tighter grip on her flashlight, telling her imagination to cool it, she gave Patsy's leash a tug, pointed the beam at the walking path that branched from the main drive, and, moving the light back and forth, walked forward.

Twenty minutes, six turns, and two paths later, Sarah ended on Alice's front porch. The sparse woods, mostly birch and white pines, had been free of Uncle Lenox—rampant or couchant—and it now occurred to her that if he was as befuddled as Eliot claimed, he might just have wandered into the cottage and gone to sleep.

Sarah fastened Patsy's leash to the porch support and examined the screen door. It was unlocked, as was the front door itself. She stepped into the building, fumbled for the light switch, and was rewarded by a glow from two table lamps and an overhead fixture.

I'm glad Alice isn't roughing it, she told herself. No doubt kerosene lamps were more in the spirit of the simple life, but the electric lights were reassuring and drove away the shadows.

It was a large room in a large cottage—the sort of cottage that many people would consider a house. A brick fireplace flanked by bookshelves filled the back wall. Decrepit wicker and oak chairs and tables did for furniture, and a large Navajo rug stretched down the middle. All in all it was a pleasant space. Except for the junk. Snuffed-out cigarettes overflowed in ashtrays; magazines and newspapers lay scattered about the floor along with a collection of muddy boots and dirty sneakers. Odd articles of clothing hung from chairs; a guitar leaned by a door; a dog leash hung over a lamp. On the walls hung several faded watercolors done by an amateur hand, a print of a Georgia O'Keefe skull, and a poster—a collector's piece, no doubt—of the early Rolling Stones.

But no Uncle Lenox Cobb. Sarah checked the sofa—and behind it—the screened porch off the living room, the kitchen, and then an overflowing curtained alcove that did service as a closet and held no room even for a man built like a praying mantis.

So on to the bedroom. Sarah, feeling now more intruder than searcher, walked across the room to the first of two doors, found the light switch, flipped it, and walked in. Guest room. The bed was made but covered with heaps of blue jeans, jackets, canvas hats, and a pyramid of rolled posters. A folding easel. A small loom strung with a woolly-looking length of something.

But no Uncle Lenox.

Leaving the guest room, bracing for the mess that must be in Alice's own bedroom, Sarah felt her sneakered foot lift with reluctance and looked down. The floor was tacky. She shone her flashlight and found herself looking down at a dark patch of something. Juice? Maple syrup? Blood?

Of course it was blood. She knew it must be even as she pulled her sneaker loose from the spot. She moved her flashlight forward and was rewarded with other spots. Or splatters.

Splatters that led straight into Alice's bedroom.

And now she hesitated, thinking not of Uncle Lenox but of people behind doors. Persons under beds, in closets. Persons curled up ready to spring out from behind bureaus, trunks, desks. Intruders rolled in comforters pretending to be Red Riding Hood's grandmother resting in bed.

And Sarah, for once, was sensible. She turned and ran to the porch, put two fingers between tightened lips, and gave a whistle that cut through the night air like a knife. Then she untied Patsy and retired behind a very large pine tree and waited.

"So I'm a coward," she whispered to Patsy, "but I don't like it in there."

And Patsy, sympathetic to her voice, rose on his haunches, put both paws on her shoulder, and began the reassuring business of washing her chin.

Sarah hissing, "down, bad dog, stop it," didn't see Alex until he was almost at the cottage's front step. She called out, thinking at the same time, okay, now I've warned whoever it is—if there is someone—that we're here for the taking. Or the shooting or knifing, she added, remembering the dark splotches on the floor.

Alex paused, moved his flashlight, found her, and ran up. Sarah explained in five words, and together, this time with Patsy front and center, they cautiously and silently reentered the cottage. Then Alex, picking up a poker from the fireplace, moved quietly to Alice's bedroom door, paused, gave it a hefty kick, backed up out of sight, and waited.

The door stood wide open. Nothing happened. Two minutes. Five minutes. And then Patsy, pulling against his leash, began a whine that rose to an eerie pitch, a whine that would waken the dead. In case someone was dead.

Sarah came up behind Alex, slipped around him, thrust one arm into the room, and hit the light switch at first try.

The room was empty. The bed mussed, a blue and red comforter falling off one side, a cotton nightgown hanging from a bedpost, the bedside table holding a mix of filled ashtrays, paperbacks, a radio, a box of Kleenex, a jar of face cream.

But on the floor on the far side of the bed, in the narrow space between the wall and the bed—Lenox Cobb.

On his back, staring at them—or at the ceiling; it was hard to tell which. He lay, fitted into the space as if into a coffin, his legs neatly together, toes pointed up, gnarled and veined hands across his chest, head cradled between an overturned wastebasket and a shopping bag. His face was wearing what Sarah first thought was a sort of dark lopsided mask but on closer inspection—she leaning past Alex's shoulder—saw was made of the same viscous material that befouled the floor.

Alex, pausing only for a second, taking in the scene, making sure that any portion of Lenox was not being supported by the bed, grabbed the headboard and, assisted by Sarah, moved it out of the way, then knelt down, ready to begin a preliminary examination.

Meanwhile, Sarah had her hands full with Patsy, who began to show a great interest in the recumbent figure. Finally, pushing the dog into the living room, she returned to hear Lenox asking in a high reedy voice, "What kept you so long?"

"Just lie still, Professor Cobb," said Alex, putting his hand gently on Lenox's shoulder.

"What kept you so long?" repeated Lenox.

"You're all right," said Alex.

"We didn't know where you were," Sarah tried to explain.

"What kept you so long?" said Lenox, his voice rising.

"I'm trying to tell you," said Sarah. "We found you just now at Alice's cottage."

Alex twisted around to Sarah. "Head injury. Loss of immediate memory. Happens a lot after this sort of thing. They repeat and repeat. Hand me my flashlight. Thanks. I'll just check his pupillary responses while you call the ambulance. Proffit Point Rescue Squad. Then go on out and give another of your famous whistles and see if you can raise Eliot."

"Why are you here?" demanded Lenox. "I didn't ask you to come. It's time for bed. Where's Elena? I didn't ask you to come."

"Just lie quietly," said Alex, gently lifting one eyelid and shining the flashlight.

"I didn't ask you to come," said Lenox, now in a fainter voice.

"Yes," said Alex, in a soothing voice. "Easy does it."

"Womoahwamamaaooooo," said Lenox, giving a prolonged groan.

"What's he saying?" said Sarah, returned from the telephone.

"He's leaving us for the moment," said Alex. He ran his fingers lightly over Lenox Cobb's disordered head. "It's not a bad wound. Not a fractured skull as far as I can tell."

At which Lenox gave another groan mixed with an unintelligible mumble that sounded to Sarah's ears like some sort of Eastern dialect. Fortunately, the rescue squad was a speedy outfit, and before long Lenox Cobb had been packaged, loaded onto the ambulance, and whisked into the night, Alex in attendance.

Sarah, after the flurry of activity centering around the ambulance departure, found herself back at Great Oaks' entrance trying to fend off the attentions of Eliot and Masha. She must come back to the house. Mrs. Beaugard wanted to thank her. It would mean so much. Sarah was such an old friend.

Balls, she said to herself. And then aloud, "I have papers to correct for tomorrow's classes. I'll come up for just a minute and then I have to go."

This, of course, was easier said than done. Mrs. Beaugard, in common with the rest of the family, seemed to be under the delusion that Sarah and Alex—"thank heaven for Alex"—were friends and supporters of such long standing that they were ready to shuck their own needs in order to stand by the beleaguered Beaugards. "Just leave Patsy in the front hall. He can make friends with Willie," said Eliot.

Sarah, plied with cider and brownies, found that she was now elevated to the position not only of indispensable family friend but of Alice's special companion. Expected to take over the care and perhaps the feeding of Alice. Ready to hear the plaints of the family on the subject of Alice. And, now, on the subject of poor Lenox, who, in Eliot's words, was obviously wacko.

"Well, it was a head injury," said Sarah. "No wonder he's not entirely sensible."

"He hasn't been very sensible for ages," said Masha. She was sitting on a stool at her mother's feet holding wool in two hands while Mrs. Beaugard made hard work of winding a skein into a ball.

"Jesus, Uncle Lenox's never even been close to sensible," said Eliot. "How did Bowmouth stand him? And now obsessing about his glasses. Why didn't he call his optometrist and have a new pair sent out?"

Mrs. Beaugard paused abruptly in her wool winding. "Leave Jesus out of this, Eliot. He is not responsible for Lenox losing his glasses. But I agree that Lenox hasn't seemed himself lately. And so cross because I haven't turned to him for everything. He's been wanting to take over where my poor Dolly left off. Help me manage my affairs, balance my checkbook, but I really think—"

"Yo, Gran," said a voice from the door. "I'll manage your affairs. I got an A in math last year. And I'm going into pre-algebra now. Hello, Uncle Eliot. Aunt Masha. Old-home week, I guess."

Sarah looked up to see a boy in faded jeans, dirty sneakers, and a black sweatshirt standing in the doorway, a large duffel bag and a book backpack at his feet. The boy was tall and slender, and although his hair was dark, almost black, and he wore steel-rimmed glasses, he was so like Alice—the same sharp face, cheekbones, pointed chin—that she knew at once this must be Jonathan.

"So here I am, Gran," said Jonathan. "I think it's a pretty good time for me to move in because Aunt Dolly's dead and you probably need someone else around. Someone young."

"Jonathan," said Mrs. Beaugard faintly. "Jonathan, I'd forgotten, what with everything. Did your mother, the court . . . ?"

The boy stepped into the room, and Sarah thought that here was a youth absolutely assured. No self-image problems, no inner doubts. He walked across the room as if he owned it, bent over his grandmother, kissed her cheek. "Not to worry, Gran. The court thinks it's okay even though the judge must be out of his tree, what with Aunt Dolly's body floating in on your cove. I mean it isn't exactly a wholesome environment, is it?"

"Jonathan," repeated Mrs. Beaugard, apparently not able to go beyond that one word.

"Listen, Gran, it's okay. My shrink said so and Mom's shrink said go for it. And Dad's happy because he's up to his ears in the Bowmouth College scene. And Mom thought it was a great idea because then she could stay in her own cottage and smoke and play the guitar, and I could stay with you in the big house and fight off intruders and burglars and alien androids."

"Oh, Jonathan!" exclaimed Mrs. Beaugard, pushing her glasses back on her nose and sitting up straight. "Oh dear, what am I going to do with you? Eliot, did I know Jonathan was coming?"

But here the boy turned, held out a hand to Eliot, shook it, walked toward Masha, gave her a peck on the cheek, and then confronted Sarah.

"I'm Jonathan Epstein. Alice is my mother. I had dinner with her and Dad tonight, and it's all arranged for me to spend the year here with Gran and help out. I'm at Martin Academy over in Rockland, which is private and there's a car pool and that means then I can bat back and forth between parents if I have to. The human yo-yo, that's me. Are you a friend of Aunt Dolly's?"

Sarah stood up, shook his hand, and introduced herself, adding, "I'm just here for a few minutes. I was part of a search party looking for Professor Cobb, who's gone off in the ambulance. He hurt himself in the woods looking for his glasses."

Jonathan subsided in a chair next to his grandmother. "Hey, you mean old Uncle Scrooge is out of it? The only bad thing about coming here for the year was that we can't get along. I've tried, but he just wags his finger at me and calls me 'boy' and goes on as if I'm the sort of scumball who's ruining America."

Mrs. Beaugard reared up. "Jonathan, Uncle Lenox is not Mr. Scrooge. He's just not himself. Unwell."

"He was well enough to chew my head off when he saw me the other day at IGA grocery store in Camden. But I'll try and behave, okay, Gran? And I'm sorry about Aunt Dolly. I mean she wasn't the most fun person in the world, but she took me sailing every summer. When I came for vacation and it was Mother's turn to have me for a while. Or Gran's, because Mother wasn't always around."

Sarah twisted around to face him. "Dolly took you sailing?"

"Yeah," said Jonathan. He reached over to the plate of brownies, helped himself to a square, and took a large bite. Then, mouth full, he nodded, chewed again, and swallowed. "Yeah, Aunt Dolly was my sailing teacher. She wouldn't let anyone on the *Sweetheart* but me. I was the privileged person. I think she thought she was rehabilitating me or something. Because I was from divorced parents. From a broken home." Jonathan took another bite of his brownie and chomped down.

Sarah gave the conversation a forward push. "She let you sail her boat? By yourself?"

Jonathan gave an heroic swallow, reached for the pitcher of cider, filled a mug, and gulped. Then returned to Sarah. "Nope. Never on my own. Just me and Aunt Dolly out on the wide Atlantic Ocean. She never let anyone touch the *Sweetheart.*

Never even put a finger on it. She told me she did all the scraping and painting and stuff in the spring and hauled it out with her own trailer in the fall. She didn't do sports much, so I guess this was kind of her hobby."

"You mean," said Sarah slowly and carefully, "she did all the maintenance herself."

"Yeah," said Jonathan. "Like it was her own baby or something. I mean it was sorta weird calling it *Sweetheart,* but she didn't have any kids or have any men drooling over her—"

"Jonathan, that's enough," said Elena Beaugard.

"Okay, Gran, okay," said the boy. "I'm just answering questions about sailing."

"Did you ever capsize in the *Sweetheart* or have trouble in a big wind?" asked Sarah, trying to keep her tone casual.

Jonathan appeared to consider this. Then he shook his head. "Not real trouble. If the wind got too strong, we'd make for the lee of some island. A couple of times I came about too fast or let her jibe—you know, turn away from the wind, not into it— and the boat flopped around. But no capsize. Aunt Dolly said the *Sweetheart* could handle tough weather." Here Jonathan paused, seeming to follow the implications of what he had just said. "You're sort of saying that it's funny-peculiar that Aunt Dolly flipped over last week in the *Sweetheart,* but I suppose everyone does something dumb every now and then. Even Aunt Dolly."

"That, Jonathan, is enough," broke in Elena Beaugard again.

And Eliot looked at the boy with obvious dislike. "Watch your lip, buddy. Caroline and I don't let Colin speak to his grandmother like that."

But Jonathan only grinned and gave a shrug. "But actually, Uncle Eliot, I don't mean to be rude, but I was talking to Ms. Sarah Deane, not Gran. And Colin's only about nine, isn't he? So he doesn't dare say much."

Sarah, hearing Jonathan skating on the near edge of insolence, turned away and found herself again facing the big fireplace and the portrait of the four Beaugard children. And now it seemed that Dolly, erect and stiff in her white painted dress on her painted garden bench, was looking directly at Sarah with her tight smile, her wide-open blue eyes, her lifted chin. It was as if Dolly were radiating determination and stubborn purpose, and it had the effect of making a hard knot form in the center of Sarah's stomach. It was amazing how some people can be such an active presence even though presumed safely dead and gone. Sarah wrenched her gaze from Dolly's face, swallowed hard, and determined to get home, back to the tedium of her own chores. Confronting the family group again, she realized that Elena Beaugard was addressing Jonathan.

"Your mother"—she said the word with obvious disapproval—"will probably come home late and go right to her cottage. Vivian is there now cleaning up after your uncle Lenox. So you may as well take your things upstairs and unpack. You can have the green room on the north side. You must have some homework and then it will be time for bed. You may kiss me good night."

Jonathan jumped to his feet and leaned over and again brushed his grandmother's cheek. "And I'll say good night to all the nice people and be a good boy and wash my hands and brush my teeth. And hey, Gran, tomorrow I'll take over your business affairs. You can be my social science project." And without more ado, Jonathan walked swiftly to the door, picked up his bookbag, shouldered his bulging duffel bag, and vanished down the hall.

"Christ Almighty," said Eliot. "Does that kid need a crash course in manners. Which he certainly won't learn from Alice." He reached over and patted Mrs. Beaugard's hand. "Poor Mother. A useless big-mouth kid for the winter."

Sarah in her turn prepared for departure, shook hands all round, left the room, and collected Patsy.

Eliot was wrong, she told herself as she opened her car door. Wrong because Jonathan, no matter how rude, had not proved himself useless. In fact, it seemed to her that Jonathan—the chosen sailing companion of Dolly Beaugard—showed great promise as a source of special information.

7

SARAH, arriving home well after ten o'clock, gave up on the idea of correcting papers and was in bed within the half hour, Patsy snoring by her side. And so soundly asleep were both that Alex's midnight return took place without either moving a muscle.

Thursday morning came too soon. The alarm clock purchased especially for its strident bell came to life at six A.M., and Sarah reached over and slammed a hand down on the control knob.

"Damn," she mumbled. It was her invariable response to the morning summons. Then, rousing slightly, "How's Lenox Cobb? Alive and kicking?"

Alex sat up and ran his hands through his disordered hair. "He's not doing too much kicking, but he's alive. CAT scan normal—consistent with a concussive injury. He doesn't remember the where and how of what happened. Which is what I expected."

"The whole family—well, Masha and Mrs. Beaugard and Eliot—seem to think he's gone completely gaga."

"The family can have a neurology workup if they want. Frankly, he didn't act too differently from a hundred other people with a head injury."

"But the hospital will keep him?"

"For a few days. His regular physician, that's Joe Foxe, has the situation in hand, and I very gladly bowed out." Alex stood up, stretched, and then took hold of one of Sarah's hands. "Rise and shine forth. It's a new day with no rain forecast until tomorrow. So did you escape the hospitality of the Beaugard clan?"

Sarah reached for the comforter and dragged it up to her chin. Then looked at the clock and reluctantly sat up. "No. It was cider, brownies, and Jonathan Epstein. Alice's boy. Mr. Cool. Flip and mouthy. I'd say Eliot wanted to brain him, and with considerable justification. And his grandmother hasn't a clue about what to do with him. Jonathan walked into that living room and spread himself. Says he'll handle Elena Beaugard's business matters as a social studies project, and he may just do that. There's a vacuum in the house, what with everyone doing no more than bemoaning Dolly's disappearance."

"Lenox will be home soon, and taking care of Elena Beaugard's affairs ought to be a permissible activity for him."

"Unless his mind is on a real skid."

"Don't listen to family opinion. Families always think their members have a few loose screws." And Alex disappeared into the bathroom for his shower.

But Sarah, washing and dressing slowly, was perfectly willing to believe that Lenox Cobb was losing his grip. She hadn't taken to him on their first meeting, and the kindest thing to think was that his mind was affected.

But Dolly was another matter. Dolly, that bland fair-haired, dumpy woman, was beginning to haunt her. Perhaps there was more to her than the person of good works. For instance, why would Dolly, the proper pillar of the community, bother about an eleven-year-old smarty-pants like Jonathan? Why was Dolly a solo sailor—except for the dubious and occasional company of Jonathan?

These questions she present to Alex over his oatmeal and

coffee. "Why this penchant for sailing alone?" Sarah complained. "Picnics, tennis, possibly golf, would seem more her style."

"When you live on the seacoast, sailing alone in a small boat isn't an oddball activity," Alex reminded her. "If Dolly had taken up martial arts or skydiving, I might have wondered."

Sarah poured herself a bowl of Grape Nuts—she needed something to crunch down on—and settled opposite Alex. "Dolly dressed like something left over from the fifties, lived this life of service—especially to her mother and the church. In fact, planned for her mother to give the big house to the Episcopal Church for the greater glory of God. Or her mother. Does that all gibe with the fact that not only did she handle her own boat, she put it into the water in the spring and hauled it out on her trailer in the fall? I mean, come on, Alex, that's a hell of a lot of work."

"So maybe she needed a little exercise."

"Hauling boats is miserable grungy work. A sixteen-foot wooden sailboat, with or without lead ballast, is a bitch to float onto a trailer even with a good winch. I know. My brother, Tony, and I had a boat like that we kept at Grandma's, and she made us put it in every summer and haul it out before we went back to school. It's no fun, and to do it by yourself, I mean really. Flats mud and cold water and big high rubber boots and fooling around with trailer axle grease."

"You may have a point. A small point."

"So I'm asking why? Why would Miss Prim and Proper, a woman with money to burn, with all sorts of working hands available, bother with the toil and hazard of dealing with a heavy wooden sailboat? Scraping, painting, and varnishing it in the spring? And ballast. Jonathan said that he and Dolly had never been in trouble sailing the *Sweetheart*. He claimed the boat behaved in all weathers. Just like the *Zippo*. So there *must* have been ballast of some sort. Maybe Dolly put ballast, lumps of lead—something heavy anyway—into the boat in the spring and took it out in the fall."

"That's fairly interesting," said Alex, moving on to his toast and coffee. "But keep your hair on, love, the lab is busy going over *Sweetheart*'s hull looking for ballast evidence."

Sarah frowned. "Maybe Dolly took it out a little while back to get ready for the hauling out. To lighten the boat so it would be easier to maneuver onto the trailer."

"And then had an overwhelming urge to go sailing in a big breeze? And forgot she'd taken out the ballast?"

"Well, why not?" said Sarah defensively. "You know how it is. Summer is gone, winter's closing in, and here's a chance for one last spanking sail. It's like the last ski run of the day, the last season's climb up the mountain trail. You get sentimental and you forget you're tired or it's too cold . . ."

"Or you've removed a few hundred pounds of lead bars from your boat. Right, sure."

"It's possible," Sarah insisted. "I might forget something like that. Say Dolly tries for that last sail and goes too far out in the cove before she finds out the boat is unstable. And the wind whoops up and she's in trouble."

"Peace," said Alex. "Let the lab churn out its report. Put Dolly out of your head. At least for now. I'll meet you at the hospital at six. Dinner and a movie. I'm not on call."

But the dead woman did not depart from Sarah's head. All through the day Sarah returned to the enigma of Dolly Beaugard. The result of this preoccupation was that her students were allowed to get away with fatuous remarks and crude jokes on the subject of Chaucer's "The Miller's Tale," groans over the stupidity of Oedipus, and even indifference to Defoe's description of the plague.

The trouble, thought Sarah, packing her briefcase after her four-o'clock class, is that I've been given a canned biography of Dolly as the stolid hardworking family saint. But no one has mentioned that Dolly was interested in rehabilitating the young—nor had a fondness for children, let alone a smartass eleven-year-old. Dolly had helped direct the Sunday school, but she didn't teach classes. She hung out at the hospital information desk; she didn't push the gift cart or move patients in wheelchairs. She worked the office side of the Girl Scouts; she didn't hike out with a bunch of squealing girls. Dolly wasn't the hands-on type. Except. Except for mucking about with her boat. And sailing with Jonathan Epstein.

"Damn, damn," said Sarah aloud as she stamped out of the English office and made for the parking lot. What was really annoying about this preoccupation with Dolly was that the woman—from her own memory and from family report—was so bloody boring. If I have to be haunted by someone, she asked herself, why can't it be the ghost of someone interesting? What was Laurence Olivier doing these days? Or Charles Dickens? Or Jane Austen, Charlotte Brontë? Cary Grant and Ingrid Bergman. Mozart, Leonard Bernstein? Mrs. Patrick Campbell, George Eliot. Oscar Wilde, Mrs. Pankhurst. But no, she was stuck with Dolly Beaugard embedded in her brain like some sort of heavy and unearthly burr.

In the parking lot, standing at the gate, she met, like two hovering fates, Alice and Jonathan. Alice in gray sweats and Jonathan in regulation skateboard attire: baggy pants and oversize jacket.

"We're here to see Uncle Lenox," said Alice.

"*She's* here to see him," added Jonathan. "I'm just an extra. Part of Mother's support system. Uncle Lenox hates my guts."

"Jonathan, you don't have to say anything but hello," said Alice. "Listen, Sarah, we need to talk. I called the English office and they said you were coming out this way, so we stayed in ambush."

Sarah sighed and lowered her briefcase. "About Dolly? Or about Uncle Lenox?"

"Both," said Jonathan.

Sarah frowned, looking at the boy who stood almost as tall as his mother, his arms folded, his baseball cap set backwards on his head so that the strap made a line across his forehead.

"It's okay," said Alice. "I've told Jonathan that I think something's weird about Dolly drowning. But I don't know what's weird. And Jonathan's one of the people who really knew Dolly and liked her."

"Because she took me sailing," said Jonathan. "She was captain and I was crew, but sometimes we switched around and I sailed and told her what to do. She was nicer on the boat than she was on land. On land she acted like Uncle Eliot. Like she wanted to put me in a home for dysfunctional kids."

"How do I fit in?" asked Sarah. "Because I haven't the time or energy to do much. I'll go up to the hospital with you, if you want. I was meeting Alex in his office anyway."

"We can walk over," said Alice. "It's just across the campus and I'm on a fitness kick. Aerobics. Webb says I'm flabby."

"You probably are," said Jonathan. "We do sit-ups and run a mile before soccer. You should try it. Anyway, I really do think it's crazy that Aunt Dolly went out sailing and tipped over."

"But you never saw her put in any sort of ballast or take it out," said Sarah, taking care of this neglected question.

Jonathan shook his head. "I was allowed to sail, not fool around with the *Sweetheart*. But I didn't see any ballast, not weights or pipes or blocks or anything. There could have been, but the floorboards were always in place when I went out. Aunt Dolly was supercareful. We had this checklist before we cast off. Everything had to be done in order. Like take off the canvas cover, put it away, get out the life jackets, undo the sail stops, untie the rudder, haul up the jib, haul up the mainsail. Check the wind direction. Decide which tack we're going off on. Cast off. Pull in the jib sheet. Fasten it down. Same with the mainsheet. The whole thing like we were in the navy."

"You see," said Alice. "Dolly was organized in her sailing routine just like she was in everything else. No one else in the family is that together. I mean, Eliot runs his marine insurance business, but he has a secretary. And Masha practices her music and knows when her next concert is. But that's about all. Mother thinks she's organized, but she's never done much more than delegate and give orders. Vivian does a lot of the running of household things, but Dolly was the executive. I think Mother was glad that her arthritis and her bad eyesight gave her an excuse to turn it all over to Dolly."

Sarah, wanting to get back to the matter of ballast, turned to

Jonathan again. "If Dolly was so careful, didn't she always check before she went sailing to see if the ballast was in place?"

"You mean pull up the floorboards?" asked Jonathan. "Why would she do that? Not if it hadn't been raining like crazy. Even then the canvas cover kept the water out. If there was ballast, like lead blocks or something, they'd stay put. Ballast isn't like sails and lines and stuff that move around or wear out."

"So Dolly never talked about having ballast?"

"Nope, but hey, maybe the *Sweetheart* had a heavier centerboard than the other Scooters. Maybe she had some custom-made centerboard that weighed a ton and kept the *Sweetheart* stable. Or a weight fastened on."

Sarah stared at the boy. Yes, why not add weight to the centerboard? Something permanent. An extra weight at the bottom of the centerboard might have come detached on that last day. Might have broken loose if the boat had scraped a ledge or hit a rock.

"Good point, Jonathan," she said. "We'll have to ask if the *Sweetheart* centerboard exactly matches the one on *Zippo*. Or if there are signs that a weight was added and it broke free."

Jonathan shrugged modestly. "You have to think of all the possibilities, don't you? And you didn't. And I did. But," he added, "you might have later on. Maybe you don't sail that much."

Sarah, knowing that her sailing experience was most often that of an absentminded passenger, nodded agreement. Jonathan, if she saw much of him, might at a later date require a heavy squashing action, but for the moment he was still a handy source of information.

Alice broke it up. "Move," she said. "We can cut by the library and around to the hospital. Use the stairs. Uncle Lenox is on the fourth floor and the exercise will be good for you, Sarah. You have shadows under your eyes. I think you're out of shape."

Sarah gave her a look. "Have you tried spending the entire day going back and forth from classrooms to offices? Or sitting and correcting papers? It's not a healthy life." To herself she thought, this is Alice Beaugard, relict and waif, Alice who smokes like a chimney and drinks like a fish—or at least she used to—and she's telling me about health. Well, I'll show her. "Come on," she said aloud, and strode forth across the parking lot toward a line of trees edging the Bowmouth College Library.

But Alice, remarkably, kept up the pace, her usually pale face flushed, her thin arms and legs in their sweatsuit pumping, and although she was breathing in gasps by the time they reached the hospital, it was a creditable performance. Jonathan, of course, like an overgrown puppy, had circled, jogged, run ahead, and was sitting on the hospital steps waiting when the two women arrived.

"Room 440," directed the woman in the green volunteer smock at the desk. A blonde woman with her hair tied back so reminiscent of the deceased Dolly that Sarah almost gaped. Was Dolly coming back in body as well as by specter?

The three climbed up the stairwell, four flights, their feet echoing in hollow taps on the cement steps. Taking first one corridor, then a turnoff, the party reached a group of huddled nurses, but since the four nurses seemed to be in the midst of some argument, they pushed on and reached Room 440.

Alice, in the lead, gave the half-open door a knock, and then stuck her head around the door "Uncle Lenox," she said.

But the room was empty.

"In the john," suggested Sarah.

But the lavatory door stood open and was likewise empty.

"Down to X-ray?" said Alice. "Or gone for lab work?"

"Professor Cobb has gone," said an annoyed voice from the doorway, and Sarah looked up to see a nurse in green scrubs. "He signed a release and discharged himself. He said he was going to take a taxi home."

"The lobby," shouted Jonathan. "I'll bet he's down there waiting for the taxi." And without waiting for an answer, the boy ran out of the room and down the hall.

Jonathan opted for the stairs, Sarah and Alice for the elevator, but all three made it to the lobby at the same time. Made it in time to see a sticklike figure wrapped in an oversize trench coat, a crutch under one arm, standing by the lobby entrance.

"Uncle Lenox," called Alice, advancing on him.

The figure turned slowly, and began an unsteady advance upon the trio. Then, "Ah, Alice. It's about time someone in the family appeared. I've waited the entire afternoon and then realized that no one was coming to take me home and I must fend for myself. I've called a taxi. They took me down in a wheelchair because I presume the hospital didn't want to be sued if I fell."

Alice, with Sarah and Jonathan assisting, managed to settle Lenox Cobb in a chair, all the while urging him to return to bed and the tender mercies of the Mary Starbox Memorial Hospital. He looked ghastly, thought Sarah, backing away. Old age, extreme pallor, bruised eyes, and a bandaged head combined to create a picture of a man teetering at death's door.

But Lenox resisted Alice, making his point with a thrust of his crutch into the calf of his niece.

Jonathan, who had been listening to the pleadings of his mother and Sarah, now joined the fray. "Hey, Uncle Lenox, if you don't want to stay and you feel okay, well, why not blow this place? I mean, who wants to be in a hospital like in some sort of animal cage?"

Lenox Cobb regarded his great-nephew with interest. "That, boy, is the first sensible thing I have ever heard you say."

Jonathan grinned. "Thanks, Uncle Lenox. That's a pretty cool coat you've got. It's plenty big, too. I like gigantic clothes."

Lenox looked down at his tentlike trench coat with satisfaction. "The nurses took away all my own clothes. Blood all over them. And no one brought me any clean things."

"We thought you'd be in the hospital for a while," said Alice.

"Don't interrupt, young woman. Except for these dizzy spells, I am perfectly well. But I couldn't leave the hospital in that disgusting hospital nightgown, so I waited until the nurses were all in their station—they spend all their time fussing over charts and ignore the patients—and I went to Room 439 across the way because I have noticed that the occupant was unconscious with oxygen and tubes and an IV drip in his arm. So I slipped into his closet and borrowed his coat. And his shoes." Here Lenox stuck out his thin bare matchstick legs, showing feet encased in a well-polished but obviously outsize pair of oxfords.

"Hey," said Jonathan. "Neat work, Uncle Lenox. You could make it as some sort of international spy."

Lenox didn't answer, but he looked mildly pleased. "Now," he said, "Alice, you must cancel the taxi and then drive me home. There is no use in spending unnecessary money. I will send back the coat and shoes, although it seems unlikely that Room 439 will ever need them again."

"What," said a voice, "is the meaning of this?"

Two physicians. Dr. Joseph Foxe, primary-care physician to Lenox Cobb, and Dr. Alex McKenzie. Both frowning.

"The meaning," said Lenox Cobb, with satisfaction, "is that I am no longer under the care of Mary Starbox Memorial Hospital and its collection of quacks. Alice, after you cancel the taxi, bring your car around to the entrance. Jonathan will stay here and help me into the car when you arrive. I will be leaving shortly. Miss—what *is* your name?"—this to Sarah—"Thank you for your attentions. I trust I will not be needing your assistance again. Or Dr. McKenzie's. Or that of Dr. Foxe. Good afternoon to you all."

"I have reached the point," said Sarah to Alex that evening over dinner, "of never wanting to see, speak, or interact in any way with a member of the Beaugard family."

"They're a little on the indigestible side," admitted Alex. "But they have amazing resilience. Lenox Cobb certainly surprised me. I thought he'd be down and out for forty-eight hours at least. Joe Foxe is mad as hell. Called out last night from a dinner party forty miles away to deal with the old boy, and then to have him take off like that."

Sarah nodded sympathetically. They were having an early dinner at Miranda's Café in the town of Rockland and planning to take in the movie. After all, as Sarah said, even student papers and unread medical journals could not compete with watching Emma Thompson and Anthony Hopkins go through their paces at the Strand Cinema.

Alex, after attending to the remains of fettucini Romeo, returned to the question of Lenox Cobb. "I suggested to Joe Foxe, on the basis of what the family said about his being a little goofy lately, that a neurology workup might be in order. Joe said he'd already suggested it to Elena Beaugard, who waffled, so then he'd tried Masha and Eliot. Masha said it sounded expensive and Eliot said what was the use, that Uncle Lenox was obviously disoriented and what could anyone do, anyway, if they found he had some kind of senile dementia. Joe Foxe had suggested that more tests might eliminate a chemical imbalance or some undetected pathology, but Eliot told him to wait. There was plenty of time. In a few days, after he'd rested and recovered, let Lenox come home and settle in. And see what happens."

Sarah rolled up her napkin. "And Uncle Lenox beat them all to the punch. So that's that." She pushed her chair back and then hesitated. "Do you think someone—person or persons unknown—banged Lenox on the head? Either when he first lost his glasses in the woods or before I found him in Alice's cottage?"

Alex frowned. "No, I do not. Not the first time, not the second time. My God, the man is elderly. I think he stumbled, lost his glasses, walked into a branch. Second time out when he was hunting for them, I think he did the same. Remember, now he's searching around *without* glasses and he's blind as a bat . . ."

"And stubborn as a mule," put in Sarah.

"Right. So it was almost dark, and for the second time he walked directly into a tree or a limb. And really clobbered himself. Staggered off, ended up in Alice's cottage, missed the bed and ended up on the floor."

"It does sound plausible," admitted Sarah. "The only reason I can imagine anyone wanting to go after Lenox Cobb is if he happened to be a witness to someone messing around with

Dolly's boat. Or just happened to be around when someone was lacing the Gattling whiskey bottle with dope. But if so, well, why not do the job properly? It would be easy to finish an old man out walking by himself. But he was only damaged. And why would anyone bother to do that? Not because he's a cantankerous old curmudgeon. The state of Maine is filled with people exactly like him."

"The proper description of Lenox Cobb," said Alex firmly, "is a man with a self-inflicted injury. An accident. And, to clear your mind of other clutter, Mike Laaka called and said the lab hasn't come up with any signs—yet—of lead ballast on the *Sweetheart.* The centerboard—which is the original one—hasn't had extra lead fastened on. Inboard under the floorboards there are signs of wear, but not severe enough to suggest lead ingots. Only canvas."

"Canvas? How do you mean canvas?"

"Canvas. Heavy cloth. Familiar nautical material. Canvas fibers have been found. Rubbed, worn canvas fibers."

Sarah subsided heavily in her chair. "Canvas. Not weights. And the centerboard hasn't been weighted. Well, damn. But canvas . . ."—and here Alex could almost see her mental machinery shifting gears—"Maybe, just maybe, Dolly used sandbags. Canvas bags filled with sand. For ballast. What do you think?"

"I think," said Alex, rising and reaching for Sarah's hand, "that we're going to be late for our movie, and since I am deeply in love with Emma Thompson and you are wild for Anthony Hopkins, we had best be off so as not to miss a minute."

"Sandbags," repeated Sarah. "Canvas sandbags. I wonder if they're ever used as ballast."

"They're used to hold in the Mississippi River in flood time," said Alex. "Now, let's move it."

But even the best of movies with greatest of actors cannot deflect a human with a bee in her bonnet, and Sarah emerged from the movie theater shaking her head. "I'm going to write a novel. It's going to be called *The Haunting of Sarah Deane.* I'm bedeviled by Dolly and Uncle Lenox and Alice, and I couldn't keep my mind on a good movie. Let's hope the enchantment wears off before I'm fired from my job."

"Let's just hope that when we make it home, we don't find Alice on our doorstep," said Alex.

They did not find Alice Beaugard on their doorstep; they found Alice Beaugard and Webb Gattling in their kitchen watching a rerun of "Cheers."

8

"YOUR Patsy is one lousy watchdog," said Alice, reaching over and switching off the television. "I knocked and yelled and then we walked right in. You still don't lock your doors, do you? Anyway, this is Webb. Webb Gattling. One of the notorious Gattling boys."

"For Chrissake, Alice," said Webb Gattling in a deep and, to Sarah's mind, sinister voice as he extended a hand the size of a fielder's mitt.

Webb Gattling was enormous. Long tawny hair, a tawny beard that flowed to his chest, eyebrows that sat like hairy shelves over his pale blue eyes, ruddy skin, and shoulders built for heaving the caber or felling large trees. Sarah, extending her hand gingerly, almost expected him to greet her with a resounding Fe Fi Fo Fum. He was the sort of man, she thought, who brought forth images of animal skins and horned helmets. And Alice reinforced all Sarah's previous ideas of Alice-the-waif, looking like some sort of windblown elf standing next to Webb Gattling.

"Hey, there," boomed Webb, "Sarah. Heard a lot about you.

From Alice. She said you and she were always in trouble as kids."

Sarah bit her lip to stop herself from saying that she, Sarah, had been the wimp half of the team, and Alice the real thing.

"I mean," said Webb, "I'm glad Alice had one friend anyway. Some of the things she's told me, hell, it's a wonder anyone around's still speaking to her."

"And this," said Alice, as if presenting a prize horse, "is Alex McKenzie, who married Sarah, and they're both going to find out how Dolly died. Who did her in. This summer he and Sarah were mixed up in some weird murder on a horse farm, so what we've got here is our own undercover investigation unit. I mean, who needs the police and all those pathology creeps? Right, Sarah? Right, Alex?"

"Wrong," said Sarah, as Alex reached out to have his hand crushed by Webb. "You do need the police. And the labs. The whole machine. We aren't the police. We're only . . ." Here she hesitated and then finished lamely, "Friends of the family."

Alex recovered his hand and tested it for bone damage. Then he confronted Webb. "Sarah's right. We just did some low-level looking around for her aunt Julia. So how about a beer and maybe half an hour of friendly conversation, and then Sarah and I both have some work to do. That okay?"

Alice, worried, looked over at Webb. He nodded. "Okay, a beer. Ale. Whatever you've got. Thanks. And half an hour. We ought to be able to spit it out in fifteen minutes."

Alex paused on his way to the refrigerator for the beer. "You mean something that hasn't been spat already."

"Well, sorta," said Webb. "Nothing new, but maybe . . . well, something from a kinda different angle."

"What sort of angle?" demanded Sarah, suddenly fearful.

"Like Webb was out in his boat the day Dolly went sailing and he saw her capsize," said Alice. "That sort of angle."

Oh God, Sarah said to herself. Wouldn't you know. The Gattling connection. Not just Alice's old boyfriend but a Gattling on the spot. Trying to pull her thoughts together, she busied herself with a tray, four beer mugs, a piece of cheddar, crackers, and a bowl of nuts. She looked over at Webb, whose size diminished the entire kitchen. What he needs, she thought, are a mead hall and tankards. And meat bones to gnaw on. Fe Fi Fo Fum.

Putting the laden tray down on the kitchen table, she said, "Okay, Webb, you saw Dolly capsize? Or just a boat like Dolly's?"

Webb reached for the green bottle of Heineken, poured it with a practiced hand into the mug, took a slow appreciate sip, then shook his head. "Didn't actually see the boat go over. I was out a ways when I saw it first. It was sailing out past the point and I didn't take a good look. Had other things on my mind. Then I saw it later when it'd gone over, and I came alongside to see if I could help. One of those damfool Weymouth Scooters, those centerboard jobs that flop over if you even breathe on them. Knew Dolly Beaugard had one, but I didn't see the name on the stern because the boat was near sunk to her gunwales. Full of water. And man, I sure hoped it wasn't a Beaugard boat."

"The trouble with Webb," put in Alice, "is that his name is Gattling, and Marsden and Junior had just washed in on the Thursday and Friday before."

"But the Gattlings—" Sarah began, and stopped. She was unable to come up with something positive to say about the Gattlings.

Webb clenched his fist and then slowly relaxed it and took up his mug again and drank long and fiercely. "Okay. Go on. Say it. The Gattlings are the scumballs of the earth. Half of 'em are in prison and the rest should be. Right? Right?"

"I didn't—" Sarah began, and then stopped again. She did and she had.

"Look," said Alex, always the moderator. "Let's forget the Gattling part and tell us what you saw."

"He can't," said Alice. "I mean, he couldn't. Because being a Gattling is why he didn't square with the police before this. Nobody would believe him. They'd have him in maximum security just for saying he was out in his boat the same day Dolly went sailing. You've got to deal with the fact his name is Webb Gattling."

"And I'm not ashamed of it," said Webb, his expression truculent. He again thumped the table, this time so hard that the mugs and bowl of nuts and plate of cheese bounced, and Sarah again thought of giants. Or was it ogres?

"I mean, hell," growled Webb, "Gattlings are all over the place. Gattlings been around since the year one. And sure there are some lousy ones—like Marsden and Junior. And yeah, some of them are kind of wild and some of them like to take a deer out of season. But holy shit, there're some damn good Gattlings like my dad and my kid brother, Davy. And Mom. Or take Captain Jim Gattling. He was my great-grandfather. Good on discipline. Good citizen. Everybody forgets about the decent Gattlings."

Here Webb took a gulp of beer and then went on. "What I'm saying is that because there are a few rotten apples named Gattling isn't a reason for every policeman around to look at the rest of us like we're planning to burn down the town or start a riot."

"Or think you flipped over Dolly Beaugard's sailboat?" said Alex.

"Yeah," said Webb. "And that's what they'd think. So I didn't tell anyone that I was out in the cove that day. Listen, everyone in our whole family is on the hot seat because of Marsden and Junior being dead. And drunk. And their boat loaded with drugs. So the cops think the whole friggin' family's running some kind of a ring, taking little packages of coke around to the islands. And they act like one of us Gattlings got jealous and came out and knocked the boys overboard. Plus the cops are asking the family about what kind of prescription medicine anyone has on hand, so it doesn't take a genius to guess that someone spiked Marsden and Junior's whiskey."

"You see," said Alice impatiently, "Gattling is a local buzzword. Sarah, did you know there are Gattlings at Bowmouth?"

Sarah jerked her head up.

"Don't look so surprised," said Alice. "Sharon Seavy—she was a Gattling—teaches biology or something like that. And Jeff Gattling works maintenance."

"Like he's a janitor," put in Webb. "But he's a good guy." This Webb added because Sarah's expression almost gave away her conviction that here was at least one of the causes of what Bowmouth officials euphemistically called "inventory depletion."

"Back on track," said Alex. "Start when you first saw Dolly's boat. Then when you saw it filled with water."

So Webb, draining his ale, settled back into his narrative. It was a simple story. He was out in his fishing boat—"beaten-up old rig, eighteen foot with a sixty horse"—because he wanted to get away from his family, who were raising holy hell about Marsden and Junior being drowned.

"Gattlings stick together when it's something like this. Two brothers dying, even if they were a couple of real losers. Well, I'd about had it with Aunt Doris and Uncle Lem and their other son, Parson, blubbering about how they were angels in heaven and had been such good loving boys. I mean shit. Those guys weren't going to live to a nice ripe old age. It was just anyone's guess whether they'd be shot in hunting season accidentally on purpose or run off the road in the night. Or be knocked overboard."

"So you took off in your boat to get away," repeated Alex.

"Yeah. To be by myself. Took off around three o'clock, I think. Pretty good wind by the time I went out, so I kept pretty much in the lee of the islands. Didn't see any point in trying to fish, so I didn't put a line down or anything. Just chugged around and then saw this sailboat come out through Proffit Point narrows and didn't pay it much heed. Maybe I noticed it was one of those damn Scooters, but I wasn't thinking about what that meant—that there was too much wind for such a crappy boat. My head was full of Marsden and Junior and the family being in a sweat about them."

Alex put down his beer. "Okay, Webb, wait up. I think we're crazy to be listening to this. You've got to tell the police. Right now. Sarah and I are sympathetic, but we are not the police. Not the proper people. So, okay. Can I call?"

Webb turned on Alice. "You said they wouldn't. You said Sarah Deane was your old buddy. What the hell. I mean fuck it. The police. I'm getting outta here."

Alice looked at Alex. "I thought we could trust you . . ."

"Webb, keep your shirt on," said Alex. "How about this. Not the state police. Just Mike Laaka. You know Mike, don't you, Alice? And, Webb, you know him, I'll bet? You must be about the same age. Went to school with him, maybe? Rockland High School."

Webb, who up to that moment had been looking more and more like the ogre of Sarah's imagination, subsided slightly. "Yeah," he said. "I know Mike. We were on the track team. I threw the hammer. Mike did the mile. But he's some kind of detective with the sheriff's office now, so I don't see much of him. Except he came around asking questions when Marsden and Junior washed in."

Sarah, pleased at finding that Webb did indeed throw heavy objects in sporting events, cut a piece of cheese, balanced it on a cracker, and handed it to Webb. Food to soothe the savage.

"So how about it?" persisted Alex. "I can call Mike. He'll only take in what's useful. He's not going to put cuffs on you just because you were out in your boat last Sunday."

Silence. Then Webb, his great shoulders rising in a shrug, nodded. "Okay. If it's Mike. Not that state police guy with the frozen balls. George Fitts."

Alex, losing no time, strode to the telephone, dialed, got Mike on the second ring, and in two short sentences made his point.

"Okay," he announced. "Mike's on his way."

"Alone?" demanded Alice.

"Alone," said Alex, adding, "So put up your feet, have another beer, and keep cool."

"Cool, hell," said Webb in a voice of thunder. "Why should I be cool? Even if it's Mike Laaka, I'm going to have to prove I didn't tip Dolly Beaugard into the drink, that I haven't been selling her coke. That I never had the hots for her, that I never got into her underpants. Or wanted to."

Alice reached across the kitchen table for Webb's hand and pulled it toward her and then folded it around her own small claw. "Webb, take it easy. If you come on like that, Mike's going to think you and Dolly had something going for years. Just tell your story and try not to throttle the guy. Mike's okay."

"Yeah?" said Webb. "How do you know he's okay?"

"Picked me up for operating under the influence," said Alice, "and was kind of nice about the whole thing. Made me walk a straight line, which I couldn't, touch my nose with my finger with my eyes closed, which I couldn't, and then did a breath thing."

"So what was nice about that?" demanded Webb.

"He didn't hassle me. Just did his job and drove me home and talked about how he heard me sing at the Lobster Festival when I was a kid. Came to see me once in Augusta when I was supposed to be drying out and getting counseling."

With that conversation ebbed, Sarah replenished the cheese supply, Alex called the hospital about two new admissions, and before long Mike Laaka was at the door.

And Webb Gattling reverted to his ogre mode. Mike's attempts at easy pleasantry were ignored or answered in mono-syllabic grunts until finally Alice shouted in exasperation, "For God's sake, Webb, stop acting like an ax murderer and tell Mike what happened."

"And what did?" prompted Mike.

It all came out. Sentence by sentence. Webb looking at the table or off at the fireplace. Never at Mike. How he, Webb, had been out in Davis Cove—out from his own mooring in the Meduncook River—had seen the sailboat go out, how he had lost sight of it, had chugged about around the islands, and then had come across the sailboat wallowing, mast broken, sails down. And no one around.

"You looked?" asked Mike, breaking into the recital.

"Christ Almighty, of course I looked. Cut my motor and put a line around her starboard cleat. Saw a life jacket tied to another cleat. Took my boat hook and lifted up the sails to see if any-one was under there. But the wind had raised such bad chop that the two boats were banging the hell out of each other, so I cast off."

"So you went home?" said Mike.

"No, by God, I didn't. I started looking for Dolly. By then I'd figured it was Dolly Beaugard's boat—the *Sweetheart*. It's the only Scooter in this area. I throttled down to half speed, which with all that wind meant I couldn't maneuver very well, and I went around in big circles and then motored off leeward, but I didn't see anyone floating or trying to swim. Stayed out for almost an hour, but then I was running low on gas, so I headed back into Proffit Point Harbor. Was going to tell Tad Bugelski, but he wasn't around."

"Who *did* you tell?" demanded Mike. "Anyone? The coast guard? The Beaugards? Or did you wait to read about it in the papers?"

"You know," said Webb, "Alice here has been telling me you're a nice guy. I remember you as okay back there in high school, but right now you couldn't prove that by me. You're another hardheaded Finn who thinks he's God Almighty's gift to the Maine coast. You're acting like I'm some sort of an accessory or something."

Mike stiffened, and Alex, who knew his old friend had a temper, waited for the explosion. But Mike held it back, took a deep breath, tapped a pencil on the table. And waited.

And Webb Gattling subsided rumbling.

Finally, after what Sarah considered was a too long and too deadly silence, Mike said softly, "Did you tell *anyone*, Webb?"

Webb looked up, his expression haggard. "No. Not directly. I went into Tad Bugelski's house—the door was open and no one was there. Used his phone to call the coast guard and said I'd found a sailboat half-sunk and I hadn't seen anyone floating around. Then I hung up before they could ask me who was calling. And that's the goddamned truth." Webb stared at Mike defiantly.

"Okay," said Mike. "Better late than never, I suppose. But Jesus, Webb, don't be so hung up on being a Gattling that you can't even function in the real world. You know that I can't just sit on this information. State Police CID is going to have to know. So when did you tell Alice?"

"Next Monday. Noon. Saw her in Rockland. Heard about the body on the local news."

"So both of you have been sitting on this information," said Mike, "since Monday. And tonight is Thursday. And the police have been beating the bush for four days. For anything. Sightings, confirmed or unconfirmed."

"I'm sorry," said Alice in a small voice.

"I'm not," roared Webb. "You know damn well, Mike, that I'd be in custody by now. For Dolly and maybe for Marsden and Junior. Listen, Dolly is dead because she drowned. Her boat went over and she drowned. She wasn't strangled or burned to death or poisoned or hit on the head by a blunt instrument. She fucking drowned."

"How do you know?" said Mike quietly.

"Well, she did, didn't she? Tad Bugelski told me she did. He was around when her body washed into Little Cove."

"Tad Bugelski," said Mike succinctly, "doesn't know the half of it. Dolly drowned, all right. But someone fiddled around with her boat. Just before Alex called, I got the report from the lab. The *Sweetheart* did carry ballast. Lead pigs in canvas covers. Laid fore and aft along the centerboard under the floorboards. But no ballast found when we hauled the boat in Monday."

"So the ballast got loose," said Webb.

"The lab thinks no. They've done some measuring and checking the rub marks, and those lead babies were snugged in like it was a custom fit, probably so they wouldn't move around when the boat heeled. So we're not talking death by mischance. Not anymore. We're talking death-through planning and through a lot of hefty removal work and careful preparation. We're talking homicide."

Alice turned first to Sarah, then to Alex, and then swiveled around and looked Mike full in the face.

"So," she said. "What else is new?"

And for a moment Mike turned to stone. He jumped to his feet and stood there staring at Alice, looking, Sarah thought, with his white blond hair, his broad features, and big shoulders, like some Nordic monument. A monument with egg on its face. But Sarah, who knew that since Monday Alice had been muttering about Dolly being murdered, simply rolled her eyes at the ceiling while Alex drummed the table with impatient fingers. But Webb nodded his big shaggy head as if to back up Alice's question.

"I mean," Alice went on, "it's no surprise, is it? Dolly wouldn't have off-loaded the lead ballast and forgotten she'd done it. Dolly remembered everything. She kept lists and made charts and kept books. She could run a small country. She could have organized OPEC or the European Common Market."

"Easy, Alice," said Webb, putting his arm around her—an arm that looked to Sarah like part of a python.

But Alice shook him off and gathered steam. "And she wouldn't commit suicide by dumping the ballast and then going sailing. What a stupid way of killing yourself. Dolly wasn't superbright, she could hardly spell, but she did things straight on. If she wanted to kill herself, she'd read up on it, buy the right kind of poison or the proper kind of gun, and do the thing efficiently. Listen, Dolly was planning to live forever and get all of Knox County under her thumb. She already had half of it roped and tied. As well as Mother. And the whole bloody Great Oaks estate."

"Okay," said Mike, recovering. He found that he didn't like the investigative initiative being snatched away by the disheveled likes of Alice Beaugard. "Maybe you can come up with some reason for your sister's death. Like Dolly might have made enemies, people that—"

Alice broke in impatiently. "Of course Dolly had enemies. Doesn't everyone? But I don't suppose Dolly's enemies would call themselves that because they were all into doing civic things together with her. Or under her. They probably called themselves coworkers or colleagues or some crap like that. But Dolly had her finger in a lot of pies. She probably drove a whole bunch of people straight up the wall."

"Whoa, wait up there," said Mike. "You can't just throw out wholesale accusations." He fished around in a back pocket and produced a notebook and pencil. "Okay, now. Names. Persons who actually hated Dolly. Were jealous of her. Wanted her jobs or whose toes she stomped on."

Alice frowned and brushed a stray strand of hair from her face. "Well, I'd say never mind about St. Paul's-by-the-Sea because Dolly had talked Mother into giving the Great Oaks family house to the Episcopal diocese. For some sort of retreat or meeting place. Father Smythe started salivating whenever he saw Dolly."

"Stop," called Mike. "You mean Dolly was behind her mother's leaving the house away from the family, giving it to the church?"

"I just told you," said Alice. "Try and listen, will you, Mike? We all knew about it and I heard Mother telling Sarah's grandmother. The point is that even if a lot of people around town might have wanted Dolly to disappear, I think it's someone in the family who got rid of her. Maybe someone who wanted the house."

"But didn't all of you want the house?" asked Mike.

"God no. The cottage is good enough for me, and Eliot and Caroline have that big pile on Tidal Cove. And Masha doesn't like the acoustics and says the damp is ruining her wooden recorders. Fogs them up. So who does that leave?"

"Okay, who?" said Mike, sighing.

"Professor Lenox Cobb, that's who. Dear old Uncle Scrooge. He's moved back into our house and he's settling in like he is going to die in the master bedroom."

Here Sarah came to life. "Your uncle Lenox is older than your mother. Why would your mother die first?"

"Uncle Lenox—even with a bump on his head and half-goofy—is in terrific shape. Oh sure, his balance isn't great, but he's all sinew and gristle and mean as they come. Mean people last forever. Mother has glaucoma and arthritis and diabetes and some sort of cardiac condition. There, you've got my opinion. Last Monday night I asked Sarah and Alex to poke around in the family nest, but now it's pretty damn clear. Uncle Lenox is the guy to nail. Okay, Webb, let's go. You've done your civic duty." And with that Alice reached out for Webb's hand and together they rose from the table. But then Alice turned again to Mike.

"To be fair, I should mention Vivian."

"Who?" said Mike, startled. "You mean the housekeeper?"

"Of course. Vivian Lavender. She's a widow and she's been working for us almost thirty years. When the house goes to the Episcopal Church she might be out in the cold. I don't think they'd keep her on; she's Catholic. I mean, even a nice pension wouldn't make up for Vivian having her own rent-free apartment. So I suppose you'd have to add Vivian to Uncle Lenox as suspects. Maybe they're working together. Except I think that Vivian's a sexy lady, and I doubt if Lenox can perform to satisfaction. I mean, can you picture Lenox bonking Vivian?" Alice grinned up at Webb and then the two started for the door—Alice scurrying to keep up with him.

"Not so fast," called Mike. "Webb, you'll have to sign a deposition. A description of what you saw last Sunday. And, Alice, don't go around accusing people, even a crank like Lenox Webb. Or Vivian Lavender. Cool it. And you two hang around. Brother George Fitts will want to have a chat with you both."

"The hell," shouted Webb, "he will." And without a backward glance Webb took hold of Alice's shoulder and gave her a push, and with the kitchen floor shaking under his footsteps, they departed.

For a moment, dead silence. Then Mike reached for an unopened bottle of beer, pried open the cap, and drank straight from the top. Then, putting down the bottle, he delivered himself of a weary sigh. "Jeezus, that Alice will be the death of me. Webb, I can take. I understand Webb. Where he's coming from. A decent Gattling in the middle of a bunch of lousy Gattlings. A damn good cabinetmaker from what I've heard. Anyway, I can see why he didn't want to go running to the police."

Alex paused in the act of loading the tray with empty mugs. "You can understand Webb Gattling. Will George Fitts?"

"Of course not. George won't give a damn about Webb's tender sensibilities. He'll put Webb onto his grid and proceed to grind and mince and shake out whatever facts there are to be shaken."

Sarah, who was now delivering the loaded tray to the kitchen sink, stopped. "Never mind George. What do you think about Alice's idea of Lenox as the villain? With or without Vivian Lavender."

"Because of the house going to the church?" asked Mike.

"Yes. It's a fair enough reason. But not only the house. Dolly was managing the whole estate, and as Alice has said, Lenox doesn't like being managed. And I'll bet he didn't much like Dolly."

Mike rose to his feet. "Bullshit, Sarah. Listen, whoever took that ballast out of the *Sweetheart* had to do it in the night. So you and Alice are saying that the old boy found his way down to the beach, maybe with Vivian holding a flashlight, got into a dinghy, rowed out in the dark, climbed aboard a wobbling sailboat, and off-loaded lead bars and rowed back. Dug a hole somewhere . . ."

"Or dumped them overboard," said Alex.

"And crept back to bed—in that creaky old house where all the floorboards snap and groan—without a soul knowing it. Or without that great shaggy dog Willie barking his head off."

"*The Hound of the Baskervilles,*" murmured Sarah. "The dog that didn't bark."

"Come off it. Willie hates Lenox. When we first interviewed the Beaugards, Willie snarled and growled whenever Lenox Cobb came near him. Listen, you're talking about the kind of action that would be tough on a forty-year-old man. This is the guy who walks into tree branches and ends up in the hospital. Here's a suggestion. You and Alice get busy and write the great American seashore mystery and use Lenox Cobb as a murderer. Put in Vivian Lavender while you're at it. They could elope after the murder and escape to Tasmania. Pursued by a robot helicopter. Hey, I've missed my calling. Need a plot? I'm your man. Good night, all, and thanks for the entertainment."

And Mike saluted Sarah with the last gulp of beer and followed Webb and Alice into the night.

With that the telephone rang. And Sarah, rinsing mugs, wrapping cheese, could tell from the sound of Alex's voice and his one-word answers that he didn't like what he was hearing. He put the receiver down and joined her at the sink.

"Tasmania isn't such a bad idea. I'm beginning to think that we're the ones who should escape. Take a Weymouth Scooter with or without ballast, a few clothes, Patsy, and a six-pack of beer and just weigh anchor. Or try the robot helicopter."

"All of which means?"

"That was Elena Beaugard. Her primary-care physician—my friend Joe Foxe—is off to some medical conference in Oslo and she wants me. She doesn't want the doctor he's turned his patients over to because—get this—she doesn't know him. I mean hell, who *knows* their doctor these days? She sounds like she will only go to someone to whom she's been properly introduced."

"Like you."

"Like me. Because—you guessed it—we're almost family. It seems that brother Lenox seems a bit disoriented. More ornery than usual. Or is this her imagination? Or her hearing? Perhaps she needs her hearing checked. Anyway, will I make a house call? Tomorrow afternoon, which is Thursday, which is also my half day off."

"And you said?"

Alex walked to the sink, grabbed a handful of beer mugs, and dumped them into a dishpan of water, breaking only one in the process. "What do you think I said?"

"You said: 'Love to. Certainly. Of course. Happy to oblige. House calls? No problem. Neither rain nor sleet nor gloom of night . . .'"

"You got it. And she asked if dear Sarah could come and comfort Alice or listen to Masha practice or amuse Jonathan when he got home from school."

Sarah picked up her sheaf of student papers and stuffed them back in her briefcase. "Unfortunately, dear Sarah has a freshman seminar and two meetings and so will not emerge until after five tomorrow afternoon. Much too late for social calls. You, my dearest Alex, are strictly on your own."

9

FRIDAY morning, October seventh, broke dank and damp, and by nine o'clock a drizzle had begun falling over midcoast Maine. By eleven the drizzle had turned to a determined rain, and large red and yellow maple leaves began to fall and plaster themselves on the ground, turning roads and sidewalks into a patchwork quilt.

This picturesque phenomenon was pointed out by Deputy Katie Waters, sitting in the backseat of Sergeant George Fitts's unmarked state police sedan. Next to the empty driver's seat sat Mike Laaka, who wished that he could have driven Katie to Proffit Point by himself and so be spared the presence of George. However, he and Katie were under orders to join the sergeant in yet another investigatory strike on the Beaugard ménage. This time with a greater sense of urgency since the word "homicide" had reared its head.

"Look at the leaves, Mike," repeated Katie, who was by nature a woman with a sunny disposition. "They're absolutely beautiful. Like someone planned to make a quilt and zoom, along came the rain and down they came."

"You can have the leaves," said Mike morosely. He'd spent the previous hour in the state police barracks getting George's opinion of sheriff's deputy investigators who choose to fly solo, visiting with informants and possible suspects in private houses.

"The trouble with you and George," continued Katie, unabashed, "is that your minds are so loused up with crime that you can't appreciate the beauties of nature."

Mike made a half turn from the front seat. "Listen, Katie Waters, you had better start getting your head together. Plan your approach. George is having you interview Vivian Lavender. He's done one session with her, but he wants another, and he's going to be tied up with Mrs. Beaugard and Masha, and I'm going to be tracking down Eliot and his wife, Caroline, and some of the people who work on the place. You've never met the family, have you? I mean, not face-to-face?"

"I was on the sailboat detail," said Katie. "Crawling around on rocks and getting gunk all over my uniform, ruining my shoes."

"So this is a promotion. You're plainclothes now and you can ruin your own things. You'll be meeting live people. So forget the leaves and what a pretty quilt they'd make."

"I have a theory," persisted Katie. "It's that anyone who sees too much of George Fitts is contaminated and starts acting like him. He needs to find some normal people, but he wouldn't know normal if it bit him. I think he needs a really desperate sex experience. A real kinky session. Like for instance—"

"Shut up, Katie, here he is," growled Mike.

Katie smiled a radiant smile. "Hello, George. All set for a day at the seashore? Should we stop for sandwiches?"

George Fitts gave Katie his wintry smile, nodded at Mike, and slid neatly into the driver's seat. "You can forget about fun at the seashore. But we'll stop for sandwiches. This is going to be an all-day thing. Back to square one." George reached over, turned the ignition, stamped on the accelerator and moved the car onto Route One, turned it south toward the Proffit Point Road.

"How do you mean square one?" said Katie, who was determined not to sit in silence throughout the twelve-mile drive.

"When we first interviewed family members about Dolly Beaugard and talked to the estate workers, the gardener, and to Tad Bugelski, we were thinking it was a drowning accident."

"And," put in Mike, "we were up to our ears with the Gattling brothers washing in, and that one didn't look like an accident."

"Mike is correct," said George. "Dolly Beaugard's death looked like misadventure, but the disappearance of the ballast has changed everything. Now we have to find out who had access to the boat. Find out when Dolly last went sailing in a stiff wind and *didn't* capsize. And work up the Gattling connection. I have an appointment with Webb Gattling late this afternoon and with Alice Beaugard this evening."

"I told Webb that you'd be getting ready to sink your gaff into his backside."

"Thank you, Mike. No wonder I have trouble with interrogations. And, Katie, don't you go trying any of Mike Laaka's tricks. Interviewing material witnesses over beer at a friend's house."

"Webb Gattling," said Mike, as he had said several times to George earlier that morning, "wouldn't have told you the time of day. I went to school with Webb, he knows me. And Alice is a friend of Sarah's, plus Alice is an old girlfriend of Webb's and they seem to have picked up with each other again. George, if you'd been there with your notebook, you would have destroyed the—what's the word?—the camaraderie."

"The last thing you need in a criminal investigation is camaraderie, so I suggest you take—"

"Camaraderie and shove it?" suggested Katie.

George accelerated slightly but otherwise ignored his backseat passenger. "Forget fellowship. Mike, that's the trouble with you knowing Alex McKenzie and Sarah. Those two are always getting mixed into an investigation, and you encourage them."

"Now, hold it, George," Mike almost shouted. "Hold it. These are small towns. Proffit Point, Diggers Neck, Thomaston, Union, Port Clyde, and the rest. Rural America. Stopovers with one or two gas stations, three churches, and a country store. A grange hall and a fire station. A feed store and a boat dock. Sometimes a Masonic lodge. Or the Elks. Rotary. Every damn soul for miles around knows or is married to or is a cousin of or went to school with every other damn soul. You're from the big bad city, and you still don't get the idea that small-town people and rural folk are so intertwined with each other that you can't mess with one person without messing with forty more. You can't run a big-city-type investigation in the boondocks. You need informality, breakfast in the diner, a drink at a bar. Be grateful to Sarah and Alex. Amateurs like those two—and even that nutcase Alice Beaugard—just happen to know a lot of people. Are related. With those three you've covered the summer colony, the residents from 'away.' Add Webb and me and Katie here and guys like Tad Bugelski to the stew, and you've got the native, the old-time Mainer connection. The blue-collar opinion."

"Simmer down, Mike," said George. "I get the point."

"I'll bet you don't. What I'm saying is, you need me to have beer with Alice and Webb. You need Alex to help take Lenox into the hospital, and Sarah to make condolence calls with her grandmother. All these people are useful. Besides being friends, they are just goddamn useful."

"Okay, Mike. But after this, let me in on your little visits. I may have information that makes these fellowship gatherings inappropriate. Or dangerous. Sarah Deane is always skating on thin ice. I don't need any more trouble than I've already got on my plate."

"But," protested Mike, "you wanted Sarah to keep an eye out when she visited the Beaugards. You told me to tell her."

"Right. An eye out. By daylight, in a house, with other people around. But not an after-dark search for Lenox Cobb, who may or may not have walked into a branch. So let me know what you're up to. I can make allowances. I am human."

"Couldn't prove it by me," muttered Katie under her breath.

"And I have excellent hearing," continued George smoothly. "And like it or not, we three are a team and we're going to work as a team. Got it?"

"Eliot Beaugard," said Mike. "He's the one who orchestrated the Lenox Cobb search. Didn't want the police around because he claimed his family was becoming notorious."

"We will speak to Mr. Eliot Beaugard," said George firmly. "Business executive types can be even more dangerous than well-meaning amateurs. Now, here's the general store. I'll pull in and, Mike, you can pick up lunch. I'll have a tuna and a Pepsi."

"Egg salad and a root beer for me," said Katie.

Mike, ducking his head against the rain, went into the store, and Sergeant George Fitts leaned his head back against the car seat and closed his eyes. He had spent a long night dealing with a newly delivered lab report showing that the well-known tranquilizer Valium had been added to the whiskey bottle found in Marsden and Junior Gatling's skiff. Valium was probably in the medicine cabinets of half the citizens of Proffit Point, but one had to start somewhere. He intended to research the Beaugard collection of medications, ease of access to the supply, and get a rundown on the Beaugard prescription history. And look into the fact that the whiskey consumed by the Gattling brothers wasn't your ordinary popular blend but an expensive Canadian whiskey put out by Seagram. Not apparently the choice of Marsden and Junior, who invariably guzzled something cheaper. Here George allowed himself to appear asleep, but behind closed lids visions of whiskeys of all shades and prices passed in a parade before his inner eye.

Sitting in the backseat, Katie Waters had time to contemplate the rear of George Fitts's head and wonder at her recent elevation as an assistant deputy in the investigative arm of the sheriff's department. Until a few months ago, Katie had been detailed to some of the more loathsome and tedious jobs in the uniformed branch. Now she was in plain clothes—slacks and a wool jacket—and assigned to Mike, who worked, often in uncomfortable tandem, with George.

George probably caused, Katie thought, as much discomfort in his coworkers as he did in those he was investigating. What a creep. The top of his head was as bald as a lightbulb, steel-rimmed spectacles glinted around pale blue eyes, and his mouth was like a narrow cut in a rock. Now she stared resentfully at the bristles at the back of George's clipped neck. Even in plain clothes—starched shirt, knife-creased trousers—he looked as if he were in uniform.

But before Katie could formulate any clear thoughts about resigning her job or asking for a transfer, Mike reappeared with a paper bag and a six-pack of Pepsi, George started the car, and they were off. Turning left and on down the Proffit Point Road, the windshield wipers racing back and forth, the wet autumn leaves splattering on the hood, on the road.

The first mile of the drive down the Proffit Point Road toward the Great Oaks estate was slightly enlivened by a broken windshield wiper and the pleasure this event gave Mike Laaka and Katie Waters as they watched George Fitts, standing in puddles by the side of the road, his black raincoat whipping around his legs in the wind-driven rain, struggling with its replacement. This entertainment, however, was replaced by the sound of an approaching vehicle.

Katie had twisted about in her seat. "Hey, here comes an ambulance. Behind us. Do you suppose?"

"You want more bodies? Listen, Proffit Point has more families than just the Beaugard tribe. Besides, it's no emergency. Not speeding. No lights, no sirens."

"By which we deduce," said Katie, "that the ambulance is returning to its place of origin—the fire hall . . ."

"Wrong," said Mike, "the fire hall is up the hill behind us. The ambulance is on a mission."

"And that means either the ambulance is returning some incapacitated patient from the hospital or . . ." Katie paused and smiled at Mike. "Or is returning a body to the place of origin. Or is picking up a just-certified dead body to take it to the morgue, and in all cases no need to step on the gas."

Mike smiled. "Head of the class, Katie." He peered again out the rain-washed window. "Poor George, I'll bet he bought the wrong-size wiper . . . No, he's got it."

With which George Fitts, face and slicker gleaming with wet, climbed back into the car, turned the ignition, and stepped on it. Stepped on it so completely that in five minutes he found himself on the narrow, winding Proffit Point Road behind the ambulance, which was going along at a leisurely twenty-five miles an hour.

"Goddamn," said George, who almost never swore.

Katie decided that George needed distraction. "You're stuck behind that thing for a while at least, so tell me about the Beaugards. What are they really like? I've seen the house from the beach, but I've never seen it up close. Or met any of the family. If I'm supposed to interview this Vivian Lavender, I should know something about them."

"The family," said Mike with feeling, "are mostly a bunch of rich loonies. Except for Dolly. She was pretty normal."

"And look," said Katie, "where that got her."

George shook his head. "Thinking of the Beaugard family members as 'rich loonies' is not going to be helpful when you start asking questions. All right, I'll give you a quick briefing. Mike can fill in what he calls the human interest parts. Mrs. Beaugard—her first name, which you will not think of using, is Elena. Summer resident with her husband for forty years, then full-time for the last ten. Husband was a patent lawyer who has a library of illustrated editions. Apparently a valuable collection. Responsible citizen from what I've heard."

"Was a total snob," said Mike. "Went around like he was Boston's gift to Maine. Tennis, golf, hunting with the Union Valley Hunt Club. Always had a big boat. Last one was a fifty-foot ketch named the *Peregrine* because he was a bird nut. Wife still is. Keeps a bird-feeding station. Anyway, Mr. Beaugard—name was Arthur—kept the boat moored in Little Cove. Both the senior Beaugards pretty much kept to their summer friends, a lot of Massachusetts migrants. Mrs. Beaugard's in her seventies now. Semi-invalid but still plenty bossy."

"Three daughters," continued George. "Masha, she's a musician. Not married. Teaches private students in Boston and hereabouts. Her group gives concerts all over New England, so she's rarely home. Dolly Beaugard, you know about. Next is Alice, age thirty-one, who has been in trouble for driving when intoxicated, for disorderly conduct, for disrupting public meetings, possession of illegal substances—and a number of other things. Two marriages, both ending in divorce. A son, Jonathan, by Alan Epstein, the writer. Custody to the father."

"Like I said, Alice is out in left field," said Mike. "Masha is a cold fish. But you've left out favorite and only son Eliot. Marine insurance business. Has a yacht, the *Goshawk*. Yachts seem to run in the family genes. Does cruising and racing all over the map. Gobs of money. New house. One kid, named Colin. Wife Caroline has this discontented glassy look. Sort of out of focus. I'll bet she's taking something. Or shooting it. I think her elevator doesn't go to the top floor. But she's decorative."

"And that, Katie, is the sort of thing not to listen to. That's Mike at his most dangerous. I have nothing on Mrs. Eliot Beaugard, so wipe that remark right out of your head."

But Mike was squinting through the windshield. "Whoa up. That ambulance isn't turning off. It's heading right for Great Oaks. There it goes, right through the gates. You don't suppose that it really is going to pick up another body? What d'ya bet old Lenox Cobb has self-destructed, which wouldn't be that much of a loss?"

George, slowing down for the entrance, turned his head in the speaker's direction. "Mike Laaka, for once, will you just shut up and wait and see what happens?"

Mike grinned at Katie and reached for a briefcase at his feet and extracted a notebook and a small tape recorder, and in silence the three drove through the splashing rain, the falling leaves, under arching oaks and sentinel white pines until they emerged into the wide circle drive that brought them to the front door.

Well, not quite to the front door. The front door was blocked by the boxy white ambulance with the big orange lettering: PROFFIT POINT RESCUE SQUAD.

George stopped his car on the driveway circle, the better to view the proceedings. He was rewarded presently by a figure on the porch with an umbrella. Who stood and waited while the back doors of the ambulance opened and a small blanketed person with a leg thrust stiffly out was lifted into the arms of the driver and was followed by one of the rescue workers carrying a wheelchair.

Mike, who had been squinting through the windshield, turned to his companions. "My God, I think it's the kid."

"Kid?" said Katie. "What kid?"

"Alice's kid. Jonathan. Right age, right size."

But now George Fitts, like a hound who has sniffed the trail, was out of the car and on his way to the front door, turning at the last minute to shout over his shoulder, "You two, stay put."

"Great," said Katie. "Just great. We sit here and watch the rain and count the leaves, and George has all the fun."

"He may want us to stay in the car in case we have to move fast. Go and get something."

"You don't believe that, do you, Mike?"

Mike sighed. "Nope. I think George sometimes doesn't like to be crowded with lowlife like us. Wants to be big man on campus. Likes deference. Everyone backing up and turning pale when the state police arrives."

"Okay," said Katie. "So we sit here. How about some briefing about this Vivian Lavender? Faithful servant. Loyal and true. All that sort of stuff?"

"She must be faithful because she's been working here for years. Good-looking in a middle-aged way. Tall, dark wavy hair. Real old-fashioned hair in a bun with hairpins. Probably quite a dish when she was younger. And hey, George is waving."

This was true. George Fitts stood under the portico holding the door open with one hand, and gestured.

"Nothing serious," he said as Katie and Mike joined him in the front hall. "Jonathan Epstein took a bad fall during a school field trip to Little Cove this morning. Broken leg and dislocated shoulder. He'll be out of action for a while. Which I gather is not an entirely bad thing."

"Hello, Sergeant Fitts," said a voice. It was Alice. She extended a hand toward Katie. "Deputy Waters, isn't it? I'm

Alice. Alice Beaugard. I don't use any of my married names. I never had them long enough to get used to. So do I call you Deputy or what? I mean, I know I call him Sergeant, and Mike, Mike because I've known him for a while."

"Call me whatever you want, Ms. Beaugard," said Katie, looking with a certain puzzlement at the thin untidy figure before her. Reeking of cigarettes, thin face like a starvation victim, huge eyes with shadows. And clothes directly from a yard sale. "So," she added, trying to sound businesslike, "I'm supposed to see Mrs.—or is it Miss Lavender?"

"She's 'Mrs.,' " said Alice. "Married Phil Lavender, but he cut himself up in a chain-saw accident and died, and Vivian went to work for Mother. Been here ever since. But listen, you guys. Now I've got you here in the hall and before Eliot or Mother grabs you, I want you to look into this thing about Jonathan's so-called accident. I've spent the morning at the ER and he's going to be stuck at home for weeks."

"But," said George, looking at his watch, "it was an accident, wasn't it? A school trip. He fell down."

Alice looked over her shoulder, then walked to the door leading into the living room and shut it firmly. "I have doubts," she said in a hoarse whisper. "It was one of those crazy field trips private schools dream up that are supposed to bring everyone together. An early breakfast cookout for the sixth grade. I mean, in this weather, really. With the rain the breakfast had to be indoors in our family boathouse on Little Cove. I mean, heaven forbid Eliot and Caroline should have their house messed up with a bunch of kids. Anyway, Vivian—Mrs. Lavender—arranged to send along the food—bacon, eggs, sausages—as Mother's contribution to all the foolishness. After breakfast the kids and their teacher were going out in Eliot's boat to motor around in the rain talking about navigation or something educational like that. The boat's called the *Goshawk*. All the family use bird names for their boats. Except Dolly, who, of course, had to be different. We've had *Lapwing*, the *Gannet*, the *Peregrine*. I mean talk about totally boring."

"Not an accident, you say," said George, moving the flow

back to the mainstream. It was one of his gifts—not letting witnesses float more than a few sentences away from the subject.

"Yes. I mean no. Not an accident. I mean, what do you think? First Dolly and now Jonathan? The point is that someone shoved Jonathan down the gangway. You know, the ramp that goes to the float. It was low tide, so the ramp went almost straight down. Jonathan said he felt a hand on his back. He lost his balance and wham, bang, down he went. Dislocated shoulder and broken leg. Not a bad break, but he's got a cast. They've given him a sedative and he's going to be out of action for a while. I mean, can you picture it? Mother and Lenox *and* Jonathan together in the house. All under the weather. My God."

"Go back, please, Miss Beaugard, to the accident. You say Jonathan felt a hand against his back."

"Yes, and Jonathan doesn't make up things like that."

"How many children were on this field trip?"

"What?"

"It's important to know how many children were trying to go down that ramp. If there was a crowd of them, pushing, shoving, as kids do, well, it's likely it was an accident."

"Oh," said Alice. "Well, I guess that might have happened. But there aren't too many in this sixth grade class. Jonathan's has about twelve kids in it. But guess who else was around."

"Tell me," said George.

"Besides brother Eliot—he was handling the boat—and Vivian, who was picking up the breakfast dishes and leftovers, there was my uncle Lenox. He'd been invited for the cookout. You know, that reach-out-to-the-elderly crap. Jonathan's teacher, Mr. Griffin, apparently had Uncle Lenox at Bowmouth in some Shakespeare class."

"Your point?" prompted George.

"I told Mike last night." Here Alice looked reproachfully at Mike Laaka, who was standing, notebook open, pencil busy, next to a silent and listening Katie Waters. "I told him to watch out for my uncle. That he doesn't want the house to go to the Episcopal Church. That was Dolly's idea. Mike, didn't you tell

Sergeant Fitts about what I said? About Uncle Lenox being dangerous?"

"No," said George Fitts. "He didn't. I heard about Webb Gattling sighting the *Sweetheart* but not a word about Lenox Cobb."

"I thought you guys told each other things," said Alice. "Okay, now you know. Uncle Lenox is perfectly capable of leaning over and giving Jonathan just a little push. Uncle Lenox is a loose cannon around here, so you'd better keep an eye on the guy."

George, whose cheek muscles were now in motion, gave Alice a short nod. "Thank you, Miss Beaugard. I will keep an eye on Professor Cobb. And," added George, "I will also keep an eye on Deputy Investigator Laaka, who is another loose cannon."

10

GEORGE Fitts turned again to Alice Beaugard. "We'll want to talk to each of you again—separately—but first I want to meet with the whole family. Please ask your mother where that would be convenient."

"Frankly," said Alice, "Mother would never think any place was convenient if it's the police. The idea of having you here in the front hall just about gives her hives. Nothing personal, but she's one of the old guard who thinks that the only time you should meet a policeman is when you cross the street. But I'll ask her. Do you want Uncle Lenox to sit in? The chief suspect."

"Miss Beaugard," said George, "there is no chief suspect. Maybe there never will be. And yes, if Professor Cobb is feeling up to it, I'd like him there."

"And Vivian?"

"Mrs. Lavender? Certainly."

"How about the gardener and all the little busy gnomes who cut the grass and sweep up leaves? Or my son, Jonathan, who right now is in bed zonked with a sedative?"

"No," said George patiently. "Let Jonathan stay put. As for the rest, we'll get around to them after I have my meeting."

"What meeting? Have I missed something?" The front door stood open and Alex McKenzie walked into the hall. He stopped and took stock of the four persons now grouped in front of a heavy oak seat and mirror affair that sprouted hat racks made from deer antlers. "Hello, Alice. Hi, Mike, George. Katie. All the big guns huddling in the front hall. What's up?"

George Fitts looked at Alex without pleasure. "What are you doing here, Alex?"

"House call. I'm reviving the custom. Beloved Dr. McKenzie making the rounds of his grateful patients."

"I bet," said Mike. "You're here on a private snoop?"

"I don't snoop," said Alex. "And never on my day off. Snooping is Sarah's thing. I'm legitimate. A call from Mrs. Beaugard last night about Lenox Cobb being more than usually fuddled. Or is it her eyesight or hearing?"

"We can combine," said George, taking charge. "Alex, sit in with us while I ask everyone here some general questions. Miss Beaugard, please ask your mother which room we can use."

Alice, shaking her head, opened the living room door and reappeared almost immediately. "The library. Mother doesn't use it much except to check on the bird-feeding station outside the window."

"I'll just go and report to Mrs. Beaugard," said Alex. "I want full credit for a house call."

Mrs. Beaugard, a wool shawl over her shoulders, was fixed in a living room wing chair by a glowing fireplace. She welcomed her substitute physician with slight inclination of the head, giving Alex the impression that on her social scale, doctors ranked well below the electrician and the plumber.

"I'm worried about my brother, Professor Cobb," she began. "I think he's had one of those invisible strokes. You know, when what someone says is all garbled. But my hearing aid makes this dreadful buzz if I turn it up. And his face seems strange, but

I do have glaucoma, so it's just possible I'm not seeing his face clearly. So do you wish to examine him now?"

"I think," said Alex, reaching for Mrs. Beaugard's cane and holding it out to her, "that Sergeant Fitts wants to see everyone. You suggested the library, didn't you?"

"The police have been sent simply to plague me," said Mrs. Beaugard in complaining voice. "With my daughter dead, you'd think there would be a sense about what is fitting. And Jonathan injured. His shoulder *and* his leg. From carelessness, I'm sure. The boy just plunges about, not looking where he's going."

Alex absorbed this new information without comment and contented himself with reaching for Mrs. Beaugard's arm, assisting her to her feet, and placing her cane in her hand. "Let's go into the library together and get it over with," he said.

Together they made slow progress across the room, through a dim passageway, and into a gloomy book-lined chamber. The library.

Being in the room was, Alex thought, as he settled Mrs. Beaugard in an armchair before the unlit fireplace, rather like inhabiting an aquarium. Rain-streaked windows and French doors gave out on an unrelenting dark gray sky and a cluster of dripping evergreens, while the green wallpaper and the glass-fronted bookcases inside reinforced the sense of being underwater. Books, in Alex's opinion, usually gave color and warmth to a room, but here glass doors covered with a wire grille obscured row upon row of books concealed in identical green slipcases, and the effect was to reduce the shelves to a uniformly depressing backdrop.

"My husband," said Mrs. Beaugard, looking about her with ill-concealed irritation, "collected illustrated editions. He had special slipcases made to protect them. And to discourage the children."

"The children?" repeated Alex, puzzled.

"Of course. Many of these are children's books. *Robinson Crusoe, Alice in Wonderland, Heidi.* With well-known illustrators. First editions. Many of them signed."

"But off-limits to the children?" said Alex.

"Naturally. Arthur was afraid the children might try and read them. He said children wouldn't appreciate fine illustrations. Children, especially ones like Alice, don't care what they do to a book. Arthur once caught Alice crayoning in a first edition of *The Wizard of Oz.*"

"Mrs. B!" exclaimed a voice, and Alex looked to see themselves confronted by a tall, middle-aged woman. Vivian Lavender, wasn't it? Alex tried to remember what Alice had said about the housekeeper. Something about being Catholic and having a nice apartment in the house. Dressed in red wool, rounded in the right places, she was a handsome woman with an oval face, brown eyes, full lips, ruddy complexion, and dark hair, center-parted and fastened into a knot at the nape of her neck.

"Mrs. B., you're sitting here in the dark. We need more light and a fire. Sergeant Fitts and the two deputies will need to see to take notes. I've been asked to sit in along with the family."

"Vivian," said Elena Beaugard in a testy voice. "The room is fine just as it is. I don't want to settle down here; I want to keep this meeting as short as possible."

"Just a little fire," said Vivian, kneeling on the hearth and reaching for a clutch of kindling poking out of a copper tub. "Think of Professor Cobb. He's been so shaky since his accident. And I like a warm room myself." Here Vivian Lavender smiled up at Mrs. Beaugard and began crumpling up a page of newspaper. "Here they all come. I've started the coffee for later, but I'll make sure the police have theirs in the kitchen."

Mrs. Beaugard nodded approval. "Yes, that will show them that they can't have the run of the place. And two logs will be quite enough."

Vivian settled two birch logs on top of the kindling, produced a match, lit the fire, and smiled with satisfaction. "There now, Mrs. B. Much cozier. And is this the doctor?" She stood up and stretched out her hand. "Dr. McKenzie. How do you do. We're so glad you could come because there's hardly a physician left who makes house calls. Mrs. B., would it be all right if the doctor took a quick look at Jonathan? After the meeting. He's asleep now, but judging from his color, he may be running a fever."

Alex had begun the ritual protest about other physicians' patients when the library door opened and in trooped the family, Eliot, Alice, and Caroline. Followed by George Fitts, Katie Waters, and Mike Laaka—Katie with a notebook, Mike with his tape recorder.

The group broke apart and settled into the corners of the room, and Alex was again reminded of the aquarium—now a more brightly lit one—in which the fish were turning and twisting and settling into their respective nooks and crannies, under plants, in dusky corners, by the rain-splashed windows. Even the gray and green woven carpet suggested the pebbled bottom of a tank. There was George Fitts, the barracuda, lurking over there in a stiff chair by the bookcase, his face in shadow. Katie Waters, small, wiry, with her short blond curls, a tropical species, undersized but feisty. A butterfly fish perhaps. Mike? Mike might be something playful and porpoiselike. Eliot Beaugard? An expensive and high-class fish, like the Atlantic salmon. And Alice? Something raggedy, perhaps a sculpin or one of the skates. And Caroline . . . ?

"Don't you think so, Alex?" said Mike.

Alex jerked his head up and found a roomful of Beaugards and police staring at him.

"The Weymouth Scooter," prompted Mike. "You know all about them. You had one. That they're unstable."

Alex pulled himself to the surface, seeing the fishlike features of the assembled company fade and take on familiar human characteristics. "Yes," he said, fumbling for words. "The Scooter as it was originally designed flops around in a stiff wind. For Dolly to have sailed without trouble all these years must have meant that she modified her boat—or used extra ballast. Which I gather she did."

This seemed to satisfy the company, and George took over the narration. He seemed to be embarking on a discussion of the hazards of sailing small boats on ocean waters, but as the audience settled back in their corners, eyes shifting, hands twisting, feet tapping, Alex could see that this was one of George's ploys: Given a group of contentious family members, it was a good idea to lull them with recitation, wait until boredom and mild exasperation had set in, then strike. Alex settled back and waited for the strike.

Katie Waters, who was also familiar with George's methods, chose to make the most of the opportunity to check out the interior of one of these old summer "cottages" about which she had heard so much. Her first impression involved the word "shabby." Used. Dilapidated. Leather chairs with slightly gaping seams; a wicker table by the windows in need of fresh paint. And those awful pictures. Dark oils showing sailing ships on greasy waters, hunting prints depicting ducks falling out of the sky or someone holding a dead fox out to openmouthed foxhounds. And, like Alex, Katie thought books normally added a lot to a room. She herself had recently joined a book club and considered the rows of brightly covered jackets gave her little apartment a lot of zip. But these books in their glass prison, with their green slipcases, added to her growing negative view of the Beaugard ambience. Old Boston money might be a great thing, Katie concluded, but if you're not using any of it to cheer up your living space, well, what was the point? The whole room made Katie think about mold.

Mike Laaka, as George wove his way through a description of Proffit Point boating facilities, was repeating the word "snob" to himself. Like Mrs. Beaugard, who acted as if the police had head lice and body odor; like Eliot Beaugard, who referred to small motorboats as "stinkpots" and fiberglass vessels as "Clorox bottles." Like vacant-eyed clotheshorse Caroline or snooty Masha with her recorder group playing that weird music he'd seen on her music stand: gavottes and pavanes and other such stuff. And then Lenox Cobb, an academic snob with the disposition of a wolverine. And the boy Jonathan. Another spoiled kid going to that private school, probably making pottery and weaving blankets. As for Alice—hell, wasn't there always an Alice in every proper family? An Alice to keep the family off balance. What they all needed, Mike thought, was a twelve-hour-a-day job sluicing out fishing boats.

Mike looked up to see that George had given Katie Waters a signal to begin taking notes, which meant it was time for the tape recorder. Mike fished in his briefcase and held it aloft. "Any objections?" he asked.

"I hope not," said George smoothly. "We tape-record these sessions more as a check on ourselves than to intimidate you."

"Yeah," said Alice. "Right. Sure."

"So, okay?" asked Mike, hand on the on button.

Silence. Only a slight shifting of bodies, bottoms on their chairs, a recrossing of arms, a movement of feet.

Then Alice again. She was perched on the lower step of a set of library steps by the bookcase, her arms wrapped around her blue-jeaned legs. "If we object, we're guilty. Of something. Murder, arson, assault, forgery, drowning of Dolly. Right?"

"Alice!" said Mrs. Beaugard. "Let the police get along with whatever they think they're doing."

"Harassment," said Eliot.

"Bunch of dogs!" shouted Lenox Cobb so loudly that everyone, even George Fitts, jumped. "Dogs," he repeated. "The watchdogs bark. Dingdong bell. Hah!" And Lenox subsided with a throaty cackle.

Alex came to. He had been drifting about with his undersea fantasy and had been about to assign Lenox Cobb the role of the spiny spider crab. Now he took a hard look at the man. Color good, no discernible lopsided droop of the facial muscles, voice perhaps a little slurred and hoarse. But what was this business about dingdong bell? Maybe the family was right about Lenox. He was sliding off the deep end. Alex shifted slightly in his seat, the better to keep Lenox Cobb in view.

"Mrs. Beaugard," said George quietly. "We're here to tell you that your daughter's death may not have been accidental, that the ballast her sailboat carried was not in place when the boat was found, and that it's possible the lead was removed sometime prior to Sunday afternoon, October second, when she went sailing."

"She could have forgotten she'd taken it out," said Masha,

speaking for the first time. She was wearing a deep green wool skirt and high-necked top and was draped elegantly on a small sofa at the other end of the windows. A green moray eel, decided Alex, looking over at the musical daughter.

"Dolly Beaugard," said George, still in the same low non-threatening voice, "from all accounts was an organized person. It seems unlikely that she forgot that she'd gone through the tedious job of removing the ballast. Remember, we also know that she took care of every detail of the sailboat's maintenance. So why did she go out in a stiff wind in a boat without ballast? Probable answer: Dolly went sailing that Sunday thinking the ballast was in place. We aren't sure just what happened when the boat foundered, but we must consider her death as a possible homicide." George paused and looked about the room, his usually impassive face wearing an expression that could almost be described as welcoming.

"Mrs. Beaugard," he said, "weren't you concerned about your daughter going out in her small sailboat on a day when the winds were increasing and small-craft warnings had been issued?"

Elena Beaugard came to life. "Sergeant Fitts, I've always been aware of the dangers of sailing, but Dolly would never have listened to me. She went out whenever she pleased."

"So," said George, "you did absolutely nothing to stop her."

"Now, see here, Sergeant Fitts." It was Eliot who rose from his chair by the window and strode across the room to take a protective stance by his mother's chair. "My mother," said Eliot in a threatening voice, "isn't well. Saying something like that is inexcusable. You just cut it out."

"Eliot," snapped Mrs. Beaugard. "I can handle this myself. Sergeant Fitts, I did point out at lunch to Dolly that the wind was coming up, but I knew that she often went out in just such weather and was an experienced sailor. And she always took a life jacket."

"Did you perhaps remind her to check over her boat? The condition of the sails, the tiller. The presence of the ballast?"

"Sergeant Fitts," roared Eliot, "I said cut it out."

But Mrs. Beaugard reached for her cane and snapped it across her son's shins. "Eliot, stop trying to interfere. I've met people like this before. Sergeant, I'll say it again. Dolly never needed to be reminded about safety."

"Did she usually sail on Sunday afternoons?" asked George.

"Yes. After Sunday dinner. We always had a proper Sunday dinner even if only Dolly and I were there to eat it. Vivian and Dolly prepared a meal, usually a roast, so that it would be ready for us after church. Then later she would go for a sail."

"This was generally known? Dolly's Sunday afternoon sail?"

"It was no secret," said Mrs. Beaugard. "Everyone on the point knew Dolly sailed on Sundays. She was so busy with her committees that she often didn't have much time during the week. But her Sunday afternoons were special."

"I see," said George. He turned to Eliot Beaugard. "You're an experienced sailor. Was your sister, Dolly Beaugard, competent in a small boat? Able to go out by herself in all weather?"

Eliot paused, appeared to be weighing Dolly's qualifications, and then nodded. "I wouldn't say she was an expert. But sure, she was okay in a small boat. Could handle most weather problems that came up. But I guess she really screwed up last Sunday. Misjudged a squall, got knocked overboard by the boom swinging over. Who knows? If the ballast was gone, I'd say she probably took it out herself. But then maybe couldn't resist one last sail before putting the boat in dry dock. It's a god-awful tragedy and my mother's just about had it up to here with the police."

George nodded briefly, then turned again to Elena Beaugard. "She always sailed alone?"

"Except for Jonathan," put in Alice. "Dolly took Jonathan sailing all the time."

"But not on the Sunday of October the second?"

"No," said Mrs. Beaugard. "Jonathan was staying with his father. Mr. Alan Epstein."

"Did Dolly usually haul her boat in by the end of September?"

"About that time," said Mrs. Beaugard. "Because of hurricanes. We always worry about hurricanes in the fall."

George nodded and then directed his attention to Vivian Lavender, who had chosen a particularly uncomfortable-looking straight-backed chair.

"Mrs. Lavender, can you remember the last time Dolly Beaugard went sailing in a strong wind and came home without mishap?"

This question produced the housekeeper's reminder that Sunday afternoon was her half day off. "So I wasn't usually around to see Dolly sail, except perhaps in midsummer when it was warm enough for me to go to the beach. But not in late September."

George threw the question open to the floor and garnered a variety of conflicting answers. Dolly had sailed the Sunday before she drowned and had come in early because there wasn't enough wind (Mrs. Beaugard); Dolly had sailed that previous Sunday but had stayed out almost two hours because there was a good wind (Eliot); Dolly said she cleaned the boathouse that Sunday, so there must have been a dead calm (Masha); Dolly had gone sailing late just the Wednesday before she died, and there had been a ton of wind. It had been windy all week, and Masha was wrong about the previous Sunday—that had been windy, too (Alice).

George then spoke his appreciation for their cooperation and said that now he and the deputies would meet separately with members of the family in various parts of the house. And Deputy Waters with Mrs. Lavender. In the kitchen. He rose, walked to the library door, opened it, and then paused, about to speak.

But Alex beat him to it. On his feet at the same time as George, he glanced at his watch and then, addressing the now rising company, "Anyone know what the weather's going to do? I know it's still pouring cats and dogs, but I had plans for tomorrow and . . ."

Although perhaps surprised by the sudden question, almost everyone had something to say about the weather. Mrs. Beaugard said Alex should watch the six-o'clock news. It gave the weather. Perhaps tomorrow would be brighter. Masha Beaugard shrugged and said the rain had better stop because it was affecting her wooden recorders—she'd have to start practicing with plastic ones. Eliot proclaimed that the barometer was going up and promised clearing skies by tomorrow night with a wind shift to the southwest, and added for good measure that the high should be in the fifties and that there would be a half moon. Vivian Lavender remarked that she only paid strict attention to the weather just before her day off, and Alice said for heaven's sake, Alex, look out the window and make a guess. That's all those dingbats at the weather bureau do. And Lenox Cobb, who now stood next to his sister and, like her, clutched a cane, said it was stupid to ask a group of people who had no scientific background to make any sort of a prediction. He, Lenox, usually knew what the weather would be because he considered all the variables, including not only air pressure, unstable airstream, cloud formation, whether stratocumulus or nimbostratus or the more dangerous jet stream cirrus, and—

"Thank you, Professor Cobb," said Alex. "I'm no weather scientist, but I'd be glad to have you tell me about your interest. Your sister suggested that since Dr. Foxe is out of town, I take a look at you. See how you're doing after your accident. How about your bedroom in ten minutes or so? Just a short examination."

And Lenox Cobb subsided and began a slow uncertain shuffle out of the room. Pausing at the door, he jerked his head at George Fitts, then jabbed his finger at the waiting Mike Laaka and Katie Waters. "The police. Bowwow. The watchdogs bark. Bowwow." And departed.

The family filed out and Katie Waters headed for the kitchen after Vivian Lavender. But George and Mike lingered.

"Well, Alex," said George in a none too pleased voice, "you stole my thunder."

"Sorry, George. Couldn't resist it. Thought you might not be getting around to asking."

"It may not mean a thing," George reminded him.

"I know," said Alex. "But anything's worth a try."

"What in God's name are you nattering about?" demanded

Mike. "So Lenox Cobb is a frustrated weatherman. So what. In Maine everyone pays attention to the weather."

"Thank you, Mike," said George. "Now catch up with Masha Beaugard and run through her time-and-place schedule for the week before Dolly's death. And ask her what prescription medicines she's taking and if she keeps medications in this house when she's away. As for you, Alex . . ."

"Time and place with Lenox Cobb?"

"No, that's police business. But you might ask him if he drinks Canadian whiskey."

Alex sighed. "The way he's acting, he'll probably kick me in the teeth for examining him, let alone asking questions."

Mike grinned. "What's that old rhyme? 'I do not like you, Dr. Fell, Why it is, I cannot tell.' Well, I've no trouble telling why I don't like that old fart. Bad-tempered bastard. Watchdogs and bowwow. Jeezus. You'd better commit him, Alex."

"What I'd better do is examine the man and the boy Jonathan. And then get out of here. Salvage an hour of my day off."

And Alex strode out of the room and headed for the stairs.

11

ALEX, mounting the stairs toward the upper regions of the Great Oaks house, had a reaction something like that of Katie and Mike. But Alex's response to his surroundings was tempered by his familiarity with the genus Maine Summer Cottage. Sarah's grandmother, Mrs. Anthony Douglas, lived in just such a house, but hers was older and gloomier. And indeed his own mother and father had a smaller and livelier version of the same out on Weymouth Island—its interior freshened by white paint and his mother's watercolors. But there was something uncanny about this enormous house, too many contentious generations lurking like dubious ghosts behind the hodgepodge of furniture. Alex trudged upward on the uncarpeted stairs and found his attention attracted by a series of ancient black-and-white framed photographs that rose along the walls. Summer events: The Croquet Party, The Costume Ball, The Regatta, The Island Picnic, Fourth of July Tennis Tournament. They were like illustrations for an Edith Wharton novel, but Alex doubted that the Beaugard family had ever been as carefree and joyous as these pictures suggested.

"Taking your time, aren't you?" It was Lenox Cobb clinging to the top of the banister.

"Wonderful old pictures," said Alex, reaching the last step.

"What you don't see," said Lenox, pointing his cane at a photograph showing four smiling men in white flannels holding pear-shaped wooden tennis rackets, "is that half the people in these photographs were always ready to kill, shoot, strangle, the other half. Arguments over whose serve it was, which ball was let, who had forgotten the mustard, what boat had not yielded to starboard tack, which family had taken which other families' tennis hour. On and on. Ad nauseam. And now? These police all over our house like hound dogs. I did say dogs, didn't I?"

"Yes, Professor Cobb, you certainly did."

"I'm losing track of what I do say. It's that swipe on the head. The attack on me. I have these blurred periods. And my balance seems off. I can remember a tennis tournament in 1928 and weather details because meteorology is one of my hobbies, but then I blank out completely. Damnation."

"Let's go into your bedroom," said Alex soothingly, "and let me have a look at you."

"But where is Dr. Foxe? He's my regular doctor. He should be here. Although he never seems to want to make house calls."

Alex reminded Professor Cobb of the reason for Dr. Foxe's absence and, after an initial resistance, managed to assist the professor into a cavernous room with a canopy bed.

"Where's your black bag?" complained Lenox, after he had been seated on a wooden chair with claw feet. He pointed to a small green carryall such as fishermen use for their gear.

"Black bags have gone the way of the horse and buggy," said Alex, opening the box and extracting a stethoscope. "Too many people around looking for black bags with drugs. Now, if you'll let me help you off with your shirt."

And Lenox grumblingly submitted to an examination by rubber hammer, stethoscope, otoscope, and ophthalmoscope. Alex thought as he probed and touched and listened that he himself—a healthy and strong man in his mid-thirties—must seem almost an insult to the elderly professor sitting bare-chested before him. For Lenox Cobb's body had pretty much settled into an assemblage of sinew, gristle, bones, and loose freckled skin. A body closely resembling a plucked and starved turkey.

"Pretty sound," said Alex, closing his bag. "But it might be a good idea to come into the clinic for a neurology workup. Or if you're not too uncomfortable with this 'blurred' sensation you describe, you could wait for Dr. Foxe to come back."

"It's only that I wanted to help Elena get her affairs in order. I'm the only one who understands how this house should be run. Elena depended too much on Dolly. And the Christmas Bird Count needs organizing, but I have trouble concentrating. Even with my new glasses. They don't seem to work as well as the ones I've lost. Alice telephoned in the prescription and she probably left out some information. On purpose."

"You *did* have a concussion," Alex reminded him. "At your age you can't just spring back into action."

"My age, my age. Everyone in this family acts like anyone over sixty is ready for the boneyard. Alice, Eliot, Masha. Bunch of harpies. Waiting for Elena and me to go under. And Dolly wasn't much better, giving our house away. God knows what else Dolly planned. Deeding all of Great Oaks' land to some ladies' auxiliary knitting team or the Bible-thumping crowd over at St. Paul's."

"I didn't know Episcopalians thumped Bibles," said Alex.

"As for me," went on Lenox in a peevish voice, "I'm finished. A relic. Show me a butt of malmsey and I'll jump in. Or retire to Pomfret Castle and talk of graves, of worms, and epitaphs."

"What!" said Alex startled.

"Shakespeare, Richard the Second, you muttonhead. Physician, cure thyself. And leave me in peace. And, Dr. . . . . What *is* your name?"

"Alex, Alex McKenzie," said Alex. "And one more suggestion. I don't know if you're much of a drinker, but I'd take it easy with alcohol for now."

"I am a man of the grape," said Lenox Cobb. "Cognac—Courvoisier—and sometimes a dry sherry. I detest other liquors. But I will take your advice and be frugal."

"Splendid, Mr. Cobb."

"It is Professor Cobb."

"Professor Cobb. And now I'm supposed to check on young Jonathan."

"Ah, yes, Jonathan," said Lenox, seizing his cane. Then pausing at a small bookcase, adjusting his glasses, he selected a blue-bound volume. "I'll come with you."

"I think not," said Alex, firmly.

"I think yes. I need to see what's happened to the boy. Out there on the dock with that bunch of young hoodlums from his class. They should have been in school and not having cookouts in the middle of the school week. That's what's wrong with the world. Sixth graders who can't spell their own names out on field trips."

"Which room is Jonathan's?" asked Alex, giving up on the idea of shaking himself loose from Lenox.

"This way," said Lenox, pointing with his cane.

Jonathan was discovered sitting up in bed, one arm in a sling anchored across his chest, the other trying to drag a pair of blue jeans over his leg cast. His mother, Alice, hovered nearby with a dish of melting ice cream.

"He doesn't seem to want to eat anything," she said almost plaintively—quite a different tone from the usual Alice voice.

"Moth-er," said Jonathan. "I'm thirsty, not hungry. Because of the sedative. It dries your mouth. Ice cream will make it worse. How about some ginger ale or a Coke or a nice cold beer?"

"I think," said Alice to the two men, "he's feeling better and he doesn't have a temp. Did you know I can use a thermometer? Took a nurse's aide course once. But I didn't graduate. All right, Jonathan, I'll rustle up something to drink."

Alex introduced himself to the invalid. "I know you've met Sarah. My wife. In this house and at the hospital when Professor Cobb discharged himself."

"Correct," said Lenox, moving closer to the bed. "Now, boy, how do you feel?"

"Hi, Dr. McKenzie," said Jonathan. "Hello, Uncle Lenox. I feel peculiar. And sorta mad. Like I've really screwed up. I was on the soccer team and now I've blown it. Or someone blew it for me. Gave me a nudge down the dock."

"And no one believes you," said Lenox with satisfaction. "They think you stumbled. My case exactly. I think there's someone out to destroy the Beaugard family. Or the few with brains."

Jonathan nodded agreement and then turned to Alex. "Okay, Dr. McKenzie, Mother said you wanted to look at me. You know what they said in the ER? Distal fibula fracture with slight bone exposure plus a dislocated shoulder. I'm taking antibiotics in case of infection and my shoulder hurts like anything and my leg is beginning to sound off, but I want to get up."

"I've just been telling your uncle to take it easy, so I'll say the same to you, Jonathan. Didn't the doctor at the hospital say to keep your leg up for a couple of days? Normally, after that you'd be able to use crutches, but with your shoulder, it's going to be a wheelchair for a while. Did they give you anything for pain? Yes? Okay, don't be a martyr. Take as directed."

"It's not that I'm sick. I just hurt. And I'm stuck here. With the family."

"Join the club," said Lenox Cobb unexpectedly. "You and I are trapped in the confines of a hostile family. And I can't read. Not more than a few pages because my eyes tire. So I have a proposition for you. You read to me—a book of my choosing—and I will pay you a small stipend for your trouble. You can put it in your college fund."

"More like my Nintendo fund," said Jonathan, managing another grin. "But are you going to make me read Shakespeare and gruesome stuff like that? Or poetry?"

"A compromise," said Lenox, pushing a chair close to the edge of Jonathan's bed. "I choose one book, you choose the next."

"But you'll choose Shakespeare? It's what you taught at Bowmouth, wasn't it?"

"I had the Susan Addinbrook Ransom Chair in Elizabethan

Literature. And yes, I dabbled in Shakespeare. Lectured to thickheaded undergraduates for thirty-five years. However, in view of your extreme youth, I will choose from various works. I have brought a volume with me. Something suitable since I assume you prefer a horror story with all the trimmings. We can begin immediately. After this man—Dr. whatshisname—leaves us alone."

With which Dr. Whatshisname nodded his good-bye and slipped quietly out of the room, hearing from the hall Jonathan's high-pitched boy's voice: " 'The "Red Death" had long devastated the country. No pestilence had ever been so fatal, or so hideous. Blood was its Avatar and its seal—the redness and the horror of blood. There were sharp pains, and sudden dizziness, and then profuse bleeding at the pores . . .' "

Alex descended the stairs, scribbled a quick note for George to the effect that Professor Cobb was not a whiskey drinker, handed it to Katie Waters, who was just emerging from the kitchen, and then headed for the front hall. And ran head-on into Masha Beaugard.

Masha, instead of sliding away after a brief greeting as Alex expected her to do, lingered and indicated distress. Her car was in Camden. Being fixed. Something about the manifold. Was he by any chance going that way? Because didn't he live somewhere in Camden? Near Bowmouth? A lift would be perfectly marvelous.

Alex, who would have given much to drive home in absolute peace, said yes, of course. Just as soon as he'd spoken to Mrs. Beaugard. About her brother.

"Uncle Lenox has gone wacko, hasn't he?" said Masha, reaching for a glossy purple raincoat. "That's what Eliot thinks and Mother's trying not to think. I mean, one minute he's with it and the next he doesn't know his own name."

"I'll be with you in a minute," Alex said, and made for the living room door, where he found Eliot Beaugard standing at the window staring at the dripping landscape while Elena Beaugard, in her accustomed wing chair by the fireplace, confronted

George Fitts. George seemed to be winding up proceedings and thanking Mrs. Beaugard for being so helpful.

"I know none of this has been pleasant," George was saying, "but it has to be gotten through. And we do have some news for you. The laboratory is releasing your daughter's body for burial. Sometime this weekend. Perhaps you can let us know if there is a funeral director whom you want to manage things."

Eliot jerked around. "Hell, it's about time. Do you police always hang on to bodies like that? Mother's been worried sick about it. The funeral should have been today."

"Mr. Ouellette of Thomaston always takes care of the family," said Elena in a faint voice. "We can have the funeral Monday. Or Tuesday. Eliot, will you call people? Father Smythe. Put a notice in the paper. Do what's necessary. Oh, Dr. McKenzie. How is Lenox? Is he recovering properly? He seems so confused at times that I thought he might have had a very tiny stroke. And just when I was thinking of letting him help me manage the estate. Take care of some of the accounts. The things Dolly used to do for me. But now I'm afraid he's not up to it."

"Well, not yet," said Alex. "He's in pretty fair shape, but a neurology workup wouldn't be a bad idea. After all, he had that blow on the head. Twice."

"Walking into a tree," put in Eliot. "Wandering around in the dark without his glasses. But hey, Alex, thanks for coming, letting Mother drag you all the way out here. And don't worry about Uncle Lenox. We'll all keep a close eye on the guy. Alice ordered two pairs of spare glasses for him, so we shouldn't have any more searches in the woods. Maybe we'll put an alarm on his belt. The way they do with little kids."

"Not a bad idea," said Alex, saying to himself, not a bad idea in more ways than one.

"And listen, he and Jonathan can buddy up. Couple of invalids and both a pain in the ass—sorry, Mother. I'd say they could neutralize each other."

Here Eliot paused and then patted his mother's shoulder.

"Okay, sorry again; I know Uncle Lenox is your special only brother. But sometimes I've had it with him. He spews out so much piss and vinegar that it's hard to stir up much sympathy. And, Alex, don't forget tomorrow. Saturday. You and Sarah. Drinks at our place. Around six. We need to get Mother out of the house. Just a few close neighbors. The family, Masha, and—"

"And Alice," said Alice, coming into the room, followed by Mike Laaka.

"Hell, Alice, you don't need to get out of the house; you're hardly in it. But come along. And bring your current boyfriend if you have one. As long as he's remotely civilized. Not out on parole or spaced out on drugs. A cross-dresser with a size C bra. Nothing to upset Mother here, who isn't exactly New Age. Hey, look out." This as Alice advanced menacingly across the floor. "Just kidding. Okay?"

"Kidding, my foot," said Alice, glowering. "Listen, Eliot . . ."

And Alex made for the door. And into the front hall, where he collected Masha, who stood sheathed in her raincoat, a handbag over her shoulder, a folding music stand tucked under one arm, and a bulging leather musical instrument case in her hand. "I have a rehearsal after I pick up my car," she explained.

Mike Laaka caught up with the two just as Alex had settled into the driver's seat.

"I'll stop in tonight."

"Why?" demanded Alex, turning the ignition.

"Because I love you," said Mike. "I love Sarah. I love all mankind. And because George says so."

"Get lost," shouted Alex, shifting into first and turning the Jeep toward the drive.

For the first six miles he and his passenger drove in silence, and then when Alex was beginning to feel a relaxation of tension and contemplating which tape would not only soothe him but please a player in a recorder group, Masha came to life.

"It's bizarre," she said. "Or ironic."

"What is?" said Alex. "Dolly's death, the Gattling brothers, or just life?"

"Well, all those, though I suppose everyone expected those two Gattlings to come to a sticky end. I meant Lenox and Jonathan. All poor Mother needs is to have those two underfoot all day, every day. Jonathan with his big mouth and Lenox with his bigger one. Like having a pair of crabs scuttling around."

Alex glanced over at his companion. A beautiful woman. Very white skin, which was odd after the more than usually hot summer, so perhaps she spent most of her time under umbrellas or in rehearsal halls. Her auburn hair was cut straight across her high forehead, hanging straight and short around her head; her arched nose, her wide mouth, her firm little chin, her sleek compact person, all these came together in a way that made Alex think of sophisticated females of the twenties. The Jordon Bakers or Gatsby's Daisy, or better, a Siamese cat. Yes, Masha Beaugard would do very well as a Siamese cat.

"Just like crabs," repeated Masha. "Don't you think?"

"You have a point," said Alex, coming to and wondering where the conversation was going.

"Mother at this time in her life needs peace and calm. Dolly gave her that. Dolly might have seemed a bit much to everyone, and God knows she did drive Eliot and me up the wall twenty times a week. But she took care of Mother."

"Did you mind about the Episcopal Church? Alice told me about your mother's idea of giving Great Oaks to the diocese. Fairly soon, not after she died."

"I don't really mind," said Masha slowly. "I haven't any sentimental attachment to the stuff in the house. But if I'd had a say, I'd have given the house over to a music group. For a permanent music school and summer youth program. Tanglewood north. We've got enough churches around, but not enough music facilities. I'd like to see our recorder consort have a permanent home here. But that's just my interest. I don't think anyone else in the family knows Beethoven from the Beatles. Except maybe Alice. She has a terrific voice and won't sing a note. Sheer orneriness. But that's Alice for you."

"Won't you all inherit all the land around the big house?

Along with Lenox. If none of them are interested in keeping the place, you might have your music school after all."

"God knows about Uncle Lenox," said Masha crossly, "but Eliot would be sure to sell off his share. And get big bucks for it because it's shore land and has deep water for moorings. Then he could buy another new boat or add a wing to that house of his. Alice would probably sell out, too, since it's ten to one she'd be in some sort of jam and need cash."

"Dolly didn't have any plans for your mother to dispose of the rest of the property? As far as you know? The Nature Conservancy, for instance?" Alex asked this carefully, having long thought that someone as superorganized as Dolly Beaugard must have considered the future of more than the house. All those cottages, several acres of woods, a sand beach, a pebble beach, and two coves.

Masha was silent. She looked out the window, scowled at the rising mist, the still-falling rain, and then tapped her finger on her knee. Then returned to the window and seemed to take an interest in the scene—Madison's General Store, a sheep farm—and then almost at the Thomaston town line, she nodded.

"You're right. I can't believe that Dolly stopped short at the house. She did everything to the nth degree. She must have had an estate plan for Mother that included disposition of every damn thing on the property, down to every acorn in the woods and pebble on the beach. And she probably wrote it all down somewhere. But the police have been suctioning up everything Dolly owned, and I haven't heard a word about an estate plan. Or Mother's will."

"The police," said Alex with feeling, "are not into sharing. They may be incubating Dolly's Line-a-Day Diary, but they won't be telling you about it. Not yet."

"Because we're all suspects," said Masha bitterly.

"Everyone in Knox County is fair game," Alex pointed out. "This is a homicide. Apparently."

"Because of the lead ballast? Honestly, I think it was exactly like Eliot said. She couldn't resist one more sail and forgot she'd taken out the ballast. Dolly *did* make mistakes. She once gave Mother the wrong medication for some stomach bug and Mother threw up all night. Dolly wouldn't have admitted it, but Vivian found the empty prescription bottle in the wastebasket. Dolly was one of those people who is never wrong, and if she was, she'd cover her tracks like crazy. Okay, Alex, you can let me off at the garage on the next block. Thanks a lot. And listen, Mother likes you. I can tell. And Sarah. See if you can make a suggestion about leaving some property for a music school." Masha paused, the car door open, then shrugged—"Don't listen to me. As Eliot would say, 'just kidding.' "

And Alex pulled the Jeep to the curb, and Masha, clutching bags and music case and music stand, departed.

Sarah was discovered kneeling on the fringe of a patch of rough grass referred to optimistically by the owners as the lawn. Even though the rain had somewhat abated, the ground was sopping. But rain or no rain, Sarah was planting peach trees. Five of them. Alberta peach trees.

"At this time of year?" demanded Alex, examining the tags.

Sarah pushed a mound of peat moss around a slim twiglike trunk, then straightened and wiped a wet and grimy hand across her forehead. "I think it's safe. Spring or fall is okay. But you have to wrap the trunk because of mice. I wanted something to grow and bloom and have fruit. We can make peach pie or *pêche* melba. The trees are a sort of an antidote to *l'affaire* Beaugard." She pushed another handful of peat in place, rose, stamped on the squelching ground, and then gathered up the half-empty bag of peat. "Let's go in and you can tell me about your adventures at Proffit Point."

An hour later, sprawled in chairs, drinks in hand, the two reviewed the day.

"So," said Sarah, "how did the house call turn out? Uncle Lenox has gone gaga or is he being maligned by evil forces within?"

"Uncle Lenox—whose brain does seem a little on the fuzzy side—is being read to by young Jonathan Epstein. Who is also out of action. I think they've found each other and have each decided that they've been pushed into or off something. By the evil forces or visiting aliens. Jonathan has a broken leg—simple fracture apparently—and a dislocated shoulder."

"I suppose they deserve each other."

"Don't knock it. It keeps two potential antipersonnel bombs out of everyone's way. Lenox actually proposed the reading program and will pay Jonathan. The professor's eyes are not up to snuff."

"His brain *and* his eyes?"

"They sometimes go together, those two things. Anyway, I left Jonathan and Lenox and Edgar Allan Poe going at it."

"While George and Mike . . ."

"Plus Deputy Katie Waters. Busy with more interviews. The family more or less accepts that Dolly is a possible homicide. George asked when Dolly last went sailing safely in a strong wind. A point on which there was much disagreement—short-term memory loss all round. Then I stuck my long nose in and asked a weather question and beat George Fitts to the punch. Here's the question: What's the weather going to do? How would you answer that?"

"You're kidding."

"No, serious."

"Well, I think it'll stop raining. It usually does."

"That's it? Your complete opinion?"

"I'm not planning a garden party tomorrow or a track event, so I don't much care. I mean I'll be glad to have sun, but I can live with rain. Good for the peach trees. So what's this all about?"

"You made the point yourself. You don't much care about the weather because you haven't planned anything that relies on it."

"So?"

"So what if you planned to do in a woman by taking ballast out of her small sailboat? Wouldn't you want to do it when a strong wind was predicted? No point in lifting the lead if there was going to be a long period of dead calm or light breezes."

"And you found out that the Beaugards all go around with barometers, holding their fingers into the wind?"

"Mrs. Beaugard listens to the six-o'clock news; Vivian Lavender checks when her day off is coming up; Eliot knows exactly what the barometer is going to do; Alice told me to look out the window; Masha worries about her recorders; but Professor Emeritus Cobb—get this—is the weather bureau personified. Statistics, the variables, the air pressures, all the appropriate jargon."

"So Eliot and/or Uncle Lenox, cohorts in crime, dumped the lead ballast."

Alex made a low rumbling sound that suggested disgust. Then he stood up and made for the oven, from whence the smell of chicken emanated. "I think the weather idea may be a bust. It would only make sense if everything else was in place. So let's eat before Mike comes to spoil dinner."

"Mike's coming? Tonight? Oh shit. I'm fond of Mike, but . . ."

"But oh for an evening without him."

"Tell him he has exactly twenty minutes of our precious time and then he's out on his ear."

"Make it fifteen and I'll agree."

12

AT eight-thirty a heavy hand sounded on the kitchen door.

"Twenty minutes," Sarah announced as she opened the door to Mike Laaka. "And only twenty minutes," she added, as she led Mike into the kitchen, his slicker gleaming from the still moist air. "Alex and I are trying to have these little pockets of normal evening life, and there's no room for you."

But Mike only grinned, patted Patsy, accepted a mug of coffee from Alex, and settled down in one of the overstuffed kitchen armchairs. Then, after a few moments spent in discussion of rain, mist, and drizzle and the question of Hurricane Griffin, now hovering somewhere west of the Azores, Mike got down to business.

"As you know, Alice claims Wednesday afternoon as the last time she saw Dolly out sailing. We didn't really believe her because Alice hardly goes about with a calendar in her head. Or much of anything else. But we've a report from a fishing boat that a boat like Dolly's *was* out then. And confirmation from the weather gurus that last Sunday afternoon the wind was offshore and blowing east. Or east northeast. Tide turning and flowing out. Which means—"

"Which means," Alex interrupted, "that Dolly would cast off from her mooring in Back Cove and run out through the Proffit Point narrows into open sea with the turning tide, before the wind, not need ballast or a keel—may even have left her centerboard up—and wouldn't have hit trouble until she let down the centerboard, hauled in sail to go off on another tack. Or tried to come about."

"You got it," said Mike. "If wind had come from another direction—say the usual southwest—she would have known right off something was wrong, could have made it back to shore or at least dropped her sails and grabbed a paddle. The *Sweetheart* apparently carried an emergency paddle."

"So," said Sarah, getting into the act, "our weather expert knew in which direction the wind was going to be blowing. Or took a chance on it. That means Lenox Cobb or Eliot Beaugard. Or both working as a team. End of case. Good night, Mike."

"Sarah, Sarah," said Mike, settling back against the pillows and taking a healthy gulp of coffee. "After all we've been through together. Listen, if you get rid of me, you'll only have George infesting your kitchen. What I've come here to say—in part, and this is between us—is that old George is a bit thrown by the Beaugard family. It's not his scene. Not that it's mine, but George is in charge, not me. Like some decayed royal family— old lady Beaugard acting like Queen Victoria; Eliot, the crown prince and their dad, papa Arthur Beaugard, with his illustrated editions, most of them kids' books, for God's sake, because I heard some adult talking about Daddy's first edition of *Peter Rabbit.* I mean, Christ, a grown man collecting books about bunnies."

"Your point?" said Sarah.

"My point? I think our Sergeant George, for once in his life, is almost glad that you're in the mix. He actually said to me he'd like you to hang around with the Beaugards and keep your ears open. Chat about Peter Rabbit. Goldilocks. Socialize with Alice Beaugard. And Webb Gattling."

Sarah sat up straight. "Oh, good Lord, bugger off, Mike. We've done what we could. We haven't much extra time for much more. Not for Alice. Or Webb. We have jobs, remember."

"Actually no real effort is needed on your part. I gather the Beaugards will hang around you. Light up your life. Just don't discourage them. There's this cocktail thing tomorrow night. And Dolly's funeral. You can network like crazy. Mingle."

"All that and Alice and Webb Gattling," said Alex. "You mean Sarah and I can double-date?"

"Go for it. We really need to firm up the Gattling place in all this. Right now Webb and Alice are the only links."

"Are you now saying the Gattling drownings do fit in with Dolly's drowning?" said Sarah.

"It's being thought about. The lab is reexamining the Gattling skiff looking for canvas fibers. Looking around for supplies of Valium. Both Mrs. Beaugard and Caroline—Eliot's wife—have prescriptions for it. Actually, Mrs. Beaugard has about twelve different prescriptions for this and that. And Caroline admits to enough stuff to stock a pharmacy. As for Alice, God knows what she's got stashed somewhere in an old shoe. Everything from hallucinogenic toadstools to castor bean candy bars."

"Alice says she's trying to kick the alcohol habit, so maybe she's trying to stay away from drugs," put in Sarah. "So how about the Gattling family prescription collection?"

"No Valium in Marsden and Junior's immediate family. But the Gattlings have probably ripped off a few drugstores in their day. Let's just say Valium is very available and that some of the Beaugards have a supply."

"Weak, weak," said Sarah. "Won't stand up in court."

"And the whiskey bottle found in the boat. Seagram's V.O. Canadian Whiskey. Not your ordinary rotgut stuff that Junior and Marsden liked to pour down their gullets. So, Sarah and Alex—"

"Oh sure," said Sarah, "we're to go to Eliot and Caroline's cocktail party with a little notepad and an instant camera and check out the liquor supply. See if Canadian whiskey is featured."

"I knew you'd cooperate, Sarah. If we find any tie—even a flimsy one—between the three drownings, then we'll have a—"

"Real mess," said Alex. "Good night, Mike."

The next afternoon—Saturday, exactly ten minutes after six— found Sarah and Alex driving down the Profitt Point Road in the direction of Eliot and Caroline's new and splendid house. Neither passenger, however, was rejoicing at the lifting of the rain and the clearing of the air.

"It's like being taken hostage or something," complained Sarah. "Getting dressed up to come all the way over here to be with people we don't much like. Except Alice. There are moments when it's possible to like Alice. Away from her family, that is. Anyway, we could have gone to the movies and seen Anthony Hopkins and Emma Thompson again. Or rented a video. *Godfather Seven* or *The Return of the Slime*. Something uplifting."

"We have a mission," Alex reminded her. "Case Eliot's liquor inventory. We're looking for Canada's finest. Seagram's V.O."

"Well, I hate whiskey, so I hope they have rum." Sarah paused for a moment and took in the passing scenery. And like Katie Waters before her, she gave herself a minute to marvel at the patterns of colors left on the road by the fallen leaves. "Not exactly Shelley, but the colors are hectic enough."

"Shelley? What's he got to do with anything?"

"It begins 'O wild west Wind, thou breath of Autumn's being' and goes on about dead leaves . . . 'like ghosts from an enchanter fleeing, / Yellow, black, and pale and hectic red. Pestilence-stricken multitudes . . .' And so forth and so forth."

"In the first place," said Alex, ever practical, "there isn't a whisper of a wild west wind today, and those leaves aren't going anywhere. They're plastered flat. 'Pestilence-stricken multitudes'? Phooey. Shelley should have run into a few real pestilence-stricken people."

"Poetic license," said Sarah. "Shelley's using the leaves to go somewhere else. Never mind poetry. You don't deserve it. What we have to do now is brace for this evening because it isn't really supposed to be a 'cocktail party.' Not with Dolly dead. It's for family distraction and moral support. With drinks on the side."

"To quote Eliot, it's to get 'Mother out of the house,' " said Alex. "We'll do a slow spin around, bare our teeth, press hands and admire the view of Tidal Cove, case the whiskey. And duck out."

"Forget the view. They have a brand-new house. They'll want to show us all over so we can gasp with envy."

The turn in to Eliot Beaugard's drive was marked by one of those mailboxes whose fiberglass sides are impregnated with the likeness of mallard ducks or cardinals—in this case a schooner with all sails set, and beneath, the name E. BEAUGARD in large black print. The chief reason for Sarah and Alex's scrutiny of this everyday object was that, uprooted from its guardian position by the side of the drive, it lay directly in the path of the Jeep.

Alex slammed on the brakes and cut the engine.

"Wild west wind?" said Sarah.

"Wild west people more likely," said Alex, grimacing. He climbed out of the car and hauled the mailbox, its post still attached, to the edge of the drive and propped it on a stone. Then he bent, reached into the open flap, and extracted a rolled newspaper, a copy of *Time*, a copy of *Business Week*, one of *Yachting*, a few catalogs, and several letters.

"Guess no one's been down for the mail today," he said, returning to the car. "I'll do a hand delivery. Looks like a chain saw got it. What is it about mailboxes? They've become a universal target. In hunting season they're shot full of holes, and in the winter they get trashed for the fun of it. You know, why go bowling when you can just crowbar a few mailboxes?"

The drive was not a long one, but it wound left and right through spruce and hemlock, then dipped suddenly and went via a narrow stone bridge over a brook before rising toward the house.

And for the second time, Alex slammed on the brakes. A figure had suddenly risen from beside the bridge, jumped into the road, and held out his arms.

"It's Webb Gattling," said Sarah, frowning at the man standing spread-eagled in front of them. She looked again. Standard Maine rural wear: jeans, black and red checked shirt, black baseball hat. High-laced boots. But the man was too short for Webb. She shook her head. "No, it isn't Webb. It's just a lot like him. Big head and hairy. Like Webb if he'd been shrunk in the wash."

"Damn," said Alex, "we're going to be good and late." But he rolled down his window and poked out his head.

"Help you?"

The man approached the car, making sure he still blocked the drive. "Maybe," he called. "You the police?"

"No," said Alex. "We're not."

"Well, you the Beaugards? Any of them?"

"No," said Alex, "and if you'll please move . . ."

"Please, can you prove you're not the Beaugards?" said the man, maintaining his position but giving a backward glance over his shoulder that suggested to Sarah he had an adjunct in the vicinity.

"Believe me," said Alex, "we're private citizens making a visit."

The man moved three steps closer, and now Sarah could see that he was at least two heads shorter than Webb, his hair was darker, more brown than blond, and his beard lacked Webb's fullness.

"But you're going to see the Beaugards?" said the man. "So I've got a holy message. From me. And all of us. My whole family. We have our sacred grief, too. Marsden and Junior are gone to glory. Brothers in Christ and now in rapture with Him. Praise the Lord. I'm praying that the Beaugards will tell the police to leave us in peace. Okay, you understand that, my brother?"

"I understand," said Alex, "and now could you please move?"

The man did, but only another step forward so that he almost leaned across the hood of the Jeep. He peered at Alex and then squinted at the windshield toward Sarah. "I've seen you before.

Both of you. Around with Mike Laaka. With that state trooper, George Fitts. They are godless folk and I pray for them. Daily I pray for the police, but they are blind to God's perfection."

Here the man became increasingly agitated, almost hopping from foot to foot, his bearded chin quivering. "Go and tell unto the Beaugards that we are innocent of Dolly Beaugard's blood. That Dolly Beaugard was a saint on earth. And some of us have taken action which I do not condone. But remember Jesus among the money changers. The mailbox shall be a sign unto you."

"The mailbox was your work?" said Alex.

The man shook his head. "I would not lift a hand to do such work. Praise the Lord. But there are those that would. Listen, brother, tell the Beaugards that Parson was praying for them. For the truth to trample out the vintage where the grapes of wrath are stored. Bless you." And the man jumped back down from the bridge—amazingly agile for one of his bulk—and disappeared into the lengthening shadows of a late October afternoon.

"Good grief," said Sarah. "The Troll of Proffit Point. Or the Mad Hermit. Parson. Who on earth is Parson? I mean, it's obvious that he's related to Webb, but is he one of the 'good' Gattlings or one of the bad ones? Or just the craziest. Bitten by the Lord."

"Frankly," said Alex, gunning the Jeep over the bridge and up the hill, "I don't care. Good, bad, crazy. But he's certainly in touch with someone who has a penchant for mailboxes."

"The police must be leaning on the Gattlings and they're feeling the heat. Every available Gattling has probably been worked over about Dolly as well as about Marsden and Junior, and they probably think the Beaugards are pointing accusing fingers."

"So some Gattlings are fighting back with mailboxes, and others are praying," said Alex, as he swung the car up to the house, rounded the circle, and parked behind a sleek dark vehicle with the familiar BMW logo on its butt.

The news of the fallen mailbox and the meeting with Parson Gattling—if that was truly his name—did much to change the tenor of the cocktail gathering. In any event, the gathering Sarah guessed from the subdued murmurs and lack of movement coming from a wide-open living space overlooking the cove, was more dedicated to the details of Dolly's death and upcoming funeral than to anything else.

Alex had no sooner made his report to Eliot, who had opened the door, than Eliot swore loudly, strode into the living room, and made the announcement. "My mailbox. Cut down with a chain saw. Those goddamn Gattlings. Alex and Sarah met one of them at the bridge. Parson. Says he's praying for us but seems to think we're blaming them for Dolly's drowning. That's close to blackmail, so I'm going to telephone the police." And Eliot stamped out of the room.

Leaving Caroline Beaugard to do the honors. Which she did in a disinterested, almost disdainful way, standing, languid hand outstretched. She was wearing a turquoise caftan and her hair fell like honey down her back, but her beauty had an unreal quality as if she were not involved in anything she said or did. She was a real puzzle, Sarah thought. A druggie or into something spiritual? Cosmic awareness. Finding her inner—or outer—self, transcending the mundane world of house and home.

The introductions went forward: the assembled Beaugards—minus Jonathan, but including Professor Lenox Cobb, who must have been dragged protesting to the party. A dark-clad figure, scowling and clutching his cane, he sat hunched on a white and pink flowered sofa. Besides the Beaugards there were several strangers, a couple by the name of Roxford, an intense-looking man whose first name was Helmann. A young woman—Amy—clasping the arm of an older man, Duncan. Plus two middle-aged second cousins of Elena Beaugard with names straight out of Tolstoy: Nicholas and Katerina Smeltovich or something like that.

"Do you want to wait for Eliot to fix your drinks?" asked Caroline. "Or fix them yourselves; everything's there." With this gracious offer, Sarah and Alex walked as directed to a table laden with bottles, lemon slices, orange slices, olives, cherries, seltzer waters, plain waters, and mixers of all sorts.

Alex helped himself to Scotch and water and returned to the other guests while Sarah considered possible choices. It was a full bar, she noticed as she reached for the rum and mixed up a rum and orange juice. Thus equipped, she turned to study the scene. Alex seemed to be engaged with Masha reenacting the confrontation with Parson Gattling. Alice Beaugard was sitting on a bench with one of the Tolstoy cousins, and Caroline floated—there was no other word for it—from guest to guest, pausing only to bestow her vague smile, listen to a few words, and then turn and join another guest.

Then Sarah remembered. The mission. Whiskey. Well, it was a perfect moment for an inventory. She turned and tried to register varieties and types. Dry sherry, Bristol Cream, Dubonnet, a burgundy, Chablis on ice. Then brandy, rum, vodka—all in high-priced bottles. Tanqueray gin. Whiskey and blends. Chivas Regal, Jack Daniel's, and three pricey bottles of Scotch. No Seagram's V.O. But wouldn't any sensible malefactor involved in lacing whiskey with Valium get rid of his supply of Canadian?

Sarah, with regret, placed her glass of rum and orange juice behind the fat bottle of Bristol Cream Sherry, and walked over to join Alice and wait for Eliot's return.

It worked as predicted. Eliot, somewhat red in the face, rejoined his guests. "The sheriff's office is sending a deputy right over to check around. See if there's any damage beyond the mailbox. I asked about this Parson Gattling and I got zip. The guy even laughed at me. Parson's probably wanted for something, but do you think those birds would let on?" Here Eliot paused and seemed to remember that this was a festive occasion—or at least semifestive. And that there were two newly arrived guests. And that one of them stood empty-handed.

"Sarah, where's your drink? Didn't Caroline? Well, never mind. What would you like? Name your poison."

"I don't suppose you have any Canadian whiskey?"

Eliot frowned. "I don't know. You may have caught me on that one. No one in our family drinks it, but then, I should have it on hand. Let's go over and see." And Eliot marched to the long table and began examining bottles. Then he excused himself, left the room, and came back empty-handed. "Sorry, Sarah. Thought there might be some hidden away in the pantry, but I guess we've never had anyone ask for it lately. Caroline," he called over his shoulder. "Next time you're in town, pick up some Canadian whiskey, will you? Sarah, we'll have to have you back some evening for a solo drink. Now, what other kind of whiskey can I interest you in? Or how about a nice Scotch?"

"Actually," said Sarah, repressing her relief, "rum would be fine. In juice if you have it."

Eliot smiled. "That's a switch. Whiskey drinkers don't go for rum. Never mind, I've got the makings." He turned back to the table and began busying himself with bottle, ice, and glass. And returned with Sarah's drink. "You're not alone. Someone else went for orange juice and something and left it behind the sherry. Now, in a proper mystery scene, we would have to check the glass for fingerprints."

"Fortunately," said Sarah, "we're not in a proper mystery. And your house, it's marvelous." Confident of the perfect distraction, she waved a hand at the surrounding walls and expanse of seaward windows.

It worked. Sarah was taken in hand and given the tour. It was all splendid: soaring ceilings, high beams, glass—every window facing the sea—the land walls hung with contemporary tapestries, abstract oils, and glass shelves featuring small ship models.

Returned to the living room, she fortified herself with a handful of mixed nuts from a bowl, and a piece of hard cheese sitting on a small cracker quite meager pickings, she thought, considering the general upscale ambience. Probably Caroline's choice. On the flowered sofa she found Lenox Cobb had been joined by Alex, and the two men were deep into a detailed discussion of the coming Christmas Bird Count: species seen, species hoped for. The possibility of a king eider, the scarcity of the red-necked grebe. A recent sighting of a number of Bohemian waxwings. It was a subject, in Sarah's opinion, that did not grab. She looked about and settled on a bench next to Alice, who was still occupied listening to one of the Tolstoy cousins, Katerina, describing the experience of putting her life into the hands of Weight Watchers while at the same time editing a book on home cooking.

"I drool all over the manuscript," she was saying.

This did not seem promising, so Sarah shifted her attention to the Roxford couple, who were engaged in a hissing argument on the question of admitting new members to the Proffit Point Tennis Club.

"Fifteen families are too many," hissed the female Roxford. "We don't get enough time on the court as it is."

"But Dolly Beaugard is gone. That leaves a vacancy."

"She never played anyway, and neither do the rest of the Beaugards. Except Eliot. What we need to do is get rid of one of the full-time families . . ."

Sarah turned back to Alex and Lenox Cobb. Counting birds began to seem more attractive. And Lenox for the first time seemed relatively affable. He was sitting up and vigorously extolling the virtues of a new field telescope.

Lenox, Sarah thought, listening to the professor, might have redeeming qualities after all. And he seemed to be having no speech difficulties of the sort that Alex had described. She had just decided that the visit had lasted long enough and was wondering how to extricate Alex from Professor Cobb's orbit when Eliot Beaugard saved her the trouble.

"It's time for Mother to go home," he announced, and with this there followed a putting down of drinks, a general rising, and a murmuring of thanks. And because of recent events, there was much clasping of hands and meaningful looks of condolence.

Sarah and Alex joined the general exodus, but were stopped at the doorstep by Eliot. "You're both in cahoots with the police, aren't you? Mother knows all about last summer with

Sarah's aunt Julia Clancy and that business of the groom murdered by a horse."

"Not by a horse," said Sarah, "a human. And we're not in cahoots with the police. It's just that—"

"I've got you," said Eliot. "I won't say a word. But if you could just find out about this Parson Gattling. He sounds dangerous. As well as cracked in the head."

"Really, you'd better let the police handle it," Sarah began, and then saw Eliot had turned and was staring in the direction of the shore where, in the fire red of the setting sun, the dock, the little dinghies, the moored sailboat, the islands and peninsula beyond, stood out in dark profile like cutout silhouettes.

"Beautiful," said Alex. "These fall sunsets. If you took a picture, no one would believe it."

"I never get tired of sunsets," said Eliot. "Even my old *Goshawk* looks terrific." He waved at the sloop, which sat out on the flat dark waters of the cove as if it had been painted there.

" 'A painted ship upon a painted ocean,' " said Sarah, happy to move away from police matters.

"Rime of the Ancient Mariner," said Eliot. "But it's a magic boat. You wouldn't believe where I can go in that old thing. Right up in coves and through shallows."

"A centerboard?" asked Alex.

"You've got it. A big centerboard in that baby means I can take her where boats this size with a keel wouldn't think of going. Hell, when I'm cruising I can sneak into little inlets, drop the hook, and have a night's peace while all the other guys are stuck out in a crowded noisy harbor."

"But a retracted centerboard must take a lot of cabin space."

"That's the downside," said Eliot. "And old *Goshawk*'s getting a little creaky." Then he seemed to remember what had brought him outside. He extended his hand to Sarah. "Thanks so much for coming. It means a lot to Mother to have old friends around at a time like this. And don't forget about Parson Gattling, will you? Prior convictions, what he was doing when Dolly drowned."

Alex and Sarah turned and walked in silence to the Jeep. And in silence completed the first ten miles down the Proffit Point Road.

Then Sarah drew a long breath and said, "That meeting with Parson Gattling does give me the shivers. Talk about weird."

"Just your everyday nut with a religious flavor, I'd guess," said Alex. "But I will ask Mike when I see him."

"Oh shit!" said Sarah suddenly. She pointed at her feet.

"Oh shit what?"

"Look there. The mail. Eliot's mail. Caroline's mail. From the mailbox. We forgot to take it in."

"I'm not going to turn around. We're halfway home. We'll get it to them tomorrow."

"What's the penalty for mail theft?"

"Probably years in a federal prison."

"One of those minimum-security ones, I hope. We can learn basic skills, how to run a laundry and play volleyball. Not a Beaugard in sight. It's sounds wonderful."

Alex nodded and, to the great hazard of safe driving, reached over and kissed Sarah on the cheek.

13

SUNDAY promised to be a day of clear autumnal weather with a surcease of trouble from the direction of Proffit Point.

Sarah and Alex sat lingering over a very late breakfast since Alex was not on call for what was left of the weekend. And Sarah had spent the dawn hours finishing a pile of papers on Defoe.

Both were therefore in an unaccustomed state of mellowness.

Alex yawned and stretched and shoved away the sheets of the *Maine Sunday Telegram* that lay strewn around the breakfast table. "A whole day free. Where will we go? How about a hike? Climb Megunticook. Or something bigger?"

"How about Mount Dessert? If we left now, we could drive up Cadillac Mountain and—"

"Hike, not drive. Patsy would enjoy a little muscle flexing, wouldn't you, Patsy?" Alex reached over and ruffled the gray head.

"Anything you say. I've corrected every paper in my possession. And I have Defoe and *A Journal of the Plague Year* to thank for some almost good writing efforts. Bubonic plague seems to turn students on. It's better than the incest in *Oedipus* because that takes place offstage, which is no fun at all. Students want their incest close up and in living color."

"I think," said Alex, "that you're on to something. Lenox Cobb had Jonathan reading 'The Masque of the Red Death,' and according to reports, Jonathan—Mr. Junior Cool—was fairly gripped. You might consider a curriculum of plague literature next year."

Sarah nodded absently, examined her teacup, found it empty, and reached for the teapot. "Well, speaking of plagues, what about Lenox Cobb? He was almost genial last night, sitting there on the sofa with you. Birds seem to be his thing. Or one of his other things. Along with the weather and Shakespeare."

"He wants to manage the south Proffit Point end of the Christmas bird count, but I think it's beyond him. He's still on the fragile side and complains of headaches and blurred vision. And he did repeat himself yesterday, got himself tangled into some more quotations from *Richard the Second*. Anyway, I said I'd help out with the count. Along with you. It's the Saturday before Christmas."

"I can't believe you're thinking about anything connected with Christmas. It's October, for heaven's sake. But when the time comes, I'll be your recorder. But I will not count birds."

"Understood. And Lenox is going to have to accept help other than mine. Even help from nephew Eliot, who's apparently an acceptable birder, but a man Lenox cannot stand. As well as the whole high-style profile of Eliot and Caroline's."

"Eliot and Caroline. Oh my God!"

"What?" demanded Alex, alarmed.

"The mail. Their damned mail. Saturday's mail. Eliot and Caroline's. We'll have to deliver it. Right now."

Alex gave a long gusty sigh. "I knew it was too good to be true. A whole day."

Sarah pushed herself away from the breakfast table. "We'll have our day. Only a small slice of it goes to mail delivery. Get your jacket and I'll put Patsy on a leash. He needs fresh air. I think he's been a little under par lately."

"We've all been under par lately," said Alex, standing up and stretching. "Okay, we deliver the mail and I'll take binoculars. Practice for the bird count."

Driving toward Proffit Point, Sarah returned to the subject of plague. "It's not only my students and Jonathan. Pathology, violence, has certainly turned the Beaugards on. They're fairly quivering. And it's not just the very real grief. The whole family's more, well, alert. Ready for action. It's very peculiar."

"Actually," said Alex mildly, "the Beaugards are just catching up to the rest of the world, where peace and calm is what's peculiar. The Beaugards—except for Alice—have always been pretty quiescent. Sheltered, staid, and stolid. Frozen into a past of social propriety. Big houses with gates and protectors. Gardeners and housekeepers and nannies. But after Dolly washed in, they've had a look at the real world."

But Sarah had moved on. She had been holding the heap of Eliot and Caroline's mail on her lap when several envelopes slipped to the floor of the car. In retrieving them, she brought a glossy brochure to the fore.

She turned it over in her hand. A handsome two-masted sailboat photographed against roiled waters with a message in gold: GREETINGS FROM SEAOVER YACHTS. YOUR BROKER FOR THE FINEST SAILING VESSELS AFLOAT. THE SEAOVER 36 SLOOP; THE SEAOVER 40 YAWL; THE SEAOVER 46 CUTTER-RIGGED SLOOP; THE SEAOVER 55 SCHOONER.

"Hey," said Sarah, waving the folder in front of Alex's face. "Do you suppose Eliot's going to dump the faithful *Goshawk?*"

"I don't suppose anything. But I do know you're reading someone else's mail."

"You sound like my grandmother. This is just a brochure. Fair game. Practically public property. There's a catalog from Brooks Brothers and Lands' End. And L.L. Bean. Winter Fun in the Outdoors. And from Orvis. All quite high-toned stuff. As for personal mail, I wouldn't dream of glancing at any."

"I'll bet."

"Well, just turn it over carelessly in my hand."

"Give me those letters," said Alex, reaching over.

"Certainly," said Sarah, pushing the pile back in shape and slipping it onto his lap. "The rest is pretty boring. Bills from the telephone company and cable TV."

The delivery of the mail went without a hitch. Caroline answered the door and accepted the bundle without a word and halfheartedly invited them in for coffee. "Or a Bloody Mary or something. Eliot's out on the *Goshawk.*" Caroline pointed in the direction of the cove where the sloop sat at its mooring and a rubber Zodiac raft bobbed at its stern.

Alex and Sarah declined the invitation with thanks, and Alex asked if the sailing season was coming to an end.

"I guess so," said Caroline. "Eliot's going to run her over to Little Cove this afternoon and have her hauled out for the winter. Well"—she hesitated—"thanks for the mail. We wondered. Sorry you won't come in." And she turned and closed the door.

"What's with that woman?" complained Sarah as they started back to their car.

"Be grateful. You didn't want to go in, did you? To help her read her mail."

"Oh, shut up. No, I didn't, but she has as much charm as a doormat. All looks and nothing else. Maybe it's low blood sugar."

"Maybe, my love, she doesn't like us. Doesn't share the Beaugard lust for our friendship. Ever think of that?"

"Actually, she reminded me of a rabbit. A well-dressed irritable rabbit who doesn't want to come out of its hole."

"A pretty expensive hole, that house," said Alex. Then as they reached the Jeep, "Oh hell, Patsy's jumped out. Didn't you close the window?"

"Didn't you?" retorted Sarah.

"Your dog," said Alex, reaching for the leash.

Patsy, excited by low-flying seagulls, making bounding and barking progress around the muddy margins of the cove, was corralled after a forty-minute pursuit.

"Damnation," said Sarah, looking at her spattered trousers. "Wouldn't you know it was almost low tide. And look at Patsy." She looked down at the dog, whose wiry gray hair was thoroughly wet and streaked with dark and inky swaths of flats mud.

"Home," said Alex. "Bath, change, put dog in run, and then we'll have our day. Even if it's midnight, we're going to have our day. Now, put that mutt in the car."

"Irish wolfhound," said Sarah, hauling at the leash.

"Mutt," said Alex, opening the rear door of the Jeep.

The rest of Sunday, the evening that followed, remained in Sarah's mind as a delightful parenthesis. A brief period of tranquillity undisturbed by the demands of medicine, academe, or a single member of the Beaugard household. Even Alice, with or without Webb Gattling, failed to turn up at the kitchen door, and the twilight sighting of Parson Gattling holding a placard across the street in Rockland did not upset equanimity.

But then came Monday and the funeral of Dolly Beaugard. And the funeral of Marsden and Junior Gattling—all three bodies having been released to their families the past weekend. As if indeed the circumstance of their deaths, the sharing of the drowning waters, had brought the trio into a sort of synchrony.

The first event took place at two o'clock at the Diggers Neck Baptist Church; the second two hours later at St. Paul's-by-the-Sea in Camden. Thus, it was just possible for a mourner to make the Gattlings' obsequies and then gun it to Camden in time to attend Dolly's event.

Several people managed to pull this off, among them Sergeant George Fitts, Deputy Michael Laaka, and Alice Beaugard—she sitting in the rear with Webb Gattling and holding tightly to his clenched hand.

Alice, meeting Webb around the corner and just out of sight of the church, had a fierce argument with Webb on the subject.

"Webb," she pleaded, "look at me. Wearing a gray skirt and black coat at least a size too big. And this blouse with a ruffed neck. It was Dolly's. I mean, God, I look like something out of

Hamlet. Just for your family because mine doesn't care if I go in a clown suit. I mean, they expect it of me."

Webb, his beard combed smooth, his hair slicked down, a giant trussed up in a dark suit and tie, looked down at Alice with approval. "You look okay. If you looked the way you usually do, like you're some kind of refugee from what's that place, Bosnia, hey, you'd scare my relatives to death. They're not so damn happy about the Beaugards as it is. Parson's been going around making sermons about the cops and your family. We'll sit in the back. But I'm not ashamed of being with you, so it's time everyone knew it."

"Me, too," said Alice. "I mean, it's time my family knew about you. So if I'm going with you to Junior and Marsden's funeral, then you can come to Dolly's and sit with me."

Webb frowned down at her. "You don't get it, do you? Look, in plain English, your family can always come slumming. Give us the benefit of their presence. Doesn't work in reverse. You're one of the summer people who've sort of moved in full-time. You guys live in houses with names like Great Oaks and go sailing for the fun of it. Or like Dolly, you don't have to earn money, so you can volunteer. Or Masha, playing in a little artsy-crafty group. Don't get me wrong. You know I like music, even her stuff. You took me to a concert, remember. It wasn't so bad. But for a living? I'll bet she couldn't make a living out of playing the recorder without family cash behind her. Or how about you, batting around, letting your family pay your rehab bills?"

Alice, who normally would have been shouting with anger under such an attack, found tears racing down her cheeks. "Hold it," she choked. "Goddamn you, Webb, I'm not like them. Not really."

"Let me finish. First, I love you. Hope you love me. And I don't care who your family is. But be real. To your mother we Gattlings are just lowlife scumballs. And if I go to Dolly's funeral, hell, it'll be as if some kind of Al Capone turned up. Someone who might have tipped Dolly over in that goddamned boat. Or dumped the goddamned ballast. Yeah, I've heard all about that. So I won't go to your funeral. But you'll come to ours. Because even if my family hates Beaugard guts, they don't think the Beaugards killed Marsden and Junior, except for Parson, who has fleas in his brain. So let's get to the church. Me not ashamed of you, you not ashamed of me. Then I'll drive ninety miles an hour and drop you at Dolly's funeral. And tonight we'll go out for dinner and forget what our last names are."

And Alice, her face collapsed into a strange mix of defiance and agreement, allowed Webb to take her arm and bear her off.

George Fitts and Mike Laaka, fortunately, had no problems—psychological or social—with attending the Gattling double funeral. George believed in covering all bases, and this was an event featuring two suspect deaths. Two possible homicides. And in George's experience, it sometimes happened that the murderer was in attendance. Anyway, no harm in keeping an eye out for untoward arrivals. And for once, George was glad to have Mike along. Mike was local and could sort out who was there—like any of the Beaugards, for instance—and then they could research any persons who did not fit into the Gattling mourner profile.

Together the two men left the car, George's green Ford Escort—unmarked but well known by half the county; together they walked up the steps to the church and at the top step split, George to the left, Mike to the right. Each in possession of a memorial program.

If that's what they're called, thought Mike, settling himself in a back pew, far to the right, and opening the double-folded piece of cream paper. Embossed lilies—in silver—on the front. In silver the words IN BLESSED MEMORY OF MARSDEN JOSEPH GATTLING AND EDWARD "JUNIOR" WILLIAM GATTLING. REST IN PEACE. Opening this up, Mike could see that a number of hymns were interspersed with the service and that interment in the Sunny View Cemetery would follow. But for now the crowd was thickening, streaming down the aisles, looking for space in the pews. Women in floral dresses and dark coats, men whom Mike knew spent their lives wearing jeans, coveralls, and high rubber boots, and now looked, as did Webb Gattling, strangely constrained in suits and ties. Mike knew most of them. Gattlings of all flavors, of course. And there was Tad Bugelski, Proffit Point's harbormaster and finder of the bodies. And the postmaster. And the guys from the Texaco station. And, for God's sake, Alice Beaugard and Webb: Alice in that outfit, dressed like some sort of visiting nurse, and looking as if she'd got something in her throat that wouldn't go down, hanging on to Webb's arm. Was this an announcement? Or an "in your face" appearance by the two of them? Mike twisted his neck sideways and was rewarded with the sight of the two clambering into a rear pew opposite his own. So they weren't going to flaunt themselves and mix it up with the family up front.

Mike now examined the front of the church. Two caskets side by side. Closed. Well, he supposed that even the most skilled cosmetic treatment couldn't restore those two boys to healthy looks. Up front, lecterns, a sort of semicircular painting with Jesus and people wading around in blue water. And a real tub—did Baptists call it a tub? Or an immersion vessel? A font? Never mind, Laaka, pay attention. They're not paying you for guessing about what Baptists duck their members in. Who else?

Mike turned around to face the entrance. One of the cashiers from the Camden National Bank. Was she a Gattling? And that real estate salesmen, what was his name? Levensitter, Tom Levensitter. Was *he* a Gattling? And Digby Reynolds. Well, he went to all the funerals, did Digby. Music, shelter, and sometimes free coffee and food. He'd probably make it to Dolly's, too, if he could find a ride. And, well, would you look at that? Vivian Lavender. Navy blue with a yellow scarf. Standing there as big as life by the middle door. On enemy territory. A Beaugard spy. Or a second spy if you counted Alice. Mike allowed himself a stare and just then Vivian looked his way. Their eyes met, Mike saw a visible wave of relief move across her face, and before he could think about changing his seat, he was joined.

"Thank heavens," whispered Vivian. "Someone I know."

"You grew up around here," Mike reminded her. "You know as many people as I do. You know the Gattlings."

"Yes, of course I do. But you know, working for Mrs. Beaugard, living at the house. All these years." Here Vivian lowered her voice so that Mike had to lean toward her. "I just don't feel quite right about being here."

"Then why are you?" said Mike.

"Eliot convinced me. Said his mother would have wanted it. Because both Gattling men washed in on Beaugard property. Into Little Cove. Eliot said he felt that some gesture . . ."

"Why not send flowers?" asked Mike. "Or make a donation?"

"They did that, too. Everything proper."

Mike couldn't resist. "Guilty conscience?" he suggested, and was rewarded by the shock on Vivian's face. But now the Gattling family began filing in and seating themselves one by one in the front row. Large, small, old, young. Giants like Webb and shorties like Parson Gattling who brought up the rear.

Then, in a loud voice from the front of the church: "I am the Resurrection and the life, says the Lord our God. He who believes in me even though he is dead, yet he shall live . . ."

Mike allowed his attention to wander. Vivian Lavender. In the flesh. Sent by Eliot. Well, according to George's theory, this is significant. The unexpected mourner. Right beside him in her navy blue suit with the stylish yellow scarf knotted about her neck. The housekeeper. Well, Mike had read *Rebecca* as a kid. Seen the thing on video. He knew all about housekeepers. An evil bunch.

Suddenly Mike was aware of a poke in his side and the presentation of a hymnal. "Top of the page," whispered Vivian.

They stood and Mike found himself singing, baritone to Vivian's alto, both very tentative:

> "Blessed assurance, Jesus is mine!
> O, what a fore-taste of glory divine!"

The service went on, Pastor Bob Bonner promised a place in heaven for Junior and Marsden besides other Gattling loved ones, and the whole thing ended with, in Mike's opinion, a strangely selected hymn that went on about

"Fainting struggling sea-man, and
Some poor sailor, tempest toss'd,
Trying now to make the harbor,
In the darkness may be lost."

"And even Vivian seemed to think this an improper ending.
May be lost! Didn't they read the papers?" she demanded, collecting her handbag. "Well, I'm off to St. Paul's. Goodness, what
a day."

The housekeeper, repeated Mike to himself. But how? And
why? Putting Valium into Canadian whiskey and smuggling it
aboard the Gattling skiff. Impossible. Or nearly. The Gattling
brothers had put out from Digger's Neck across the cove. At
night. With packages of cocaine. Even Sarah's overactive imagination couldn't put water skis on Vivian and send her out to
meet them midcove. Well, then, how about Alice? Webb's girlfriend. And Webb has a skiff. But why? And what for? Oh hell.

These thoughts he shared with George Fitts on their high-
speed trip across Knox County to St. Paul's-by-the-Sea.

"Vivian Lavender's been with the Beaugards for ages," said
Mike. "I might be able to talk myself into thinking she had it in
for Dolly. You know—jealousy, Dolly managing everything in
sight, stepping on Vivian's toes. But why kill the Gattlings?
Come on."

"You always want to rush," said George. "I'm making out a
time chart for the entire Beaugard and Gattling setup. See if
there's any intersecting. People in the wrong space. Don't go
leaping into the dark before you have a single fact."

"Okay, okay. But don't you think it's funny about Vivian turning up?"

"I'm paying attention to her being there. And Eliot sending
her—if he did. And Alice turning up. I didn't expect that."

"Webb must have a good grip on Alice," said Mike. "Anyway,
I think Vivian's a damn handsome fully packed female. I'll bet
Dolly wasn't crazy about her. Now, if Vivian had drowned and
Dolly—"

"Mike, relax. I'm not forgetting Dolly. I've been asking

around. She seems to have not only done good works, but she tossed an enormous amount of money into her various projects. Gifts to the hospital, the church. We've had an auditor going over the estate books, but so far nothing seems to be out of whack. Dolly must have used her trust fund income."

"Saint Dolly," murmured Mike as Camden came into view.

Sarah, after only a token protest, had been pressed into service at the church in the hours before the funeral. While Masha arranged the flowers from the family around the altar, Sarah was handed the job of the "other" flowers. Because although the newspaper notice—rushed into Monday's paper—had said "flowers gratefully declined," there were always those who sent them. These had to be marshaled, their donors noted, in the Beaugard Room of the Parish House—"where the family will receive guests following the service." Beaugard Room? wondered Sarah.

Having no classes on Monday, Sarah simply canceled her student appointments and spent the day at the church figuratively and literally with her sleeves rolled up. Then, as noon approached, she was pressed into arranging tea things, dealing with a caterer's delivery of small cakes and tiny cookies. In this she was assisted by a tall young woman who announced that she was Mary. Mary Dover, the assistant rector of St. Paul's, her office being attested to by Mary's round collar, her black dickey, and the silver cross that hung from her neck.

"Such a loss," said Mary. "Why, we could never have finished the Beaugard Room without Dolly. Never in a hundred years."

"Oh?" said Sarah.

"Well, we had the space, but it was a wreck. More of a storage area really. For Sunday school supplies and blackboards and so forth. But we needed paint and plaster and a decent rug. New beams, tables, chairs, a modern kitchen. And along came Dolly."

"Very generous," murmured Sarah, busy stacking tea saucers.

"That's why it's the Beaugard Room," said Mary. "Of course, Dolly said her mother was behind the donation. But Dolly was the engine. And when we needed a whopping big sum of money all at once, there she was. Well, now, everything looks in order. I'll go and review what I'm going to say. So much about Dolly that was truly inspirational. What an example to all of us."

So, said Sarah to herself. Dolly not only did good works. She funded them. So big deal. The Beaugards have money dripping out of their pockets. But a whole room? Then turning around, "Oh, hi, Alex. Lunch?"

"Just have time. A quick lunch, then back to the hospital."

"Okay, but can you pick up Grandmother Douglas around three-thirty? She can't bear to be late for anything. I have to come back after lunch and deal with all this. Flowers up the yin yang. I'm trying to make the place not look like a gangster's funeral parlor. All those orange and pink gladiolas from the Girl Scouts and the St. Paul's Dorcas Society. Didn't any of them read the notice in the paper?"

"Appropriate, though, gangster's funeral parlor. Whiffs of homicide along with the incense."

"Don't say that to Grandma. She takes funerals seriously. I wonder if they'll sing 'For All the Saints.' "

Eliot Beaugard arrived at three o'clock dressed in somber oxford gray with a navy tie, and confronted Sarah. "Hey, there, great job. How did we ever get along without you?"

How indeed? said Sarah to herself. Aloud, she thanked Eliot and asked if the family had arrived.

"Ready to roll," said Eliot. "Literally, as far as that young squirt Jonathan goes. He's in a wheelchair. Alice is missing, natch. And Vivian is on an errand—well, not of mercy. Say diplomacy. I told Mother that since those Gattlings washed in at Little Cove, we should at least acknowledge them at the funeral. Vivian's gone as the family representative."

"But Vivian . . ." Sarah objected.

"You're going to say she's not a Beaugard, not one of us," said Eliot. "But Vivian's been with us so long, she *is* one of the family. A damn important part of it. She's local; the Gattlings will accept her." And Eliot, after a quick glance at his watch, made off toward the stairs leading to the church proper.

"You," said Sarah aloud to the tea service, "are full of it." Then to herself she added, no way will Vivian be thought of as a Beaugard substitute. In fact, it'll be damn lucky if she's not considered an insult. And Sarah gave her short hair a quick smoothing, pulled down her sleeves, wrapped herself in her green wool coat, and headed for Dolly Beaugard's last public appearance.

14

RATHER than leave the church and enter by the front steps, Sarah chose to slide in via an anteroom that opened into a side aisle of the nave. The room was one Sarah remembered from other ceremonial occasions as serving as a holding tank for the chief attendants at funerals, weddings, and christenings.

This choice gave Sarah a good look at the Beaugards en masse. Since they were all occupied with each other, she was able, by slowing her steps and angling her head, to take in the main features. Uncle Lenox Cobb, in a gray suit, blue striped shirt, a crimson bow tie. Seated. Hands on cane. Glowering into middle distance. Next to him Jonathan. Wheelchair, cast-covered leg stuck out in front of him, left arm strapped across chest. Pale angular boy's face, hair brushed, khaki trousers—one leg slit to accommodate the cast. White shirt. Crimson bow tie. Two red bow ties? Was it a club and Jonathan and Lenox the only members? The Masque—or the tie—of the Red Death?

She checked her watch. Still thirty-five minutes to go. She hesitated and then found a bench behind a potted fern where she could be seen if wanted, but was not obtrusive. No point in rattling around in the church among the empty pews; she'd hang in here for another ten minutes and then see if she could spot Alex and her grandmother coming in. Who else had turned up? Not Alice. Good old unreliable Alice. Where was she? But Masha had made it. Masha in a knit maroon tube thing, turtle-neck to ankle, was sitting alone by the window—one of those fake Tudor casements—and studying a piece of music. A leather instrument case stuck out of a large open handbag. Deduction: Masha was part of the service.

And ensconced in a leather chair, the mother. Mrs. Beaugard. Entirely in black. From head to toe. Shoes, stockings, dress, jacket. And hat. With a veil. Black veil. No one wore those any-more, did they? Well, yes they did, because here she was, Elena Beaugard looking exactly like those old photographs of bereaved wives and daughters: Mrs. Woodrow Wilson, Sarah Delano Roosevelt, Queen Mary, the Queen Mum, Queen Eliza-beth.

Eliot was leaning over his mother in a consoling posture; Vivian Lavender, the hired family diplomat, hovered on her opposite side. Vivian, to Sarah's eyes, looked rather flushed, and the bun at the back of her neck had let loose a lock of dark hair. That hasty trip from funeral one to funeral two had no doubt taken its toll. But the flush was becoming, and as far as healthy looks went, Mrs. Lavender, along with Eliot, was a clear winner.

Caroline Beaugard provided the real contrast. What was that song—or was it a poem?—something about pale hands, pale lips? Caroline, sitting by herself, had chosen a gray many-layered silk costume, and the general effect was of someone recently brought up from the grave. Or about to descend into it. And the heir apparent, nine-year-old Colin Eliot, in navy blazer and flannels and navy tie, stood well apart from his mother, intent on some electronic gadget in his hand. A pocket Nintendo, Sarah decided.

And here was Alice. Rushing in, wearing clothes at least a size too big. Kissing her mother and having trouble with the black veil. And judging from her mother's gestures, she was being reprimanded and then forgiven, her hands patted by the black gloves.

And now the organ. A great thundering groan from the partially opened door. Glorious Things of Thee Are Spoken/Zion City of Our God. Or if you preferred: *Deutschland, Deutschland, Über Alles.*

Time to go. Sarah slid out from behind her fern, waved at Eliot and his mother, and made for the church.

Right on time. Alex with Grandmother Douglas bent on his arm stood at the rear. Sarah hastened forward and all three made a stately entrance and settled into a middle pew, a choice that prevented Sarah from checking out those who preferred the rear.

After the bowing of heads, however, Sarah sat up and let herself drift. What was it about Gothic-type churches with their vaults, ribs, piers, those stained-glass windows—Mary and Martha, the Loaves and Fishes, the Marriage at Cana? These out-of-world artifacts together with the trappings of the funeral, the groaning organ, the somberly clad people, the flowers, all had a fatal effect on concentration. The more one tried to focus on the virtues of the dear departed, the more the mind darted off into distant byways and dubious side alleys.

At first Sarah made an honest effort to focus. She opened the memorial service folder—cream paper, black print. Prelude, hymns, readings, a Psalm, the homily, another hymn, another Psalm, prayers, the commendation, the blessing. And Dolly's real name: Dorothea. Sarah had forgotten that. Dorothea Sophia Beaugard. Seeing it spelled out that way gave Dolly herself a certain exotic flavor. Where had the Sophia come from? Oh yes, those two cousins at the party. The Russian connection. But Sarah was sure that, in Dolly's case, the stodgy Beaugard DNA had probably tamed any wild impulses from the Volga and the steppes. And as far as Dolly's death went, nothing exotic about it. Just good old homegrown homicide.

Sarah drifted away again. She found herself reviewing a college course in the history of architecture. What was the crucial development? Oh yes, the stilting of the longitudinal rib. From thence came buttresses and vaults, the pointed arch, the whole bit. At St. Paul's-by-the-Sea, even the secondary spaces and rooms were determinedly Gothic. Even the Beaugard Room with its fan vault.

A fan vault. My God, that must have been expensive. Had Dolly and her mother funded the vaulting as well as the kitchen? Sarah, dimly aware of the opening chords from the organ, stood up, gripping one side of the open hymn book. But instead of joining in with "Lead on O King Eternal," she began taking inventory of the Beaugard Room. Spacious. Approximately eighty by forty. Refinish the floor, panel the walls, which looked like oak. Or oak veneer. Say $4,000, plus or minus. Oriental-type carpet—it couldn't be the real thing, could it? Or perhaps Dolly had rolled up a spare from the Great Oaks attic and presented it. Suitable footing for Beaugard shoes. Put down $5,000 for an imitation, $25,000 for the real thing. Compromise at $10,000. Refectory oak table, at least eight straight chairs with leather seats. Two armchairs. So for furniture—being conservative—three grand. Curtains: lined, plum brocade for six windows: $400. At least.

And the kitchen. Ye gods. Sarah and Alex had finally upgraded their 1930s farmhouse kitchen, and she knew what a kitchen could do to a budget. Wouldn't there be a six-burner institutional stove and megasize sink and fridge?

"Sarah," hissed Alex. "Stand up."

Another hymn. As predicted: For All the Saints Who from Their Labors Rest. Saint Dolly. Or Saint Dorothea. Was she the martyr beheaded for refusing to be raped? Or was that Sofya or Sophia? Sarah had a poor grip on saints.

Sitting down, Sarah allowed her attention to center for a moment on Masha Beaugard, who now stood by the organist and joined him in "Sleepers Awake." But the Beaugard Room exerted too strong a pull and Sarah returned to her accounting. Let's see. Add those four mullioned windows that matched the rest of the parish house. Plus the handsome etchings of English cathedrals: Ely, Salisbury, Wells, York. Hardly garage-sale stuff. Then the fan vaulting, which might be a fake, not structural.

Well, however you sliced it, the total was sneaking up on $100,000.

"Good God!" Sarah said aloud in a shocked voice.

"Sarah," said Alex. He indicated her grandmother with her head bowed. "Our Father Who art in heaven, hallowed be Thy name," he said in a threatening voice.

Sarah adjusted her posture and began reviewing the Beaugard Room, item by item. Maybe more than $100,000.

"Amen," said Alex.

"Amen," said Grandmother Douglas.

"Good God," repeated Sarah, shaking her head. And she'd probably left a lot out. The kitchen utensils, the china, the glasses, for instance. Even if it all came from Wal-Mart, there had to be a lot of it. And that tea service looked new. She glanced up and found Father Smythe looming benevolently over the congregation. ". . . be gracious unto you. The Lord lift up His countenance upon you and give you peace, both now and evermore. Amen."

"Amen," said Sarah belatedly.

The church crowd surged into the aisles forward, through, and up—to the Beaugard Room—or to the front doors and fresh air.

Mrs. Douglas was collected by the faithful Hopkins, who had sat in the back, and Sarah and Alex edged out of their pew.

"Okay," said Alex. "What's next?"

"The Beaugard Room wherein the family will greet guests. Named for chief benefactors, the Beaugards. Especially Dolly." Here Sarah paused and observed the somberly dressed crowd pressing toward the entrance to the Parish House stairs. "Look," she added, "there's no point in fighting our way into the room until later. Let's go outside for a while and then go back in."

"Sorry, I've got to be back at the hospital. I'll push up and shake hands now and you dribble in later."

This plan agreed to, Sarah joined those retreating to the rear of the church and found herself shortly on the wide stone steps. And almost into the arms of Parson Gattling. A Parson Gattling in a navy blue serge suit and a stack of small cards in one hand.

They stared at each other, both realizing that they'd had an early encounter of a questionable nature.

Sarah, her mouth running ahead of her brain, said, "It's Mr. Gattling. Aren't you at the wrong—I mean, wasn't there another . . ." She stopped, closed her mouth, and tried to regroup.

Fortunately Parson Gattling was a man with a mission. "I'm here today," he said, "because of getting God's justice done. On all you Beaugards and us. After what was done to Marsden and Junior and Dolly. And I'm praying for Beaugards because they are deep into sin with the Lord. And I am praying for the repose of the sacred soul of Miss Dolly Beaugard. Rest her in peace."

Sarah, vastly annoyed, grabbed at the second sentence. "I'm not a Beaugard. I'm not even related. My name is Sarah Deane, and what do you mean, 'deep into sin with the Lord'? As far as I know, all the Beaugards have done is lose their daughter."

"The Beaugard family has a date with God," said Parson Gattling, in his gravelly voice. "We in the Gattling family do not cry out for vengeance, but vengeance is mine sayeth the Lord God of Israel." Parson hesitated and then extended one of the cards from his pack. "Read and beware," he said. "Forgiveness is divine, but first comes prayerful confession."

Sarah found curiosity overtaking irritation. What was the man talking about? "Explain, please, Mr. Gattling. Who should be confessing? And why? What *are* you talking about?"

"Let those who have done evil come forward," said Parson Gattling. "I'm not saying it's you who should come forward if your name isn't Beaugard. But all of us have sin on our shoulders and have consorted with evil. And I'm here to say that Marsden and Junior have not died in vain." And with that Parson shot his head forward rather like a turtle and gave Sarah a meaningful look. Then he turned and joined two men hurrying down the steps and presented each with his card. Both men, Sarah noticed, seemed too surprised by the offering to refuse, and by the time they came to, Parson had accosted another departing party.

She turned the card over. It looked like a homemade printing job. But the message was simple enough. BEWARE OF FALSE PRIDE IN THOSE WHO ARE NOT NAMED. TRUTH WILL OUT EVEN THOUGH IT IS NOT SOUGHT. IN MEMORIAM: MARSDEN GATTLING, EDWARD "JUNIOR" GATTLING. ALSO MISS DOLLY BEAUGARD. R.I.P.

Oh, for heaven's sake, Sarah said to herself. It's like a very bad thriller. Parson—was that his real name?—sneaking around by wrecked mailboxes and infesting other people's funerals and handing out nasty cards. But since the encounter had rather tainted the hoped-for fresh air, Sarah turned on the steps and headed through the church toward the Beaugard Room. And toward Alice. Find out about this Parson person. But first the proper expression of sympathy to Elena Beaugard.

"A wonderful service," said Sarah, who had hardly heard a word of it.

"Thank you, my dear," said Mrs. Beaugard. For a moment she retained Sarah's hand in a now-ungloved hand. The hat and veil, too, were off and she seemed simply a tired, white-haired woman.

"And Masha," said Sarah. "She plays beautifully."

"I should hope so," said Mrs. Beaugard, sounding a little more like herself. "Five years of college and study in England. It cost a small fortune."

And what, said Sarah to herself, after she had left Mrs. Beaugard, does she think the Beaugard Room cost? But I suppose there are priorities. Musical training is hardly in the same category as a room dedicated to the greater glory of God. Or the greater glory of St. Paul's-by-the-Sea.

Sarah found Alice nibbling on a cookie by a casement window. "The Beaugard Room," she said. It was all she needed to say.

"I am absolutely damned," said Alice. "I didn't have a clue. I mean, I heard Dolly and Mother go on about fitting up some old storage space in the church, but you know I don't hang around at St. Paul's the way they did. Except for weddings and affairs like this. I mean, look at the rug. It's not from Great Oaks, so it must have cost a bundle. Talk about benefactors. You'd think

Mother was the Arthur Vining Foundation or the Margaret Milliken Hatch thing on Public Television."

"It's all pretty impressive," Sarah admitted.

"It's pretty scary," said Alice with vehemence. "I wonder if there's any cash left to pay the oil bills this winter."

"Did Dolly have an allowance?" asked Sarah. It was a touchy sort of question since if Dolly was being subsidized, so probably was Alice. And Dolly at least worked for it, what with all the household management and driving her mother to and fro. Alice had been, Sarah was sure, a continuing drain on the family coffers. Masha was no doubt part self-sustaining, and Eliot completely, but how about Lenox Cobb? Was he part of the Beaugard support system?

"We all have allowances from the trust fund Father set up for each of us. Not huge but good enough for food on the table and clothes on our backs. Good enough except for me because I've been kind of a major expense." Alice gave a hollow laugh and pushed her hair off her forehead. Her face was pinched and wan, she licked her lips continually, and her gray skirt and black coat, rumpled from sitting at two funerals, hung unevenly from her thin shoulders.

"Would Dolly's trust allowance have funded the Beaugard Room?" Sarah persisted.

"Are you kidding? No way. Oh, maybe a chair or so. The table. A set of dishes or a coffeemaker. No, this must have come straight from Mother. With Dolly's encouragement. Dolly going on about lay not unto yourself treasures and that sort of stuff."

Sarah nodded and changed the subject, determined not to let Alice disappear until she'd cleared up one more thing. "Parson Gattling. What do you know about him? And is that his real name? Is he some kind of minister or something?"

Alice shrugged. "He's Parson, all right. It's his name. Maybe he thought he had to live up to it. He's a sort of preacher at one of those little churches no one has ever heard of. Like Blood of the Lamb Tabernacle or Evangelical Wonder Church. He's not a bad guy, but he's cracked about religion, and right now he's all riled up about Junior and Marsden. I think it's because of Dolly dying at the same time. He apparently admired Dolly. It's all totally boring. That's what Webb thinks, too. That Parson's not a bad guy, but he's got a few loose screws in his head. I went to the Gattling funeral; did you know that? Parson did a sort of eulogy. You'd have thought they were burying the Archangel Gabriel and his twin brother. And now I'd better see about getting Jonathan and Uncle Lenox home. Or getting them a ride because I should stay here and hold the fort. I mean, I *am* stuck here and then I'm supposed to meet Webb. You don't suppose, I mean, would you . . ."

Sarah saw the handwriting on the wall. Oh well, what the hell? It was something useful she could do, and it got her out of the now-congested Beaugard Room, heavy with the mixed scent of the massed floral arrangements and industrial-strength coffee.

It was all arranged in a minute. Professor Cobb was detached from an argument with Father Smythe on Shakespeare's use of biblical images, and Jonathan in his wheelchair was relieved of a coffee cup filled with sherry. Together the three made a slow progress down the stairway ramp—St. Paul's was accessible to the handicapped—and with Alice's rather distracted help, the invalids were fitted into Sarah's Subaru.

"The funeral wasn't so bad," said Jonathan, as Sarah turned the car out of the church parking lot. "I mean, it wasn't the greatest way to spend the afternoon, but I was going stir-crazy inside the house stuck in a wheelchair, and besides, I think Aunt Dolly might have liked it. All those readings and the music and the hymns and stuff. She was sort of traditional."

"The Episcopal Church has abandoned the King James version at its peril," said Lenox. "One more nail in the coffin of the literate world."

"You mean all the thees and thous," said Jonathan. "Like Shakespeare?"

"Jonathan, what are you reading now to your uncle?" said

Sarah, anxious to move away from a lengthy condemnation of all contemporary society.

"We're finishing up Edgar Allan Poe," said Jonathan. "He's pretty neat. I like 'The Fall of the House of Usher' best so far. It's really creepy, that part about Lady Madelaine being buried alive. But next week I can choose the book."

"And what are you going to choose?" asked Sarah.

"Well, Uncle Lenox didn't stick me with Shakespeare right off the bat, so I won't stick him with anything too gruesome. Maybe some sci-fi stuff. But hey, what did you think of the Beaugard Room? It must have cost a million bucks. Or a thousand anyway."

"Far more than a thousand," said Lenox. "I must talk to Elena. I would like to do her books, but my eyes are still a bother. But I think Dolly may have been dipping into capital. I wonder if she had power of attorney."

"No, she didn't," said Jonathan unexpectedly. "I came into the room one day last summer and Aunt Dolly was having an argument with Grandma about it. And Grandma said no. That she wasn't in the grave yet and hadn't lost her mind and it would just cause trouble with her other children."

"Elena never said a truer word," said Lenox sharply. "Power of attorney in Dolly's hands would have ruined the family in the first week. The entire estate would have been given away. Dolly was obsessed with giving."

"Hey," said Jonathan, "you can say that again. And she was really obsessed with sailing."

Which remark caused a blight to fall on the conversation and Sarah drove her passengers home in welcome silence.

15

THE funeral services for Marsden and Junior Gattling and for Dolly Beaugard marked for many the end of the first phase of the three Proffit Point drownings. A conclusion of sorts. A resting.

After all, the bodies of the three victims no longer lay in the limbo of the state pathology laboratory but had disappeared—after appropriate graveside obsequies—from sight. Dolly had indicated in a note found in her desk that after cremation she wanted half of her ashes interred (in their receptacle) in the Sunny View Cemetery. This was done with Vivian Lavender, Masha, and Alice in attendance—Mrs. Beaugard and Lenox abstaining. The remainder of the ashes, Dolly had requested sprinkled over the ocean beyond Little Cove, a task that Dolly's brother took care of on a calm October morning. However, since Eliot did not make the effort to row his rubber Zodiac raft much beyond the tidal zone of his own cove, it seemed likely that every twelve hours at low tide some fragments of Dolly Beaugard might return on the incoming tide to familiar shores.

The Gattling family, on the other hand, opposed cremation

on the basis that resurrection seemed more hopeful for a set of bones than for a pile of ashes. Thus twin graves in the same Sunny View Cemetery received the mortal remains of Marsden and Junior, and in a curious twist of fate, ensured that Dolly and the two Gattling brothers would continue their unlikely association.

The other persons concerned in what were now being considered by the constabulary as three possible homicides hiding under the name of "death by misadventure" settled back into their daily lives and attempted to deal with the changes wrought by these events.

Elena Beaugard, driven by housekeeper Vivian Lavender, made a number of trips to see her lawyer, Mr. Snagsby, about altering her will and adjusting the disposal of her estate without a Dolly to advise or to inherit.

Alice continued to see Webb Gattling for evenings of argument and lovemaking. And to hand over her black shaggy dog, Willie, to his care, fearing that Lenox Cobb's dislike of dogs might bring harm to the animal. Also Alice continued to drop in unexpectedly at Alex and Sarah's kitchen to ask about progress in what she referred to as the "cover-up" of Dolly's death.

Masha Beaugard departed for a concert tour of Vermont, intending to return at intervals and certainly for Thanksgiving.

Lenox Cobb, still afflicted with uncertain balance, occasional confusion, blurred vision, and recurring headaches, continued to try and advise his sister on the management of her estate and to listen without undue adverse comment to wheelchair-bound Jonathan Epstein, who, after finishing with Edgar Allan Poe, read his way through *A Hitchhiker's Guide to the Galaxy* (Jonathan's choice), *Macbeth* (Lenox's choice), and *Dune* (Jonathan's).

Eliot Beaugard returned to his office and the world of marine insurance, and at home to the business of hauling out his boats and float for the winter. To these activities he added a number of filial visits to his mother to request that she put the estate management in his hands. This always refused.

Caroline Beaugard was known to consult a psychic in the town of Tenants Harbor on subjects unknown and to sign up at the local community college for a course in computer competence. From which she was dropped due to lack of attendance.

Deputies Mike Laaka and Katie Waters, already burdened by the Gattling-Beaugard investigations, were forced to look into a series of break-ins among the summer cottages not only at Proffitt Point but in several nearby coves, inlets, and harbors. In the time left over, the two deputies continued to check out purchasing records of Seagram's whiskey and the filling of Valium prescriptions.

George Fitts, while awaiting the lab report on cloth fibers found in the Gattling skiff, busied himself by seeing to the dragging of Proffit Point Harbor and Little Cove with an eye to finding—or not finding—ballast ingots of lead from Dolly Beaugard's little sloop, the *Sweetheart*. At the same time he instigated the undercover pursuit of the Gattling-Beaugard link through Webb Gattling and Alice.

Parson Gattling continued his confused demand that the Beaugards admit their sinful complicity in the death of his younger brothers, Junior and Marsden, and of Dolly Beaugard, for whom he seemed to entertain a strange admiration. These efforts involved handing out his printed cards on street corners as well as standing, a placard held high, as a reproachful presence at the entrance of Great Oaks. Sometimes, particularly in the evening, Parson could be heard by passersby chanting a sort of dirge or, as some claimed, speaking in tongues.

Vivian Lavender continued in faithful service to Great Oaks and its owner, adding to her many duties the answering of sympathy notes from the beneficiaries of Dolly's volunteer efforts.

Alex McKenzie retreated into the practice of medicine, ready to face the approaching flu season and trying to accept the unwelcome news that Elena Beaugard had decided to retain him, not Dr. Foxe, as the family physician. Periodic house calls on the several ailing members of the household, Mrs. Beaugard reminded him, would be appreciated.

Sarah Douglas Deane returned to her classes, to the serving

up of Defoe, Chaucer, and assorted Greek tragedies to her sometimes resistant undergraduate students. And in what remained of her time, to wondering about the cost of the Beaugard Room. And then asking herself whether the Beaugard Room was a lonely phenomenon or were there other rooms? Other bequests or endowments among the institutions Dolly favored with her volunteer activities.

In such a way did the first three weeks of October pass. Two threatened hurricanes went out to sea and so missed the coast of Maine. The deciduous trees came to full glory of red, yellow, gold, and russet, and the humped and rolling blueberry barrens of Hope, Appleton, and Liberty turned crimson and purple. Jugs of cider and bushels of apples and baskets of pumpkins and acorn squash decorated roadsides. The air became keen with the temperature dropping below thirty degrees at night so that sea smoke rose from the still warm ocean coves and ponds.

And then it was over with a driving rain and a wind switch to the northeast, the wind increasing to gale force, the rain becoming opaque. Becoming sleet. Becoming snow.

"Damn," said Sarah, emerging from the warmth of the Bowmouth Library late one Saturday morning and hesitating. Then she retreated from the steps to the doorway and addressed the head librarian, Miss Murdstone, who was struggling into her raincoat. "Snow. I can't believe it. It's only October."

"October twenty-ninth," said Miss Murdstone. "Almost November. But *The Farmer's Almanac* is predicting a mild winter."

"Well, the National Weather Service isn't," said Sarah testily. "And I'm not even finished with summer, let alone fall."

"Weather," said Miss Murdstone, "is a state of mind," and she tied her raincoat belt, lowered her head, and bucked her way into the driving wind.

"The hell it is," said Sarah to no one in particular. She backed up into the library anteroom and considered the options. She had planned to finish wrapping the newly planted fruit trees against the ravages of hungry mice. But not in this storm. So back to work? No, she'd already spent the morning wrestling with conflicts in the midterm exam schedules. To the gym for a workout? No, an intercollegiate basketball game was planned for the day.

And then Dolly Beaugard's name wiggled into her brain. It had, of course, only been temporarily pushed underground. So why not a little expedition to find out what other lucky institutions St. Dolly and her mother had supported? The figure of Dolly in her green volunteer smock rose before her. It seemed to beckon. Sarah returned to the main desk of the library.

"Where," she asked the librarian's aide—an undergraduate who was working on her eye shadow—"could I find a list of bequests? Contributions, that sort of thing, to the Mary Starbox Hospital?"

"Hey," said the aide, "I don't know. Try microfilm. Plug yourself into the scanner. Or go to the hospital library."

But ten minutes in the hospital library brought forth from a publicity pamphlet nothing beyond the fact that the Beaugard family was listed as a "friend" of the building fund. Over $5,000 made you a benefactor, $1,000 a patron, $500 a friend. Alex, Sarah was interested to note, was a "contributor"—in the $100–$200 range.

But she supposed there were other veins to be explored. Other gifts. Weren't people always being urged to contribute to a new X-ray gismo, a new MRI, a neonatal unit? The chapel? With the word "chapel," Sarah found her thumbs pricking. The pious Beaugards, if they gave anything, might be attracted to the hospital chapel. A stained-glass window, a pew perhaps. Sarah left the library and, following hall signs, hurried down the hall in the direction of the emergency room and the pathology lab. And the chapel.

The Beaugard Chapel.

A small polished brass plaque on the door proclaimed it such. And as luck would have it, a man of the cloth—round collar, dark suit—was just leaving.

Sarah buttonholed him. The chapel. How long had it been the Beaugard Chapel?

"Oh," said the man. "About four months. It never had a name before, but then the Beaugards—Miss Dolly and her mother—gave the money for refinishing the pews and the red carpet and those two stained-glass windows. A new font—we do have baptisms here—and an altar cloth. Wonderful additions. The patients, their families, really appreciate our chapel." The man hesitated, apparently thinking that standing here before him was a troubled person.

"You may come in to pray and rest just anytime," he offered. "Or ask for counsel and comfort. Someone of your denomination."

Sarah assured him that she was not in need, would not detain him, just wanted to look around. And the man, looking faintly relieved, departed.

Crimson runner going up the short aisle to the little altar space. Polished oak pews with crimson seat cushions. Kneeling stools also covered. Window on the right: Jesus touching a woman with his hand, she rising from a bed. Window on the left: Jesus and a circle of children, background a flock of lambs.

In Sarah's head, a cash register. The chapel, to be sure, was nothing on the scale of St. Paul's Beaugard Room, but even so, this was a substantial outlay. Add to the Beaugard Room's total and the donation thermometer might be up as high as $120,000.

And what other pricey good works had Dolly and her mother been up to? Sarah reviewed in her head what she knew of Dolly's volunteer record. The Godding Museum of Art, The Farnsworth Museum. Paintings? Special exhibits? How about the Girl Scouts? The Midcoast Audubon Society? Sarah looked at her watch. Ten past twelve. She headed for Alex's hospital office.

A half hour later, Alex returned from rounds and Sarah announced their plans for a wintry Saturday afternoon.

"A wintry afternoon," Alex reminded her, "can happen at home by the fireplace with a good book and beer available."

"It can happen at museums and organizations dedicated to the nurture of youth and the environment," said Sarah.

"Now what?" demanded Alex impatiently.

"One hundred and twenty thousand dollars, give or take a few thousand," said Sarah. And she explained.

"Well," said Alex thoughtfully, "I knew about the Beaugard Chapel; I pass it every day. But I didn't think much about it. Figured Mrs. Beaugard with Dolly pushing her had coughed up some cash. Not remarkable. People with large incomes do it every day. Older people especially. They know they're getting on and think it's time to do some good in the world. Visible good."

"So people can say how wonderful they are—or were?"

"Sure. So what's the excitement?"

"The chapel and the Beaugard Room at the church."

"I still don't get it."

Sarah paused and then shook her head. "It's just that I've had the impression from Alice that money was tight. And Dolly didn't have power of attorney, so even if she wanted to have rooms and plaques all over the state, she couldn't. She had an allowance for household spending plus a modest income from a trust fund. All the children had that, even Eliot, who doesn't need it."

Alex walked over to a coat rack and hung a slicker over his arm, walked over to his office door and held it open.

"Exit please. So your idea of a smashing Saturday afternoon is to prowl around and see how much more cash has been thrown at deserving institutions. Okay, I'll drive around, visit museums and waste time. But consider this. Mrs. Beaugard has no strings on *her* income. Can't you assume that Dolly made the suggestions and Mrs. Beaugard wrote the checks?"

Sarah walked out into the corridor and then turned back to Alex. "I could, but I'm not going to. Mrs. Beaugard's got a reputation as a tightwad. Grandmother Douglas suggested as much. Small donations, not rooms and chapels. Hospital 'friend,' not 'benefactor.' Dolly headed committees, wore smocks, but I've never heard she personally gave out great wads of money."

"How about Eliot? He may be the man behind all this."

"Eliot strikes me as someone only interested in feathering his own beautiful nest."

"Stalemate," said Alex, as they both, shoulders hunched, heads down, dove out into the snow and wind and made for the parking lot.

"Your car or mine?" he shouted.

"Follow me home and then we'll take yours. What we've got to do after hitting the museums and Scouts is to nail George Fitts to his office desk. He's got the Beaugard estate books, but he may not have seen the chapel and the Beaugard Room, and if the estate books don't show the donations and tax deductions, then something's amiss."

"But he won't let us know."

"He'll let Mike know and we'll squeeze it out of Mike."

For once, Sarah's plan moved forward on oiled wheels. The Godding Museum of Art in Rockport sported two large marine oils and a Thomas Eakins labeled as gifts of the Beaugard family. These just acquired and hung within the last six months. The Farnsworth Museum secretary was pleased to acknowledge the acquisition of a Fairfield Porter depiction of a summer sailing scene. Purchased with a donation by the Beaugard family.

The Girl Scouts were less fortunate. Only two camping scholarships for deserving and needy girls. The Midcoast Audubon director, Joe Bartlebury, admitted to the Beaugard funding of a lecture series on native Maine birds. Arranged six months ago.

"Not big bucks," said Sarah as she climbed back into Alex's Jeep after this last visit, "but add it to the chapel and the church room and it's impressive."

"I'm beginning to wonder at the timing," said Alex. "Everything in the last two years."

"Yes, the Beaugard Room was finished last month; the chapel, ditto. I wonder," Sarah went on thoughtfully, "if Dolly had intimations of mortality."

"Or immortality via conspicuous donations. Although," he went on, "Mrs. Beaugard's getting on and she's not well. She'd be the one to be worrying about her life expectancy."

"Let's hit George Fitts. Lay this on him. See if we can make his eyebrows shoot up."

"It would take more that a few hundred thousand dollars to get a rise out of George," said Alex dryly.

This proved the case.

George received Sarah's report in his state police office—a beige space without charm or the distraction of pictures, carpet, or comfortable chairs.

"Interesting," said George, without sounding or looking interested.

"You'll look it all up, won't you?" said Sarah. "I mean, what if there's not a single record of all this giving out?"

"I would be surprised," said George, who was never surprised.

"But if there's nothing," pleaded Sarah, "then wouldn't you think that someone's siphoning off some cash?"

"How?" said George. "As you've said, no one in the family has or had power of attorney."

"Could Dolly have sold off some of her own jewelry?" asked Sarah. "That is, if she had any."

But George shook his head. "We have access to Dolly's safe deposit—because of the possibility of homicide—and no jewelry is missing. She had a diamond bracelet, a sapphire ring, sapphire earrings, and other fairly valuable pieces. It's all being held until the estate is settled. No records of Dolly having sold any."

"You don't suppose Dolly got her mitts on her mother's jewelry?" said Sarah.

"Forget jewelry, Sarah," said George. "We've checked. Four years ago Mrs. Beaugard divided her jewelry among her three daughters and Eliot—for his wife, Caroline. Mrs. Beaugard kept only her wedding and engagement ring and a small diamond-set watch."

"And everyone still has the stuff?" demanded Alex.

George smiled his smile—the slight upward bend of thin lips. "Yes. Except Alice. She sold most of it about three years ago and the rest last year. Rumor has it the money funded a new pickup for Webb Gattling."

"But you will go through the estate account books and see if

Mrs. Beaugard's been shelling out big hunks. To Dolly or directly to the church and the others," said Sarah, returning to the matter of greatest interest.

George inclined his head. "Yes, we will. Thanks for your efforts, both of you. Believe me, the whole investigation is under control. And now, if you'll excuse me . . ."

The telephone rang. George reached for the receiver, listened, nodded, said yes, no, no, right away. And hung up. Then, without changing the expression on his face—a face that Sarah had long ago decided was made of an exceptionally hard rubber like erasers—George said, addressing Alex, "That was Mike Laaka. He's heading down to Proffit Point. Beaugard place. The entrance. A delivery van driver just called in to the sheriff's office. A body's turned up. Or two bodies. No details."

Alex took a deep breath. "You want me to come?"

"You're one of the medical examiners, aren't you?" said George.

"A body? You mean homicide?" ventured Sarah.

"Homicide?" said George, as if the word were new to him. "At the moment it's an unattended death. Or two. Wait and see."

"At Proffit Point? But who?" persisted Sarah.

George rose, flicked an invisible piece of lint from a sleeve, and reached for his black raincoat hanging on the door hook.

"No ID at this point. Not even a decent description. The driver— he was on an outing with his family—is fairly incoherent. One of the bodies, at least, appears to be male. That's as far as the report goes. Except that even when we get there, identification is going to be difficult."

"Oh?" said Alex, eyebrows lifted.

"One body disfigured," said George. "Head battered. Sarah, go with Alex and see if you can keep the Beaugard family away from the scene until I get a trooper up to the house. The Beaugards might listen to you since you're such a friend of the family." And George wrenched open the office door and pointed the way out.

16

JONATHAN Epstein slapped the copy of Frank Herbert's *Dune* closed and groaned.

"I've had it," he announced to his uncle, who sat beside his wheelchair.

"You mean the book?" said Lenox. "I thought it was one of your favorites. Favorite books can be read more than once. You have no patience. None of your generation has any patience."

"Cripes," said Jonathan testily. "It's not the book. I still like *Dune*. It's this house. Being trapped. The whole thing sucks."

"Wonderful expression. So defining."

"Well, it does suck. What I'd really like to do is make a video of *Dune*. Do a screenplay, though I guess I'd have trouble with the technology. But now it's your turn to choose a book, and I suppose I'll have to read *Hamlet*. Or one of the others. Or something gruesome like a poetry collection."

"No," said Lenox. "I thought we'd try Stevenson. *Treasure Island*. I haven't read it since I was twelve years old. Although I realize you cannot believe I was ever twelve."

"Nope, I can't," said Jonathan. Despite his obvious discontent, he almost smiled. "I think you were born Professor Lenox Cobb with a copy of *The Complete Works of William Shakespeare* in your mouth. And I haven't read *Treasure Island* because everyone was always saying I should."

"I think you may take to the book. A few murders, some gunfire, swordplay, a bit of madness, alcoholism, a sailing ship, and a treasure map. With fine illustrations by N. C. Wyeth. I assume there's a copy somewhere around."

"Probably," said Jonathan gloomily. "But I don't want to start reading it right away. I want to blow this place. I've got a walking cast on so I can put my leg down. If I can manage with one crutch to go to the bathroom, I can make it outside."

"You probably could," said Lenox. "But you shouldn't. Besides, it's snowing and blowing a gale. Also it's getting dark."

For a moment Jonathan hesitated and then looked down at his watch. "It's only quarter of five, and the sun doesn't go down until almost five-thirty."

"What sun?" demanded Lenox. "There's a snowstorm going on. The sun isn't out."

"I don't care," said Jonathan defiantly, "if it's pitch-dark. I want to get out of the house, and you can't stop me."

Lenox looked at the boy without expression. "I wouldn't dream of disturbing myself so far. Go on. Get it out of your system, and if you fall down and fracture your other leg or pull your arm out of its socket, I do not wish to be blamed."

Jonathan paused in the act of hoisting himself out of his wheelchair. "Will you do one thing, Uncle Lenox? Just help me downstairs. Help me balance. It's a little tricky. I tried it yesterday. Please, Uncle Lenox. Then I won't bother you. Honestly. And I'll wear a jacket. And don't let Grandma know. You know she'd go crazy. Mother wouldn't, but Grandma would."

"You want me to be an accomplice, is that the idea?"

"You got it," said Jonathan, grinning. He pulled himself up with his one good arm—his right one—reached for the crutch that lay across his bed, pushed it under his armpit, and stood up. Then, awkwardly, his leg in its cast thumping down on the floor, he hopped and wobbled his way to the bedroom door.

Lenox Cobb followed.

Downstairs at the front hall coat closet, unmolested by Grandmother Beaugard or Housekeeper Lavender, or any other member of the family, Jonathan struggled into a windbreaker, pushed one arm into a sleeve, then fastened it around his neck and buttoned it below his sling—this procedure watched but not assisted by his uncle.

Jonathan hopped to the door, wrenched it open, and for a moment paused as the snow, blowing slantwise, stung him in the face. The moment's hesitation allowed Lenox to jam a knitted hat over the boy's head.

"Be off with you," said Lenox. "And if you cripple yourself for life, I don't want to hear about it."

With which Jonathan swung himself out onto the front porch, reached back, and slammed the massive front door shut. Then, clinging to the rail, he hopped down the three front stairs and disappeared into what strongly resembled a minor blizzard.

In the front hall Lenox Cobb moved to a narrow side window and squinted through the snow-streaked windows into the increasing dusk. For a moment he stayed without moving and then, abruptly, he jerked himself around, reached into the coat closet, grabbed the first garment that came to hand—an ancient black chesterfield topcoat belonging to Elena's dead husband, Arthur—nothing was ever thrown away at Great Oaks— whirled about and snatched a cane from a carved mahogany umbrella stand, and reached for the front doorknob. This he turned, tugged open the door, stumped out, slamming the door behind him.

"Goddamn that boy to hell," shouted Professor Cobb into the snow and wind. And, enveloped in the oversize coat, cane first, he stepped off the front steps and into the storm.

It wasn't easy. Jonathan, after the first rush of exhilaration produced by his escape from the house, began to falter. Began to think seriously of turning back. The wind was sharp as a knife; the snow was blowing straight into his face and down his neck.

His crutch and his one good left foot kept slipping in the accumulating little drifts, and he couldn't use two hands for balance. And it was really dark. Almost like night. Besides, hadn't he made his point? Sticking it to them all. Showing Uncle Lenox that he was not just a kid who could be treated like some invalid baby. That he had real guts.

The trouble was, he didn't want to be back in the house. To be almost suffocated in the seventy-four degrees of heat his grandmother dictated for her thermostat setting. Stuffed back there in his wheelchair reading *Treasure Island* to Uncle Lenox. *Treasure Island*, Jonathan was sure, was one of those books adults thought were good for you. Stevenson, yuck. He was the nerd who'd written that *Child's Garden of Verses* which had been dumped on him when he was too old for junk like that. Stuff about "I have a little shadow that goes in and out with me." Total yuck.

And then as Jonathan, stooped over on his one crutch, was hesitating, there came one of those sudden switches in weather for which the state of Maine is so justly infamous. This time, however, uncharacteristically, the switch was toward benevolence. The northeast wind abated, stalled, considered, and then grooved over to the southwest. The snow ceased driving, regrouped, and began to float straight down. Even the dark gray gloom of late afternoon seemed to lighten and the black lines of the oak tree trunks and feathered branches of evergreens became visible.

Jonathan, caught in the middle of turning about, blinked. Stopped, and then, bracing his shoulders, stumped forward down the sloping driveway. Carefully. Mindful of each step, each putting down of the crutch into the white-covered ground.

Where was he going? Nowhere in particular. Just out, out, out. He began to hum to himself, counting his steps, one-two, one-two. Foot-crutch-foot, foot-crutch-foot.

Moving steadily if awkwardly, Jonathan made good progress. The spruce trees along the verge of the drive with their widespread branches acted as a canopy, and the snow was not so heavy on the ground. He kept moving, almost rhythmically now, warmed by his exertions, until he reached the exact halfway point between the house and the big stone entrance pillars. He knew it was the halfway point because the narrow road off to the left led around to his mother's cottage, branching off on a narrow path that descended to the beach below Little Cove. Jonathan knew the beach well. It had a nice stretch of sand and had long been the focal point of children's summer swimming lessons, rowboat and canoe excursions, and family picnics.

So how about the beach? He paused, considered, and rejected. Early bravado had faded; his shoulder was beginning to ache with the strain of the walk; the end of his broken leg, even with a protective sock over the cast, was soaking wet. No, he'd just go on to the entrance gates. The whole driveway from house to the main road was slightly over half a mile long. Both ways added to a mile. Far enough.

Almost a quarter of a mile to the rear, moving at the pace of an uncertain but angry snail, came Professor Lenox Cobb. Although, unlike Jonathan, his limbs were sound and his arm was not strapped to his chest, he was having a great deal of trouble getting over the ground. He was still suffering vertigo from his concussion, and his vision, always imperfect, was now partially obscured by snow falling onto his glasses. Furthermore, the black chesterfield coat, snatched so hurriedly, was several sizes too large and flapped and blew about his knees and tangled around his legs so that he resembled nothing so much as an ambulatory tent.

When the kindly change of wind came, Lenox, as had Jonathan, came to a halt. He, too, had been thinking of turning back. Let the boy fall down and freeze to death. Ungrateful brat. Loudmouthed unmannerly snip. The sort of personality he had most dreaded turning up in his undergraduate classes. To hell with him. But then the snow began its slower filtering, the trees on either hand became visible, and the professor, with the deep sigh of a martyred man, stuck his cane into the ground and pushed forward.

The last hundred yards of the Great Oaks drive slopes more sharply toward the level of the Proffit Point Road. Standing just before the descent, a viewer has a clear picture not only of the foot of the drive and the top of the stone entrance pillars but of the mailbox, which stands lone sentinel beside the left-hand or beach-side pillar.

But not this afternoon. Even in the increasing dark, Jonathan could see a muffled figure standing in front of the mailbox. Leaning back against it, in fact. A figure holding up a placard like some sort of prophet. Or from one of those sci-fi books that blast people—prophets and monks and witches in medieval dress—into future centuries. Jonathan shivered, with excitement rather than cold because he was now almost too warm, sweating from his efforts. He took off the knitted hat and with his one hand stuffed it in his windbreaker pocket. And then shuffled a little closer, a few yards down the drive. Yes, even with the snow falling, there he was. Parson Gattling.

He was sure it was Parson. I mean, he told himself, who else? Everyone had been talking about Parson since Aunt Dolly's funeral. Parson standing on the steps of St. Paul's handing out printed cards, Parson railing against the sin of the Beaugards and the drowning of his brothers Junior and Marsden as well as Aunt Dolly. Parson hanging around the Great Oaks entrance.

This was better than any sci-fi movie. And now Jonathan could hear him. A sort of chanting, a monotonous rise and fall of a rusty voice. Jonathan couldn't exactly make out what he was saying, just isolated words. Something about God and miserable sinners.

Jonathan had no intention of confronting Parson. Not face-to-face. But he wanted to watch him, listen to him for a little while. Maybe if he was lucky, he'd catch Uncle Eliot or Aunt Caroline coming over to visit and seeing Parson. Talking to him, getting mad at him. Trying to send him away. Uncle Eliot and his grandmother had said that it was time to call the sheriff.

Charge Parson with vagrancy or harassment. His own mother had said no, he was harmless, just mixed up. Maybe his mother would come home now and talk to Parson. Or Dr. McKenzie would drive up and stop, because he knew his grandmother wanted to have the doctor make house calls. Or even Aunt Masha might come home from her concert, though she wasn't as likely to make as interesting a scene as Uncle Eliot.

Jonathan really wanted a scene. He'd been bottled up in that house for too long reading about scenes. But here was the real thing. Almost like a video. Or a good action-suspense movie. Jonathan had long since decided his future lay with the movies. To be a director, like Steven Spielberg, that was the ultimate. Now he worked his way to the edge of the drive, then stepped off into the brush, stepped behind an oak tree, and began inching his way—foot-crutch-foot—down the slope. Quiet now, he mustn't alert the enemy. Was Parson the enemy? Or just some sort of alien presence. Jonathan, fresh from the world of *Dune*, was up for an alien. It would be fun to pretend that he, Jonathan, alone of all earthlings, had spotted an intrusion from another galaxy. Perhaps an escapee from the starship *Enterprise*—Jonathan was a faithful "Star Trek" fan.

Now closer, Jonathan could see that Parson—or Parson's clone, the alien—had subsided on a large rock and that his placard on its stick rested like a musket over his shoulder. Well, Jonathan didn't blame him; he must be plenty wet and cold. Unless, of course, he came from a planet that specialized in inner-body heating mechanisms the way the *Dune* people worked their moisture conservation. Jonathan took two steps down and stopped. And shivered.

Actually this was stupid. It was getting pretty dark and now he'd have to go uphill to get back. His shoulder was really hurting and the toes on his broken leg felt like they had turned into little ice cubes. Oh shit. Anyway, Parson wasn't that interesting. In fact, he was totally boring. And forget the crap about aliens. That was for little kids. So Parson was hanging around the Great Oaks mailbox. Big deal. Jonathan planted his crutch in the ground and turned to go. And froze in place.

Something dark, something black, was moving just below him. Like a bent-over man. Or woman. Or something. It was moving and twisting through the bushes and trees, stopping almost every step and twisting around looking. But there was no face. Just a sort of oval shape like a big black olive stuck on top of shoulders. Black arms and legs. Sliding, slipping a little, but hardly making a sound. It was heading for the road. Little by little. And carrying something. Something sort of round and light-colored.

Jonathan planted his crutch deeper into the not-yet-frozen ground. And stood there frowning into the soft falling snow, seeing the black shape getting closer and closer to the road. Closer and closer to the hunched figure of Parson Gattling, who sat on his rock, his placard slung over his shoulder.

Suddenly Jonathan knew what he was seeing. Without knowing it, he let out a strangled yip, lost his balance, and tumbled forward into a tangle of snow-covered leaves and brush. And then lifting his head off the ground, he saw, as if he were watching some sort of old black-and-white horror film, the figure in the black hood raise the light-colored object and bring it down like a hammer, like a splitting maul, on Parson's head.

Heard the dull thud, a sort of gasping breath—perhaps it was his own gasp, perhaps the black figure was gasping—saw the black arms raised again, the object descend, heard a second, softer thud. Saw Parson sway to the left, slip off the rock, and crumple on the ground like a bundle of dirty laundry.

Saw the black figure stand up, turn, and stare directly at him. At the very place of leaves and bush where Jonathan lay prone, legs splayed, crutch fallen under his chin. And then, running lightly, the black thing started toward him up the gravel drive.

And like a well-timed bit of choreography, down the drive stumbled Professor Lenox Cobb, cane raised on high, yelling like someone leading a cavalry charge straight into the firing line of the enemy.

17

MIKE Laaka for once in his life wished that George Fitts were there keeping things from going totally haywire. Cool-hand George managing everything. Jeezus, it was like he had to hold down an octopus. Put cuffs on it. Here he was stuck with securing the scene of the crime, nursemaiding all the passengers of the delivery van—FRIENDLY FLORISTS—FLOWERS FOR ALL OCCASIONS. I mean, said Mike to himself, you don't usually have a whole frigging family finding bodies.

As he told Alex later, "Take Jake Marooni, the driver. If he hadn't stopped on the other side of the Great Oaks entrance just because his kid Ben had to pee, then he'd have driven on by and someone else without the whole family in tow could have found that goddamn awful bloody mess by the Beaugard mailbox. I mean, there was a snowstorm going on, but this kid can't wait. And the kid has a modesty fit because his mother and sister are in the van, so he goes way up into the woods to unzip, and then Jake gets impatient and gets out of the car and all hell breaks loose. Jake finds the body, its head mashed like a Halloween pumpkin, the whole mess being lit up by that highway lamp that's right by the entrance. Well, then Ben Marooni comes out of the woods yelling he's seen a covered-up body and a live man's head next to the body and runs crashing down through the woods and back to the entrance gates, and he sees this other body by the mailbox and sees his Dad vomiting. So the kid keeps up yelling and, natch, out of the van comes Mom and little sister Rachel and they see the body and everyone starts carrying on. Like there was a major massacre, which it sure looked like. So I've got to call in for help and guard the body by the mailbox and at the same time see what in hell the kid is yelling about. Has he really found a body and a head, or was he just spooked being in the woods when it's dark? I mean, talk about triple trouble."

Mike, as he went on to explain, decided that it was best to pursue the living the live head—rather than stand guard over body number one, about which nothing immediately useful could be done. Shouting at the Marooni family to stay put, to stay away from the corpse, to touch nothing and to keep an eye out for the police—they were coming Mike took off. But in the excitement he hadn't taken his flashlight, and although he heard someone calling, he couldn't find the source of the voice. Particularly as the voice was indistinct, and this was probably because the Marooni family were still crying and shouting up a storm down there at the end of the drive. Mike swore and damned the lot of them.

Stumbling in the dark, cursing himself and the world in general, he turned back, sped slipping and sliding in the snow back down to his car, grabbed his flashlight, yelled at the Maroonis to for God's sake just shut up, and dashed back. Up the drive, into the bushes, half-blinded by the snow that cascaded down from the low spruce tree branches.

And then he found them. Two more bodies, it looked like. Or a burial mound. Two human shapes under . . . under what? A black tarp? A blanket? Mike swung the flashlight around and discovered two black shoes attached to two legs, one foot in a sneaker, and the other foot covered in a sodden-looking cast. And one head. Rearing itself out from under the black blanket.

Professor Lenox Cobb.

"What took you so long?" demanded Lenox in a hoarse voice, echoing the very words he'd used before when he had been discovered by Sarah behind the bed in Alice's cottage.

"This boy," said Lenox, indicating the lump beside him, "has had a severe shock, and I'm sure he's suffering from exposure."

"I'm okay," came a muffled voice, and the second head rose out of the black cover. "It's just I can't stop my teeth from chattering. It's a sort of biochemical thing."

"Hold your tongue, Jonathan," said Lenox, "and keep your head under. Heat escapes from the top of the head. I gave you a hat and you've lost it. Hypothermia is a serious condition. We are both at risk. I'll thank you to call the rescue squad and the police immediately. It's fortunate that I had the sense to bring a coat at least two sizes too large."

"Stay where you are," commanded Mike.

"We have little choice," said Lenox Cobb's head. "Jonathan has broken his crutch and I am completely enervated. As well as," he added severely, "in danger of pneumonia."

But at that moment came the sound of sirens whooping, cars, trucks squealing to a stop, their roof lights whirling. "Hang in there, Professor," Mike yelled. "Help is on its way."

And it was. Help in the form of sheriff and police, uniformed and plainclothes. Help in the form of the ambulance, the Proffit Point Rescue Squad, the scene-of-the crime crew, and all the minions and apparatchiks of the law. And medical examiner Dr. Alex McKenzie. And Beaugard close family friend—she had given up protesting this title—Sarah Deane.

Jonathan Epstein and Professor Cobb, attended by two members of the rescue squad, left in the ambulance, which also carried Katie Waters with notebook and tape recorder ready for statements.

Sarah was escorted by Sheriff's Deputy Riga on a circuitous route through the snow-filled woods and back to the drive—the drive entrance having been surrounded with yellow scene-of-the-crime tape. "What you've gotta try and do, according to

Mike," said the deputy, "is you gotta keep the Beaugard family in place. Not have them coming down here and causing trouble. We got everything under control, and we'll send someone up to the house just as soon as a few more of our guys show up. Right now everyone's busy at the scene and looking around. So tell the Beaugards that all their family members are okay, that the old man and the kid are just going to have a little checkup in the ER and probably come home good as new. Okay, you got that?"

Sarah, wishing she were anywhere but on a difficult visit to the Beaugard headquarters, said yes, she'd got that.

"If they ask you what's going on, just say there's been an accident. You don't have to go into it. You don't have to say a body's been found or anything like that. Just an accident. And you don't know who it is, probably no one connected with anyone around Proffit Point. A vagrant, maybe someone from out of state."

Sarah stopped and looked directly at Deputy Riga. "I heard Mike say when the ambulance left that it was Parson Gattling. Mike heard the boy—his name is Jonathan Epstein—say he'd seen him standing by the mailbox."

"Hey," said Deputy Riga, "don't go jumping. No ID yet. The guy's head was stove in, so we'll have to wait for prints. Wallet, contents of his pockets. Dental records."

Sarah, who had been trying not to think of Parson—or anyone—with a "head stove in," grimaced. "I'll try and keep the family at home until you send someone up," she said. "But I can't prevent someone like Alice Beaugard—she's Jonathan's mother—from getting involved. Getting in a car and coming on down to the end of the drive."

"We've called the boy's mother at her cottage and she's not home. Not up at the big house either. We're setting up a roadblock on the main Proffit Point Road and one midway down the Great Oaks driveway. We're counting on total family cooperation,"

"Good luck on that," was all Sarah could think of saying, and in silence they crunched their way the distance to the main house.

Sarah was at first received with gratitude. Vivian Lavender opened the door and ushered her into the living room, where Elena Beaugard sat in her commanding wing chair by the fire. Mrs. Beaugard seemed more outraged by her grandson's and brother's absence from the family hearth than by any possible harm they might have suffered.

"Thank heavens, Sarah, you're at least someone we know. I couldn't believe it when another of those dreadful deputies called in to say that Jonathan and my brother were off to the hospital but that they were just fine. Just a little chilled. What on earth did they mean by that? Of course they were chilled. It's been snowing all afternoon. Why were they out by the road? Jonathan's fault, I'm sure. He isn't supposed to leave the house, but then, he is so spoiled and headstrong that he must have taken off and poor Lenox went after him. Lenox is not well enough for that sort of thing. And besides, it's past dinnertime. Vivian has been keeping everything warm."

Sarah, obeying orders, said her piece, adding that the nature of the accident had not been determined, and as far as she knew, it did not involve anyone known by the Beaugards. Which, if the "accident" is Parson Gattling, she said to herself, isn't exactly true. He may not have been "known" by the family, but all the Beaugards were certainly aware of his almost daily appearance with his placard at the foot of the Great Oaks drive.

"An accident?" repeated Elena. "That's what this deputy said. But what kind of an accident? An automobile? A hit-and-run?"

"I don't know," said Sarah truthfully. And again she added to herself, accident, hell. When she had climbed out of the car she had kept her head averted from the bundle by the road, but even if she dodged seeing the bludgeoned skull of the late Parson Gattling, the twisted limbs and blood-soaked clothes had caught the corner of her eye. That was no accident. She swallowed hard and tried to respond to Mrs. Beaugard's invitation to dinner.

"There's plenty of food," said Elena, "because of Jonathan and Lenox not being here, nor Masha. And I never know whether to expect Alice, so we always have too much."

To this less than gracious invitation, Sarah pleaded absence of appetite. The last thing she wanted right now was a plate of food. Parson's death was a much too recent event to allow for anything but nausea.

Fortunately, the quadruple arrivals of Caroline and Eliot and Alice and Masha distracted Elena, so Sarah was spared further urgings.

"What in hell is going on?" demanded Alice. She had stamped into the house, hair plastered against her face, patches of snow clinging to her coat, her heavy boots dark with wet. "I mean," she went on, "there's a bloody great police barricade set up at the gates. Yellow tape and squad cars, the whole nine yards. No one would tell us a thing, and the police made us drive away from the gates and take the harbor road all the way around to Back Cove."

"Yes," said Masha, her pointed nose red with cold. She unwound a long scarf and began stamping her fur-edged boots. "The Back Cove Road," she added, "and it's a mess. We never use it in the winter. We had to ditch our cars by the Back Cove boathouse and walk from there. I've driven from Vermont and they made me leave all my clothes in the car and carry my instrument case."

"Hounded by a deputy sheriff," complained Eliot.

"Did you all come together?" asked Sarah, interested, as the group straggled one by one into the living room. It seemed strange that the entire family through some sort of telepathy had arrived simultaneously at the Great Oaks entrance.

"Hell no," said Alice. "I don't travel in a caravan. But the police had a roadblock. Bunch of other cars stacked up. We had to wait until we were all checked over. Name, address, age, color of eyes, weight, purpose of visit. Whole crock of shit."

"Alice!" said Mrs. Beaugard.

"Okay, Ma, but talk about a waste of time."

"And the taxpayers' money," said Eliot.

Alice turned to her brother. "I know why I'm here. I live on the property. So does Masha when she's free."

"Right now I am," said Masha. "For a few days anyway."

"But why are you here, Eliot?" demanded Alice, asking the very question Sarah wanted answered. "And you, Caroline?" Alice went on. "Is there a party? And I'm not invited? Sarah's here. Why? Not that she needs an invitation, but why would she want to ruin a perfectly good Saturday night eating beans and cold ham?"

Eliot looked slightly offended. "I don't need a reason to turn up at my mother's. But if you must know, I was finishing a shower and drying myself and looked out the window. Saw all those police cars racing down the road, their lights going like blazes. So I got dressed and went out down to the end of our road. Saw the Great Oaks entrance gates looking like a police circus. Came back and dragged Caroline away from the tube."

"I was getting dinner," said Caroline in her dull voice. "I always watch the news then."

"Anyway," said Eliot, "we had a problem even getting out of our driveway. My car—the Explorer—had a flat tire. Happened this noon; I ran over a big nail. That's the problem of a new house. Nails are always coming to the surface. Anyway, it was blocking Caroline's BMW. So we had to do a bit of maneuvering."

"And here you are," said Masha impatiently.

"There's nothing like an accident," said Alice sarcastically, "for bringing families together."

Eliot ignored his sister. "We drove down the road and were caught in the jam with all the cars held up by the roadblock."

"The point is," said Alice, "what the hell happened? Who's hurt? Or dead? Or hit by a car? No one told us anything."

Mrs. Beaugard shook her head. "None of us knows a thing. But at least it's no one in the family. And Jonathan and Lenox will be coming home soon. They're quite all right."

"Christ, what do you mean they're quite all right?" shouted Alice. "Where is Jonathan, anyway?"

This question took some time to answer, and since no one in

the living room knew the exact reason why Professor Cobb and his grandson were visiting the emergency room, a certain amount of arguing and general restlessness resulted until Alice called the hospital and was told that the two patients in question were doing fine and would shortly be coming home. A matter of exposure and repair to the boy's leg cast. Thank you for calling.

"They said Deputy Waters—that's Katie Waters—was with them," announced Alice. "Something's going on and we're being jerked around. At least I am."

"No, you're not," said a smooth voice from the doorway. George Fitts slid on little oiled wheels into the living room. "I knocked, but you were all talking. Mrs. Lavender let me in and said to tell you dinner was getting cold, and would Mr. Eliot carve the ham if he's staying?"

Alice ignored the possibility of dinner. "If we're not being jerked around, why does it feel like we are?"

"The police," said George quietly, "have been extremely busy. The accident is a complicated one. Now, if you'll please go in to dinner, I'll prepare to take statements from all of you. And from Jonathan Epstein and Professor Cobb when they arrive. I'll also tell you as much as I can about what's happened. And Dr. McKenzie is coming in and can answer any appropriate medical questions."

At which point Dr. McKenzie, on cue, came in. Looking, to Sarah's eyes, like an accident himself. His face had been raked, probably by branches, and bore several long scratches. His hair, his clothes, were wet and his boots clotted with mud. He looked down at these apologetically. "I'll take them off," he said.

"You need not bother," said Elena Beaugard. "Everyone else is dirty." It was a true statement. The walk from Back Cove had rendered the Beaugard arrivals unfit for proper living rooms.

"So," said George Fitts, taking charge, "if the members of the family will please go in to their dinner, I will be ready for them when they come out. Dr. McKenzie and I have to go over some ground together. I assume we can use the library again?"

With which, like oversize children, the Beaugard clan trooped out the door, one by one, and headed for the dining room, but the docility lasted only to the hall. Then Sarah heard loud questions, expostulations, and Mrs. Beaugard's thin querulous voice rising above the others. What was that old play, Sarah asked herself, with Tallulah Bankhead? Or Bette Davis? Or both. *The Little Foxes.* That was it. Family members trying to have each other for lunch. Or dinner, as the case may be. Sarah followed the others to the library and confronted George Fitts.

"I am not a nonperson, George. I'm involved. I've been sent up here as a buffer or a placater or something. I've been used. So give: What is going on? That god-awful thing down there on the road which I tried not to see. Was it Parson Gattling?"

George settled himself in a leather lounge chair and opened his ever-ready notebook. "Yes, it was Parson. Massive injuries to the skull. Alex can give you the details later if you want. He said there were depressed fractures to the cranial and occipital areas of the skull."

"I don't want the details," said Sarah. "I can imagine."

"Unconscious immediately," continued George. "Death soon after. Probably not self-inflicted wounds since the damage was to the top and back of the head. From a very quick examination, it looks like the weapon was used more than once. A repeated blow."

"The first one would have done the trick," said Alex. "Another was probably insurance."

"Or temper," said Sarah.

Alex nodded. "Whatever. The weapon? Who knows? I'm not going to second-guess the pathologist, but it looks like our friend the blunt instrument. No sharp indentations, tears, knife-like slashes."

"Poor Parson," said Sarah. "Standing on street corners holding his pathetic sign and chanting about sin and forgiveness and the Beaugards."

"Not just in town, standing at Great Oaks' entrance," Alex reminded her.

"If you were out to get Parson," said George, "a quiet country road in a snowstorm when it's getting dark would be a good choice." He looked up from his notebook. "Parson's death gives us the same problem we had with Marsden and Junior. Is killing Parson part of a 'get the Gattlings' scenario? Or did Parson's public campaign suggesting Beaugard complicity in his brothers' deaths point to some sort of Beaugard-Gattling relationship we don't understand? Also, Parson seemed to admire Dolly. Why? Whether from hearsay or actual knowledge we don't know."

"Well, there's the Alice-and-Webb connection," said Alex.

"I know," said George in an annoyed voice. "I've had them tailed for weeks and nothing has come of it. Even Webb's sighting of Dolly's sailboat isn't that helpful. Why would Webb—Alice's boyfriend—try and kill Dolly? Unless Alice put him up to it. But why would she do that? Is that in character for Alice?"

"You know Alice is a flake," said Sarah. "And she's a little devious. But I don't think she could possibly have pushed Webb into destroying Dolly, no matter how jealous she was of her sister. Alice has been living on the wild side, but it was a sort of self-destructive unfocused wildness. She seems more stable lately—maybe thanks to Webb. And I think she's got a soft heart, plus she really seems to have appreciated Dolly's efforts in taking care of Mrs. Beaugard. All that driving around and taking her to church and bridge and to her reading group."

George nodded. "Well, we'll keep our eyes on Alice and Webb. All we're sure of is that the Gattlings don't accept Alice, and Webb would be an outcast among the Beaugards. The two of them have kept away from both families. Alice keeps her dog, Willie, and her clothes at Webb's cabin. She's living two lives."

"That's nothing new," muttered Sarah. "And as for Parson, I just can't see either Alice or Webb bludgeoning the poor man. Webb's a sort of gentle giant. Paul Bunyan."

"Sarah, don't get stuck in literary types," said Alex. "There are giants and giants. And ogres. But, George, you do have two witnesses to the attack. Professor Cobb and young Jonathan."

"Katie Waters phoned in a report. She rode in the ambulance

with them and tried to get some answers. Stubbed her toes right away on the professor. He clammed up and told Jonathan to keep quiet. But I gather Jonathan did see something of the assault on Parson and that Lenox Cobb came screeching in on the scene just when the perpetrator was heading in the boy's direction. And that scared him off."

"The murderer, him?" demanded Sarah.

"Or her," said George. "Except Katie said that she had the impression Jonathan felt he'd seen something strange. Not just the killing, which must have been frightening in itself. But that the attacker looked weird. Jonathan kept referring to 'it.' "

18

IN spite of the family objections—Mrs. Beaugard demanding, Lenox Cobb forbidding, Alice pleading—George descended on Jonathan within twenty minutes of the boy's return to Great Oaks.

"Strike while the iron is hot," George told Alice. "The boy isn't going to forget what he's seen, but he may start elaborating. Or denying. Substituting. Giving in to his imagination. We need answers and it's lucky Jonathan's a bright kid who doesn't seem like the hysterical type. Then I'll follow up with Professor Cobb."

"Not Lenox," Elena said, sounding her cane on the floor. "He isn't well. He gets muddled and has those awful headaches."

"The report is that Professor Cobb was perfectly rational in the ambulance," said George. He paused and looked at his watch. "It's just nine now. Give me and Mike time with Jonathan and then I'll see your brother. And I expect everyone in the house to stay put. Thank you. And you, Alex . . ." The sergeant looked over to Alex, who stood by the living room entrance hoping to grab Sarah and depart for home. "Alex, stay with Professor Cobb, will you? The library. Out of everyone's way. I don't want him questioned by the family. And, Sarah, you may as well go to the library with Alex. Keep to neutral subjects. Understand?" And George, followed by Mike Laaka, walked into the hall and toward the stairway.

"Thus spake Zarathustra," said Sarah to Alex.

Alex grinned ruefully. "And let no man put asunder. But hell, I thought we'd be able to slide out of here about now."

"No way," said Alice, appearing at their side. "You might as well get used to being Beaugard adjuncts. Miserable with the rest of us. But I hope that Sergeant Fitts doesn't pounce on Jonathan and turn him into a basket case."

"From what I've seen of your son," said Alex, "it'll be the other way round. Kids like Jonathan nowadays cut their teeth on blood and guts. Think of the daily dose on the tube. I'll bet Jonathan doesn't stay tuned to the Disney Channel."

"Jonathan," said Alice defensively, "is quite sensitive. He puts on a good act, but a lot of it is just that. An act."

Curiously enough, Alice Beaugard was on target. About both the sensitivity and the act. And George Fitts was correct in believing that kids allowed their imaginations to take control of facts.

The result was that George had a hard time of it. Jonathan was discovered reclining on his bed, his leg in a fresh fiberglass cast stuck out in front of him, his arm in a clean sling, and a copy of *Doomsday Comics* resting on his stomach. He was wearing cutoff jean shorts and a black T-shirt with the legend in white letters: STOLEN FROM THE MAINE STATE PRISON.

Jonathan's act was a variation of the "what, me worry?" stance; his sensitivity to recent events shown by a repeated licking of his lips and a tremor in his speech. Led through his arrival above the Great Oaks entrance, his distant view of Parson Gattling, hearing Parson chanting his message, the arrival of the attacker, the bludgeoning of Parson, the attacker running toward him, and the appearance of Lenox Cobb, the yield was sparse. George recited and Jonathan said "yes," "no," and "maybe" in appropriate intervals.

Finally George put down his notebook in exasperation and withdrew to the window with Mike Laaka while Jonathan, with an ostentatious yawn, picked up his comic book. "Okay, Mike, you want to try?" asked George. "Because I'm getting nowhere . . ."

"You need to go at it differently," said Mike, realizing that for George to admit failure was a rare event. "The kid is shook but isn't going to admit it. You need an angle."

"And what angle do you suggest?"

"I don't have an angle, but I know someone who would."

"Oh?" said George suspiciously. "Not his mother?"

"Sarah. She's an English teacher. She's up to her hips with kids every day of the week."

George sighed. "I was hoping not to involve Sarah in this one beyond her help as someone who knows the family. Besides, Sarah teaches college students, not eleven-year-old boys."

"The difference isn't always that great," said Mike. "Listen, trust me. And trust Sarah. She does know kids and she has a younger brother who's over twenty and sometimes acts twelve."

George shrugged, nodded, and Mike went to find Sarah, who, along with Alex, was trying to interest Lenox Cobb in a discussion of the finer points of backgammon. A subject selected by Alex as being almost devoid of emotional content.

"The problem," said Mike as the two climbed the stairs, "is that George wants to start at _A_ and end at _Z_. He usually takes a witness over the jumps in order, backs 'em up when it's needed, gives a loose rein for a little, then hauls 'em back on track. But no dice with this kid. He's doing George's thing right back at him."

"I'll try," said Sarah. "I have one idea. Jonathan belongs to the media generation, and Alice told me once that his hero is Steven Spielberg. Let me try that angle. It might work. It means beginning as if nothing was real. It didn't really happen."

"That's not going to make George happy. It did happen."

"You two stay in the background," said Sarah. "Don't butt in, and if I strike out, okay, I strike out."

George and Mike retreated to the far reaches of the room by the window, partially out of sight but within earshot.

"Okay if they hang in?" asked Sarah to Jonathan. "I mean, they *are* working on this business. They have to earn their salary."

"No sweat," said Jonathan, turning a page of his comic book, and Sarah could see a space vehicle exploding in a splash of yellow and red fire spots.

"Why do you think I'm here?" asked Sarah, helping herself to the bedside chair usually occupied by Lenox during the reading sessions.

"Oh, the police guys probably think that I'll go all mushy because you're a female and a friend of my mother's," said Jonathan, turning another page showing a two-headed crocodile in orbit.

"If you were making a movie and had a scene with a witness and a detective, how would you handle the interrogation? If the witness wasn't exactly spelling out what happened?"

Jonathan lowered his comic book. Then raised it up again. "I'd hypnotize the witness," he said. "Make him relive it. Like in *Dead Again.*"

"That was a pretty neat movie," said Sarah. "So let's say you're the director of a movie. Or a TV show. A horror movie. You want a lot of suspense and action. About a kid with a broken leg who is taking a walk in a snowstorm and happens on a murder."

"You don't like the hypnotizing idea?" said Jonathan.

"Yes, it might work. But you've got to have the boy relive the experience. Show him being put under and at the same time move the boy into the scene. How would you handle that?"

Jonathan, still holding the comic book, frowned. "I suppose I'd do a fade-out. Fade out from the hypnosis scene and gradually make the boy look solid in another setting. A spooky one."

"Like a snowstorm? When it's getting dark?"

"I told Sergeant Fitts everything I know."

"Listen, Jonathan, take yourself out of what happened. Just for a little while. Be the man behind the camera. I've heard you're interested in directing movies. Okay, here's your chance. Who would you cast for the boy? Not Jonathan, but who?"

Jonathan frowned. "Not a kid. Maybe someone like Indiana Jones. Harrison Ford."

"Okay," said Sarah. "Set the scene."

"It's not snowing. It's Africa. And there's a gang of murderous extraterrestrial smugglers around. They smuggle skins of endangered species for their own planet. Which doesn't have solar heat. It has a double cold moon." Jonathan put down his comic book and sat up. "It takes place at a hunting lodge."

Oh brother, said Sarah to herself. I hope George and Mike can keep their shirts on through this. Aloud she said, "Okay, set the scene and roll the camera."

"His name isn't Indiana Jones, it's . . . it's Roderick Usher. He's a reincarnation. Of the first Roderick Usher."

"Okay," said Sarah.

"He's had this fever and now he's a lot better. The fever is due to gangrene in his foot and he has to use a crutch. And his shoulder is tied up because he was mauled by a Bengal tiger."

"Got it," said Sarah.

"And he's tired of being stuck in the hunting lodge with this old medicine man named . . . named Edgar Allan Poe. He's another reincarnation. Actually this is the twenty-second century and everyone is a reincarnation. I mean, there's an Abraham Lincoln and a Magic Johnson around. Well, Roderick, he starts down the road in the rain. It's monsoon time. Do they have monsoons in Africa?"

"Go ahead and have one if you want."

"I want this to be accurate."

"Sure they have monsoons," said Sarah recklessly.

"And he goes miles and miles down this dirt road and suddenly he sees down by the mailbox . . . no, not the mailbox, the road sign pointing to the next village. It's raining hard, but he sees this beggar. The kind of beggar that wears an orange sheet and carries a begging bowl. And the beggar—he's a Buddhist—is singing a mantra. And Roderick Usher listens and all of a sudden . . ." Jonathan paused and took a deep breath.

"Bring the camera in," suggested Sarah.

"No, bring the sound up. Sort of bushes being mashed down by the wind and background of Elton John. His early stuff. And then the camera picks up this thing like a man. Or a woman. Wearing black. It comes out on the road and it's carrying a round thing and you can't even see its face because it's an alien and doesn't have a face. And it lifts the thing it's carrying . . ."

And Jonathan subsided. "That's all. The camera scans uphill and picks up the old medicine man, who is totally naked except for lions' teeth around his neck, and he comes screeching down the road, but the alien's gone. He's vaporized. That's the end of the scene. And that's all I'm going to do tonight. I'm hungry. Ask Mother if she can send up some pizza."

"Just one more thing," said Sarah. "The head of the alien. Is it totally absolutely black? No face?"

"Sort of shiny black. Like the rest of him. Because it was raining. He looked like one of those people in books about the Middle Ages. We've been doing the Middle Ages in school. Knights and serfs and varlets and that sort of stuff."

"What sort of Middle Ages person did he look like?" asked Sarah softly.

"Like an executioner," said Jonathan, picking up his comic book. "With the ax. He's called a headsman and he wears this black hood and chops off people's heads when the neck is put on a block of wood. It's called a beheading. So do you think you could ask about the pizza and maybe some ice cream? Chocolate nut or Toffee Crunch if there's any left."

George and Mike escorted Sarah downstairs.

"It's a ski mask," said Mike. "A perfectly dressed murderer."

"A shiny ski mask?" asked Sarah. "Aren't they usually wool? Something knitted."

"Neoprene or some synthetic," suggested George. "I'm not

sure that session was very useful. Aliens and Indiana Jones and Africa."

Sarah turned on him. "George Fitts. You and Mike said you were getting zilch out of Jonathan. Never mind the frills and native village and medicine man stuff. Now you know the man—or woman—was all in black and wore a mask and a hood and carried something round."

"Or something that looked round," said Mike. "George, thank the lady."

"Thank you, Sarah," said George. "I suppose we're a step ahead with that description. But someone all in black isn't much help. Now, please join Alex again in the library and tell Professor Cobb I'll see him in about ten minutes. I want to fill in my notes about Jonathan's scenario."

"I think," said Sarah, "he's got a future in cinema. Watch out, Steven Spielberg."

Arriving in the library, she found that Alex and Lenox Cobb had exhausted the possibilities of backgammon and were arguing about what an eleven-year-old should be reading.

"Shakespeare cannot possibly hurt him," said Lenox. "He's a spoiled boy, but he's not without intelligence. He got through *Macbeth* without trouble. I'm thinking of renting the video. Later on we can try *Julius Caesar*. Then *Hamlet*. After all, he's subjecting me to extraterrestrial mayhem."

"How about the good old classics?" asked Alex. "King Arthur, Jules Verne, or Rider Haggard?"

"*Treasure Island*, I thought. One chapter tonight. It will take his mind off what happened. The business of blind Pew and the Black Spot is quite diverting. There should be a copy around. I can't reach the top shelves here, but I know that Elena had a set of Stevenson somewhere."

"I'll help you look," said Sarah. She looked around the room. One wall was covered in ceiling-to-floor open bookshelves; the other two longer walls, by the glass-fronted cases holding Arthur Beaugard's collection of illustrated books. And there was a library stepladder ready and waiting. At least, looking for

Treasure Island would distract Uncle Lenox. She began the search, starting low and working up to the top. Stevenson was discovered three rows from the top of the open set of shelves. But no *Treasure Island.*

"I don't think it's a complete set," she called down to Lenox Cobb. *"Treasure Island*'s missing, and so is *David Balfour* and *Kidnapped.* I suppose those were the popular ones and they're floating around somewhere."

"Eliot probably took them off to his house," said Lenox crossly. "He thinks since he's the only son, he's entitled."

"I'll keep looking," said Sarah. "Maybe they're misplaced."

"Never mind," said Lenox, "I can borrow one of the illustrated editions. It's not as if we're going to spill soup on them. I'll make Jonathan wash his hands."

At which juncture George Fitts appeared and summoned his other witness to the murder. Or witness to the postmurder attack on Jonathan. "In the breakfast room," announced George. "I've set up a tape recorder. I didn't use one with Jonathan because I was afraid it would disconcert him, but you as a professional will be quite used to it."

A good touch, thought Sarah. Nothing like appealing to Lenox Cobb's overstuffed sense of pride.

"You can help look," Sarah told Alex, who had settled down comfortably with a dog-eared copy of *Huckleberry Finn.*

Alex smiled up at her. "It's all yours. The exercise will do you good. I've been crawling all over the driveway entrance out in the snow. I need rest."

So Sarah continued the search. Up and down. Leather, cloth, old paperbacks, early Everyman editions; even *Kidnapped* came to light next to *The Scarlet Letter.* It was clear, she thought, that no one in the family had paid much attention to order; the books were stuffed in regardless of author or subject—Gibbon next to *Gulliver's Travels*, which leaned cozily against *Pride and Prejudice.*

"I'll try the illustrated editions," said Sarah. "Besides, I'm dying to look at them. Do you think anyone would mind?"

Alex looked up. "No one in the family seems to be exactly book-oriented," he said. "Just don't drop them."

But Sarah had already advanced on the first glass bookcase. Unlocked. So much for security. Or was it that no one cared? Maybe they weren't all that valuable. But they were certainly dreary with their green cloth slipcases and the uniform black and gold titles giving the names of the books and the illustrators. Like those on the open shelves, these, too, were shelved without regard for author, title, or illustrator. Any proper librarian would have a fit. As expected, the majority were children's books. Sarah ran a finger lightly over the titles. *Peter Pan in Kensington Gardens*—Arthur Rackham; *The Arabian Nights*— Maxfield Parrish; *The Dance of Death*—Albrecht Dürer (an adult title departure); *Wind in the Willows*—Rackham again, and also the same title with E. R. Shepard's illustrations. Sarah would have dearly liked to stop and ruffle through a few volumes, but *Treasure Island* came first. She climbed one step higher and there it was. N. C. Wyeth, the illustrator. The last slipcase at the end of the top shelf, right next to *A Child's Garden of Verses*—Jessie Wilcox Smith.

Sarah climbed to the top of the library steps, reached, and pulled the slipcase toward her. It came, light as a feather.

So light, it almost flew out of her hand. Puzzled, she pulled the two parts of the slipcase apart. Empty. No *Treasure Island*. She scowled at the slipcase halves. Well, someone had beat Lenox to it. A family Stevenson fan. Or the volume had been sold. Traded. Auctioned off. Or . . . ?

Sarah reached toward the middle of the top shelf for the Rackham *Peter Pan*. As light as *Treasure Island*. And as empty.

Then from the top shelf she drew out an *Alice in Wonderland*—Teniel; a *Don Quixote*—Vièrge illustrations; and a "Night Before Christmas"—W. W. Denslow. All empty slipcases.

"Alex!"

"What now?"

"They're empty. The slipcases. The whole top row. It's a false front. Just for looks."

Alex rose from his chair, joined her, and reached to the end of the second from top row and pulled out Defoe's *Robinson Crusoe*—Cruikshank, the illustrator. Empty.

"What on earth," said Sarah. "The collection is just a sham."

Alex shook his head. "It wasn't a sham ten years ago when Arthur Beaugard was alive. My mother is crazy about Arthur Rackham illustrations, and she went to an auction in Portland and stubbed her toe on Arthur. It was a limited edition, bound in vellum, signed by Rackham. It went for big bucks, too much for Mother, but Arthur outbid everyone. She told me that he was bidding high all day. Illustrated books, first editions, signed editions, editions with letters bound in." Alex stepped down and then walked to the center of the bookcase and pulled out *The Story of Miss Moppett*. Beatrice Potter. Not empty. The opened case revealed a small gray book with green lettering and a color paste label. And an envelope filled with a typed file card. This Alex extracted, read, and whistled.

"What's the matter?" demanded Sarah, who stood with an empty case of *The Knave of Hearts*—Maxfield Parrish—in her hand.

Alex read aloud. "*The Story of Miss Moppet*. London: Frederick Warne and Company, first edition in book form; 1916. Dust wrapper. With letter from Beatrice Potter to a 'young friend.' Purchased at auction, Kennebunkport, 1982. Thirty-five hundred dollars." Alex looked up. "And I'm in medicine when I could have been collecting children's books."

He reached again toward the middle of the shelf. Again heft and weight. A copy of *The Nutcracker*, by E. T. A. Hoffman, illustrated and signed by Maurice Sendak. Limited edition, 1984. Bought by Arthur Beaugard for a mere $950. Another three books from the center of the bookcase all proved to be filled with the labeled books, with prices going in one case as high as $7,000. But when Alex checked the ends of the top and the bottom shelf, he came up with empties.

"There's a pattern," he said. "The stuff in the middle is good goods. The hard-to-reach books are hollow."

But Sarah was dragging the library steps over to the second

of the glass bookcases. Also unlocked. She opened the door and mounted the steps and reached. Top row, last book on left. *Sleeping Beauty*. Illustrator: Edmund Dulac. Hollow.

She climbed down and withdrew *The Tempest* from the front and center. Arthur Rackham. Filled with a large quarto with a vellum back and gold stamping. White dust wrapper with red lettering; 1926. The file card announced with two exclamation points (was it glee or was it sorrow?) that Arthur Beaugard had bought the Rackham signed book from a Boston bookseller for a mere $2,600.

Sarah put the book down on a small table by the window. "Good grief," she said. "We are in the wrong business. Well, someone's been doing some secret reading. Or borrowing."

"Or dipping into the honey pot," said Alex.

"Or buying large sailboats named *Goshawk*," said Sarah.

"Or helping Webb Gattling purchase motorcycles or buying expensive rosewood recorders. Masha told me good recorders start around three thousand dollars. And she has seven of the things."

Sarah paused, opened *The Tempest*, and contemplated Arthur Rackham's signature. Then she said, "Or just maybe, someone has been furnishing a space called the Beaugard Room."

19

FOR a moment Alex stared at Sarah, and Sarah stared at *The Tempest*. Then, holding the book gingerly, she slid it back in its slipcase and placed it back, front and center on the shelf, and closed the bookcase. And turned to Alex. "Now what?"

"Try and put those books back in order."

"They aren't in order, they're all mixed up. I think I've overdone it looking for *Treasure Island*." Sarah subsided in the leather chair by the fireplace. "What shall we do? Anything? Pretend we weren't snooping?"

"Speak for yourself," said Alex. "I wasn't snooping."

"You're an accessory. But is this anybody's business but Mrs. Beaugard's? For all we know, she may have been selling off books for years. Perfectly legitimately. She's not a collector."

"Or," Alex added, "Arthur Beaugard may have been—what's the museum word?—deacquisitioning. It's not our business, and I doubt if it has anything to do with Dolly being dead or with anyone else being killed. It's one of those messy irrelevant facts."

"Maybe an embarrassing fact. It doesn't look exactly on the

up and up. Leaving the filled books front and center and the empty cases on the top shelves and at the end. Keeping up the appearance that the collection is intact."

"Maybe if Mrs. Beaugard's behind it—or her husband sold them off—they didn't want to leave empty shelves. Okay, okay"—as Sarah began shaking her head—"granted, it looks as if someone has been helping themselves."

"And I'm afraid," said Sarah in a disappointed voice, "it wasn't Saint Dolly. She didn't need to pawn books. She had the access to her mother. If George Fitts comes up blank with the estate accounts, we'll have to think again. But for God's sake, it's not as if Mrs. Beaugard doesn't know about the donations. She's been in the Beaugard rooms taking bows, getting credit for Oriental rugs and stained-glass windows. She must have known generally about the cost, though maybe not down to the last penny."

"So you have another candidate with sticky fingers?"

"I'm afraid so. It's Alice. Eliot doesn't need money, and Masha seems to live fairly modestly even if she owns expensive musical instruments. Recorders aren't in the same class as violins and cellos. But Alice's life has been an absolute shambles. All those drying-out sessions and medical events and starting and stopping careers. Doling out cash to Webb from time to time. Selling her own jewelry. Besides, there's Jonathan."

"But Alan Epstein must be paying child support for Jonathan. Even here at Great Oaks. And before that, Alan had the whole expense of the boy. But granted, Alice seems to be the needy one."

At which interesting point Alice Beaugard poked her head in the door. "I'm coming in. I've had it with Eliot and Caroline. They're arguing with the police about whether they heard anything of the so-called accident out on the road. George Fitts keeps saying 'are you sure,' and Eliot says how much can you hear if you're in the shower, and Caroline says she was watching the tube. The police really want to know if Parson was on the Beaugard payroll, but he wasn't on anyone's payroll. Picked up odd jobs but never worked at a steady one."

Sarah made a sudden decision. "Alice, do you know where there's a copy of *Treasure Island*? Your uncle Lenox wanted to start Jonathan off on it. Their reading program."

Alice yawned and wiped her hand across her mouth. She looked exhausted. "I suppose there's one around. Did Uncle Lenox look?"

"He asked me to. No copy on the regular shelves, and the copy from the special collection is missing. Just the slipcase."

Alice threw herself down on the sofa, pulled off her boots, and lay back on tapestry cushions. "So someone's borrowed it."

"Actually," said Sarah, "someone's borrowed a lot of books. I was looking for *Treasure Island* and found out that some of the slipcases are empty."

Alice shifted into a sitting position and eyed Sarah with a certain amount of pleasure. "That's what I mean. Snooping is in your blood. You can't help it. It's like a cat with mice. You have investigative DNA. That's why I asked you to help with Dolly's death. And see what came of it. We all finally know that Dolly was murdered. But now that poor goof Parson has been killed. And now Sarah the Snoop has found empty slipcases."

"You're not surprised?" asked Alex, speaking from an opposite sofa. With the three of them settled by the fireplace, any visitor would have assumed that here was a late Saturday night gathering of friends, a pleasant scene with the light of the flames flickering on the brass andirons, the marble clock ticking sonorously on the mantel, the snow falling soundlessly against the glass windows.

But now a small amount of color crept into Alice's cheeks. "No, I'm not that surprised. I mean, anybody could help themselves, and they probably have. The cases aren't locked. And I know what some of those buggers are worth."

"Oh?" said Sarah encouragingly.

"Well, Dad always said they were valuable. It was no secret, what with all the time he spent going to auctions. The books are just sitting here asking to be lifted. Oh, okay, if you want to know, I did get into the collection. Sort of. Just before Dad died, he gave Jonathan a Christmas present. You know, the first grandchild, and Dad wanted him to have something special. Jonathan was about three. It was a first edition set of the Winnie-the-Pooh books. All four of them. With dust jackets, which I guess makes them more valuable. Signed by A. A. Milne with an extra sketch by E. H. Shepard in the front of each. It was a neat present, but I was totally out of cash and I told myself, what the hell, Jonathan doesn't care if he reads a first edition. So I bought him a brand-new set and sold off the valuable ones. For a nice hunk of cash, believe me. I spent it fast on back rent and a new therapist."

"And that's all?" asked Sarah. "No other books?"

"Once more. I was desperate again. I'd just been divorced and fired from my job and I couldn't keep asking Mother for handouts. So I palmed *Peter Rabbit* and *Jemima Puddle-Duck*, both first editions. I had them hidden in a wastebasket when Dolly came pouncing in. Caught me holding *Tom Kitten*. Quite a scene, so I put *Tom Kitten* back and she promised not to tell Mother. Dolly, our little family watchdog. Except I did have the two Beatrix Potter books, and you wouldn't believe what I got for them. Enough to buy a very good secondhand car. But that's all there is to it."

"Not quite," said Sarah.

"You mean someone else has been lifting books?"

"A lot of the top slipcases and the end ones are empty."

Alice sank back on her cushions and rolled her eyes. "Well, well. I'm not alone. Wish I'd hit the shelves for more while I was at it. Now I suppose it's too late because you and Alex know and you'll probably leak it all to the police."

Sarah shook her head. "We don't think it's any of our business. It isn't as if it has anything to do with Dolly dying. But if you're interested in insurance or tracing the books, you should probably report it."

Alice was silent for a full minute and then a smile spread over her face. "Or I could just ignore the whole thing and finish the job. Siphon off the rest of them, and who's to know? Mother's never given a damn about the collection, Masha is a music-only type, and Eliot reads sailing magazines and spy stories. And Caroline, the only stuff she reads is off-the-wall psychological books."

"What *is* wrong with Caroline?" said Sarah. "It's as if she had a glass door between herself and the world."

"What's wrong with Caroline," said Alice succinctly, "is Eliot. The marriage from hell. Yeah, I know I'm a great one to talk, but those two are impossible together. Eliot's the outdoor action and social party type; Caroline complains and turns her head away from everything. Life with her eyes closed. The thing they had in common is a big new house, but the novelty's wearing off. Of course, there's Colin. He's nine and he's learned to keep his distance from his parents and make his own space. Jonathan likes him, so he couldn't be all bad."

"So who's lifting illustrated books?" said Alex, returning to topic A.

"Anyone," said Alice. "The butcher, the baker, the candlestick maker. Family members or someone who works on the place. Listen, I don't think I'll tell anyone. Not yet. No point in laying any more stress on Mother by going public. She's called a family powwow for tomorrow. Wants to talk about the estate, about Dolly's own plan, she says. Make sure we're all happy with it and know we'll be taken care of. Cottages, trust funds. So bringing up missing books will snarl everything. Eliot will go on about estate valuations and inventories and all that shit."

"Your family will have to know sometime," said Alex.

"Yeah, sure, but I don't think it's going to cause major trauma. Mother might get a little sentimental because the collection was Dad's pride and joy. Though when he was alive, Mother used to bitch about the time and money he spent on the books. All those auctions. Running off to Portland and Boston and New York. To say nothing of L.A., Dallas, London, Rome, and you name it."

At which Vivian Lavender appeared in the door. "Professor Cobb wants to know if you've come up with *Treasure Island*."

Sarah rose, went to the open bookcase, and brought out a volume. "*Kidnapped*. A good substitute."

Vivian disappeared and Sarah turned to Alice. "Mrs. Lavender. Would she . . . ?"

"Have snitched books? It's an idea. She might have. To feather her nest. Or her future nest, since as you know, Mother plans to leave the house to the Episcopal Church, and Vivian's RC, so she'll probably be given the boot. With a nice pension."

"As a matter of fact," said Sarah, "I've seen her coming out of St. Paul's-by-the-Sea when I've dropped Grandma off. Maybe she's switching gears."

Alice raised her eyebrows. "Smart move, smart move. If she really has. I didn't give Vivian enough credit. It's a good way to ensure future employment. And it's just a step sideways, isn't it? Drop the pope and support married priests. But church or no church, Vivian deserves what she can get. All these years of coping with this house and all of us. If she's lifted a few books, I'm not going to start yelling 'stop thief.' After all, I took some, why not Vivian? Or anyone else. It's a wonder we have any left."

"So how about locking the bookcases?" asked Sarah.

"You mean not give the rest of the world equal opportunity? Okay, not a bad idea. And for now our lips are sealed. Too bad I can't tell Jonathan. He'd love it."

"Nix on Jonathan," said Alex. And then seeing the door open and the bald dome of George Fitts appear around the corner, he stood up. "Okay, we're excused, George? Enough is enough."

"Yes," said George. "We've wrapped up interrogations for the night." He turned to face Alice, who was back on her cushions feigning indifference. "I've told your mother we're leaving a team down at the site by the entrance. And I'm putting two men up at your house at access points. Your mother's not happy about it."

"Mother," said Alice, "is probably having kittens. The idea of men to whom she has not been properly introduced lurking in our bushes will drive her bananas."

"Actually women. I should have said women. Female troopers," said George, who had grave reservations about female troopers.

"Even worse," said Alice. "Mother doesn't approve of female troopers. Mother's barely accepted the vote."

"Good night, Alice," said Sarah, pulling herself to her feet. She walked to the door and opened it. "We'll be in touch."

"You can bet your sweet life we will," said Alice. "You, Sarah, and you, Alex, are under contract."

"What's she talking about?" demanded George suspiciously.

"Not a signed contract," said Alice. "A verbal agreement. But binding. Isn't that what the lawyers say? Or call it a moral obligation to deal with whatever accidents, murders, drownings, general attacks, and pails of shit are thrown our way."

"No, you don't," said George to Sarah.

"Right," said Sarah. "No, we don't."

"Good night," said Alex loudly. He strode to Sarah's side and seized her sleeve. Stopped by George.

"You can take the main drive back out; we've put a tarp over the site. And we're doing the post on Parson Gattling at seven A.M. Path lab in Augusta. You'll have to leave by six to make it."

The snow had stopped, the wind had died, and Proffit Point lay under a soft shroud of white.

"So beautiful," Sarah sighed. "The first snow in a quiet woods. It always makes me think of those stories where a snow wizard steps in front of the sleigh, raises a hand, and the prince or the maiden is transported to some iceberg kingdom."

"Instead," said Alex, whose moments of fancy, always somewhat limited, were now completely short-circuited by an intense desire for home and hearth, "we're transported to the land of yellow scene-of-the crime tape."

"You, Alex," said Sarah with irritation, "could drive anyone to the brink of murder—no, damn it, I didn't mean murder. See what a noxious influence you are. Sometimes I absolutely loathe men of science. Well, this maiden will be transported, but the prince will turn into a block of ice and serve him right. I say the snow is beautiful and I say to hell with the yellow tape."

Alex, now arrived at the entrance, slowed the car to a crawl, and guided by a series of posts and policemen, maneuvered the car out onto the highway and in the direction of home. "Okay, I'm willing to think about the snow," he said. "Now that we're out of Great Oaks. You talk about noxious. That place is super-noxious. And tomorrow, most of the morning anyway, will be blighted by Parson's autopsy."

But Sarah had subsided. "You know," she said, "I think we're both living on at least three levels. At least I am. It's like having a multiple personality disorder. First, there's my everyday life—teaching, feeding the dog, going to see Grandma Douglas, calling my family in Vermont. On another level I'm living in the middle of the Beaugards, tangled into that huge emotional net. We may not have started out as bona fide 'friends of the family,' but we are now. Whether we like it or not. Whether we like *them* or not. After all, some of the Beaugards may have alienated the entire neighborhood, and we're fresh fodder. But I am sorry for them all. Talk about your family stew."

Alex shook his head. "But taken individually, not beyond recall. Mrs. Beaugard marches on, a little damaged but intact. Masha has her musical life, Alice doesn't seem to be drinking, Eliot is obviously in good shape, Caroline doubtful, but Professor Lenox is perking up. Seems sharper, less fuddled. And the Jonathan reading scheme seems to be working out. Good for both of them. Couple of ego types having to make do together. So what's the third part of your personality disorder?"

"That," said Sarah, "is a side of me I like to pretend doesn't exist. It's Sarah the Nosy Parker. Sarah the machine, sifting facts, making comparisons. Collecting trivia, asking questions."

"What questions, for instance?"

"Okay, here's a sample. Why did Alice take only a few of those illustrated books? It could have been a steady source of income at a time she badly needed money. Yes, Dolly caught her at it, but why not try again? And then how about Mrs. Beaugard and this estate-planning business tomorrow? What's she up to? Doesn't sound like a blueprint for family harmony. Think of the trouble things like that cause. At least it does in Agatha Christie novels. And what's with Eliot? Is he really concerned only for his mother's welfare? Wanting to be helpful handling her accounts? And my God, Caroline, What's eating her? Is she a space case or sniffing glue? Or had a recent lobotomy? And Vivian Lavender. The faithful housekeeper. Is that an oxymoron?"

Alex, now frowning at an approaching snowplow, simply made an assenting motion with his head and then, after the plow had added a sheet of snow to the windshield, cursed, flicked on his wipers, and said, "Okay, beloved. You may now return to personality one. The feeding of our dog, the preparation for the bed, the thoughts for the morrow. Sunday. You can correct papers and shuffle about in the snow and I'll be in Augusta viewing—as they say—the remains."

"Parson Gattling," mused Sarah. "Such an oddity. What do you think? A latter-day prophet or just a public nuisance?"

"Something the pathologist won't concern himself with. Just the blunt instrument. Its size, shape, material, weight, height. How delivered. With what force. From which angle. From above or below or from the hip. Backhand, forehand, left hand, right. Or by tooth and claw."

Sarah sighed. "The pathologist's life seems so simple. Just the facts. The gruesome facts."

"The whole goddamn business is gruesome," said Alex with a sudden fervor as he swung the Jeep up the drive and jammed on the brakes. "But here's home and dog and a night's sleep."

"To knit up the raveled sleeve of you know what," said Sarah as she reached for the car door.

"Only it didn't," Alex reminded her. "Try another quote."

Sarah gave him a small smile. " 'Oh sleep it is a blessed thing/beloved from pole to pole.' "

"That," said Alex, "only puts me in mind of a dead albatross and a boatload of bodies."

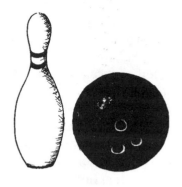

20

THE next morning—it was Sunday—Sarah, although tempted, did not hunt about for a treatise dealing with multiple personality disorders. Instead, she let her thoughts move, albeit uneasily, from the world of academe to the more volatile world of the Beaugards, all the time trying to dampen her over-developed bump of curiosity. This last effort naturally proved impossible. The contradictions and crosscurrents, the three drownings and the murder of Parson Gattling, refused neglect. Thus, when Alex came home for lunch after his session at the autopsy table, Sarah demanded information.

"Not a blunt instrument," said Alex, throwing himself full length on the sofa. He was feeling particularly sorry for himself. He had really wanted nothing more of the afternoon than to consider the questionable prospects of the Boston Celtics—now with Larry Bird forever lost to them—and perhaps to start the new Elmore Leonard paperback he'd picked up the day before. But at one o'clock he had come home to five messages from his answering service on the subject of new admissions.

And he wasn't supposed to be on call. Someone had blundered, the backup system had faltered.

"What do you mean it wasn't a blunt instrument?" Sarah demanded. Sarah, who had labored wrapping fruit trees, correcting papers, taking Patsy for a run in a road now slick with frozen patches of yesterday's snow, was, in Alex's opinion, not able to leave bad enough alone; he regretted bringing up the subject.

He moved a pillow under his head, pushed Patsy's cold wet nose away from his face, sighed, and then repeated himself. "Not a blunt instrument. Well, not really."

"You mean a sharp instrument?"

"No. Just not a blunt one."

"You're not making any sense."

"Neither did the pathologist, Johnny Cuzak. He seemed to think that whatever did the damage was made of a smooth heavy rounded material because there weren't a lot of bone fragments in the skull, the sort you see when something sharp is used. Like an ax or shovel."

Sarah pulled his ankles to one side and settled herself on the end of the sofa, a cup of tea balanced in one hand. "If it's not a blunt weapon or a sharp one, what are they talking about?"

"They're not. Not talking. Johnny doesn't speculate. Two things seem sure. Two blows on the head. Parson was unconscious immediately. Death shortly after the second blow."

"But smooth and rounded?"

"Or curved. Judging by the wound configurations. Beyond that, it's anyone's guess. Okay, shall I pick up some chicken for tonight on my way home from the hospital?"

"If we keep having chicken," complained Sarah, "we'll both start to cackle. But thanks, yes. We can soak it in something Japanese and add mushrooms. And now I'll probably spend from today until Christmas thinking about things round and hard. Like baseballs or field hockey balls or those giant wrecking balls they knock down buildings with. Or bowling balls." Sarah suddenly stopped. "Bowling balls! Well, why not? Perfectly round, very hard—I've dropped them on my foot—and portable. Just tuck it under your arm and when you want to use it, there are those little finger and thumb holes."

"I suppose," said Alex, "it's a perfect weapon."

"And it could be cleaned easily and put back with a bunch of other balls and rolled down an alley into the pins, accumulate a lot of strange fingerprints, and no one the wiser."

Alex looked at her with respect. "You know, Sarah, you have a talent for coming up with oddities. I'll bet George and Johnny haven't even considered bowling balls."

"It's a wild stab. Didn't Jonathan say his executioner figure was clutching something to his stomach? So let's see if we can find out who bowls. Which of the Beaugards. The Gattlings. Vivian Lavender. Whether any bowling alleys are missing balls."

"People have their own bowling balls. They have their names on them, keep them in special bags."

"Whatever," said Sarah impatiently. "But after using the ball as a weapon, it could be put back in the alley, as I said, or it could be deep-sixed anywhere along the coast. But I think the subject is worth a little amateur effort."

Alex picked up *The Boston Globe* Sunday edition from its scattered position on the floor and shook out the sports section. "I'll call George and see if he likes the idea. You, my dearest love, please stay put and wrap fruit trees."

"I've done that. What I need is a little drive into town."

But Alex wasn't listening. He had unfolded the sports section and was deep into the convoluted world of the Celtics.

So Sarah pulled on a jacket, loaded Patsy in the car, and drove directly to The Happy Family Lanes outside of Rockland.

"What d'ya mean you don' wanna bowl?" demanded the stubby hirsute manager whose name just happened to be Eddie Gattling. This unnerving fact caused in Sarah a brief shiver, but swallowing hard, she persisted.

"I'd like to look at the balls, see if I can lift them. In case I want to take it up. My husband loves to bowl," lied Sarah, "and I'd like to join him. If the ball isn't too heavy."

"Hey, no problem," said Eddie. "Lots of ladies bowl like

almost seven days a week. It's a big thing for ladies. They got leagues and auxiliaries and teams. Special shirts embroidered with your name and league colors. Go to Rockland Embroidery. Say Eddie sent you. Manager's my cousin. Ten percent off. Shoes, too. You're gonna need shoes. And listen, we got balls all weights. Kids' balls, too. You name it."

"I have a sore arm, an accident," said Sarah, thinking she might as well go all out in the matter. "I'd need a lightweight ball. Do you know the different weights?"

"Didn't I tell you," said Eddie, "ladies' balls? An easy lift. Or kids' balls. Designer colors. Pink and blue. Sort of marbled like. And finger holes for ladies' fingers. Hey, let's try you out. Come on over here and we'll just see how you do. A pair of shoes, we rent 'em. You can try a few balls. See how it feels. Just don't dump the ball down hard. Let 'er roll. Follow through. Eye on the pins. Watch me once. Footwork is half the game."

Sarah's friendship with Eddie Gattling was cemented twenty minutes later after six gutter balls followed by two strikes and a split. After which Sarah admitted that she expected to bowl not only with her husband but with her close friends Alice Beaugard and Webb Gattling. Well, why not? she told herself. The way things are going, I wouldn't be surprised to find myself bowling or on a high wire or leaving for Fiji with the two of them.

Webb's name produced the desired effect.

"Hey, he's my cousin. On my dad's side. Webb's built like a gorilla. What an arm. Listen, if he wanted, hell, he could clean up bowling. Go on the tour. But that ain't his interest. And that Alice, she's not too bad. Just sorta scatterbrained."

Half an hour later, Sarah, now Eddie Gattling's future protégée—"hey, you got a good eye on you"—left Happy Family Lanes with the promise to come back with her hotshot bowler husband and maybe Alice and Webb, "to try out that pink ball."

From the bowling alley, Sarah, with Patsy slumbering comfortably in the backseat, took herself to the town of Camden and the AbaCaDaBra Bookshop, a well-known institution dealing in secondhand, out-of-print, and, in a locked room, rare books.

Once in, Sarah ferreted out the manager, Mr. Rafferty, a small man with a goatee and gold-rimmed glasses wearing a striped apron. To him she described herself as an ardent fan of illustrated books. A fan who wanted to start a collection. First editions. Signed editions. Extra illustrated editions. For instance, did they have any Oz books?

"I hope," said Mr. Rafferty severely, "you have some idea of what beginning such a collection will cost?"

"Money," said Sarah, now a slave to untruth, "is no problem. I just don't know quite how to begin. Children's books, I suppose, are the best source."

"They are a good source, but not the only one," said the man. "The Oz books—first editions with dust wrapper intact—have gone out of sight."

"How far out of sight?" asked Sarah.

"We're talking three, four, five thousand dollars," said the man. "*Ozma of Oz*, first edition with a dust jacket, just brought well over four thousand dollars at auction. A second printing. And you're interested no doubt in first printings."

Sarah acknowledged that first printings were of the utmost importance to her. And she did want them signed.

An hour later, Mr. Rafferty had turned quite red with excitement. The locked door of the rare-book room was unlocked and Sarah had been given a full view of the shop's high-priced spread. Very high-priced. Sarah was shocked.

Finally, after much backing and filling and expressions of admiration and wonder, Sarah extricated herself on the excuse of a consultation with her husband, who was also very interested. Alex is so useful, she thought, especially when he isn't around.

Feeling fulfilled, she returned home, dragged Patsy on a second walk up Sawmill Road, and presented Alex with a summary of her day's efforts.

Alex eyed her with annoyance. "I've told George about your

bowling ball idea. He said you're to avoid any investigatory visits and not to join a bowling league. Especially don't ask about who bowls where and when. You have his permission to think about other round portable objects. Johnny thinks the thing must have weighed something over ten pounds and been delivered with considerable force from a strong right hand."

"Bowlers," said Sarah, "sometimes have arms like John Henry."

"Or Webb Gattling?" suggested Alex.

"But," said Sarah, changing direction, "you don't have to be a John Henry. Or Webb Gattling. Bowling balls come in all weights. They have lighter women's and kids' models. Pink and blue with a marbled effect. Very fetching."

"George," said Alex, "is now researching alleys and the whole scene. Private bowlers, teams, leagues, collectors of old balls—there are such—but he thanks you for your continued interest."

"My continued interest has also dragged me over to a rare book dealer in Camden. Illustrated editions, eighteenth, nineteenth, and early twentieth in good condition, signed, with dust jackets, are big bucks. Enough of them could furnish a chapel or two."

"Why not come to the obvious conclusion? Mrs. Beaugard dipped into the collection. Along with Alice and maybe the rest of the bunch from time to time. But first and foremost, Mrs. Beaugard."

"Encouraged by Saint Dolly, who handled the marketing end. I'll have to see if Mr. Rafferty remembers her. He's my new friend. I'm the customer to whom price is no consideration and who wants to start a collection of illustrated books. First editions, first printings. Dust wrappers. Signed. The very best."

In the days that followed, winter established itself with two more short snowstorms followed by a freeze, a sleet storm, a lengthy thaw, and then a dip by the thermometer into the single digits. With the increasing rawness of the weather in midcoast Maine, the faces of its inhabitants began to assume that look of grim endurance that characterizes the visages of northern peoples from November through the frozen mud season of March. The fact that the *Farmer's Almanac* had predicted a mild and pleasant winter with southern zephyrs did nothing to soften local tempers.

But Sarah hardly noticed that November had tightened its grip; the weather, compared to what was going on in her life and the lives of her dear friends the Beaugards, was simply a damned nuisance. She brought out her quilted coat, oiled the leather of her winter boots, pulled on her knitted hat, and trudged forth from classroom to classroom, from her Grandmother Douglas's to the living room of the Beaugards, and from time to time dropped into a bowling center to admire the variety of balls on sale or for rent, and to a number of secondhand bookshops to inquire about the availability of first editions of illustrated books. And sometimes, when both their schedules permitted—as on a certain mid-November Wednesday—Sarah made it to the hospital cafeteria to meet Alex for lunch and compare notes on things temporal and spiritual.

"Turkey loaf today," said Alex. "And fun in the afternoon. Office hours and another house call to make on Mrs. B. She's complaining of weak spells, feeling a little dizzy. Thinks Jonathan's shoulder isn't much better. Which, of course, it isn't, what with throwing himself on the ground the way he did. He's stuck in his sling for another few weeks or so. And I'm supposed to check up on Uncle Lenox, who seems to be better and brighter."

"That's supposed to be a good sign."

"Son Eliot—this from Mrs. B.—feels it's a bad one. The light before the dark or some such garbage. I think Eliot is dying to stick Lenox in a nursing home and get him out of the family manse. He seems to think his mother defers to brother Lenox and not to him. Eliot isn't used to being number two. But actually, I need to talk to the professor. He's supposed to be putting together this Christmas Bird Count business, but I doubt if he's up to it. I think the whole thing should be turned over to Eliot, who's done it for years as Lenox Cobb's second-in-command. They usually split the Proffit Point territory. Eliot takes the north and Lenox the south."

"You just said Lenox was much better. Let him get on with it. Why trouble trouble? Getting caught between family cross fire."

"Better doesn't mean perfect. He's wants to go out in the field and do the actual count with a team. This in December, which usually features blasts of wind and snow. He'd be spending six or seven hours slogging about in it."

"He won't take it kindly if you ground him."

"I'm not going to ground him out of hand. Just suggest that he take it easy. Cover only part of the territory. He'll snarl and I'll change the subject. But the idea will be planted. Anyway, I probably won't make it home until after six."

"And guess who's coming for dinner. Actually, they're bringing the dinner."

"Surprise me. No, don't. It's our new buddies, Webb with his bowling arm and Alice, probably with her monogrammed bowling ball. Okay, who needs a quiet evening?"

"Webb might be helpful, because I'd like to know more about Parson," said Sarah. "Whether he was simply a religious nut, or paranoid, or privy to special information. Did he actually know Dolly, and was he the real link between the two families? I don't think Webb is the link. He seems too straightforward."

"Are you saying Webb is uncomplicated? That uncomplicated doesn't mean trouble? You're thinking in stereotypes, which is something I'm sure you tell your students never to do. You have this picture of Webb as John Henry, Paul Bunyan, or the Jolly Green Giant. A muscleman unable to do more than bed Alice and lift weights. But not someone—because he's so uncomplicated—who can bash cousin Parson over the head or tote lead sailboat ballast or spike a bottle of whiskey with Valium. Here's what I think. You've taken to Webb Gattling and have a sneaking old-time fondness for Alice, so you'll be damned if they have anything to do with murder."

"That," said Sarah, "is complete hogwash. I'm being completely objective."

"Right, sure," said Alex. But Sarah had picked up her brief-case and was walking rapidly to the door of the cafeteria.

As predicted, Professor Cobb would not hear of any curtailing of his efforts regarding the forthcoming Christmas count. Alex had finished examining Mrs. Beaugard, expressed sympathy for her spells of feeling "weak and dizzy," and suggested a workup at the hospital clinic sometime in December. Following this, Lenox Cobb was tracked down in the library together with Jonathan. The boy was explaining why *Robinson Crusoe* (Lenox's choice) was a really totally lousy book but might make an okay movie. If Jonathan had the job of cinematography and was in charge of the casting, the lighting, the script, and special effects.

But the subject of the Christmas count, once broached, brought vehement response from the professor. "You're in league with Eliot. You think I'm too old and out of my head because of that concussion. Want to put me in restraints and cart me off to a nursing home. Well, I am damned if you're going to. Eliot can work with the north Proffit Point people and stay out of my hair. You, Alex, can help me with the South team. Elena will watch her birdfeeders and keep track of the different species that come there to feed. Jonathan can help her. His eyesight is excellent and it is not beyond his capability to identify a common bird."

"Jonathan," said Jonathan, "doesn't know a bird from a bird nest. So I won't."

"We shall see about that," said Lenox Cobb, with a look at the boy. "Your school wants you to do a biology project while you're stuck here. A bit of ornithology ought to take care of the matter."

"The only good bird is a dead bird," said Jonathan. "I want to dissect a dead bird. All its organs and digestive canals. That'll make a great project."

Lenox wisely ignored this passage, and Alex made one more try. "Professor Cobb, if the day of the count is clear, the sun out and no wind, well, maybe you could go out for a few hours. But if we have a stinker of a nor-easter, something like that, think about staying home and helping with the feeder count."

"That suggestion," said Lenox, "is totally unacceptable."

And Alex let it rest and took his leave.

The evening found Sarah and Alex and their buddies Alice and Webb making an evening of it at Happy Family Lanes. Sarah had suggested it over dessert, and Alice was enthusiastic.

"You mean," said Sarah, "you bowl? You know how?"

"Of course. My father loved to bowl. We had our own alley at Great Oaks, though now it's used for storage. It's out behind the vegetable garden attached to the potting sheds. Duckpins, we called them. Or candlepins. My father felt it kept us safe at home. But when we kids were older, had wheels, we'd escape and go and do real bowling in Rockland."

"You were serious about bowling!" Sarah exclaimed.

"Hey, Sarah, I'm not serious about anything," said Alice. "But bowling was sort of a cool thing to do. It wasn't fashionable like tennis or sailing, and Mother always thought the commercial alleys attracted scumbags."

"Scumbags like me," put in Webb, who was polishing off his second piece of squash pie.

"Dolly even had her own ball," said Alice. "She kept it in a blue canvas bag with her monogram. A real Dolly touch. The rest of us just used the balls of the alley."

"Her own ball?" said Sarah.

"Yeah. Her very own. Fitted. Dolly had small stubby fingers and said she had to have her own ball."

"Where is her ball now?" asked Sarah, trying to make the question offhand, careless.

"God knows. Maybe Sergeant Fitts impounded it with the rest of her stuff. Maybe he's a bowler. Actually, I heard that Dolly tried to start a hospital league, but it fell through and she gave up the game. Anyway, even if she did have her own ball, she was always better at candlepins because the ball is smaller. Lighter."

Sarah, who was now gathering coffee cups and stacking

them on a tray, paused and absorbed this piece of information.

But Alex, who read Sarah's mind, answered the unasked question. "Smaller, lighter, and no finger holes."

"So," said Sarah slowly, "you wouldn't have much control with a ball like that. It would be slippery, wouldn't it?"

"Honestly, Sarah," said Alice. "You kill me. What are you planning to do with it? Go fishing? Juggle it? You just throw the damn thing down the alley at these thin pins. Candlepin bowling in Maine is big. Where've you been all these years? You're culturally deprived, that's what you are."

"Let's get going," said Alex. "We'll bowl for an hour and that's it. I've got a heavy day tomorrow."

And Sarah, wrestling with the idea of two types of bowling balls, simply nodded, promising herself to check up on the world of candlepin bowling at some future date. In the meantime she had neglected Parson Gattling. It had not seemed proper to introduce the subject during dinner. After all, digestion came first, and Parson's death was a singularly bloody event. But now it was time. Sarah made a point of making Alice sit in the front seat of the Jeep with Alex and she planked herself down in the small space left by Webb's bulk in the rear seat.

"We're still so sorry about Parson," she began. "I never knew him."

"Well, why would you?" said Webb unhelpfully. "Being a Gattling and all that. But listen, no one knew Parson. None of us did. Always was on the weird side. Think it was his name. I mean, if your parents name you Parson, isn't that asking for trouble?"

Alice twisted around from the front seat. "Parson thought he had a sort of mission. To testify. But no one was ever sure what he was testifying about. One minute he was in a lather about the size of lobsters, and the next he was standing on the street corner with signs about gays in the Boy Scouts—or not in the Boy Scouts, I can't remember which, maybe both. And then for a while he went on about God not being dead."

"You got it wrong," said Webb. "God was dead in New York and Boston and California. In Chicago. But he was alive in

Texas, Canada, Maine, and parts of Vermont. Maybe in New Hampshire."

"So," said Sarah, "you'd say he ruffled some feathers."

"Ruffled," roared Webb. "He goddamn plucked feathers out by the root. By the handful. Wasn't a family around that hasn't been riled up by Parson some time or other, felt he was kicking their ass. Of course, Parson didn't kick. He sort of mourned and chanted and hung around looking like some kind of hound dog. The Beaugards were his last project. Parson, he got all steamed up when Marsden and Junior washed in at Little Cove. And then with Dolly Beaugard drowning about the same time, well, he added two and two and came up with . . ."

"Four?" suggested Sarah.

"More like thirteen," said Webb. "None of Parson's ideas added up to much more than making people mad as hornets. I guess it sorta caught up with him, more's the pity. Hey, Alex, watch it, the alley's right there on the left."

And with that summary, Sarah, for the time being, had to be content. Bowling became the feature of the evening, and as time went on, she found her attention more and more centered on bowling balls, the ease with which the fingers slipped into their holes and gripped the ball, the size of Webb Gattling's biceps and forearm, the force with which his ball left his hand and smashed into the pins. And the accuracy and skill with which skinny Alice Beaugard hurled a man's ball down the alley.

21

SARAH, distracted by the picture she had conjured of a black-clad assassin in a ski mask creeping through the woods clutching a bowling ball, had little time to speculate on other aspects of what she thought of as the Beaugard-Gattling stew. Further, the approach of midterm exams at Bowmouth College, the threat of Thanksgiving dinner at Grandmother Douglas's, complete with a number of distant and eccentric relatives, plus the apparent need of Alice and Webb to drop in without notice, all contrived to fill her waking thoughts. In fact, it wasn't until Sarah had picked up her grandmother from her weekly trip to the hairdresser's on the Monday before Thanksgiving that another aspect of the Beaugard saga came to light. An aspect that she, Sarah, had completely forgotten.

Her grandmother, belted and settled in the passenger seat, her fine-spun white hair newly shampooed and fastened into its net, showed signs of not wanting to go immediately home.

"I would love to have a drive," she announced. "That is, if you're not too busy. Somewhere out in the country."

Sarah nodded. Luckily she had nothing going on beyond the usual paper correcting and the ongoing speculation about bowling balls.

But it appeared that there was more than scenery on Mrs. Douglas's mind. The drive was a pretext, and Sarah was amused to find that her stern grandmother was not above a little spate of gossip. The Beaugards. And who else? Sarah said to herself.

"I had tea with Elena Beaugard," began Mrs. Douglas. "Eliot dropped her off on Sunday afternoon for a visit. She is a difficult woman, but I do feel sorry for her. That business of the dreadful Gattling person."

"Which dreadful Gattling person?" asked Sarah. She turned the car in the direction of the Camden Hills. The drive promised to be a lengthy one.

"That man who stood around holding up placards. A name like Preacher or Parson. Elena could talk of nothing else. A murder at her very gates, coming so soon after Dolly's death. Elena is trying to put her life together, which is not easy because Alice is such a worry. She's been seen in the company of some sort of backwoods person. A lumberjack. And then Elena has the boy Jonathan at home all day because of his accident. And Lenox Cobb underfoot."

"But Mrs. Beaugard is coping?" said Sarah.

"She is trying to. She has been seeing her lawyer and is following through on the plans Dolly made with her for the estate. She feels that this will be a memorial to Dolly."

"I'd say the Beaugard Room at St. Paul's-by-the-Sea and the Beaugard Chapel at the hospital and the paintings given to the art galleries add up to quite a clutch of Dolly memorials."

"That remark, Sarah," said her grandmother, "shows a mean spirit. Those are gifts from the whole Beaugard family— although I must say Elena seemed a bit surprised at the extent of the furnishings. The stained-glass windows and the kitchen, the new pews at the hospital. But I suppose Elena's memory isn't quite what it was or Dolly hadn't made the details clear."

"And this estate plan?" prompted Sarah.

"The carrying out of Dolly's plans is to be a memorial to Dolly alone. Sarah, where are you going?"

"I thought I'd drive you up Mount Batty and you can see over Penobscot Bay. The roads are pretty clear and I have four-wheel drive."

This idea deflected the description of Dolly's estate plan, and it wasn't until Mrs. Douglas had viewed from the safety of a heated car the dark waters and darker islands stretching before them, had recited Edna St. Vincent Millay's poem about three tall mountains and a wood, and they had started the drive down the mountain road that Sarah was able to remind her grandmother.

"Quite extensive, the whole plan. Dolly's interests are to be remembered. The barn and cottages and the dock at Little Cove to the Audubon Society for a nature camp. To be shared with the Girl Scouts. And a piece of land and three cottages on Back Cove together with the boathouse for a summer art center."

"And no objections? How about access to the beach? Is the whole shoreline being gobbled up?" demanded Sarah, now seeing the Beaugard heirs barred from the ocean.

"Not gobbled," said Mrs. Douglas. "Given for the public use. In the true spirit of Christian giving. And the family members will retain the use of the Little Cove Beach, which stands below Alice Beaugard's cottage. We had picnics there in the old days when your grandfather and Arthur Beaugard were alive."

Before Mrs. Douglas could lose herself in nostalgia, Sarah brought up the subject of the two docks. "Won't the family need a float and moorings and a place to land a boat?"

"No one in the family has need of anything more than a little skiff than can be pulled up on the beach. No one sailed but Dolly. And besides, I am sure the Audubon people and the Scouts will allow the family to make landings if needed."

"Eliot sails," Sarah reminded her. "That big baby called the *Goshawk.*"

"You have not been paying attention, Sarah. You know that Eliot has docking facilities at his own cove."

"Is Vivian Lavender going to be turned out?"

"A pension and the single gift of a large sum at Mrs. Beaugard's death. But, quite heartening, did you know that Mrs. Lavender has been taking instruction?"

"In what?"

"The Anglican Church. From Father Smythe. After much searching, she has brought herself to see a wider truth, a more liberal and kindly way to God. The Episcopal Church. It is an heroic step. Leaving the Roman Catholics. She will be taken into the congregation the Sunday after Thanksgiving. I have met her several times in the fellowship hour after the service. And I pride myself—in a very small way—that I helped her to the light. She was quite disturbed by the idea of a woman priest—an idea to which I myself have hardly become accustomed—but I told her that God moves in mysterious ways His wonders to perform."

"That did it?" said Sarah, surprised. "Women priests for someone who's been a sturdy RC from the word go seems quite a lump to swallow. I mean, talk about indigestion."

"Sarah, instead of making smart remarks, I suggest you concentrate on your driving. If you would spend a portion of the time you devote to unseemly activities in attending church—any reputable church, by which I do not mean congregations that speak in tongues or claim to be saved—you might comprehend what I am saying. Mrs. Lavender is to be commended and her decision celebrated."

And Sarah, her mind too busy with Dolly's estate plan to be annoyed, turned the car and did as her grandmother requested.

That evening, Thanksgiving reared its festive head. A telephone call from Mrs. Douglas's faithful Hopkins brought the news that Sarah's grandmother had had a slight fainting spell; her physician had ordered rest and quiet and the cancellation of the forthcoming dinner. But, added Hopkins, her grandmother was distressed at the thought of Sarah and Alex without a place to go on Thanksgiving and had called Mrs. Beaugard and it was all arranged. They were expected to join the Beaugards in their celebration.

"Oh shit," said Sarah, hanging up the telephone and turning to Alex. "Thanksgiving. Well, shit."

"If the Pilgrims could only hear you. You'd be in stocks for a year. What's the matter?"

Sarah told him, adding, "We can't even use our family. Your mother and father are going to Montreal, and my parents are off in Chicago with Aunt Julia in tow. And Tony . . ." Here she paused. The idea that her footloose brother would ever be in one place long enough to plan a meal seemed unlikely.

"Forget Tony. You're stuck. Stuck but good."

"*We* are stuck," said Sarah. "Not just me."

"I may be on call on Thanksgiving."

"The hell you are. I've seen your schedule. And don't go offering to take over for some other doctor. Okay, we can stick it out because it might be interesting to see if Mrs. Beaugard's estate plans have rattled any cages, see if it's on the menu."

"The Beaugards certainly won't talk about anything so personal on Thanksgiving. What are we supposed to bring? Cranberry sauce or celery sticks or something major?"

Sarah made a face. "The turkey. We won the jackpot. Twenty-two pounds at least. Don't ever say Mrs. Beaugard is careless about money."

"Nor is she one to talk about it. That estate plan of hers will not be on the table. Believe me."

Driving through a new spate of what weatherpersons call "mixed precipitation," a term that covered a simultaneous fall of ice, sleet, rain, and snow, Sarah and Alex agreed that their Thanksgiving job was to act as go-betweens to the various Beaugards. But, as Sarah pointed out, since sailing, the church, sickness, divorce, death in any form, and the estate itself were forbidden subjects, they had better stick to neutral subjects like the meaning of Thanksgiving. "I'm in my best Calvin Klein copy dress and shoes that pinch like hell, but I suppose it's in a good cause."

"The cause is to prevent a Thanksgiving Day massacre among the Beaugards—a family in your opinion rivaling the Borgias."

Sarah ignored this remark and confined herself to hoping that the turkey was well done. Here she leaned over the car seat and examined a savory-smelling foil-wrapped object that lay cradled in a laundry basket.

The two began their Thanksgiving visit seated well apart from each other in the vast living room of the Great Oaks house with its forest of chairs and odd tables and stray sofas, its large mantelpiece oil portrait of the four Beaugard children in their antique summer clothes brooding over the gathering.

On later consultation, Sarah and Alex could both testify that Great Oaks' estate plan was indeed the feature of the evening. Mrs. Beaugard's—or rather Dolly's—plan was not only on the table, it was served with drinks and hors d'oeuvres, it appeared with the mushroom soup, it strove for attention with the turkey, the creamed onions, the mashed chestnuts, the glazed carrots, it got equal time with the mince and pumpkin pies, the sorbet, the Stilton and water biscuits, and it lingered over the coffee.

In fact, at the very moment of the guests' arrival there had been not a moment's hesitation before the subject was brought out like a newborn baby for all to admire. A plan apparently viewed with gladness—almost jubilation—on all sides. It was, thought Sarah, sipping gingerly at her sherry—not a favorite drink—as if the prayers of the entire family had been answered. At least this was her initial impression when the buzz and hum about the plan began bubbling up in all corners of the room. And not a single Beaugard was showing any reticence in bringing the subject to the surface.

"Well, it's all settled," said Eliot, seating himself by Sarah, a martini in one hand. "An estate plan that does Dolly proud, which is what Mother wanted."

"Including the Episcopal Church, from what my grandmother said," put in Sarah, abandoning any idea of staying away from the subject. "Your mother told her about it."

"That was all arranged last spring, but the church is only a piece of the action. But now the Audubon and the Scouts and the art community will have a slice."

"All Dolly's favorite projects," observed Sarah.

"Mother's, too. Mother and Dolly were pretty close in their interests. And Mother's none too well, you know. Breathing problems, her eyes, her arthritis. Let's face it, she may not have many more years, and now she can relax knowing that Great Oaks won't be turned into a condo development or a fish factory. In January we'll help her move into one of the estate cottages. All on one floor with a nice view and a room for a nurse if she needs one."

"And her brother, Professor Cobb?"

"A winterized cottage nearby. Perfect. Just close enough, but they won't be on top of each other."

"And you're not worried about Back cove and Little Cove taken out of family hands? The docks, the floats. Moorings."

Eliot laughed. "Who needs those things? Dolly was the sailor. Oh, sure, I am, too, but I've got my own setup, and if I want to bring the *QE2* into the harbor, I'm sure the Audubon people will let me tie up. No, I'm glad the whole thing's done with and we can get back to normal life. Alice and Masha will have their space, and Vivian is taken care of."

"Jonathan seems to be an emerging sailor. Dolly's student."

"He can go right on with his sailing career. Go to camp and learn properly. Camp will do that spoiled egomaniac good. And he and Colin—that's my boy—can sail together out of our place. Mother's right when she says we can't hold the estate together for every generation to come. And now, do you really want to drink that stuff? Mother's had that sherry for years. Let me get you something else. What were you drinking at our house? Juice with rum, wasn't it, because I was out of Canadian whiskey?"

"Rum, please, if there is any," said Sarah. "I've given up on whiskey. An allergy, I think."

Settled back with a substantial dose of rum in a tall glass while Eliot bustled off to take care of Father Smythe's refill, Sarah found herself joined by Masha. Masha with gold earrings and in a high-necked claret-colored dress that swept the floor. Probably, Sarah decided, the perfect recorder concert costume.

"Hello, Sarah. I've been meaning to come over and say hello, but Father Smythe trapped me. Wants our group to play next Sunday in church. Not giving us much notice. And he's on his third whiskey." Here Masha took a delicate sip from a wineglass. "Anyway, what do you think of our news? Great Oaks is to be the Dolly Beaugard memorial. I hope those organizations can get along without fighting, but it's no skin off our backs if they don't." She seemed suddenly bored with the subject and rose to her feet. "I'd better see what's going on in the kitchen." Then she bent over and lowered her voice. "I can't say that I'm not disappointed that one hunk of land and one cottage couldn't have gone for music. A summer fellowship program with a resident musician. Oh well, I suppose it's good that the dust has settled and we can stop fussing about the place."

And so it went.

Alex found himself the recipient of the same sentiments expressed to Sarah. Eliot had told him that it was all for the best and that he wished he could have been on the ground floor of the planning, but that was Mother for you. Next, Alice perched briefly on the edge of Alex's chair. Her holiday costume resembled an ensemble associated with early Diane Keaton movies: baggy pin-striped trousers and a wide flowered necktie. She, speaking in a hoarse stage whisper, told Alex she was bloody well tired of the whole business and was glad it was down in black and white. All that needed doing was the final drawing up of the plan. Buildings, boundaries, goods and chattels, all that crap. The whole thing should be wrapped up after New Year's. And she, Alice, was happy that the family could get on with what they did best. Normal everyday bickering and in-your-face activities.

Professor Lenox Cobb, in ancient tweeds, stick tapping, moved Alice from her perch, waved her to another part of the room, and planted himself on a straight chair facing Alex. In general he agreed with Alice, although not in the same words. It was high time that Elena made a decision about the estate. She was not in the best of health. The new estate plan wasn't one that he might have made. He, Lenox, might have considered Bowmouth College as a proper recipient of a piece of the land, but then, Elena had never listened to him. If he hadn't had that accident, had been able to function in the period after Dolly's death, things might have been different. But now that the business was decided, well, he for one accepted it. "Now, Alex, I want to discuss the Christmas count with you as I fully expect to take my place in the field. You must bring your telescope. We are always short of telescopes."

The theme of satisfaction expressed during the drink period persisted through the dinner itself—this served from the sideboard since Tad Bugelski's daughter Sharon, brought in to help in the kitchen, could not be asked to serve, and Vivian Lavender had joined the family in the role of a guest. One by one the celebrants settled about a long table made festive with mounded fruit and yellow chrysanthemums. Then over steaming basins of mushroom soup—"Aunt Ethel's Spode," announced Mrs. Beaugard—Father Smythe kicked off with grace. But even the Thanksgiving grace was not immune to the estate settlement fever. Oblique reference was made to the plan so that the general thanks to the Lord was backlighted by the example of Dolly Beaugard as a Christian woman and the generosity of Mrs. Beaugard in the arrangement of her worldly goods. Amen.

Sarah found herself flanked on one side by Father Smythe's hard-of-hearing wife, and on the other by Jonathan. Facing them was Caroline Beaugard—who just as well might have been mute as well as deaf for all the conversation she generated—and Eliot and Caroline's son, Colin, the nine-year-old cousin of Jonathan.

Jonathan, having expressed his opinion of first the mushroom soup, then the creamed onions, and now the mince pie, put down his fork and, leaning over to Sarah, whispered that he thought the whole estate plan sucked. "It just stinks. Where's the dock going to be? On that rinky-dink beach? You can't haul up a sailboat with a keel on that beach."

"You don't have a sailboat with a keel," Sarah reminded him.

"Someday I will. When I'm older. And I'll need a deep-water place to keep it. With a heavy-duty mooring. There's a good holding bottom in Little Cove. Aunt Dolly told me it was."

Here cousin Colin spoke up. His fair hair was brushed back, and just as for the funeral, he had been dressed with attention to his grandmother's approbation: gray flannels, navy blazer, white shirt. But already one end of his button-down collar had come loose and a dribble of mushroom soup showed on a cuff. Normal kid, Sarah told herself.

"You don't need to get a keel boat," said Colin. "You can buy a big centerboard boat like ours and bring it almost into the beach. Or," he added magnanimously, "you can use our dock."

But Jonathan only nodded at his younger cousin and switched subjects. "I know you're an English teacher," he announced to Sarah. "Well, I've been reading these books to Uncle Lenox because his eyes were blurred because of his concussion and my school says it's an okay project if I do something with one of the books. And I wonder can you borrow some video stuff at Bowmouth. I've asked my father—he's Alan Epstein and he's teaching there—but he says he hasn't access to any. Anyway, I'd need a camcorder, one with a zoom and a macro close-up and maybe some lights."

"I guess," said Sarah slowly, "I could borrow some equipment for you. What book are you going to use?"

"That was tough," admitted Jonathan. "First I wanted to do 'The Masque of the Red Death,' but that needs a big cast. And then Uncle Lenox thought maybe the death scene in *Hamlet* with poison and swords, but we haven't read *Hamlet* yet, so I guess it'll be 'The Fall of the House of Usher' because Gran's house will make a neat setting. I can make it look all falling down and grungy without too much trouble. Will you help? We could put it on at Christmas."

"In the true spirit of Yuletide," murmured Sarah.

Jonathan grinned. "Okay, well, maybe it's not like the *Christmas Carol*, but even that had some gruesome parts in it." Here he leaned across the table. "Colin, you can be in my movie. A video really. 'The Fall of the House of Usher.' It's totally gross. You'll like it."

Colin, who had been mashing pumpkin pie with his fork, looked up and smiled. A beautiful angelic smile. Why, thought

Sarah, startled, that's how Caroline would look if she would ever smile. Or speak. He's exactly like her.

"Could I?" asked Colin. "Is there a part in it for a kid?"

"We're not talking kids," said Jonathan loftily. "We'll take the men's parts. Like I said, there's a lot of really gross stuff. You can be Roderick Usher, which means acting crazy a lot of the time. I'm the person who tells what's happening. He's called the narrator. And we need Lady Madelaine, who gets put in her coffin alive. Maybe my mother will be Madelaine."

"You could research the costumes. Have you got illustrations in your book?" said Sarah. And instantly regretted it. Illustrated books were high on the list of subjects to be avoided.

But it was too late. Jonathan's face lit up. "Hey, sure. Grampa's collection. Our copy of Poe doesn't have any pictures, but I'll bet there's a copy in Grampa's library. Uncle Lenox"—calling across the table—"is there a copy of Edgar Allan Poe in Grampa's collection? Colin and I are going to do a video. For Christmas vacation. In this house. We need to see illustrations to find out about the costumes."

"Just use your imagination about the costumes," said Sarah hastily, but the idea was in motion, and Alice Beaugard now entered into the scheme.

"We always used to have plays over Christmas. There's a whole trunk full of things put away in the attic. Top hats and sword belts, even uniforms."

"I don't want to do plays," said Jonathan. "I want to do a video. Sarah Deane is going to get me a camcorder and some film. We'll film a story by Edgar Allan Poe."

Here Mrs. Beaugard looked up, puzzled. "I don't remember any Christmas stories by Poe."

"Oh, we can put in some Christmas stuff," said Jonathan. "Like we could have a tree set up. And a wreath on the door. And Hanukkah candles because my dad is Jewish. I haven't decided what religion I'm going to be yet. Maybe an atheist."

"As long as you tidy up afterwards," Elena said absently, and returned to her coffee. Dinner was over, the table cleared, and the elders were finishing with coffee and brandy.

"Did Grampa have a copy of Poe in his collection?" persisted Jonathan. "So we can tell about the costumes. And the setting."

"I suppose so," said Mrs. Beaugard. "He had everything under the sun. I never saw the attraction. So many of them children's books. For a grown man . . . Well, it was his hobby and I tried not to interfere, though Lord knows he spent enough money on the books and those matching slipcases. We'll have to arrange for a sale when it's time to clear out this house." Then Mrs. Beaugard turned to Father Smythe. "That reminds me. I wanted you to have a book as a memory of Dolly and me. And Arthur. Something personal. Perhaps there's an illustrated Bible. A children's Bible."

"Mother," said Masha in a tense voice. "If you're giving out mementoes, I'd like to choose a book."

"And," said Eliot, suddenly alert, "I wouldn't mind one of the Wyeth-illustrated ones. *Robin Hood* or *Treasure Island.*"

"*Treasure Island* is gone," announced Jonathan. "Uncle Lenox looked."

"Oh," said Eliot, eyebrows lifted. "Well, I hope nothing else is 'gone.' But *Robin Hood* will do."

Sarah stood up. "I hope you'll forgive us. It's been a wonderful Thanksgiving, but we really have to go. Thank you so much."

And here Alice scooted around the table and grabbed Sarah by the sleeve. "Oh no you don't."

"Oh yes we do," said Sarah, detaching Alice. She smiled at Mrs. Beaugard. "This is a private family thing and I know you'll forgive us. Alex, didn't you have to check in at the hospital?"

"Not that I know of," said Alex at his most aggravating.

"Alex," said Sarah between clenched teeth. "The family will be going into the library. Together with Father Smythe. To look for books. Illustrated books. Just the family."

Alex suddenly jerked his head up and Sarah saw that he had come to. Just in time. They both shook hands all round and made it to the front hall and had the door open when the first cries of outrage from the library fell upon their ears.

22

TIIE drive back to Sawmill Road was made hideous by sleet, slick roads, an overturned semi, and sundry cars spinning their wheels in unexpected swerves and turns.

Usually such weather would have turned Sarah tight-lipped and anxious and kept Alex silent as he peered through the snow-splattered windshield. Instead, oblivious to the weather, like escaping culprits, they found themselves prey to an unseemly amusement.

"My God," Sarah exploded, "do you think they'll start throwing empty slipcases at each other?"

"More likely grabbing the ones that still have books in them."

"And accusing each other. Yelling 'you did it.'"

"And Mrs. B. going on about Dolly's memory and her legacy, and then the awful thought will occur to her that husband Arthur . . ."

"About whom she seems to have had doubts . . ."

"Yes," agreed Alex, "there are undercurrents. Arthur away at auctions spending all that money on children's books, and he a grown man. And there've been rumors that Arthur wasn't always alone on his trips. After a murder, rumors come bubbling up like sewer gas. I heard from Mike—yesterday, in fact—that sometimes the invaluable Vivian Lavender went along to drive him. Particularly in the last few years. Like his wife, Arthur had eye problems. Look out, hang on." Here Alex made a correction in the direction of the Jeep, which had begun to slip sideways on a patch of ice toward a drainage ditch. Returned to the road, he slowed slightly. "Even four-wheel drive can't handle this stuff. Anyway, it seems that sometimes Vivian Lavender played chauffeur for the old boy."

"Vivian Lavender." Sarah ran the name around her lips. "Well, anything's possible. Or what could happen probably has. Elena Beaugard may have been an inspiring sex figure in her day, but somehow I doubt it. After all, she's Lenox Cobb's sister, and I think the Cobb blood runs cold. And Vivian is what they call 'Junoesque.' But we shouldn't leap to conclusions. Let's just say that the late Arthur Beaugard inspired doubt. At least on the subject of book auctions."

"But Arthur Beaugard was buying books, not selling them, right up until the end. By telephone, if he couldn't make it to sales." Then, as the Jeep slithered its way up the Sawmill Road hill, fishtailed up their drive, and came to rest slightly askew by the kitchen door, "We made it. Home, beautiful home."

"Let's call Mike," said Sarah, as they debarked. "See if George has found any big holes in the Great Oaks account books."

"It's Thanksgiving," Alex reminded her.

"Just try," said Sarah. "It can't hurt. But if Arthur Beaugard didn't filch his own books and Alice only took a few, and Eliot and Masha and Lenox and Vivian are clean . . ." She didn't finish the sentence but turned and handed Alex the telephone.

Mike was tracked down at his parents' house in Union, and even thanked Alex for calling. "You got me out of a game of Go Fish with six-year-olds."

Alex completed the call in four quick minutes of question and answer, and faced Sarah. "George has been working on it. He thinks the estate books have been cooked and money washing has been going on. Odd hunks of cash coming in. And going out."

Sarah shook her head. "It looks like everyone's been asleep at the switch. We should have guessed, but we were just befuddled by all the folderol about her."

"Saint Dolly."

"Yep. The hospital chapel, the art donations, the Beaugard Room at the Parish House. And Mrs. Beaugard being a little surprised by the extent of *her* generous gift. *Their* gift. Actually, Dolly's gift."

Alex corrected Sarah. "Not Dolly's, Arthur Beaugard's gift."

"To the greater glory of Dolly."

"What did Robert Frost say about the beauty Abishag and boughten friendship? Well, old Dolly may have done one better. Buying sainthood. The fact that she died about thirty years early only means that her reputation is set. Nothing like an untimely death to cement sainthood. And now the entire Great Oaks estate—give or take a few family cottages and the Little Cove Beach—will be the Dolly Beaugard Memorial, all a tribute to a woman who knew the value of books." Sarah was silent for a moment, and then, reluctant to let the subject rest, "What on earth is Mrs. Beaugard going to do when she realizes what her dear Dolly has done?"

But as the days counted down from Thanksgiving to Christmas, it became obvious to all concerned that Mrs. Beaugard did not realize what dear Dolly had done. Would not realize. Would not listen. Would not consider for a minute.

Alice was the first to give warning of the maternal deaf ear.

On the Friday morning following Thanksgiving, Alice, followed by Jonathan—now back on crutches—and his cousin, Colin, burst into the Sawmill Road kitchen. Alice wheeled on the two boys. "Out. Out. Go outside and wait for your ride. What I'm going to say isn't fit for your ears." She turned to Sarah, who was struggling with the trash. "The two boys are spending the day with Alan, thank God. He's picking them up. Lunch, dinner, movies, the whole bit."

With the retreat of the two cousins, Alice sounded off. "You lowlife slimeballs. You and Alex. You just took off and left us with that whole library scene. We almost had another murder—or four murders—on our hands. First I'm accused because I have the honesty to admit that I took a few books, and then Eliot begins stamping around and pulling books off the shelves, and Masha joins in, and pretty soon we're standing there yelling at each other and Mother is collapsing on the sofa and going on about Dolly's legacy and how the books belong to the estate. Then, if you can believe it, Uncle Lenox gets into the act and starts hee-hawing."

"Hee-hawing?" said Sarah.

"Chuckling. Sniggering. Making obscene noises like he was some sort of visiting hyena. And Mother's going on about feeling faint and she needs her pills and her heart won't take it—which it probably won't. And you two rats have left us holding the bag—or the bookshelves."

Sarah drew a string around the neck of a large green trash bag, strangled it with an angry tug, and then swung around on Alice. "Now hear this. We didn't leave you holding any bag, we left you holding your own blasted empty bookcases. And they're empty because someone in the house besides you had very sticky fingers. Listen, we did you a favor by getting the hell out of the house."

Alice raised her eyebrows. "This is Sarah Deane, my always calm and cool buddy of school days? This whole thing must be getting to you."

Sarah swung the trash bag over her shoulder and hauled it to the back-door steps, returned, and made a face at Alice. "I've never been calm and cool. It was an act. At school I was scared stiff about some of the messes you got us both into, but I was always boiling over inside. Most of the time I'm your basic wimp. But I thought I should let you know that Alex and I aren't just existing to help the Beaugard family get through each day. I have a life. Alex has a life."

"And I should get a life?" Alice grinned and settled herself at the kitchen table. "Well, I'm on the way to having a life. With Webb maybe. We'll see. Anyway, Sarah, you're involved. It was pretty clear from the yells and screams last night that none of the rest of us has been dipping into rare books, and so you know as well as I do whose sticky fingers must have been turning the books into memorial windows and chapel pews."

Sarah sighed. "Yes, Alex and I think so, too. But what about your mother? Isn't she in shock?"

"We told her and she didn't listen. Eliot was standing there ready to administer oxygen. Masha wanted to call Alex to prescribe a sedative. Vivian ran to get Mother's pills. But Mother, after flopping around and hyperventilating, dug in. Dolly, how could we think it? What sort of monsters were we? Wretched jealous children. Not a word would she hear. And so forth. Total denial."

Sarah went to the counter, examined the coffeepot, and decided that there was enough for one cup of coffee for her uninvited guest. "Okay, Alice, one cup and then I've papers to correct."

"Okay, okay, I know you're a working woman and I'm a fly-by-night. Actually today is shrink day. I'm going to talk about what happens when the family saint has befouled the family shrine and the matriarch won't believe it."

Sarah came over and took the other chair. "Shrinks like denial," she said. "Gives them something to sink their teeth into."

"Mother's the one doing the denying, but she would never be caught at a shrink's. Anyway, the point, according to Eliot, is that we should lock up the bookcases, take inventory, and move on. What's done is done, says Eliot. And Masha, too. But boy, are they burned. Me, too. We've wasted all this energy admiring Dolly, the community angel."

"Go back to Lenox sniggering. Why on earth? You don't suppose he was an accessory?"

"No way. He's only just moved to Great Oaks this fall. Before that, he had his own place near the college and rarely came over. But I'd say from the way he's acting that he isn't all that surprised. Says he always knew Dolly was too good to be true, and now she's proved herself a real Beaugard. Heh-heh-heh."

"And Vivian was shocked?"

"Yes, she went all pale and dithery. I sort of got the notion that she thought that we thought she was the guilty party. You know, the lowly housekeeper augmenting her salary. But when it came clear to all of us—except Mother—that Dolly had been busy, well, Vivian was mighty enthusiastic about the idea."

"And Caroline?"

"That was peculiar. She didn't say a word. Well, Caroline never does say much, and lately she's been imitating someone who's taken a vow of silence. But anyway, she kept quiet through the whole library wingding and then she began to cry. Silently. Just tears coming down like rain. And then sort of gulping. To cut the story short, it seems she was having some sort of breakdown right there in the library in front of everyone, and it ended with Eliot driving her to the hospital. She's been admitted. Psychiatric section. That's why I have Colin. For the weekend. Maybe for longer. Which is okay since he and Jonathan are planning some Poe horror production."

Sarah nodded. "Yes, I promised to try and get some video equipment."

"Uncle Lenox is all for it. In fact, the more horrible everything gets around the house, the more Uncle Lenox seems to like it. He just seems to thrive on all the infighting. And since rescuing Jonathan from Parson's murderer, he's been positively genial. At least for him. Still a sourpuss, but not as bad as before. So now I'll leave you to think about Dolly, who may be frying instead of floating about on celestial clouds."

"I have no intention of thinking about Dolly at all," said Sarah firmly. "I don't plan to mix it up with your family until the Christmas Bird Count—if it's still going to be held."

"Of course it's going to be held, although Uncle Lenox may throttle Eliot before it happens. Two chiefs and no Indians."

"Alex and I plan to be the Indians, and you can come with us."

"Sarah, I would no more spend a December day slogging around in the snow counting feathered things than I would swim nude in the harbor. No, I'll skip that one and make Webb take me bowling. I'm getting my own ball because I'm tired of rental ones. No one, not even the police, seem to know where Dolly's ball's gone. It seems to have disappeared completely." And with this interesting statement, Alice took her leave.

Sarah was given five minutes of peace to collect empty cans and bottles and drag them to the barn for recycling classification. There, Alice's place was filled by the arrival of Mike Laaka. He settled himself on an upturned milk crate and pulled out a notebook. "Time for a little cross-checking, and I don't mean hockey. You and Alex have been sitting on some info. Not sharing like George wanted you to. I had to find out the hard way. Eliot Beaugard called last night saying some of his father's rare books are missing."

Sarah paused in the act of reading the bottom of a plastic bottle. "Okay, I knew that. Alex knew that. Alice did, and Dolly knew that Alice had lifted a few. Alex and I decided it wasn't vital information, that it was internal family stuff."

Mike regarded her in astonishment. "George Fitts would have you in cuffs for that statement. Wasn't vital? God-a-mighty, you didn't guess it might be Dolly? Eliot seems pretty sure. No proof, but he says there's a family consensus on the matter. Except for the old lady, who wants Dolly's halo to stay on her head."

Sarah had moved on to the returnable bottles and was counting. "Three dollars and five cents, ten cents, twenty, twenty-five. Okay, that's one bag full." She turned back to Mike. "Actually, Alex and I were very slow on the uptake. Figured it was probably Alice, maybe the others dipping in when they needed cash."

"George has gone wild with the estate books. Well, wild for George, which means that his machinery is whirring faster than usual. Dolly's accounting system reexamined, rare book dealers visited, cash disbursements rechecked, and so far, there's an emerging pattern of cash deposited to a Parish Fund at roughly the same time as an outgo of cash listed for something called the Vicar's Fund. Followed shortly by donations to St. Paul's itself and to the other lucky institutions. None of that seemed significant early on. I mean, Dolly had her hands on all sorts of church funds, altar guilds, the St. Paul's white elephant sale—the Church Breakfast Fund—you name it. Nothing to suggest income from rare books, but that doesn't mean Dolly didn't keep track somehow. She was plenty methodical about everything else."

"So you didn't follow up on any of these church accounts? Go over them with Father Smythe or his secretary?" It was time, she thought, to take the offensive. Take the heat off Alex and herself and show up the police as derelict.

Mike shrugged. "No, that all seemed beyond an investigation into a suspicious drowning."

"Was there anything else in her accounts that struck you—or George—as weird?"

"I suppose," said Mike, "the shrewd amateur is going to nail something that the stupid police missed. Well, you won't. It's boring. Disbursement categories are stuff like household, insurance, employees, withholding taxes, clothing, health, utilities. All the usual, except for donations and charitable gifts, which, as you know, sucked up a lot of cash."

"And income?"

"What you'd expect. Trust funds, dividends, bonds, IRA withdrawals, and interest paid on savings accounts. Normal hefty income sources. Substantial payments from a trust fund, from dividends of stocks, bonds, interest paid on bank accounts. All perfectly normal income sources. Except for this Parish account."

"Does the income from the Parish account match the outgo into any of the other church accounts? The Vicar's Fund, for instance?"

"Nope," said Mike. "No match. The Vicar's Fund got small potatoes. But George is going over the whole thing to see if he can find an in-out match by combining several accounts."

"And what parish?" demanded Sarah.

"St. Paul's, we assume," said Mike. "I mean, that was the family church."

"But why is the parish giving money to the Beaugards?"

"Got me. Maybe a fund Dolly was taking care of. Maybe she acted as a holding tank. After all, she was knee-deep in everything that went on at St. Paul's. George now thinks the church might be into some hanky-panky. A real laundering scheme."

"That's plain crazy," said Sarah. "Churches don't go around doing that. Do they? I mean some of those evangelical TV guys are pretty sharp fund-raisers, but not the boring old Episcopalians."

"George will have St. Paul's down on its knees praying for mercy. If anything fits with Dolly's death or the church has started an off-track betting parlor—which I'd kind of like—George will ferret it out. So okay, we missed the pattern before, but hell, we all had a lot of stuff on our plate. God, three drownings or homicides in one weekend. We all just thought Dolly and Mrs. Beaugard were great benefactors. Mrs. B. didn't throw up her hands in horror when she visited those Beaugard rooms."

"You're right," said Sarah. "That's what fooled everybody. Mrs. Beaugard accepted the thanks and praise and smiled, and everyone thought she was part of the Lady Bountiful team. Well, she was, all right, but she didn't know that her husband's books had funded three quarters of the donations."

"Right," said Mike. "Dolly kept the Great Oaks estate books, so we assumed that Mrs. Beaugard peeked into them to see how her finances were going. Probably signed a bunch of blank checks. Hell, Mrs. B. *trusted* Dolly. She'd probably have noticed if the balance was way out of whack, but it never was. Not for long anyway. Dolly must have sold a load of books—for cash, no paper trail so far—maybe deposited the cash in this Parish Fund, then turned around and made the donation."

"Maybe the Parish Fund was managed by St. Paul's," suggested Sarah. "Maybe they even sold the books for her. Acted as a fence."

"I like it," said Mike. "I like it real well because here's another detail. So far—and of course, it's early—not a single local book dealer remembers anyone vaguely resembling Dolly coming into his shop to wheel and deal with illustrated books. George and his team hit the five or six dealers at home this morning before breakfast and got a solid negative for his trouble."

"So maybe Dolly did it by mail. New York dealers, Boston, Philly. Wherever."

"That involves checks, money orders, credit cards. Documentation, and so far we've got a blank. No, I'm crazy about the idea of St. Paul's as a fence. Beautiful."

"You'd better keep your mouth shut or a thunder bolt will get you. Anyway, how does this whole book-lifting business change things? Assuming for sure it was Dolly. Besides tarnishing Dolly, what does it tell you about her murder? Was Dolly killed by someone in the family because she was marketing rare books from the estate, books that belonged to all of them?"

"It *is* a motive."

"Oh, come on," said Sarah. "Why not just blow the whistle on her? Exposing Dolly—watching her wriggle in public, disowned by church and hospital and art gallery, drummed out of the Girl Scouts—all that would have been a lot more satisfying to some of her siblings than a complicated sailing murder scheme."

Mike rose from his milk carton, the crossed pattern of the plastic dividers imprinted on his pants. "Yeah, I suppose I agree. Why kill Dolly when public humiliation would have been so satisfying? There's enough money to go round the family twice over. Frankly, this book thing is just another crazy knot in the plot. With or without the church. What I want is the knot that connects Parson and his murder and the Gattling brothers to the Beaugards. And I don't buy Webb Gattling as the link."

"Nothing yet?"

"Nothing solid. The lab has mislaid the samples of cloth fibers found in the Gattling skiff. George was hoping for a match with the canvas covers of the lead bars. Boy, that would be a connection we could cheer about."

"I thought," said Sarah, "that some of the Gattling tribe must have worked for the Beaugards some time or other."

"You're right, they did. Gattlings have been part of labor crews brought in to work on the docks, the floats, the moorings, to trim trees, rake driveways. Do maintenance. The whole county, as you know, is riddled with Gattlings, so it isn't surprising we've dug up some who've been on the Beaugard payroll. Some guys—including Gattling relatives—have confessed to beer given out by Vivian from time to time, but no contact with the family. Eliot apparently had a couple of Gattlings as part of a construction crew when he had his dock put in. Dolly had a crew rebuild the Little Cove boathouse, and Parson Gattling was one of them. No, don't get excited. Even if Parson turned up outside Dolly's funeral, I don't think it means a damn. So far as we can tell, none of the Gattlings or any of the other workers seem to have been on friendly terms with the Beaugards. I mean, why would they, the Beaugards being such snobs? Except for Alice. And Alice," went on Mike with a certain edge to his voice, "has the luxury of playing the free spirit, the sot, the sensitive female—even the slightly loony one—because there's that nice squishy Beaugard money cushion behind her. Shrinks, private school for the kid, a cottage, home when she wants to come back to it. Sometimes people like Alice plain make me want to puke."

"Ease up, Mike. Alice is just one of those people who never fitted in at home or anywhere else, and now she's found Webb. Someone stable. Going out with Webb, sleeping with him, going bowling—and hey, I almost forgot, Alice is buying a new bowling ball."

"So?"

"Bowling ball, bowling ball, bowling ball," shouted Sarah in exasperation as Mike turned to leave. "The weapon. Round, smooth, heavy, absolutely lethal. The perfect weapon. Well, Alice says the police haven't got Dolly's ball, and no one in the family has seen it, so she's buying a new one. So where do you suppose Dolly's ball has rolled to? I'll bet right in Proffit Point Harbor. Or out past Little Cove."

Mike's face took on a quizzical look. "Okay, so the bowling ball is a terrific round weapon, but forensics called in yesterday and they've recovered a micro-size chip of paint embedded in Parson's skull."

"Not a bowling ball chip?"

"They're looking into bowling ball composition, but this is a paint chip. Light tan. Hard paint. Or paint that goes on metal. Or marine paint. Lab tests not finished."

"Metal, marine!" Sarah almost shouted it.

"Metal. Sea hammers, pry bars, sledgehammers, wrecking balls. Marine. Seawater. Ocean. Boats, docks, hulls, masts."

"How about a painted bowling ball?"

"Sarah," said Mike, sighing heavily, "you find us a painted or retouched bowling ball or a seagoing bowling ball or a metal bowling ball, or the murderer's glove that just happened to have a fleck of paint on it. We'll all be as grateful as hell. See you."

And Mike turned on his heel and departed.

23

SARAH was left to her own devices, free to attend to her student papers, to the sorting out of the books for the living room bookshelves. To the hanging of pictures, Alex's mother's watercolors, Grandmother Douglas's murky oil of sheep grazing on a blasted moor, her own favorite prints. Free to call a friend for lunch, to look up, see if Anthony Hopkins and Emma Thompson were showing somewhere. Free to go about a normal humdrum life.

Here Sarah paused in the middle of these pleasant plans, then turned and gave the plastic milk case—lately warmed by the rear of Mike Laaka—a vicious kick. So vicious that it spun across the barn and whacked into the barn door. Damnation. She wasn't free.

No way. Her other life was taking over, swarming over what was known at Bowmouth College as "Thanksgiving break." Break, hell! The netherworld of Beaugard-Gattling violence had left her free to only contemplate a murder with something other than a bowling ball. Free to consider a church laundering scheme, to contemplate St. Paul's—or its minions—acting as a fence. Maybe the Vicar's Fund was Father Smythe's own special payoff. So much percent for each bookload sold. Like Mike, Sarah now found herself rather attracted to the idea of Father Smythe as the silver-tongued agent who slid about town with laden book bags. Father Smythe with his benevolent smile and soothing words for the bereaved. With his long white hands and his white hair and smooth-shaven face and his round white collar.

If Dolly hadn't unloaded the books in person, was it still possible that she had sold the things out of town? Had George checked to see if Dolly had made trips to the big book cities?

But what did any of this rather fascinating scenario have to do with the three drownings?

"To hell with it," said Sarah aloud. She marched out of the barn and was about to reenter the kitchen when she felt a waft of warmer air. The warm front. The weatherperson had promised a warm front, and by heaven, here it was. Probably the last warm front delivered to the state of Maine until May. Already she could see that the dirty patches of ice along the driveway edge were melting.

Okay, I'm out of here," Sarah announced to herself. Her brain needed a long rest. What she needed was movement. Action. Her bicycle. A plunge down Sawmill Road, a whirl around the campus, maybe lunch with Alex if she could find him free at the hospital. Lift those legs, tote that body, blow some air into her head.

It took only a minute. Mountain bike, bike helmet, windbreaker, gloves, water bottle. Her willing partner, Patsy. Patsy, who needed a break from tame walks over ice and snow and excursions into his dog run.

A sort of reckless excitement took charge, and Sarah screeched out onto the main road, hurtled down Sawmill Road, bounced over the ruts and cracks of an ill-paved secondary road, then crossed into the side campus road like something pursued by furies. Patsy, a giant gray wolflike presence bounding at her side.

But having survived the descent, she came a cropper on the

flat. Swerving around the hospital parking lot, she hurtled down the main walking path toward the English office. Fortunately, the campus was emptied of the usual teeming student population and the first hundred yards was clear. The few pedestrians encountered jumped to one side in advance of Sarah's charge.

But at the Malcolm Adam Hall—home of the English Department—a boy flung himself out of the door and raced for the sidewalk and careened into Sarah's path. Dodging the boy, Sarah confronted another figure bent over on his crutches, and this obstacle was too much. She jerked her wheel sharply to the left, the wheel hit a root of a guardian tree, and after a brief airborn flight, she ended headfirst in a clump of decorative barberry bushes.

Extrication was painful, and Patsy's heavy licking of her face made it no easier. Untangled at last, she faced Jonathan Epstein on crutches, Colin Beaugard, the running boy, and their escort, Alan Epstein, former husband of Alice. Sitting up, trickles of blood running from her scratched face, she stared. The Beaugards. Again. Was there no safe space? "I give up," she said as she clambered painfully to her feet.

The immediate result of the encounter was a visit to the English office for washing material and Band-Aids. The end result was lunch at the student cafeteria, Sarah having given up on Alex.

Lunch had an hilarious quality. There is nothing, Sarah reflected, so likely to break ice as the sight of a damaged adult. Both boys had enjoyed Sarah's collapse, and this inclined them to chatter. Alan, preoccupied with his chicken stir-fry, pretty much let the conversation run riot.

After the boys had finished instructing Sarah in the rudiments of doing wheelies, riding without hands, and jumping ditches, the subject turned to the projected video film of "The Fall of the House of Usher." Jonathan seemed torn between working out special effects, such as having Roderick Usher grow fangs and begin to slaver midway, and developing atmosphere through a number of sound effects such as wolf howls, thunder, wailing voices, and Lady Madelaine's heavy scratching as she tries to rise from her coffin.

Colin, as the unfortunate Roderick Usher, seemed fixated on everything about the video being perfect, and to this end wanted to put off the final family viewing until midwinter.

He finished the last of his french fries—dipping the last in a pool of ketchup and twirling it expertly and conveying it to his mouth. "It's my dad," he said through a mouthful. "He wants everything sort of professional. I mean, he inspects my bedroom and gives me points. And when he takes me sailing, I have to pass all these dumb tests and tie knots and figure out the course we're sailing like we were in a race or something. Like our new house. Everything had to be the best. Everything had to be perfect. Like we can't have our video look like it was done by a couple of kids."

This idea, Jonathan contested hotly.

"You try to be perfect and you're just sitting around spinning your wheels three years later. I say go for it. Creative stuff can't be made to fit into some sort of stupid rule book."

Here Alan Epstein looked up from his stir-fry. "There speaks a wise man. Listen, Colin, just get on with the project. Don't get hung up on perfect. Nobody's perfect. If I tried to write the perfect novel, I'd never have published anything."

"You just don't know Dad," said Colin. He reached for his mug of root beer and took a gulp. "He's different. Like this new sailboat that's coming. The *Gyrfalcon*. That's a big hawk. He uses bird names. Anyway, he's been yelling on the telephone to the builder and saying there's no point in launching the boat at all if it's going to be second-rate."

Sarah lifted her head. "You're selling the *Goshawk*?"

"Yeah," said Colin. "I liked her a lot, but now that Dad is going in this transatlantic thing next summer and he's the new commodore of the Profit Point Boat Club, well, he wanted—"

"Let me guess," said Alan. "The best. The perfect boat."

Colin nodded. "Maybe that's why Mom cracked up. I mean, she's been sort of out of it for a while, but she liked the *Goshawk*. And she liked our old house at Great Oaks. It wasn't a real house, just one of the cottages, but it had three bedrooms and a new kitchen and stuff like that. Anyway, we're going to see her this afternoon." He turned to Sarah. "You want to come? She's in the psychiatric part."

"I don't think—" Sarah began, but Alan forstalled her.

"I think Caroline has trouble with conversation. That's what Alice told me. So come along and we'll all keep the ball rolling."

Later, on their way to the hospital with the two boys ahead of them, Sarah wheeling her bike and walking next to Alan, he elaborated. "Caroline's in Never-Never Land. Withdrawl. I think it all got too much for her. The perfect house, the perfect this, the perfect that. She's tried floating along on the surface for a while, but I guess she just decided it was easier to slip under. According to Alice and even allowing for Alice's over- or understatement, Caroline hasn't been with it for ages. Beautiful woman, though. Looks like one of those models photographed in a fog, looking out to sea, wrapped in blowing gauze. Actually, I think she did work as a model for a bit. Never much of a mother. Didn't want a kid at all. Said children put too much pressure on you. But Eliot wanted a child—you know, keep the Beaugard line going, though why, I can't imagine— and Caroline gave in. Colin's probably part of Eliot's picture of the perfect family. But then, Eliot hasn't got much time for him. Lucky he's a self-sufficient kid, but I'm glad to see him hang around with Jonathan. They're close in age. Both very bright."

"Won't Caroline," Sarah said, "think it's odd if I turn up?"

"She won't think. Period. Any more than she'd think it odd if Alice's divorced husband turned up. Or Mickey Mouse. Or Phil Donahue. Relax and just talk about anything. Easier on the kids. Two boys can't be expected to keep up the chat with a woman who's inhabiting outer space."

The visit, like all visits to psychiatric facilities and their inmates, had the sense of taking place in a bell jar. But Sarah and Alan kept up a running conversation about weather and about the eccentricities of the Bowmouth English Department and its faculty. It was a subject that got them easily through the forty minutes while all the while Caroline sat in a turquoise vinyl chair, neatly combed and dressed in a pink cotton jumpsuit, thumbing her way through *People* magazine and occasionally directing her gaze to a framed reproduction of Monet's lily pond.

Masha Beaugard met them at the door as they left. She was carrying her recorder instrument case and looked, as usual, faintly exotic in green suede with an orange scarf around her throat.

"Any change?" asked Masha, lingering by the door, and to Alan's negative turn of the head, she nodded. "No, I suppose not. Dr. Shrank—can you believe a shrink called Shrank?—said not to expect any. Well, I'll stay for a while and go through whatever family news I can dredge up. And keep the subject away from murder and Dolly. Sarah, hey, good to see you."

Leaving the hospital, with the two boys well to the rear—Jonathan moving slowly on crutches—Alan and Sarah returned again to the pleasant business of dissecting certain aspects of the English Department, the tyranny of secretaries and the vagaries of students who flip in and out of classes, lose their texts, and respond with great self-pity if reminded of these lapses.

"But," said Alan, "I have this genius kid in one of my classes. He just laps up the stuff. Creative as hell. Working on a sci-fi short story and it's good. Rough, a little overblown, but good. Funny thing, his name is Gattling. Mark Gattling. It's as if no one can get away from the name. They're like hamsters."

"Gattlings have always been around," said Sarah, "but we haven't noticed all that much. Except when one of them is hauled into court. But now with Parson being banged on the head . . ."

"Jonathan keeps bringing up the Parson business," said Alan. "Made quite an impression. A boy's first murder. He can make hay out of it for years. His first novel, his first TV miniseries, his first film script. And wouldn't you know it, the murderer was in costume. Just like one of his horror comics."

"If you call a ski mask a costume."

"Jonathan calls it an executioner's suit, hood and all. To be serious, he was quite shaken. You know, I had qualms about letting him spend the winter at Great Oaks. Even with Alice on an even keel, all of them—Uncle Lenox, Caroline, Mrs. B.—remind me of the Munsters. Not your average warm and fuzzy family unit."

"Professor Cobb and Jonathan seem to have worked out a relationship," Sarah pointed out. "Reading his way through a list of a boy's Great Books. The book choices took some forbearance on Professor Cobb's part. I think the two are good for each other."

"Yeah, surprise, surprise, because Lenox can be a real grouch. And Mrs. B. when she goes into her royal mother act is tough to take. But you're right, on the whole it's working out. Even Alice seems to be working out. Webb Gattling seems solid—in all senses of the word—from what I've heard. Jonathan thinks he's okay, and that's what seems to matter. After all, I'm up to my eyebrows on this Bowmouth job, so parenting has to take second place for a while. Seeing Jonathan on weekends and during vacation breaks."

Sarah suddenly couldn't resist a question. "What was Dolly like early on? When you married Alice. When you were part of the family."

Alan raised his eyebrows. "Correction. Never part of the family. Adjunct. Barely tolerated. Mrs. B. never wanted any additions to the family tree. Including Caroline, which may be part of Caroline's trouble. It was Eliot who wanted to move off the Great Oaks estate, but Mrs. B. blamed Caroline because Eliot was the beloved and only son. Colin is welcomed—sort of—as carrying the precious Beaugard name, although Mrs. B. hardly gives Caroline credit for birthing the boy. As for me, she never made me feel welcome. She felt I came from a dubious background—my father designed swimming pools on Long Island—and I'm Jewish, not that I work very hard at it. However, I've asked Jonathan about her, and he says she's okay. But if it weren't for his wrecked shoulder and broken leg and Lenox Cobb's reading program, I'd probably yank him out of there and try and find a housekeeper."

"Dolly?" prompted Sarah.

"Oh yeah, Dolly. Look, Dolly and Eliot were the fair-haired children. Literally. Alice was off-the-wall, and Masha learned a long time ago to distance herself. Dolly was queen bee. Dolly was Mrs. B.'s rod and her staff, and now, it appears, her in-house thief."

"No absolute proof that it was Dolly," said Sarah. They had reached the English Department and had stopped at the side door.

"Good God, who else? Must have been Dolly. And if Mrs. B. isn't made to see the light, well, the entire estate is going to be turned into one giant Dolly memorial."

"But," Sarah reminded him, "none of the children seem to mind. Eliot seems happy, Masha only wishes some piece of land had been left for a summer music place, and Alice doesn't seem to care. Only Jonathan was mad. He wanted the dock and the boat facilities."

"Jonathan will survive. Speaking of which, I see the kids are almost on our necks and I promised Burger King and a horror flick."

Sarah extended her hand. "Good to see you, Alan. I really like Jonathan even in his uncouth moments."

"Thanks. He'll shape up, I hope." And with that the two boys presented themselves, and Jonathan announced that Colin had come up with the really neat idea that Roderick Usher should have fits.

"You know, seizures," said Colin. "I can roll my eyes up and hold my breath and I'm good at falling down."

"It's for the audience," Jonathan pointed out. "Part of the story is kind of slow, but if Roderick Usher has a fit right away in the first scene, it makes it more interesting. I mean, the audience will be more sympathetic to Roderick that way."

"I could foam at the mouth," said Colin. "Shaving cream. I could have a little plastic bag ready."

Sarah grimaced. "Awesome. Absolutely awesome." And she turned her bicycle and, followed by Patsy, rode away towards Sawmill Road.

From an investigatory point of view, the post-Thanksgiving week continued a period of relative stagnation, but the next Thursday, December first, brought not only a new snowfall but Mike Laaka with glad tidings. He arrived at the Mary Starbox Hospital in the late afternoon and cornered Alex as he was leaving his office.

"Wait," said Mike, "until you hear this."

"I can wait," said Alex, pulling on his parka and fumbling in his pockets for gloves. "I can wait for days."

"This will make your eyes pop out."

"Try me," said Alex, waving good night to his nurse, who was busy dousing the office lights.

"Don't play indifferent with me," said Mike. "That's Sarah's act, and we all know she's panting for information. Anyway, listen to this. Guess who was handling Dolly's rare book scam. Guess who was our middleman, our fence."

"Okay," said Alex, as the two men walked down the corridor, "out with it. You'll feel better."

"Parson Gattling. The mad preacher. Seems he got the goods from Dolly all neatly wrapped and packed in small cartons and took them around to different dealers. Up and down the coast. Apparently Dolly made the arrangements by phone and Parson was the conduit. He delivered the books, picked up the cash, and took it back to Dolly. Anyway, that's how we guess it worked. Then after delivery, Parson got his cut. The Vicar's Fund. Vicar—Parson, get it?"

Alex stopped dead by the doorway. "Are you sure? That's fantastic. Parson! Parson and Dolly. Those two working together."

"Crazy, isn't it? Crazy as this whole case."

"Are you all sure it was Parson?"

"Absolutely. George added a photo of Parson to those we were taking around to book dealers and we had a one hundred percent ID from all of them. It was Parson, all right."

"Good God, how did Dolly ever dream up Parson as her delivery man?"

"Who knows? We found out—and I told you this—that Parson worked on the Back Cove dock when Dolly was having it rebuilt. Or, for all we know, he met Dolly at one of those reach-out-and-touch-someone church affairs. You know, when different churches tie themselves in knots pretending they're all just loving Christians together. But however they met, Dolly probably figured that no one would ever connect the two of them."

"If Dolly hadn't drowned, they wouldn't have," said Alex. "Okay, that's news to take home for dinner."

"One more little tidbit," said Mike. "Several fibers from the Gattling skiff—the lab's located them—match the canvas covers of the lead bars. There you are. Another Gattling connection. And one that probably finished those two beauties. They helped off-load Dolly's boat and got murdered for their trouble. Dead men tell no tales. Now we'll have to sniff out which Beaugard—if it was a Beaugard—or a Vivian Lavender, or persons unknown, hired Marsden and Junior. So how about Parson himself? That's a wild idea, isn't it?"

Alex, the bearer of hot news, was greeted by Sarah that evening with her own brand of news. She was at the kitchen table engaged in sorting through her Christmas card list, adding new names and canceling the undeserving or the deceased—the latter of which included Dolly Beaugard. "You're to call Great Oaks," she announced. "Lenox Cobb has a chest cold. Or a cough. Mrs. Beaugard is worried, and she herself is feeling a little faint."

Alex hurled his parka at the corner of the kitchen and stamped his feet. The recent spell of warm weather was a thing of the past, and along with the new snow had come a sharp-edged cold front. Ten above that night was predicted. "I suppose," he said, "that puts the lid on the professor's taking the field in the Christmas Bird Count. He's too old to take chances with a respiratory problem. But Mrs. Beaugard specializes in feeling faint, particularly when things haven't been going her way."

"You mean Dolly, whose reputation is being muddied by her jealous siblings?"

"Exactly. But now she's got another reason to feel faint. The Gattling connection has really come home to roost." And Alex delivered Mike's news, adding, "I don't know which is scariest, but maybe it's the Parson-Dolly hookup."

"The Vicar's Fund, of course. Dolly didn't have the imagination to think up a better cover name for him. And the Parish Fund. That must refer to money she gave to the church."

Alex objected. "The Parish Fund lists money taken *in*—as into Dolly's account *from* the parish, i.e., the church. And then a few days later a check for cash—a fairly small one—is made out from the Vicar's Fund and the money presumably is given to Parson Gattling. For services rendered. That still suggests complicity on the part of St. Paul's-by-the-Sea. Because the donations Dolly made later to St. Paul's and the hospital, the Scouts and galleries, are listed by name. Perfectly straightforward."

"You're making my head ache," complained Sarah. "I haven't even begun to come to grips with someone hiring Marsden and Junior to unload the ballast from Dolly's boat, and certainly can't deal with St. Paul's sending money to Dolly. Unless, of course, the books traveled from Dolly first to the church and then from the church to Parson. Isn't that the way they launder money?"

"Now you're making my head ache," said Alex. He stood up and reached for his parka. "I'll go over to Great Oaks now before the weather gets any worse. See if I can talk sense into that old coot Lenox Cobb about doing what he's told to do. When I come home I expect you to have a clear explanation of the Parish Fund for me."

And Sarah did.

"No problem," she said after dinner as the two lounged together in front of the living room fire. "Parish Fund doesn't have to mean parish. Nor St. Paul's. There are other parishes."

"Don't be cute. It's been a long day and I'm not up for anything subtle."

"Take Dolly," said Sarah.

"I did. I have. Go on."

"She wasn't supersmart. Highly organized, capable, did good works. Okay? But no student. A lousy speller, said Alice."

"You're close to boring me," said Alex with a sigh.

"Not a speller. Parish, for instance. The name meant church to all of us because this whole business is tangled up with the church. But add an extra letter to Parish and what do you have?"

"You're enjoying yourself, aren't you?"

"Yes," said Sarah. "It's these little triumphs that get us through the winter. Parish can turn into Parrish. P-A-R-R-I-S-H. As in Maxfield Parrish. Noted illustrator of books. I called Alice tonight, and she said funny I should ask because Parrish was one of her father's favorite illustrators. He started his collection because he'd had one of Parrish's books as a little boy. Hawthorne's *Wonderbook*, actually."

Alex, now alert, nodded. "So the money Dolly got from selling off chunks of the collection was put in the Parish-Parrish Fund. Like Parson's payment going into the Vicar's Fund."

"You've got it," said Sarah with satisfaction. "And it may not have been a spelling mistake. Using normal spelling is a good disguise. Dolly, as we now know, was plenty devious."

For a moment the two settled back and allowed themselves to enjoy the warmth of the fire, a fire whose glow was made more welcome by the contrast it made to the snow slanting down on the living room windows.

Then Sarah roused herself. "Okay, so Dolly had a book-selling scheme that used Parson Gattling and benefited church, God, and country, but answer me this—"

Alex interrupted. "I know what you're going to say, and the idea will keep you awake."

"What I'm asking," Sarah persisted, "is not only who killed Marsden and Junior for those services rendered, but why are Parson and Dolly dead? Was it something to do with Arthur Beaugard's collection? Is there some maniac book dealer on the loose? So who killed those two? And why?"

24

THE news of the Marsden-Junior role in unloading ballast from the *Sweetheart* did not reach the Beaugard homestead. But the Parson Gattling–Dolly Beaugard alliance leaked out and created a small sensation.

Eliot Beaugard, on being queried by George Fitts about his sister's cofelon, appeared genuinely flabbergasted. "Goddamn," said Eliot. "Nothing can surprise me now. Tell me Dolly ran an underground drug ring or had a job as a hooker and I won't bat an eye. But don't tell Mother."

"I understand," said George, who had already tried Mrs. Beaugard on the subject and had almost been turned from the house because of it.

"Hot spit," said Alice, when reviewing the subject over sandwiches with Sarah at the Bowmouth student cafeteria. Alice was calling on the still-incarcerated Caroline; Sarah was between classes. "I mean, holy somoli, there was more to Dolly than met the eye. Parson Gattling! Prim and proper Dolly with her own fence. But," she added, "what was that crap about the Beaugards being sinful that Parson went on about? Do you think he was mad for Dolly and had decided that one of us did her in?"

Sarah looked up from her apple crumb cake. "Anyone's guess what went on in Parson's head."

"Well, he did show up at Dolly's funeral," Alice reminded her.

True, thought Sarah later as she trudged the stairs toward her classroom. But Parson hadn't been mourning Dolly, had he? She couldn't remember exactly what he'd said. Maybe he had assisted in her death, the ballast unloading, and was regretting it.

This untoward idea was expressed to Mike Laaka by Masha during one of Mike's continuing interviews with members of the Beaugard clan. "I think Parson did it," she announced. "Killed off Marsden and Junior because of the drug business. Parson wasn't getting his share, so he doped their whiskey. And Dolly wasn't giving him a big enough cut when here he was risking his neck carrying those books around. Maybe he even tried to blackmail her . . ."

"But then Dolly would have killed *him*," Mike pointed out.

Masha shook off the suggestion. "Say she resisted blackmail and that made him angry, so he just took care of her."

But Jonathan, in Mike's opinion, took the prize for suggestions. He ran into Alex on a chance meeting in the hospital—Mike was there to try and extract a few words from Caroline Beaugard on the subject. "Jonathan's idea takes the cake. As he sees it, his uncle Eliot wants all the Beaugard land so that he can turn it into an international yacht resort facility complete with clubhouse, marine shops, condos, heavy-duty moorings for sixty-foot jobs. Tennis courts, gift shops, lagoons, the works. Club Med in Maine."

"Jonathan thinks big," observed Alex. "Does he have any reason to think Eliot is thinking of constructing a resort?"

"He told me that his uncle might use the resort as cover for a worldwide smuggling center for the sort of microchips that do robot navigation for yachts. That maybe Uncle Eliot was working for the Japanese."

Alex shook his head. "I'd say Jonathan doesn't like Eliot."

"Very true. Jonathan's mad about Back Cove and Little Cove being given away in the estate plan, and he said that Uncle Eliot could stop it if he wanted to, but just because he has his own dock, he's not interested in doing anything."

The visit to Caroline Beaugard bore bitter fruit. She indicated by nods that she was not surprised about the Dolly-Parson tandem, nor at anything that happened. Asked if she had any hunches about who might be the murderer, or murderers, of the two, she spoke for the first time in days. "Why not Eliot? He makes me miserable. Everything I do is wrong. I choose the wrong colors for the rugs and the furniture. I wear the wrong clothes. I haven't any life at all. If it wasn't Eliot, it was probably Alice. She gets away with murder anyway. Why not the real thing?" And Caroline turned away and gazed out the mesh-covered window.

Vivian Lavender expressed herself to George Fitts as troubled on behalf of Mrs. Beaugard. "She needs to believe in Dolly." When reminded that Mrs. Beaugard had not accepted Dolly's guilt, he was told that "deep down she believes and it is destroying her."

"Is Mrs. Beaugard any worse, healthwise?" asked George, meeting Alex, who was making one of his increasingly frequent after-hours house calls at Great Oaks.

"Her heart's a little tricky and causes some shortness of breath, but for the rest, it's the chronic stuff—arthritis, glaucoma. But don't ride roughshod over her, George. And take it easy with Professor Cobb. He's not in the best of health, either. I'm going to take a look at him now."

Lenox was sitting up in a window-side chair wrapped in an ancient dressing gown of Oriental design, a large-print edition of *Timon of Athens* on his lap. He was coughing when Alex appeared at the door and made a visible effort to quell the spasm. "I am much better," he announced. "I hardly cough at all. It's the smoke coming up from the kitchen. But I still can't read even large print without trouble. But I shall be in shape for the bird count."

"We'll see," said Alex, sitting down and pulling his stethoscope out of his pocket.

During the examination that followed, Lenox reverted to Topic A—the Dolly-Parson phenomenon. "I suspected Dolly from the word go. Beware of people wearing halos, is what I say. Arthur's books were just crying out for someone to snatch them. And they weren't all children's books. Some big items. An Antonio Novelli, Honoré Daumier's *Les Robert Macaire*, and a number of Cruikshanks and Rowlandsons. A William Blake, *Songs of Innocence and Experience*. Of course, I never connected Dolly with books since she was barely literate, but she certainly knew value when she saw it. I think the entire estate plan of Elena's should be scrapped. Now, about the Christmas count. We need at least to equal last year's number of sixty-six species. They saw no owls. We must try to find owls."

Alex returned home to tell Sarah that, judging from what he'd heard around town, all the members of the Beaugard family were equally guilty of murder, everyone knew Dolly was up to something, and Lenox Cobb was in no condition to go out and count birds on December seventeenth.

"Well, I've made up my mind," said Sarah. "It's Vivian Lavender. She did it all. She was Arthur Beaugard's mistress—that's almost a fact since we know she drove him around—and she hated Dolly for taking away her job security. And she's madly in love with . . ." Here Sarah paused.

"Go on," said Alex, "in love with . . ."

"Well, it would be too easy to say Eliot and like father, like son. So how about Parson Gattling? They were probably at school together, and as I've said, I think Vivian has warm blood and Parson had that mystical quality. But then he done her wrong and started playing games with Dolly. Answer: Vivian must kill Dolly and Parson. And look ahead to bedding down with Webb. Webb has that shaggy basic strongman quality, which means that Alice had better watch out. Housekeepers know everything that goes on, they're privy to family secrets, and they want wealth and power and sex because they've been denied. Okay, do you buy it?"

"Go to bed and sleep it off," said Alex.

The Midcoast Audubon Society's annual Christmas Bird Count took place as planned on December seventeenth on a crisp sixteen-degree day that followed several days of heavy snowfall. The addition of a brisk north wind meant that the birders went forth to do their counting wrapped and layered, booted and hatted, lugging telescopes, notebooks, and binoculars, looking very much like figures out of a Norse saga.

"Just why are we doing this?" demanded Sarah, struggling into her heavy-duty lined jacket. "It's only six A.M. and dark as pitch and freezing cold. Why not count birds in the spring? There are lots more around then and we'd be comfortable."

"Birds are counted then, too," said Alex, who was folding up his telescope. "It's not a sport, though it started out that way. The point is to see which species are losing ground, which species are holding their own. How many are staying around for the winter."

"More fool they," said Sarah, winding a polar fleece scarf around her neck. "Okay, what's the drill? I'm ready with my trusty pencil; you say 'hark, look, a pink-coated yellow snapper,' I write it down. Right?"

"Right," said Alex. "Now, move it. I'll fill the thermos and take the telescope, you grab the binoculars."

"I'm not going to be sighting anything," said Sarah. "But at least the whole affair is a vacation from the Beaugard machinery."

"Not entirely. I'm going to stop in and make sure Lenox Cobb stays put in the house. I've put Jonathan up to suggesting he read *The Tempest* to his uncle as consolation. The professor did his dissertation on *The Tempest*. Colin will be staying with them, and they can both read and help Mrs. Beaugard watch and count the birds that come to the feeder."

"And then?"

"Then we meet our team—with Eliot as commander in chief at the entrance gates—and go to work."

It fell out as planned. Professor Cobb, in the last stages of his cold, after token grumbling, gave in to Alex, and the assembled bird-watchers climbed into their cars and headed for the frozen wastes and frigid shores of South Proffit Point.

Sarah, standing in the shelter of a group of pines, notebook clutched in a mittened hand, watched the members of the Proffit Point team wade through a snow-filled field trying to verify a reported snowy owl. Because of the cold and the wind, the wearing of ski masks, balaclavas, and face masks was de rigueur, and they looked, she thought, exactly like Jonathan's description of Parson's murderer. Hooded executioners, all of them.

"One snowy owl," announced Eliot with triumph—although with his black coverall and red knitted balaclava, it was hard to tell that it was Eliot. "First snowy owl we've seen in three years. And five juncos, six blue jays, nine chickadees . . ."

"And a partridge in a pear tree?" suggested Sarah.

But Eliot had no time for levity. He pointed to the scraggly branches of an apple tree. "Look over there. Waxwings, I think. Let's keep an eye out for Bohemians." And he moved off through the snow, binoculars raised.

And here Sarah found herself joined by a slender figure so muffled that again identification as to name or gender was impossible. But the figure, speaking in a high breathless voice through its ski mask, announced she was Sandi—"Sandi with an *i*"—Sandi Ouellette, that her husband was a funeral director, and they had met Sarah at Dolly Beaugard's funeral.

Sarah, extending a hand, thought with resentment, I can't get away from Dolly out here in the middle of a field. But Sandi went on to say she simply didn't know a thing about birds, but her husband had wanted her to help keep score.

"Be my guest," said Sarah, proffering her pencil and pad, but this was refused. "I can't cope with all those weirdo bird names, so I'll just hang out with you for the duration. Okay?"

Sarah said okay, and for the next three hours Sandi dogged her footsteps as the team of birders slogged through drifted snow, slid about on frozen ponds and marshes, and stood on the shore in the teeth of the north wind counting gulls, ducks, loons, and grebes.

"And four great cormorants and at least twenty black guillemots, and one Iceland gull," said Alex, the visible part of his face looking frostbitten but pleased.

"How exciting," squeaked Sandi Ouellette, and Sarah decided that she was being partnered by a Barbie doll.

The day progressed, a watery-looking sun out, the wind softened and shifted slightly to the west so that tears did not come immediately to the birders' pinched faces. This moderation, followed by a sandwich-and-thermos lunch and the sighting of a single fox sparrow and two brown creepers, put the group into a mood that could almost be described as jolly, so that when Eliot suggested they finish the day at Diggers Neck, there were no dissenters even though the area was known for its difficult footing on barren stretches of rock and ledge.

"But we'll do Great Oaks first, won't we?" asked a tall man wearing a red plaid duck-hunting cap with the earflaps pulled down—a man Sarah now recognized as Sandi Ouellette's other half, the undertaker Fred Ouellette.

"Well," said Eliot, collapsing the legs of his telescope, "I thought I might have seen a king eider out past Little Cove yesterday. An adult male. Maybe the female. But I'm not sure. My telescope wasn't set up. But I think it's worth checking out."

This announcement caused an immediate stir and there was a general movement toward the cars.

"What's a king eider?" asked Sarah, catching up to Alex.

"It sounds exciting," piped Sandi, trotting along behind her.

"A king eider," said Alex, slipping into his instructional mode, "is a stubby sea duck with an orange bill shield. The female—"

"I've found it," said Sandi. "In my Peterson. That duck is some weird." 'Weird' seemed to be one of Sandi's favorite words.

"The female," said Alex doggedly, "looks almost exactly like the female common eider, but the head is rounder, the bill looks shorter. But if we really see either, it's quite a find."

"Awesome," said Sandi, climbing happily into the front seat beside Alex.

What was awesome, Sarah said to herself, was the numbing cold. Wind or no wind, the temperature seemed to be falling. The others, undoubtedly warmed by the possibility of a king eider, seemed immune to such suffering. Suddenly, as the car rounded the circle by the front door of the Great Oaks house and stopped, she decided. "Good-bye," she said. "I give up."

Alex twisted around and eyed her—the only facial expression possible through the slits in his ski mask. "Are you sure? We're going to be hiking out to Little Cove. Maybe pick up some land birds on the way."

"You pick them up," said Sarah. "Me, I'm going in and enjoy central heating and imagine a trip to the Everglades."

"Gosh," said Sandi, "you're going to miss the king eider."

"He's all yours; go to it, Sandi," said Sarah, and she clambered out of the Jeep and walked with determined steps toward the house.

"Come on, Alex, get out of the car," said Sandi, plucking at Alex's sleeve. "The others are getting ahead."

Sarah reached and lifted the front door knocker, waited, then hearing no answering footsteps, turned the knob and the door swung open. Honestly, she thought, the Beaugards are just asking for it. Not only those bookcases but the whole house is unlocked. And the place is loaded, paintings, prints, cupboards full of china and a sideboard heavy with silver.

Once in the front hall, she called softly. Softly, because she didn't want to wake Mrs. Beaugard should she be napping in front of the fire as any sensible person should be on such a day. Then, pulling off her heavy boots at the living room entrance, she poked her head in the door. Empty. Of course. Mrs. B. was in charge of watching the feeder birds, and these could best be seen from the library window. Fine. She, Sarah, would settle in the living room. She looked at her watch. Quarter of three. It would be getting dark soon and the birders would pack it in.

But now, just to sit by the fire. Sarah took off her parka and woolen hat and sank into an overstuffed chair, closed her eyes, and let the warmth cover her like a quilt. A down quilt, she murmured. An eiderdown quilt. A king eiderdown quilt. Down, down, down. And Sarah was asleep.

Later she never remembered what had disturbed her. A door closing somewhere, the sound of steps. A car starting up. Whatever it was, she was awake instantly. On her feet. Looking at her watch. Four-fifteen. Almost dark. And the house was so quiet. Had everyone gone to sleep, too? Uncle Lenox and Jonathan and Colin over *The Tempest*. Mrs. Beaugard over her bird feeder. Vivian Lavender over whatever she was doing.

Sarah shook herself and considered. Then, aware of sounds on the stairs, she turned to the door that opened into the hall in time to see Jonathan with his crutch, his left leg still in its walking cast, Colin behind them, and riding herd, Uncle Lenox. All in outdoor clothes. Why? Perhaps to meet the birders and to hear the reports. As the front door closed behind the trio, Sarah decided she could skip hearing the details and all the excitement over the snowy owl and the king eider. She would leave the house by another route, climb into the Jeep, and huddle over the heater until Alex extricated himself from the group.

The library. It had French doors into the garden, and if Mrs. Beaugard was there, she could thank her for warmth and comfort. Sarah pulled on her parka, her hat, retrieved her boots, and walked quickly to the library. She opened the door and was immediately hit by a wall of arctic air. One of the French doors stood partly open, its guardian curtain bellied out in the light wind. And no Mrs. Beaugard. What was left of the fireplace blaze was flickering uncertainly in a bed of ashes; a white mohair shawl lay across a sofa back, a copy of *Gourmet* on the cushion. And on the floor a tablet of paper, its leaves ruffling in the breeze from the door. And oddly enough, in the corner, faceup, a tattered horror comic book, sure sign that Jonathan had made a library visit.

Sarah hesitated, then stuffed her feet into her boots and stepped across the room, intending only to rescue the notebook and close the door. She picked up the tablet, noting as she did that Mrs. Beaugard had faithfully recorded the species of birds seen at her feeder and that blue jays and chickadees led the list. This, she placed on the sofa, but the door was another matter. Part of a small hooked rug had become wedged underneath its bottom edge, and Sarah was forced to bend down and yank it away.

And it was in this position that she saw it. A late afternoon winter tableau set against the snow. For a moment, rather insanely, Breughel's painting of the returning hunters came into her head: the lowering sky, the silhouetted figures against the snow, the black lines of the trees. And then she knew what she was seeing.

Three figures. One standing stock-still, his hands raised against his masked face, the second kneeling down in the snow reaching out, touching. Touching the third figure. A third figure who showed as a long dark sprawled shape only partially visible to Sarah because it was sunk deep into the drifted snow. Snow that seemed to surround the shape with a comforting enfolding softness.

Then two of the tableau figures moved. The kneeling figure turned into Alex, who let his hand drop, rose, and shook his head at the first figure, who became Eliot Beaugard. Who in turn shook his head slowly as if unbelieving. And then the others, the South Proffit Point bird-watching team, swarmed into the scene.

And Sarah retreated. Backed out of the room and headed for the front hall. Where she intended to go, she could never afterwards explain. Perhaps to join the others gathered outside the library window. Perhaps to telephone the ambulance. Or the police. Or both. Perhaps to find Vivian Lavender. Uncle Lenox.

But the sound of an automobile motor stopped her short, and wrenching open the front door, she peered into the increasing dark and saw a sedan back out from the open garage, turn in a series of jerks around the jumble of parked cars, then move forward and, gathering speed, disappear down the Great Oaks drive.

And Sarah broke into a run, had almost reached the Jeep, when she felt her coat grabbed from the rear. Alice.

"Was that Jonathan?" Alice shouted. "In that car? I just got here and I thought I saw him get in with Uncle Lenox and someone else. Where the hell . . ."

Sarah gave her a push. "I'm going to find out. Right now. I'm taking the Jeep."

Alice gave a return shove, "And taking me with you. That's my son. That's Jonathan."

"I'm not going to argue," said Sarah. "Get in the car." She reached for the Jeep door. Unlocked. The keys? In the ignition. She climbed into place and Alice threw herself onto the front seat; the Jeep motor rumbled, coughed once, and roared. Sarah cranked the wheels sharply to the right, swung away away from the car ahead, and gunned the motor so that the vehicle shot through the snow-drifted driveway like some kind of runaway snowplow.

And hit the main Proffit Point Road just in time to see the taillights of the sedan disappear over the hill, heading south.

25

"I'M afraid she's gone," said Alex, standing up and returning the flashlight to Eliot. "Facedown in the snow like that."

"Oh my God," said Eliot. "My God. Mother. Poor Mother."

"She may have fallen, felt faint, but the signs of asphyxia—being smothered—are pretty clear. The protruding tongue, the eyes. Look, you don't want the details, but take my word."

"Smothered in the snow? Good Christ. But what was she doing out here anyway? In weather like this?"

For answer Alex pointed silently to a partly snow-covered tin. "Bird feed. She may have gone out to fill the bird feeder."

Eliot shook his head. "Oh God," he repeated. "Oh Christ."

"Listen," said Alex, "I'll stay here. You go call the ambulance and then the police."

"Police," exploded Eliot. "Why the police? Jesus, haven't we had enough of the police? Mother fell down. Had one of her dizzy spells. And smothered. Poor old thing." And then he took a step toward the partially snow-covered form. "We can't leave her lying out here. Let's get her in the house."

"We shouldn't move her," said Alex. "But see if you can find something to cover her. To keep the snow off."

"Right away. I'll do that right away," said Eliot, and he turned and headed for the open door of the library.

"Go around," shouted Alex as Eliot grabbed for the door handle. "Footprints, fingerprints."

"Oh goddamn," answered Eliot. "This isn't a crime, it's a . . . it's a tragedy."

"It was also an unattended death," said Alex. "But right now we have too many attendants." He indicated the dark forms of birders who, shifting uneasily from foot to foot, now stood at the edge of the little garden that held the bird-feeding station. "Take everyone around to the front and let them in the house. And keep them there. Do you hear?" This as Eliot stayed, apparently frozen in place by the library door.

Eliot hesitated, came forward, took another long look at his mother's body, and retreated, calling the birding team to follow.

"Mr. Ouellette," called Alex. "Come over here, please." Then, as the tall lanky undertaker detached himself from the group following Eliot, Alex beckoned him to his side. "I don't want to move the body. Will you stand guard while I make sure Eliot's gotten hold of the police?"

Alex discovered Eliot at the library door, his arms full of a wadded-up blanket apparently yanked from the nearest bed. He grabbed Eliot by the shoulder. "Not through there. Remember what I said about not walking through the area. Go back the way you came. I'll be right out."

Eliot turned, his face angry. "I've called the ambulance and the goddamned police." Suddenly he glared at the floor by the corner of the room. "Look at that. That comic book. Jonathan's been down here in the library." Then, his voice growing increasingly agitated, "That rotten kid. He probably talked Mother into filling the feeder. And didn't stay around to help her. Damn him." And Eliot turned from the room, the hem of a blanket trailing behind him.

Alex left the library, found Tad Bugelski's wife—she was an

enthusiastic birder—and stationed her at the library door. "No one in," he ordered. "Not until the police say okay. I'll be outside."

And as had happened so often in the recent past, the police, in the shape of George Fitts, Mike Laaka, Katie Waters, and other law enforcement types, together with the rescue squad and an ambulance, converged on the house at Great Oaks, and the person of Mrs. Arthur Beaugard was immediately subjected to those necessary indignities to which in life she would have vehemently protested.

George Fitts, having herded the members of the birding team into the living room, delgated Mike Laaka to corner Alex. This he did in the front hall.

"What do you think happened?" demanded Mike.

"Let the pathologist do the guessing," said Alex. "She was an elderly woman with multiple health problems including a cardiac condition. And none too steady on her legs. Out there in the snow and wind, well, anything might have happened."

"Perhaps an assist from someone near and dear?" suggested Mike.

But Alex only shrugged and then peered in the direction of the living room. "Where the hell is everyone? I mean the family. Jonathan, Colin, Lenox Cobb. And Vivian. My wife? Eliot's the only family member around."

"Masha's here," said Mike. "She was upstairs taking a nap. We had to bodily prevent her from going out to see her mother." At which point Eliot strode into the hall and announced that he couldn't find Lenox or the two boys upstairs or down. And that he didn't trust his uncle as far as he could throw him, but by God, he was going to find the three of them.

"Hold it," said George Fitts, appearing behind Eliot. "We need statements, and that's going to take time. Perhaps you could ask Mrs. Lavender to make some coffee. I'm going to let all these people call home to say they're delayed here, but I want a deputy to stand by next to them when they call."

"Have you secured the bird feeder area?" asked Mike.

"Yes," said George, "but with the wind blowing the snow

around, we haven't much hope of finding anything for now. I've sent for lights, and the lab people will be here any minute."

"You're treating it like a homicide?" asked Mike.

"Use your head, Michael," said George. "Considering the past two months at Great Oaks, wouldn't you take precautions?"

"Aaah," said Mike. "I think that's overkill. I think it's an accidental death. Most of the family was around this afternoon; she was alive at three and then the bird-watchers arrived. They may be a pain in the neck, but homicide isn't their thing. The old lady was pretty tottery. And had lousy eyesight. An accident waiting to happen, right, Alex?"

But Alex was looking again into the living room and now said, with some urgency, "The family may have been around— some of them—but where are they now? And Sarah. She was going to meet me here. Or in my car."

George scowled, turned on his heel, disappeared for the space of ten minutes, and returned with a uniformed trooper. "They've just finished a quick search of the house. The following people seem to be missing. Mrs. Lavender, Professor Cobb, Colin Beaugard, Jonathan Epstein. And Alice Beaugard. Her sister, Masha, saw her drive in at least an hour ago."

"Sarah Deane?" demanded Alex.

The trooper shook his head. "No one has seen Sarah Deane since she left the birding group and entered this house by the front door." And he added, "We went to check with Eliot Beaugard and now we can't find *him*."

Alice peered through the windshield of the Jeep. "I can still see taillights, but I don't know if they're the ones we want. But it doesn't make any sense. They can't drive."

"Who can't drive?" said Sarah, as the Jeep rose up over the second hill of the Proffit Point Road.

"They can't. None of them. I mean, if it's Jonathan and Colin and Uncle Lenox—the three you saw together—they can't. The boys certainly can't, and Uncle Lenox has double vision or blurred eyes. He hasn't driven since his accident. His car's just been sitting in the garage."

"Then they've gotten someone to drive them," said Sarah.

"But who, for God's sake? And why? Why are they tearing around at this time of night? It's still snowing and it's cold enough to freeze the brass balls off a monkey."

"The movies," suggested Sarah. "Lenox is taking them to the movies. Maybe Alan picked them up. Maybe it was all pre-arranged."

"Not likely," said Alice, grumbling. Then she stiffened. "I forgot. What was going on at the house? You started to talk about an accident. Whose accident? One of that birding group?"

Sarah, trying to keep the taillights of the car ahead in view, thought for a second how to tell someone that her mother had been found facedown in the snow and that Alex was shaking his head. And then she told it straight, describing her visit to the library, the open doors, the dark shape under the bird feeder.

"Oh Christ," said Alice. "Mother. Do you think?" And before Sarah could answer, "No, you don't think, do you? She's dead. Frozen to death out there."

"I don't know what happened," said Sarah. "Do you want to turn back? Are you absolutely sure that Jonathan's in that car ahead? Or any car?"

But Alice nodded vehemently. "I'm sure enough. And I can't do anything about Mother. I can't even take it in. But I can do something about Jonathan. And Colin. If it turns out Uncle Lenox and maybe Alan are taking them to the movies, fine. Great. I'll go home. So keep your eye on that car. If they go straight on into town and head toward Rockland, it could be the movies. Or someplace to eat. Only, Alan always drives that old VW Rabbit of his . . ."

"So what kind of car am I following? I can't tell at this distance."

"Same as Mother's. A Ford Escort. Both dark, hers black—she special-orders black cars. Uncle Lenox has dark blue."

Sarah slowed her car, the Jeep giving a little shimmy on the now snow-packed road. "Car's almost stopped ahead at the Diggers Neck turnoff. It's going right under the streetlight."

"And I see three heads. Three heads. Not four."

"And," said Sarah, through her teeth, "it's turning left. It's not going to town. I'll bet it's headed south, taking the Route One shortcut."

"Get on its tail, close the gap," shouted Alice.

"I can't. I'll end up in a ditch. But they're slowing a bit. At least I can keep up. Alice, are you sure Jonathan doesn't know how to drive? I don't mean 'does he drive,' just does he know *how*? Most kids of his age do. They get a chance to steer, to drive on farm roads, on private driveways."

"Well, as a matter of fact . . ." began Alice.

"I thought so."

"Just around Great Oaks. From the entrance on. Down to the boathouse, around back to the harbor. Perfectly legal."

"Legal's not the point. The point is that between Lenox Cobb and Jonathan, they can probably drive a car. And for all we know, young Colin probably drives, too."

Colin did drive and rather prided himself on his skill. Sitting next to an obliging adult, he, too, had taken the wheel at Great Oaks and had logged an impressive number of miles over the past two years. However, on this occasion he had been forced into the role of passenger and lookout.

"Watch for anyone following," Professor Cobb had ordered. "Jonathan and I have enough to do to keep the car on the road. And no, Colin, I will not tell you where we are going. There comes a time in life when younger people must trust the wisdom and sense of someone older. So not another word. I think I saw headlights behind us. Watch and let me know if they turn off."

Twenty-five minutes later, as Lenox applied a light braking, Jonathan, squeezed tight against his uncle, hanging on to the wheel for dear life, made the left turn from the town of Waldoboro onto Route One and headed south.

"That car's behind us," announced Colin. "I think it's the same car. Like a Jeep or something."

"If it's a Jeep, I won't worry excessively," said Lenox. "Let me know if you see anyone else on our tail."

"Okay," said Colin. And then, "I'm hungry."

"Contain your hunger," said Lenox. "We'll wait until we find a parking lot with a lot of cars. Then we try a stop."

"A pit stop?" said Jonathan.

"Precisely," said Lenox. "Fast in, fast out."

"And you won't tell us yet where we're going?" repeated Colin.

"I said I wouldn't and I meant it." And Professor Cobb folded his lips and squinted into the driving snow. Besides, he added to himself, at the moment I haven't the faintest idea.

At ten-fifteen that evening, Katie Waters watched the last of the Proffit Point South team bird-watchers climb into their cars and one by one drive slowly down the snow-covered drive while at the same time Alex stood by the kitchen telephone and received the first autopsy report from that long-suffering pathologist, Johnny Cuzak.

"I object," said Johnny, "to bodies on the weekend. It's my youngest kid's birthday and I left my wife with a house full of eight-year-old boys. I'd promised to help."

"Okay, Johnny, said Alex. "We all had other plans today. So what gives? Asphyxiation?"

"Yeah, as far as we can tell. We're lucky because sometimes these buggers don't show external signs."

"Go on," said Alex, wincing at the idea of Mrs. Beaugard being referred to as a "bugger."

"Well, as you noted, the tongue protruded; it was bitten, too. the eyes were prominent and there was evidence of slight bleeding from the nose and ears. Cyanosis of the face and petechial hemorrhages of facial skin and the conjunctive present."

"Any cardiac pathology?"

"Early stages of congestive heart failure; arteries a mess. Possible bruising around neck and shoulders. Maybe as a result of her fall. If she fell. Even if she hadn't suffocated, hypothermia might have got her. Mighty cold tonight."

"Thank you, Johnny," said Alex. He turned to George. "So

that's that. Asphyxiation. And now what news about the strays? I'm getting worried. Three cars gone, Mrs. Beaugard's, Professor Cobb's, and my Jeep. Which I assume Sarah has taken for reasons of her own. But I called home and no answer."

"Mmm," said George. "Is it possible there was some pre-arranged affair? Something they all went to? One of the bird-watchers told me that there's a big dinner after the bird count when all the reports from all the territories covered are given."

"You're right about that," said Alex. "There's always a banquet and then the reports. But no one from this house would go to a banquet with Mrs. Beaugard dead. You can scratch that idea."

"It was a long shot," admitted George. "So we've sent out an all-points. They'll be picked up within the hour. I'd bet on it."

But George lost his bet. The police of all sorts, state, town, deputies, were out in force dealing with the usual road accidents that befoul an icy winter Saturday night. Jackknifed semis, drivers under the influence, speeding teenagers, all took priority over three cars proceeding at legal speed along a heavily traveled route.

"This is a damn funny sort of chase," observed Alice. "Going along at thirty-five miles an hour."

"Fast enough in this weather," said Sarah. "Besides, the Bath Bridge is no place to put on speed. And we're keeping them in sight. They probably don't dare go any faster either. Particularly if either of those two kids is doing part of the driving."

Alice twisted around in her seat. "I'd swear that there's a car hanging in behind us," she said. "A Saab like Eliot's, which means maybe he's following us from Great Oaks. Chasing *us.* "

"Listen," said Sarah. "Saabs are all over the place. Relax." But as Sarah said it, the familiar spectral hand crept down her neck and crawled along her spine.

Alice grimaced. "I guess I'm just chronically paranoid. I wish we had Webb in the backseat. For extra insurance. Nobody messes with Webb."

"I'm not expecting a fight," said Sarah. "Just to stop them and find out what crazy thing they think they're up to. I suppose it's possible that your uncle has completely flipped his lid and the boys are egging him on into some horrible adventure. A Stephen King book come to life."

"God, I hope not. No more bodies, please. Oh Jesus, I keep forgetting poor Mother. I hope it was quick. Like being hit by lightning. They say freezing isn't so bad after the first part. Like going to sleep. But you're right that Jonathan and Colin, when they get together, well, they haven't got much of what my shrink calls a reality quotient."

"Hey," said Sarah. "They're turning in. Right toward that shopping mall. Oh brother, we're going to lose them in the parking lot. I'll bet they're going to eat."

"Take a guess. Colin loves McDonald's, but Jonathan goes for Burger King. And there's an Arby's down the line."

"McDonald's is closest. We'll grab a takeout ourselves and then hang out at the exit back onto Route One."

Settled back with two Big Macs and two Cokes to go, Sarah was able to point out a number of Saabs coming, going, and parked. This seemed to reassure Alice, but the more Sarah soothed her companion, the more she felt prickling at the back of her neck.

"There they go," said Alice suddenly, pointing. "Step on it. They beat us to the draw. They came out of Arby's."

"Damn," said Sarah, stamping on the accelerator, and with a surge of power, jammed the Jeep in front of a pickup truck. "Listen, they can't drive all night. They'll pull in somewhere, we can telephone, and we'll be home before midnight."

"You hope," said Alice.

"The point," said Lenox to the two boys, "is never tip your hand. The Jeep is still behind us, but a car that looks familiar has been tailing her. We will hole up in Brunswick and no one will find us. Academic friendships have their uses. We will make a quick turn off Route One and double around and into the back drive of my old friend, Professor Ambrose Hoffstedder. He is fortunately a widower and keeps late hours. I've rescued him several times from reaching foolish conclusions about Christopher Marlowe. Jonathan—pay attention—now I'm giving it some speed. Keep your wheel steady. Good, we turn left, down Pleasant Street, then turn again. Aha, that red light caught them. Now sharp left and left again. Let her skid, no one's on the street. Good boy. There's hope for you yet. No, Colin, you may not steer. Now turn. The garage is open. In we go. Easy does it. I'll get Ambrose to close the garage door, so stay put and I'll roust him out.

And Professor Cobb, lively as a cricket, bounced from the car, left the garage, mounted the back steps of a small shingle house, and banged on the door.

The results of these efforts were entirely satisfactory and in a short time the three were bedded down—Lenox in the spare bedroom, the boys on two living room sofas—and a clock set for five A.M. sitting in the middle of the floor.

But the comfort of Lenox Cobb meant the discomfort of Sarah and Alice, who, by taking turns sleeping and waking, wrapped in coats and a spare blanket—left over from a summer camping trip—kept vigil at an all-night Texaco station on Route One. And the Saab following the Jeep? It passed through the town, turned, returned, turned again, and finally took up a position at the parking lot of a Dexter Shoe Outlet a few miles south beyond Sarah and Alice's watch place near the junction of Route One and I-95.

At shortly after ten-thirty Sarah had taken advantage of a public telephone booth to call Alex at the Beaugards'. "We're okay," she told him. "Alice saw Jonathan in one of the Beaugard cars—I think he's with Professor Cobb and Colin. She was scared and wanted to follow them, and we're in Brunswick now waiting for them to surface. They've gone underground somewhere. And as soon as we catch up with them, we'll make them turn around and come home."

There was a pause at the other end of the wire—Alex conferring with George, no doubt, thought Sarah—and then Alex came back, his voice harsh. "Get back here on the double.

George has put out an all-points and Professor Cobb will be picked up as soon as he sticks his nose out. Eliot and Vivian Lavender are missing. His car and Mrs. Beaugard's black Ford are gone. You can draw your own conclusions. Kidnapping, escaping murderer. Murderers. You name it. And Mrs. Beaugard died of suffocation. Facedown in the snow. Maybe it was an accidental death. That may—or may not—ease Alice's mind. But what you're doing is plain hazardous. To the two boys, to all of you."

"George Fitts wants us back," Sarah reported to Alice. "And Eliot and Vivian and Lenox Cobb and the boys are 'wanted.' Three cars on the loose. An alert's been issued, so the police will pick them up any time now. And we're to draw our own conclusions."

"You mean pick a card, any card. Has Uncle Lenox stolen the boys for hostages and is making his getaway? Is Eliot absconding with Vivian? Or is he being followed by Vivian? And is Eliot trying to rescue Colin from Uncle Lenox? Or grab Jonathan. Or kill Uncle Lenox. Because Uncle Lenox or Jonathan saw Eliot kill Mother?"

"Except Eliot was bird-watching all day, and Alex says it's possible your mother fell in the snow. An accident."

Alice subsided briefly. Then, "Damn, I won't turn back. If you won't go on, I will. I'll rent a car. Flag them down."

Sarah shook her head. "Did I say I was turning back? No, let's push on. Let's be hung for a sheep, not a lamb."

Alice murmured assent, climbed out of the car, disappeared briefly inside the Texaco station ladies' room, and then clambered into the backseat and curled herself into a sleeping position as Sarah was to take the first watch. "Lucky you had all this bird-watching junk," she said. "Extra hats and jackets. I may take up the sport."

Sarah, after her watch, slept uneasily and then, on her second watch in the early hours of the morning, began to try and fit the puzzle together. Draw your own conclusions, Alex had said.

Okay. Take Lenox Cobb. Had he really been a victim of an

attack, as he claimed? An attack to limit his activities and his participation in Mrs. Beaugard's affairs. Or had Lenox just been clumsy and bumped into tree branches? Well, first and foremost, Lenox had saved Jonathan when Parson was killed. So he wasn't guilty of killing Parson. Two: Lenox could have bought Canadian whiskey and dosed it with Valium—anyone could lay hands on the stuff—but had he ever had contact with Marsden and Junior? Known them well enough to hire them to off-load lead ballast? Verdict: a hung jury. Three—and this was a nasty one: Lenox was at home during the entire day of the bird watch. He was disappointed at not being in the field but was planning—along with his sister, the late Elena Beaugard—to keep an eye on the bird feeder. The reading of *The Tempest* could have taken up only part of the day. Did Lenox resent Elena's estate plan—particularly in the light of Dolly's thievery? Lenox, as reported by Alex, had thought the family was being robbed. Could Lenox have escorted his sister out to the feeder to refill it? Tripped her. And ever so firmly kept her nose down in the snow? Verdict: a possible guilty.

Sarah, her eyes blurred with sleep, shook her head back and forth. The snow had stopped in the night, and except for an occasional car passing, everything on the almost-deserted street seemed to have come to a halt. Then, for something to keep her awake, she began to read, with the help of the streetlights, the signs of the various shops across the way, these being mostly old frame houses converted to commercial use.

Directly across, in pink clapboard: "THE KINDEST CUT OF ALL"— UNISEX HAIRSTYLES. To the left: MAZZINI'S GARAGE: MUFFLERS, FULL BRAKE JOB, RADIATOR REPAIR, ALIGNMENTS, SHOCKS. And beyond in Permabrick and stone: GORDON AND GOSS: CONSTRUCTION, EXCAVATION A SPECIALTY. And to the right: OCEANSIDE SCUBA DIVING. CLASSES, AIR TESTING, WET SUIT RENTAL. And under the lettering, the crude painting of a black-suited figure swimming underwater.

Sarah blinked. Wet suit. Hood, jacket, pants. Shiny when wet. Like a costume from the Middle Ages. Or a sci-fi movie. The hood and mask of a headsman with his ax. An executioner.

Not a ski mask. But why hadn't anyone thought of a wet suit? Because . . . because no one, not even George Fitts, could imagine a wet suit out in the snowy woods. Away from the water. Away from its natural habitat. But how simple. When it is dark and snowing, row in your rubber raft—your hard-to-see rubber raft—or better, swim, across to the Great Oaks beach, the site of so many jolly family picnics, climb up through the woods clutching your bowling ball—Sarah had not given up on the bowling ball—and brain Parson. Parson, who must have had information from his brothers about doing some sort of job for you. And was calling the wrath of the Lord—and probably the attention of the police—down on your head.

Now go back in time—to the end of September. Hire those two useful thugs Marsden and Junior to off-load lead ballast from the *Sweetheart*. Choose a period in which brisk north winds are predicted for the rest of a week. You're a sailor, you keep a close watch on the weather. Then, knowing that Marsden and Junior are out every late afternoon in their boat, you intercept them, and for a job well done you reward your helpers with a bottle of fine Canadian whiskey. You don't know their brand, but you know they drink like fish. You buy expensive whiskey because you always buy expensive liquor. You like the very best. But you have the sense not to choose a brand you keep at your own house. And you lace the whiskey with a dose of that most available drug Valium.

Later, after Marsden and Junior take off, you, in your handy wet suit, row out in the darkened cove in your Zodiac and assist in the demise of the two bad Gattlings. Or perhaps it's a hands-off operation. You supervise from a safe distance. The two brothers are drunk and zonked and fall overboard. No problem.

Next it's Dolly. Dolly the estate planner. Dolly the sailor. Out for one last sail on her usual Sunday. A Sunday afternoon when there's a big north wind and perhaps many of the fishing boats will stay at their moorings in the harbor. Besides, Sunday is a fisherman's day off, a family day. A good day for unobserved activities. But Dolly for that last sail will go out in her Weymouth Scooter, which can handle a blow because of that extra ballast. You wait for her boat to put out from the harbor, watch it blown like a leaf across the bay. You're in your wet suit waiting out in the bay—or sitting in your rubber raft or just swimming around. Wet suits are buoyant, aren't they? Divers need weight belts to keep themselves under. Anyway, there you are ready to assist the struggling skipper of the capsized *Sweetheart* to drown. The bowling ball perhaps? Or just an oar cracked on the skull. Remember those bruises and abrasions.

And it all made sense. Oh maybe some of the details were mixed up, but God, it made sense.

But why? Why was murder done? For the pleasure of killing in a wet suit? For the well-concealed jealousy of a doer of good works? For the hate of a Dolly Memorial estate plan? Why? Because you have money, house, dock, a new boat on order, the works.

And who—if anyone—pressed Elena Beaugard's nose into the snow? Sarah reviewed the possible candidates. Lenox? Masha? Alice? Vivian Lavender? But not Eliot. He, according to Alex, was fully occupied in directing the search for a king eider.

Back to the drawing board.

26

IF not Eliot, how about Vivian? Could she really be Eliot's ladylove? Certainly the unstable Caroline didn't seem to be much of a deterrent to another relationship. Or was this just an idea born of Sarah's overheated imagination? More important, was Eliot shaken by his mother's death? Really shaken. Could he have put Vivian up to it? A murder team. Sarah had bumped into a recent case in which husband and wife had worked in double harness. I have to call Alex, she told herself. She looked at her watch. Four-thirty. He wasn't on call this weekend, so he'd be at home. She slipped out of the front seat, careful not to disturb the sleeping Alice, and returned to the telephone booth.

Alex answered after one ring. He seemed wide-awake. "Why aren't you back here? Damnation, Sarah. I'm as worried as hell."

"It's Alice. She wants to keep on going. Because of Jonathan. And Colin. And to be honest, so do I. We don't know what Lenox is up to. He's disappeared somewhere inside Brunswick."

"I know," said Alex with a growl. "The police haven't found a trace of his car. They're betting he's holed up with some academic buddy. Now, why don't you turn around, because you're going to complicate the situation beyond belief. Eliot's on the loose and so is Vivian. Separately. Do you want to get brained with a bowling ball? Get back here."

"Actually," said Sarah with asperity, "we're in a good position to catch Lenox on the way out of town. He almost has to go on the interstate."

"Unless he doesn't," said Alex. "Unless he cuts off and takes a secondary road. And tell Alice that Webb Gattling is storming around like a mad bull. Mike and Webb are picking me up in a few minutes. We're coming right down there."

"Listen," said Sarah, "we're going to be sensible. No confrontations. No high-speed chases. And it *is* Alice's son. Eliot's, too, for that matter. Eliot may be chasing after Colin to save him. Anyway, it's Eliot I've called about. I think he's the man who got Parson. Wearing a wet suit, that executioner's hood that Jonathan described, and came into the woods by way of the beach. Swimming or with the Zodiac. But did Eliot seem shocked at his mother's death? Did he seem surprised? Grief-stricken? Or even sad?"

There was a pause on the other end of the line. Then Alex said slowly, almost regretfully, "Well, maybe not surprised. After all, she'd been in fragile health for some time. But yes, I'd say he was extremely upset. Shocked, as you said. He was close to tears. Of course, it could have been put on, but . . ."

"But you don't think it was?"

"Eliot doesn't strike me as someone who can fake emotions. But you never can tell. One thing I do know. He reacted like crazy after he found Jonathan's comic book in the library. He seemed to think Jonathan might have come in and suggested his grandmother fill the bird feeder, but didn't stay to see she did it safely. And it *is* possible it happened just like that."

"Look," said Sarah. "We're bound to catch up with Lenox

sometime, and remember, he may not have chosen those two boys as companions, but as hostages."

"That idea," said Alex dryly, "had occurred to all of us."

Lenox Cobb, Colin, and Jonathan finished a hastily assembled breakfast of cereal, milk, and, for the professor, coffee. And then he shook hands with his friend Professor Hoffstedder and thanked him for hospitality and the loan of his Toyota Lexus.

"It pays to keep up with one's colleagues," remarked Lenox after the boys were belted in place and the remains of a box of doughnuts placed in their laps. "I dislike being found in an expensive Japanese car which is certainly more conspicuous than the Ford, but we have no choice. The dénouement approaches, which means that we'll soon have an end to all this folderol. Jonathan, you are dribbling doughnut crumbs. You, too, Colin. You boys have the manners of orangutans. Jonathan, can you use a manual shift?"

"Sure," said Jonathan. "Automatic is no fun. Dad lets me shift for him in the Rabbit. He's says it's good practice."

"I'm glad to hear your father has some sense," said Lenox. "None of his novels indicates as much."

"But," asked Jonathan, "where are we going now? I know we're not to ask questions, but is it anything to do with my family?"

"That," said Lenox sharply, "is an understatement. Now, be quiet. Just trust me and pay attention to your driving." And he turned the key, and the car gave an encouraging roar.

Alice and Sarah, having had the foresight to fill the Jeep's gas tank to the brim, caught the Lexus at the pass. It was moving at a sedate pace past the Texaco station at five-fifteen A.M. on the almost deserted stretch of the business section of Brunswick's Route One. "That's him, that's Jonathan," shouted Alice. "And it's Uncle Lenox at the wheel and Jonathan squashed up against him steering. What in hell are they doing in a Lexus? Boy oh boy, is that sinister or what?"

But Sarah had the Jeep in gear. "Your uncle Lenox has switched cars," she muttered. "Clever. But also stupid. Now he's acting like a real criminal."

"He always has," said Alice.

At Dexter Shoe Outlet the watching, waiting Saab driver missed the Lexus leaving Route One and its left turn onto a smaller road. But he recognized Sarah at the wheel of the following Jeep and put his car in motion, apparently unaware of being followed himself by a black Ford Escort identical to that belonging to his mother. Then the parade of four cars, the Lexus, the Jeep, the Saab, and the Escort—each separated by a number of intervening vehicles—continued slowly south on a snow-covered secondary road.

"Where in God's name is Professor Cobb going now?" demanded Sarah, slowing for a red pickup that cut in ahead of her.

"Straight for Freeport, and we're being followed," announced Alice. "It looks like Eliot's car. Really it does. You can't go on pretending that the highway is filled with Saabs."

"Okay, okay, it probably is Eliot," said Sarah. "And maybe Vivian's hiding out in the backseat, except Alex said your mother's car is missing. The black Escort. Eliot and Vivian both disappeared just as the police started taking statements. And they're either tracking us or tracking Professor Cobb. Or both. Or maybe each other. Nothing would surprise me. And I'd guess either Eliot might do something nasty, or he's on a rescue mission. Saving the boys from the mad kidnapping professor."

"This whole thing is totally unreal," said Alice. She looked over at Sarah, her disheveled hair, her crumpled clothes, her red-rimmed eyes. "And you look totally unreal. Awful, like something dragged out of a rat hole."

"I feel like something out of a rat hole," said Sarah. "I've been in these clothes since yesterday morning. And you look like me. We both look like escapees from the dump."

Alice rolled down the window trying to crane her neck to see around the pickup truck. "This is so stupid. Why the hell Freeport? Does Lenox want to buy a canoe at L.L. Bean?"

"You two boys are familiar with canoes and tents?" demanded Lenox Cobb, as they neared the outskirts of the town of Freeport.

"Duh," said Jonathan.

"I don't want lip. It's an important question. Listen, you two, because I intend to frighten you. Seriously frighten you. I am going to give you instructions and you are to follow them exactly. If you do not follow them, I expect that one or both of you may be hurt. Injured. Maimed. Out of action. You understand?"

"Hey, no problem," said Jonathan, for once sounding genuinely alarmed, while Colin echoed, "No problem."

"So concentrate. For once in your heedless self-centered lives, concentrate. We are coming up on L.L. Bean."

"We know Bean's," said Jonathan. "But what's that got to do with why we're here? Listen, I know something happened to Gran because I heard Dr. McKenzie talking to Uncle Eliot. Is that why—"

"Quiet. I have chosen L.L. Bean's because they have such a big reputation that even on a Sunday morning the place will be filled with people. It will not be easy for anyone to find us alone there. But to make sure, I am going to give you directions. A script to follow. Jonathan, you want to work in the film industry. Here's your chance for actual on-location practice."

"I don't get it," said Colin.

"Quiet. Listen to me. We will drive down the main street past L.L. Bean's, turn right toward the side parking lot. After we turn, Jonathan will hand over the steering wheel to me, you will both unbuckle your seat belts. At the entrance to the parking lot I will pause, you will both get out—Jonathan will have to manage without his crutch; he'd be too conspicuous. Colin can take his arm. Then you both must head directly for the entrance, making an attempt to stay with other shoppers. Enter the front door with these people as if you were both members of a group. Once inside, go immediately to the camping section. Be casual. Pretend to be interested in the camping items, and when you see one of the salesmen looking the other way, duck under or behind one of the display canoes set up on the floor. If there is no accessible canoe, find a tent and crawl in. Close the flap. And wait. If after an hour—Jonathan has a watch—I have not returned, stick your head out and make sure that there is no one you recognize about. Check for a salesperson. The staff wear green polo shirts. Go to him or her and say you are lost. L.L. Bean salespeople are trained to be helpful and courteous—good role models for you both. Tell the salesperson you want to stay with a staff member until your father, Professor Lenox Cobb, comes for you."

"You're not our father," objected Colin. "You're too old."

"Colin, close your mouth and listen. Deny any relationship to anyone else. Including anyone from Great Oaks or whose name is Beaugard. Understand? Because if you don't do as I tell you, I will have you flayed, stuffed, and eaten for dinner." Both boys nodded, Jonathan now looking thoroughly unnerved and Colin positively trembling. "All right, Steven Spielberg and Roderick Usher, here's your chance. We make the turn, slowing because there's a car ahead of us. Safety belts off. Now we're coming up to the entrance to the parking lot. Now, out, out," shouted Lenox Cobb, his voice shrill with urgency. "Out, out, out. Get going."

And the two boys scrambled down, hit the pavement at a trot, and as good luck would have it, immediately inserted themselves into a family group of five complete with a baby in a stroller.

Lenox watched until the group disappeared around the corner and then turned in to the main entrance, immediately found a parking slot reserved for the handicapped, pulled in, and turned off the engine. Then, reaching into an inner jacket pocket, produced a small firearm, laid it on the passenger seat within easy reach, and awaited developments.

"It *is* L.L. Bean's," shouted Alice. "I mean it. Way up ahead. They're turning. My God, L.L. Bean. Now I can't see them. You don't suppose they're off on some camping trip? Uncle Lenox may have gone completely off his rocker. Eliot says—"

Sarah cut in. "Listen, I think Eliot is our murderer. I'm sure he killed Parson. Coming across the cove and through the woods. That description of Jonathan's. It's a description of a wet suit."

Alice frowned, but then shook her head. "He couldn't have," she began, but Sarah waved her into silence.

"We'll hit the parking lot and drive around until we spot the Lexus."

"And lead Eliot right to Uncle Lenox and the boys?"

"We'll decoy. If we spot Eliot on our tail, we'll keep going on. We're the ones he's following. Remember, the Saab let the Lexus go right past and didn't get into the act until we pulled out."

But now a minor traffic jam had developed in front of the turn in to the L.L. Bean side parking lot. The access road was one-way and a car coming the wrong direction had slithered on a patch of ice and had stopped athwart the traffic.

Alice twisted in her seat, opened a window, and peered out toward the rear. "I can just see Eliot's head. This is like some stupid Keystone Cop thing in slow motion and now we're just going to sit still in a traffic jam. Eliot is about four cars behind. But you're wrong, Sarah. Eliot can't have killed Parson. Remember, he said he was in the shower and looked out the window and saw the roadblock and the police lights. Caroline was watching the tube, and her car was behind Eliot's, which had a flat tire."

Sarah frowned. It was true. Eliot couldn't have been both in the shower and at the Great Oaks entrance in the space of fifteen or so minutes. Even wearing a wet suit and magic flippers or using a flying boat. Now waiting amid that tangle of cars filled with would-be L.L. Bean customers, she moved her mind back to the entrance of Great Oaks. The distance from Eliot's cove to the Beaugard beach. By water. By land. Walked herself back to Eliot's driveway, remembering the uprooted mailbox, Parson appearing like a troll. Eliot's house. The drinks. Canadian whiskey, the tour of the new house. Remembering Eliot explaining about the architectural wonders of the building. The height of the cathedral ceilings. And the view. Designed so that every window faced the sea. The sea!

"Alice," she said. "Every window of Eliot's house faces the sea."

"Big deal," said Alice. "You have money, you get a view."

"And he couldn't have seen the ambulance and the police from his bathroom window. Because . . ."

"Every window faces the sea," repeated Alice slowly. And then opening her eyes wide, "Every blasted upscale, thermo, double-glazed custom-made designer window faces the god-damn sea. Jesus Christ, what do you know? He lied. Little brother Eliot lied, and that just about nails his coffin shut. But why? Why in hell did he do it? Parson? Maybe Dolly? The two Gattlings? It's beyond me. But, and this really freaks me out, how could he kill Mother? He was the number one kid. Favorite fair-haired boy. The pride and joy. I'd have sworn that even Eliot, for whatever wild reason, would never have killed Mother. And that he'd be hit hard if she died."

Sarah nodded, "That's what Alex said." And then, "Hey, that car is out of the way. Okay, the parking lot, cruise slowly, and don't stop even if we see the Lexus. God, the place is jammed even at this hour. I hope the boys have the sense to keep their heads down."

"I hope Uncle Lenox isn't holding a gun to those heads," said Alice grimly. "Jonathan has a big mouth. He can be really aggravating. And you know Lenox has this gun. A little stubby thing. Goes on about the right to bear arms, but with his eyes he couldn't hit the broad side of a cow."

"Be quiet, Alice, I've spotted the car," said Sarah, accelerating slightly. "Pulled into a space by the entrance. Gray Lexus. Handicapped parking. Wouldn't you know."

"I see it," said Alice. "But only one head. Looks like Uncle Lenox. So Christ, where are the boys?"

"Maybe they really are keeping their heads down. Look, I'll turn at the end and circle back." But as she said this, a sick chill shook her. No boys in sight. Lenox Cobb, if he *had* suffocated his sister, might have no hesitation about using his little gun on two often obnoxious youngsters. Had he had time to stash them—alive or dead—in the store, under a nearby bush, to be claimed later for disposal? No, that wasn't realistic, but the milk of human kindness was not one of Professor Cobb's distinguishing features.

"There's the Saab. It's turning in," cried Alice. "Now back up, let Eliot see us, and we'll lead him the hell out of here."

But the decoy act was never necessary. Like the sudden appearance of feeding sharks around a clutch of open boats, there erupted from every entrance police cars. They swarmed and surrounded, lights flashing, sirens screaming, loudspeakers blaring. Men in uniform, men in jackets and wool hats, women in uniform, women in plain clothes, were everywhere.

The Jeep was covered almost immediately. "Both of you get out and put your hands on the top of your heads," ordered a harsh voice, and Sarah and Alice climbed out of the car, were assisted in flattening themselves against the side of the Jeep, and subjected to a thorough weapon search. Then ordered into the back of a squad car, where they were locked behind a grille.

"You horse's ass, you've got the wrong people," yelled Alice at the retreating policeman, but his attention was fortunately elsewhere. Both women found by twisting around and looking through the rear window, they could keep the Saab in view. And there was Eliot Beaugard, standing in a patch of icy slush, confronted by uniformed state troopers, and because the squad car's front window was open, the two women in the rear could hear the trooper's words.

"Eliot Beaugard, you are wanted for questioning in the death of Mrs. Elena Beaugard. If you wish to come with us or . . ."

And then, like an extra brought in to fill a small role in the last act, Vivian Lavender appeared. Was walked right onto the scene accompanied by a plain clothes female of impressive size and width. But Vivian looked, as she was marched into view, just as if she had just come from church. Tidy, her dark hair neatly center-parted, its bun pinned and centered on the nape of her neck, her complexion rosy. She stood there next to Eliot, erect in her black wool coat with a red paisley scarf fastened into the collar. So, thought Sarah, she really must have been following Eliot. Or following us. Or Lenox Cobb and the two boys.

The state trooper standing with Eliot addressed himself to Vivian. "Vivian Lavender, you are wanted for questioning in the death of Elena Beaugard on the afternoon of December seventeenth—"

But the sentence was never finished. Eliot jerked around and, with a single smooth motion, raised his fist and brought it down like a sledgehammer on Vivian's skull. And Vivian went down like a kind of malfunctioning doll. Her neck twisted sideways, her knees bent, her shoulders hunched, and she crumpled to the pavement.

So startling was her collapse that the two troopers, the large plainclothes detective, and Sarah and Alice had entirely missed the sight of Professor Cobb leaning out the window of his car and pointing a small pistol at Eliot. All they saw was that Eliot shuddered slightly and then fell heavily, arms outstretched, directly on top of Vivian Lavender in a terrible parody of someone protecting a fallen loved one from the onset of wolves or earthquakes.

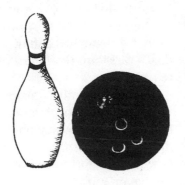

27

THE humdrum, the routine, followed—as it always does—the bizarre. Eliot simultaneously being given emergency first aid and arrested. One policeman rolling Eliot over and applying pressure to the seeping wound in Eliot's groin; another reaching around and applying handcuffs while reciting in a monotonous voice, "You are under arrest for assault with attempt to commit bodily injury. You have a right to remain silent. Everything you say can and will be used against you in a court of law. You have a right to an attorney. If you cannot afford . . ."

And catercorner from this scene, Lenox Cobb, his thin scarecrow body in its trench coat plastered against the side of the gray Lexus, his hands in cuffs behind his back, was listening to the same recitation. It was, thought Sarah, captive with Alice behind the grille, like some strange atonal musical round with Professor Cobb's Miranda warning following two sentences behind Eliot's. "You are under arrest for attempting to commit bodily injury by the unlawful use of firearms. You have a right to remain silent. Everything you say can and will be used against you . . ."

And Vivian Lavender, face livid, hair disordered, blood trickling down from one eyebrow, struggling to sit up and being firmly held down by a kneeling policewoman.

From all sides came the forces of law and order barking orders, securing the scene, escorting shoppers returning for their cars into a makeshift corral by the side of the road.

And Sarah and Alice released from their backseat cage: "Hey, sorry about that, you two. Some balls-up with the intercom message about a Jeep that looks like yours. We were looking for a couple of dames heading south after a convenience store robbery in Belfast. A couple of grungy Thelma and Louise types. You two sure fitted the bill, but then this scene blew up and I stuck around to give 'em a hand. Man, what a day."

"You can say that again," snapped Alice. She turned to Sarah. "How do you go about suing people for false arrest or false detention, stuff like that?"

And Sarah, after hours, days, even months of putting up with the general heedlessness of Alice Beaugard, stopped in her tracks. "Goddamn it, Alice, shut up. For God's sake, shut up. Try paying attention to something important. You wanted to find Jonathan and Colin. That's what's important." Here Sarah stamped a foot directly into a puddle and was rewarded with a muddy splash in the face. A result that infuriated her further. "Forget about suing the police and look beyond your own nose. You saw what happened. Eliot whopped Vivian on the head and then your crazy uncle Lenox plugged him. And we've got to find the boys. So let's—"

But the sentence went unfinished. Eliot, now alert, lifted his head from his position on the ground, twisted his neck toward Vivian, and roared. Roared at Vivian, who was being shifted onto a stretcher, roared like some damaged and betrayed beast.

"You killed her," he shouted. "You killed my mother. You bloody bitch, you killed her. I told you not to. I said watch out. I said be careful, take it easy, but you had to kill her. And now she's dead. Do you hear me, she's dead. My mother's dead. I was there. I saw her. Jesus Christ, I saw her."

But Vivian turned her head aside and with a small pink

tongue began licking away the blood as it dribbled into the corner of her mouth. And Eliot, yelling incoherently, was loaded into a waiting ambulance, and presently the disappearing wail of the siren was heard as it sped through the streets of Freeport.

"Jeezus!" exclaimed Alice. "What in hell was that all about?"

"Never mind them, not now," said Sarah. "We have to make your stupid uncle tell us where he's put the boys. They're going to be taking him away, too, for God's sake, pulling a gun like that."

But confronting Lenox Cobb wasn't necessary. A uniformed trooper approached the two women. "One of you is Alice Beaugard, right? Okay, your son and his cousin are inside Bean's. Camping section. Mr. Cobb told them to stay put until he came to get them, so we're taking him inside to help flush them out. You're to come with us so we can release the two kids to Miss Beaugard's temporary custody. The old guy's under arrest. And hey, there's a deputy from Knox County and some doctor and another man just turned up asking about you both. All mad as hell. Spitting nails."

Jonathan Epstein, settled into his mother's cottage at Great Oaks, his Portland Pirates cap pulled down on his head, lounged back on the sofa and tried to appear the cool, calm, nonchalant kid of vast experience. Mike Laaka had been given the job of interrogating the boy as well as Colin Beaugard, who waited in the kitchen with Katie Waters. Jonathan's man-of-the-world stance did not fool Mike for a minute; he had three younger brothers.

Mike began offering a waiting and anxious Alice a nearby chair, but her presence was refused by Jonathan. "Yeah, I know I'm a juvenile, but I'll just make Mother nervous. What do I say, something like I waive my rights for parental observation? That sounds good anyway."

Mike grimaced, nodded to Alice, and then addressed himself to Jonathan by expressing regret about the death of his grandmother. Jonathan, who had expected to be plunged into the matter of Lenox Cobb's drive down Route One, was put off balance.

"Gran," he said. "Yeah. I'm sorry. I guess I'm sorry. I mean, I never saw that much of her even if we lived in the same house. She took naps a lot and didn't want to be bothered, and when I was home I was supposed to go and do something else. My homework or help rake leaves. Or find Colin and play with him. She didn't like me all that much. But I'm sorry she's dead. Out in the snow. That's where I saw her lying with Dr. McKenzie and Uncle Eliot looking at her. I don't suppose Gran planned to die out there by the bird feeder."

"I don't suppose she did," said Mike dryly.

Jonathan frowned. "It was an accident, wasn't it?"

"We'll have to wait and see," said Mike.

Jonathan's frown increased. "When people say that, they always mean something bad's happened. Or is going to."

But Mike only shook his head and suggested that Jonathan describe his experience of the chase to the L.L. Bean parking lot that Sunday.

And Jonathan's expression turned to one of mild scorn. "In the first place," he said, echoing his mother's earlier opinion, "that wasn't a chase. A chase is a chase when everyone's car is screeching around corners and just missing people and knocking over fireplugs and the sirens are going. This thing was sort of a stupid slow-motion scene like it was a funeral. Anyway, we were in the front car and Uncle Lenox and I were sort of driving together because of his eyes being lousy, so I guess it would have been dumb for us to go fast because we would have had to coordinate a lot faster. I still don't know why he made us go with him, but I guess it has something to do with Gran being dead. I know she had a bad heart, so maybe she had an attack, but Uncle Lenox wouldn't tell us. He said he was getting us out of the house for our own good. But Uncle Lenox is sort of a nutcase. I mean, he's smart, but he does crazy things every now and then, and wow, does he have a temper."

Asked about the parking lot scene, Jonathan reminded Mike that he and Colin had been inside L.L. Bean's hiding out in a tent. "That was Uncle Lenox's idea, and it was a piece of cake. There was this family from Brazil ahead of us, and they wanted to buy a whole bunch of sleeping bags and backpacks and two-man tents, so they kept the salesman busy. I made Colin get into this big geodesic tent because we could scrunch in the corner if someone looked in. But after a while it was totally boring."

"Were you worried about your uncle coming back for you? Perhaps doing something dangerous?"

Jonathan considered the question for a minute and then shook his head. "Nah. Not really. In the beginning I was a little scared because he got sort of fierce, and I guess Colin believed him when he said he'd eat us for dinner. But after a while I told Colin, look, this guy is old. I don't think he's about to go and kill us. Even if he's murdered Gran. I mean, he could have killed us without driving all the way to Freeport. There's plenty of room at Great Oaks to have done it. And we drove to this house of a friend of his and he fed us and gave Uncle Lenox his own car. I guess Uncle Lenox was just trying to get us away. Away from whoever killed Parson Gattling or Aunt Dolly. Or even Gran if she was killed by some human and it wasn't a heart attack."

"Okay, Jonathan," said Mike. "You say you think that your uncle was getting you out of the house for your own good and that maybe it had to do with your grandmother. Did he give you any other reason? A reason having to do with your uncle Eliot? Or any of the other people who were following you?"

But Jonathan shook his head again. "All he said was not to ask questions and to look behind us. When I told him we saw a Jeep following, he said he wasn't worried about the Jeep. Do you know if he's going to be in jail because of shooting Uncle Eliot?"

"I don't know," said Mike, "if he's going to be held or will be allowed to post bail. But you can go now and I'll have a word with Colin. He'll be staying with you and your mother for a while until some other arrangement can be made. Or his mother gets out of the hospital."

"That's okay, Colin and I are working on a film script. But is he staying with us because Uncle Eliot is in the hospital?"

"Your uncle Eliot will be detained somewhere for quite a spell," said Mike, closing his notebook and standing up. "Now, scoot to the kitchen and call Colin."

But Jonathan lingered. "It's pretty amazing, isn't it? I mean, the whole thing. Aunt Dolly and Parson and Gran. And the two Gattlings. It's like some sort of massacre but strung out. And there's something even more amazing."

Mike sighed. "Okay, I give up. What's even more amazing?"

"Uncle Lenox. Being able to hit Uncle Eliot in a vital place. At least, one of the policemen said it was vital. In his gut or somewhere. Uncle Lenox can't see across the street even when he's wearing his glasses."

"Thank you, Jonathan."

"I suppose Uncle Lenox was trying to protect Mrs. Lavender so he can plead self-defense or something sort of like it."

"Good-bye, Jonathan."

Jonathan started for the kitchen and then turned. "Or maybe he was trying to shoot Mrs. Lavender and hit Uncle Eliot by mistake. Or he could have been trying to hit the policeman to save both of them and just missed."

"Jonathan Epstein, get out of here," shouted Mike.

The big Great Oaks house had a strange empty feeling, Sarah thought. With its matriarch gone, its resident curmudgeon, Lenox Cobb, detained, Eliot, the son and heir in irons, Vivian Lavender in custody, and Jonathan at his mother's cottage, the whole house seemed hollow, dusty, as if a fine layer of grit had settled on every surface. The furniture, the curtains, pictures, carpets, it all reminded her of a stage set left in place too long after the curtain had been rung down. And like the empty stage, the house had no meaning or purpose now that the principal players had departed and the script lay in tatters.

They were in the cavernous Great Oaks kitchen, settled around a massive walnut table, George Fitts, Alex, and herself. The kitchen had been chosen as an acceptable meeting space since George's preferred spot, the library, was ringed in yellow tape as an extension of the scene of the crime. Or, Sarah reminded herself, plural, one of the scenes of one of the crimes.

"Eliot?" Sarah asked George. "Was he badly hurt?"

George, ready for questions and interrogation, had spread before him notebooks, tape recorders, a set of pencils, a cup of coffee, and a number of telephones—portable and fixed. Now he looked up from a rough chart of the Great Oaks property.

"Condition stable. He's in the hospital under guard. Later on we'll try for a probable-cause hearing and hope the judge denies bail." He returned to his chart and with one finger circled the Beaugard estate. "A messy case," he declared. "Even arresting Eliot Beaugard."

"Why wasn't that simple?" asked Alex. "He'd hammered Vivian Lavender on the head and then, after he was shot, there he was lying there on the ground shouting at Vivian Lavender, practically announcing he was an accessory to killing his mother."

"First," said George, as if instructing slow members of the sixth grade, "Eliot wasn't under arrest until after he'd assaulted Mrs. Lavender. Before that the only legal thing we could do was to ask him to come in for questioning. But after he hit Mrs. Lavender, he could be put under arrest for assault. Unfortunately, he was shot almost at the moment of his striking her, and this meant he was incapacitated when the trooper gave him the Miranda warning. His lawyer could claim that he was in no condition to understand its meaning. Probably have the statement about his collusion with Mrs. Lavender not allowed as evidence."

"But what about Vivian Lavender? Eliot yelled, called her names. She may not be feeling very supportive about Eliot. If they really were working together all this time."

George brightened—a faint flickering across his impassive face. "We have hopes of Vivian. State's evidence. I hope she can be encouraged in that direction because I think we have her cold for the murder of Mrs. Beaugard. Lab just called and they picked up three of Vivian's hairpins—those old-fashioned long ones she wears—in the snow at the site of the body. And some fair snow-packed footprints next to the body, including an imprint on the back of the victim—we're lucky there hasn't been a thaw." Here George glanced with satisfaction at an inside-outside window thermometer showing an external temperature of fourteen degrees Fahrenheit.

"Mrs. Lavender," he continued, "has a mild concussion from Eliot's blow, but she's obviously angry with him. In fact, the detective with her says she's already made some very useful statements about the nighttime unloading of the ballast from Dolly's boat by Junior and Marsden Gattling, with Eliot supervising while Vivian kept watch at Great Oaks to make sure that the family was occupied. Eliot used his Zodiac raft, the Gattlings used their skiff. We got a search warrant this afternoon, grabbed the raft, and the lab just called to say they've recovered canvas fibers from under the floorboards of the Zodiac. As you know, we've already had matching fibers from the Gattling skiff. It was a joint murder enterprise."

"And one that younger brother Parson must have known about," said Sarah. "Which explains all those crazy biblical threats."

"Don't forget that Parson was Dolly's middleman for the rare book deals," said Alex. "Eliot was guilty—we haven't proved it yet, but it seems likely—not only of doping Marsden and Junior's Canadian whiskey with either Caroline's Valium or Mrs. Beaugard's—but when Eliot got rid of Dolly, he got rid of Parson's job. His income source. Why wouldn't Parson be sore as hell? His two brothers, his valued employer, all dead because of Eliot. So he goes public threatening, spouting curses. Made certain he'd be next."

"But was Vivian Eliot's mistress?" queried Sarah, who felt that this interesting subject was being neglected. "We guessed she might have been. Alice thought probably."

"Looks like it," said George. "We had been scouting the local motels with no luck, but after we got the search warrant, we've found evidence of their relationship in the loft of his boathouse. It's a comfortable space where he keeps boat cushions, sails, and so forth."

"Don't tell me, more hairpins?" exclaimed Sarah.

"As a matter of fact, yes. Some articles of her clothing, which she identified in the hospital an hour ago."

"But I have real evidence about Parson's death," Sarah announced. "Not just hairpins. I should have thought of it before because I've had a tour of Eliot's house. He lied about Parson Gattling and seeing the police cars at the roadblock." And she told George about the windows that faced only the ocean.

"That," said George, making a hasty note, "is very interesting. We haven't had a chance yet to really go over that house of his. Sarah, I'm glad you caught that. It saves us trouble. There are times when I forgive you for being underfoot."

"How gracious of you, George," said Sarah.

"But I don't thank you for chasing Lenox Cobb. You had Eliot on your tail and Vivian Lavender behind him and Professor Cobb in front. You could have been caught in the middle."

"Alice," said Sarah. "It was her son. We had to go."

"It would have been much safer to leave it to the police."

"George," said Sarah in a dangerous voice. "The police never caught up with anyone until L.L. Bean's. They were too busy with road accidents to concern themselves with murder and a possible kidnapping. So Alice was right to chase her son and Colin. And you know, we did provide a buffer. If Eliot had tried to pass us, we wouldn't have let him."

"And that," said Alex, rousing himself and pushing away an empty coffee cup, "is exactly why I told you to come back. Besides, there was Lenox Cobb packing a gun. It was just plain stupid."

"It was plain right," said Sarah stubbornly. "I'd do it again. But think of Lenox Cobb being armed. Alice apparently knew. What did he use? A pistol from the Civil War?"

"He used a thirty-eight Smith and Wesson Chief's Special Airweight," said George with ill-concealed fury. "Imagine that old goat with his attitude going about armed. It's a wonder he hasn't left a trail of bodies."

"But he didn't," said Sarah. "It was Eliot and his hench-woman, Vivian. But why was Eliot chasing Lenox and the boys? Did he think that Lenox killed his mother?"

"Judging from his remarks before he took off, Eliot may have thought that Jonathan, through carelessness, or possibly Lenox, might have been responsible for her death. He saw Jonathan's comic book in the library and lost his temper. Or, and this is also possible, he may have thought Jonathan, or Lenox, or both, saw Vivian doing her job on his mother and had to find out. Maybe to eliminate them because they were witnesses. But unless Eliot comes clean, we may never know."

"And Vivian, why was she following Eliot?" demanded Alex.

George picked up a notebook. "Statement from Vivian. She followed because she loved him. She actually said so. Used those very words. Like a soap opera. They had a deal. He was going to marry her after he divorced Caroline, which he'd been promising for some time. She seemed to think he was taking off without her and so she went after him. After all, where else could she go?"

Sarah nodded agreement. "Okay, I think I can understand Vivian. In the beginning maybe she was afraid she was just going to lose her job because of Dolly's giveaway estate plan. That's where the switch to the Episcopalians comes in. But then Eliot began to be an important part of her life, so perhaps she thought as Eliot's wife she was going to be the heiress presumptive of Great Oaks. But Vivian was never calling the shots, was she? Eliot was. But again why? Why get rid of Dolly? And did he knock Lenox down? Or Jonathan? There must be a reason. Some common denominator. Not money. You know it isn't money. But why?"

"And what was Vivian supposed to do to Mrs. Beaugard?" demanded Alex. "If not to kill her, what? Half-kill her? Maim her? Put her out of action for a while?"

"All we know," said George, "is that Eliot thought killing Mrs. Beaugard was a mistake. Mrs. Lavender has admitted holding her down but says she didn't expect her to die from it."

"What crap," exploded Sarah. "You push an elderly woman with a bad heart down in the snow and don't expect her to die?"

"You know," said Alex slowly, "if we can hang Lenox Cobb's injury and Jonathan's leg and shoulder, and what was supposed to be just an injury to Mrs. Beaugard, all on Eliot, then there is a pattern. After Dolly's death and the Gattling boys were eliminated as witnesses, Lenox was second-in-command. Until he was hurt. And Jonathan is a bright active kid. Maybe it was useful to slow him down. Not kill him, hobble him. And hobble, maim, injure, slow up Mrs. Beaugard. Not kill her. Leave her incapacitated and then guess who takes—"

Sarah looked up. "Hey, Alex, I think you have something, because then Eliot could become the estate manager and scuttle the Dolly memorial plan before it was made final in January. But . . . but why? In God's name, why?"

George sighed. "As I've said before, I hate motivation. I know it fascinates amateurs and armchair psychologists."

"Like me?" said Sarah.

"Exactly," said George. "The police do much better with cloth fibers and bloodstains. Real evidence. So leave it for now. As I said, it's a messy case. The public expects this neat package: the crime, the evidence, the motive, the verdict, the sentence. Well, multiple-death cases like this can go on for years. We can't prove the injuries to Jonathan and Professor Cobb were anything but accidental. But some sort of end is in sight—if we can persuade Mrs. Lavender to cooperate. Let the lawyers worry about whether Eliot's actions are tied to Dolly Beaugard's estate plan."

Sarah stood up. "Okay, okay. So I'm hung up on motivation. So I'm an amateur. But I'll say it again. Why? Eliot didn't need, want, or care about the estate. He had everything his heart desired, including Vivian nesting in his boathouse. So good night, George. Let's hope we all get through Christmas without bumping into each other. And now I'm going to check on Alice.

I lost my temper and yelled at her back there at L.L. Bean's because sometimes Alice sticks in my craw. But her mother's dead and she's looking ragged, so I can show some sympathy and see how Jonathan and Colin are holding up. Poor Colin. His father in jail, his mother in the hospital. Alex, you can join me if you want. But I don't want any more lip about Alice and my little drive to L.L. Bean's."

"Did you ever think, best beloved, that you have a singular talent for driving me as batty as any Lenox Cobb?" asked Alex as they pulled on coats and boots preparing for the drive down to Alice's cottage.

"Looking back," said Sarah, "I can see how crazy that caravan of cars was. Crazy and maybe a little on the dangerous side."

"A little!" exclaimed Alex.

"Mostly from Lenox. If I had known that he carried—what was that thing?—a Smith and Wesson something, well, I would have left more space between us. I wonder if he was really aiming at Eliot."

"All will be revealed," said Alex. "In the meantime . . ."

"In the meantime I'm going to get a grip on this business. If I can figure out *why*, then I can make sense of Eliot running around in a wet suit, dumping lead, killing Gattlings. But we forgot one person. Masha. Where was she all yesterday afternoon when everyone was looking at birds or reading Shakespeare?"

"Telephoning. Arranging the winter concerts for her group. Talk about detachment. Anyway, George has a log of her phone calls, all long-distance. Twenty or more. Masha is covered."

"As is Eliot, isn't he? For Mrs. Beaugard's death?"

"I think by thumping Vivian on the head at the Bean parking lot, he's established his innocence of that one. Not of planning a milder version of it, which involved Vivian putting his mother out of action. He used the king eider. A duck any bird-watcher would kill—pardon the expression—to see. And he made sure everyone was busy setting up telescopes and scanning the cove, leaving Vivian a free hand without bird-watchers sneaking around."

"Except for one bird-watcher. Me."

"There's one in every crowd."

"And a lot of good I was. Fast asleep in the living room. If I'd stayed awake, I might have saved her."

"Maybe, maybe not. It was probably a quick job. Talking Mrs. Beaugard into going out and filling the feeder. And Vivian probably didn't hesitate; she may have done it with a certain relish. All those years of servitude. Mrs. B. wasn't a user-friendly employer. She was a pretty autocratic woolly-minded old biddy."

"God, what a crew," said Sarah. Then, pointing, "Stop at the top of the hill. Alice's driveway is a devil with snow. We won't find any answers in there, but my conscience will be a little clearer. Alice has a good heart. At least I think she does."

And Sarah, followed by Alex, climbed out of the car and began the slippery descent to Alice's cottage, Sarah little guessing that the answer to at least one of her questions would shortly come from a highly unlikely source.

28

JONATHAN and Colin were discovered on the living room floor surrounded by sheets of paper and cardboard. They hardly looked up, simply announcing that they were working on set designs for their upcoming video. Mike Laaka was in the kitchen with Katie Waters, dealing with cocoa and a frozen pizza. "Alice is in her bedroom, but she said if you and Alex turned up, to send you in. Katie and I are feeding the boys, keeping them busy. They're okay now, but the whole thing will probably hit with a bang tomorrow."

Alice was sitting on the edge of her bed staring bleakly at a framed copy of a Matisse cutout. "I bought that during my art-appreciation period, but now it doesn't do it for me anymore. Things are so fouled up that I even think I'll quit smoking. It's a theory of mine; you know, provide a counterirritant. Besides, I promised Webb. He's coming over tonight. We're going to talk about getting married because then I might get joint custody of Jonathan, and the court might okay temporary custody of Colin."

"Well, that's good news," said Sarah. "But are you getting married just to get custody?"

"No. I really want to stay with that guy. I need something solid and massive to butt my head against. Webb fills the bill. Besides, he seems to want someone flaky and unstable and restless, and I fit that description. Another odd couple abroad in the world. Besides, he wants to keep Willie."

"How about your uncle Lenox?"

"You know what's funny? I found myself offering to take him on. My mouth just opened up and said so. That's if he gets a suspended sentence or is out on bail or something. Webb can handle the old buzzard, and believe it or not, Jonathan likes him. He wants to have Uncle Lenox come to the school and help show this video he and Colin are putting together. 'The Fall of the House of Usher,' only I think it should be 'The Fall of the House of Beaugard.' "

Here Alice gave a short harsh laugh. "The boys will probably get through this whole thing better than I will. Even Masha will handle it because she can go all remote and retire into her music. That's why I need Webb. To walk me through the next few days. And through the rest of my life."

But it was Colin who answered the question that was still buzzing like an angry fly in Sarah's brain.

She returned to the living room and found Alex on the floor with the two boys moving cardboard pieces around on a chart.

"He's helping us see spatial relationships," Colin explained.

"We've decided," said Jonathan, "to do 'The Fall of the House of Usher' in the twenty-third century. Sort of like 'Star Trek.' I think the Great Oaks house setting is too boring. We'll have a flying sailboat with all the latest technology. Our ship will be capable of landing on water and going through the stratosphere, and landing on planets in all the galaxies. It'll have a retractable keel."

"Like the *Goshawk*," said Colin. "But not like the new boat."

"The new boat?" said Sarah, puzzled.

"The one my father ordered because he's sailing transatlantic next year. If he's not in jail. He's the new commodore of the Proffit Point Boat Club, so he said he needed a new sailboat."

"Oh yes," said Sarah, remembering. "It had a bird name, too."

"The *Gyrfalcon*," said Colin. "It's fifty-six feet and a special design, but the centerboard doesn't retract like the *Goshawk*. It's got a real keel."

"So," finished Jonathan, "we'll use the *Goshawk* design and make it much bigger. Bigger even than the starship *Enterprise*."

"How about Roderick Usher?" asked Alex, now much amused.

"He'll be Captain Roderick Usher," announced Jonathan. "We'll need a bigger cast, but most of the action will be in the control room and we won't bury Lady Madelaine alive in a casket, we'll vaporize her instead and hide her in the instrument panel."

But Sarah's brain had been busy. "Wait up, Colin," she said. "How could your father keep a keel boat like the *Gyrfalcon* at your mooring? There's very little water at low tide in most of the cove. It's even named Tidal Cove."

"Yeah, I know," said Colin, now struggling with two elliptical pieces of cardboard. "These are part of the defense shield systems," he explained.

"So what was he going to do with it?" persisted Sarah.

"The new boat? Moor it somewhere else, I guess."

"Did he mention where he thought of mooring it?" demanded Alex, and Sarah could tell from the tone of his voice that he understood where her question was heading.

"Oh, maybe at Little Cove or at Back Cove. Over at Great Oaks. Back Cove is a good place if a hurricane is coming."

"But if the Great Oaks property is going to be given away—" began Sarah, but Alex nudged her arm.

"I think that's enough," he said quietly. And then to both boys, "Quite an idea bringing Edgar Allan Poe into the twenty-third century. How are you going to end the story?"

"Oh, we've changed Poe's ending," said Jonathan. "Captain Usher goes crazy, but then he has a brain transplant from a sub-alien form and he's okay. It's done with lasers and neural-sensor probes."

"And Lady Madelaine is reconstituted," said Colin. "Into an engineering-room ensign. A man. We didn't want any women in central command."

"So much for the women's movement in the twenty-third century," said Sarah as they closed the cottage door behind them.

"But you have your answer to why. Murder done for the greater glory of Eliot Beaugard, commodore of local yacht club and transatlantic blue-water sailor. I suppose it wouldn't be the first time that vanity beat out moneygrubbing as a motive."

"I doubt," said Sarah, "that George will be that interested. It's a minor piece of the puzzle for him. For us it's a biggie. Eliot didn't want the estate or the house or cottages; he wanted two good places to moor the *Gyrfalcon.*"

"Deep-water sheltered anchorages, safe from big blows, complete docking facilities. In an area served by the Proffit Point Boat Club. Those are worth more than all the tea in China, or the cash of all the Beaugards. You know that young squirt Jonathan wasn't so far off base when he suggested that Uncle Eliot wanted the Great Oaks land for an international yacht resort facility."

They reached the Jeep, and Sarah turned to look back in the direction of the Great Oaks house. "Dolly stealing books so she can be called the saint of the year, Eliot murdering left and right to be the yachtsman of the year. Mrs. Beaugard a self-centered domineering old woman. Masha retreating from human contact, Caroline off her own particular deep end. You know, it makes Alice and Lenox Cobb and the two boys seem positively lovable."

With that she climbed into the front seat of the Jeep and slumped back against the headrest, an enormous weariness like a thick blanket coming over her. She closed her eyes and sighed. "I didn't get much sleep in the Jeep last night," she told Alex.

"And properly so," he answered. "They who refuse to listen to caution, reason, good sense, and the advice of a loved one get the rest they richly deserve."

In the days that followed that particularly eventful December Christmas Bird Count, certain movers and shakers in the world of law enforcement saw to it that Eliot Beaugard, after a preliminary hearing, was denied bail, and his case was referred to the county prosecutor's office for presentation to a grand jury. This matter had been facilitated by Vivian Lavender's agreeing to turn state's evidence against Eliot in the hope of a modified sentence—manslaughter perhaps instead of first-degree murder.

Professor Lenox Cobb, after entering a plea of guilty to the possession and unlawful use of firearms, was, as a first offender, nailed with a large fine and released on his own recognizance, burdened only with a year's parole and a suspended sentence. It was observed by all who subsequently met him that although the professor spoke with regret of his departed sister, Elena, and quoted from *The Tempest* the lines about his charms being "all o'erthrown," he was, all in all, remarkably chipper. Particularly lively was the account of his rescue of the two boys from the evil Eliot Beaugard and the daring escape of the trio to the L.L. Bean parking lot, where with great coolness he, Lenox Cobb, professor emeritus of Bowmouth College, disabled Eliot with the timely use of his Smith and Wesson. This rejuvenation of an elderly man puzzled Alice until Sarah suggested to her that recent events had obviously had a highly stimulating effect on her uncle.

The body of Mrs. Arthur Beaugard was, after autopsy and the verdict of homicide by suffocation, released for burial and a small service was held at St. Paul's-by-the-Sea by Father Smythe, who twice mistakenly referred to the deceased as "Dolly." This affair was attended by the remnants of the Beaugards and by Sarah's grandmother Douglas, who, as Sarah drove her home, remarked in an annoyed voice that Elena had always been troublesome.

Webb and Alice Beaugard were married quietly in a civil ceremony attended by Colin, Jonathan, Professor Cobb, and Alan Epstein, with Alex and Sarah standing by as witnesses. Masha, driving in from Boston, arrived just in time to play a short seventeenth-century pavane on the alto recorder before the exchanging of vows.

Caroline Beaugard showed mild gratification on hearing that her husband's future residence would most probably be limited to the Maine State Prison in Thomaston. However, when offered a trial weekend to her house on Proffit Point and the company of her son, she became sullen, saying she'd never really liked children. But Colin, if he wished, could make short visits to Green Pastures, a newly established psychiatric halfway house.

Colin Beaugard proved himself remarkably resilient to what amounted to the loss of two parents. It was generally thought that this was either because he was a very tough little boy, or, more realistically, because he had always had so little attention and real affection from either father or mother that he did not now feel their absence. Thus, the last heir of the Beaugard name was quite content to move for the moment into his aunt Alice's cottage, where he and Jonathan continued to work on their script and stage mock-up of the newly named "Voyage of the House of Usher," in which latter task they were assisted by Webb Gattling's skill with saw and hammer. Colin was also initiated by Jonathan into the pleasure of receiving double the usual number of gifts through the celebration of Hanukkah with Alan Epstein and Christmas with Alice and Webb.

The first day of January dawned with one of those welcome shifts of weather from ice and zero temperatures to the beginning of a January thaw. On New Year's day the thermometer hit fifty-seven, coats were exchanged for light windbreakers, and the citizens of midcoast Maine went about smiling and lifting their pale faces to the sun. And at exactly noon of January first, the last wrinkle of the Beaugard case was smoothed and made plain.

It happened because Webb Gattling, in his new role as stepfather and stepuncle, suggested a winter picnic on the beach below Alice's cottage. A fire would be built; hot dogs, salad, cake, cocoa, coffee, rugs, and tarps would be brought, and the New Year would be given a proper push toward better days.

Sarah and Alex with Patsy in tow arrived with a hamper of sandwiches and a thermos of hot soup to add to the collection. Masha, on a two-day break from the concert world, brought a sinister-looking chocolate torte, Lenox Cobb was established with a rug, a folding chair, and a pair of binoculars in case some rare species drifted by, Alice and Webb produced a bucket of shrimp, and the two boys bore marshmallows and packages of frankfurters.

The first order of the day was the gathering of firewood. And this effort, if Sarah had not exercised remarkable self-control, might have resulted in the cancellation of the picnic. With Patsy leashed and straining toward Willie, who was tethered at a safe distance from Professor Cobb, Sarah wandered about through the spruce trees and bushes that rimmed the beach, here and there picking up a fallen branch or bundle of twigs. Until, stubbing her toe, she fell flat into a mound of melting snow. As she sat up, reaching to see what had caught her boot, her hand encountered something round. And smooth of edge. She jerked herself upright and reached under the snow. A bowling ball. A bowling ball. The words came banging into her head. Oh God, not a bowling ball. Not *the* bowling ball.

But it wasn't. It was like a ball cut in half with a neck protruding from its center. A neck with a hole in it, and fastened into the hole was a short length of chain, which in turn joined a length of dirty rope, which disappeared into the snow. Sarah probed, dug, and delivered several feet of the line and a cut and frayed end. She stared, ran a finger over the painted surface. And then seeing Alex walking past on the beach, called softly, but with urgency.

And Alex, the nautical half of the marriage, knelt down in the slush and identified the object. "It's a mushroom anchor. Good for mud bottoms."

"Like the mud bottoms around here?"

"Correct."

"It was under the snow. I tripped over it."

"It's a little one," said Alex, eyeing the anchor. "Useful for small skiffs, prams, dinghies."

"Or rubber Zodiac dinghies owned by someone in a wet suit?"

Alex stared at her and then slowly nodded. "Yes, like that."

"And it would do the same damage as a bowling ball, wouldn't it? Leave the same sort of imprint on somebody's head?"

Alex nodded again, and for a moment they were silent looking at each other. Then Sarah stood up. "Let's not spoil things. Leave it there until after the picnic. Tomorrow is soon enough. Later we can call George. He'll be happy. He likes the sort of evidence that you can measure and weigh."

Sergeant George Fitts managed a mildly pleased expression after he had arrived at Great Oaks and collected the mushroom anchor the next morning. "That was one of the missing pieces," he told Sarah, as he stowed the object in a paper evidence bag. "I never believed in the bowling ball. A bowling ball was too good a weapon. And Eliot Beaugard didn't bowl. But he owned a mushroom anchor, which is missing from his rubber raft. And this one even has his initials painted on the bottom."

"I suppose," said Alex, "that he may have dumped it overboard, and it hit a rock bottom or it didn't set itself properly in the mud, may have dragged and rolled closer to the high-tide line. As an anchor it's a lightweight affair."

"All right, Sarah," said George. "You win. It's obvious to me that even if you aren't actually looking for something, you'll stumble on it anyway. And now I've got to go up to the house for a last look round. The furniture is being moved this afternoon."

"Furniture? What furniture?" said Sarah, startled.

"From the house. I gather some is being sold, some put in storage, and the rest divided between Alice and Lenox. The Episcopal Church takes possession on the fifteenth. The gift of the house didn't depend on Mrs. Beaugard's death; she and Dolly arranged for the transfer last summer."

Sarah never knew why, instead of shaking the dust of Great Oaks from their feet, she and Alex followed George's car up the long winding drive to the house. "I suppose," she told Alex, "it's wanting to see the end of things. Closure. The end of the end. We won't be coming back here. Alice and the boys are moving to Webb's cabin in Diggers Neck, and Lenox has decided to go into some sort of retirement home for cranky academics."

The way to the front door was blocked by an enormous moving van, and a continuous stream of men and articles of furniture moved from the door to the ramp of the van. Alex parked the Jeep and both climbed out to watch. The house already seemed abandoned, shades pulled down in the upstairs rooms, curtainless windows staring from the ground floor. Sarah, standing by Alex, recognized a wicker chair from the living room, the plant table from the library, the fringed lamp that had stood next to Mrs. Beaugard's winged chair.

"I don't even feel a twinge," said Alice, appearing suddenly at Sarah's elbow. "Of course, some things are supposed to go to Eliot, but we'll store his stuff. Or give it to Caroline if she ever comes back into daylight. The church is buying the piano and keeping the dining room table and sideboard. And look, here comes the family." And Alice pointed to the front door, where two men were carrying a large painting. The portrait.

"You're not selling . . . ?" Sarah began, but Alice nodded vehemently. "I don't want it. Masha doesn't. I got word to Eliot in prison, and he doesn't. The two boys aren't interested, so off it goes. It's always given me the fidgets. Good riddance, I say."

And Sarah, Alex, and Alice stood and saw that the painting in its heavy gilt frame had been carefully leaned against the front steps while one of the men approached with a heavy comforter and a roll of tape.

At that moment the sun, which had been hesitating behind a clump of clouds, slid out and shone directly on that painted group of summer children. Stubborn Dolly with her honey-colored hair, Masha staring off into space, Alice looking for an escape, and Eliot in his sailor suit, master of all he surveyed.

And then the comforter swaddled the painting and it was

borne away, up the ramp, and fitted between two bed mattresses. And Sarah suddenly remembered.

She turned to Alice and Alex. "I knew that portrait reminded me of something. A photograph I'd seen before in a magazine. In a biography. Except for not being the right number of girls, it's just like one made of the Tsar's family."

"The Tsar?" exclaimed Alice. "What Tsar?"

"Tsar Nichols. Of Russia. You know, his family when they were at the Summer Palace. The girls in their afternoon frocks. Olga, Tatiana, Marie, and Anastasia. And the little boy, the Tsarevitch, in his sailor suit. The photograph always made me shiver because I knew what was going to happen to them."

Alice was silent and then she blew softly through her lips. "Maybe that's what I always felt. A sense of doom hanging over us. Except," she added with a tight smile, "in our case there were one or two survivors."

"What are you doing standing there moping?" said a cracked voice. Professor Cobb. "Why don't you stop gawking at furniture nobody wants and come out to Little Cove. The king eider is back."

"You mean," exclaimed Sarah, "there really *is* a king eider here?"

"Of course," said Professor Cobb crossly. "Eliot found it and took everyone to see it the day of the Christmas Count. A very fortunate sighting and a first record for Proffit Point. Eliot has many serious faults, but even Eliot would not claim a bird he had not actually seen."